The Ambassa

André Brink was born in South Africa in
1935. He is the author of eleven novels: *The
Ambassador, Looking on Darkness, An Instant
in the Wind, Rumours of Rain, A Dry White
Season, A Chain of Voices, The Wall of the
Plague, States of Emergency, An Act of Terror,
The First Life of Adamastor* and *On the
Contrary*. He has won the most important
South African literary prize, the CNA
Award, three times and his novels have
twice been shortlisted for the Booker Prize,
in 1976 and 1978. In 1980 he received the
Martin Luther King Prize, and in France
the Prix Médicis Étranger. In 1982 he was
made a Chevalier of the Légion d'Honneur
and in 1987 was named Officier de l'Ordre
des Arts et des Lettres, promoted in 1993
to Commandeur.

André Brink is Professor of English at the
University of Cape Town. He has three
sons and a daughter.

Also by André Brink

An Act of Terror★
Looking on Darkness★
An Instant in the Wind★
Rumours of Rain★
A Dry White Season★
A Chain of Voices★
The Wall of the Plague★
States of Emergency
The First Life of Adamastor
On the Contrary★

Mapmakers (*essays*)
A Land Apart
(*A South African Reader*,
with *J.M. Coetzee*)

★available from Minerva

André Brink

The
Ambassador

Minerva

A Minerva Paperback
THE AMBASSADOR

First published in Great Britain 1967
by Longmans
This newly translated and revised edition
first published in Great Britain 1985
by Faber and Faber Ltd
This Minerva edition published 1995
by Mandarin Paperbacks
an imprint of Reed Consumer Books Ltd
Michelin House, 81 Fulham Road, London SW3 6RB
and Auckland, Melbourne, Singapore and Toronto

Copyright © André Brink 1985
The author has asserted his moral rights

A CIP catalogue record for this title
is available from the British Library
ISBN 0 7493 9637 7

Printed and bound in Great Britain
by Cox & Wyman Ltd, Reading, Berkshire

This book is sold subject to the condition
that it shall not, by way of trade or otherwise,
be lent, resold, hired out, or otherwise circulated
without the publisher's prior consent in any form
of binding or cover other than that in which
it is published and without a similar condition
including this condition being imposed
on the subsequent purchaser.

IN MEMORIAM

Ingrid

. . . love is a form of metaphysical inquiry

LAWRENCE DURRELL

Author's Note

The Ambassador was the result of my first prolonged exposure to Paris as a student (1959-61) and formed part of the first wave of fiction produced by the 'Sestigers' ('Writers of the Sixties') in South Africa. Most of these works, by young writers who had spent some time abroad, were attempts to emancipate Afrikaans fiction of the time from its colonial constraints by introducing trends of thought and technique then in vogue in Europe and by breaking down taboos in the field of religion, ethics, sex and even narrative technique then prevalent in Afrikaans literature. Although there was little overt involvement with politics, the movement had surprising political side effects, as the questioning of Afrikaner morality and religion contributed towards a breakdown in the stranglehold of the authorities on the minds of the younger generation. As such, it paved the way for a later wave of fiction which was to involve itself more explicitly with the socio-political scene in South Africa and of which my novels from *Looking on Darkness* onwards formed a part.

That first exposure to Paris was in many ways traumatic for me. After more than twenty years within the comfortable, closed framework of conventional Afrikaner attitudes, values and beliefs the sudden discovery of all the cross-currents of thought and experience in Europe was a cultural shock from which it took years to recover. The fact that this sojourn coincided with the Sharpeville massacre in South Africa also introduced an unsettling discovery of what was *really* happening – what had been happening all the time – in my own country. Everything I had taken for granted had to be re-examined: tribal customs and taboos, religion, relationships with groups and individuals and with the country itself, ideas, a view of history, plans for the future. For me, *The Ambassador* was the first expression of a search and an exploration which is still continuing.

The book was originally published in Afrikaans in 1963 (*Die*

Ambassadeur, Human & Rousseau, Cape Town). An early, and embarrassingly deficient, English translation was published in South Africa under the title *The Ambassador* (Centaur Books, 1964) and in Britain under the title *File on a Diplomat* (Longmans, 1967). The present edition is an entirely new translation which is also the result of extensive revision of the text itself. The original version had been preceded by several early drafts; and in preparing this new edition I have in several cases restored earlier passages and scenes where these now appeared to me more satisfactory than their subsequent published versions. In the process I was tempted to undertake a complete rewriting, but I decided deliberately to preserve the essence of the novel in its original context.

The whole point of this edition is that it is *not* a new book but that it marks a point of departure; without it, I would not have been able to write *Looking on Darkness*, or *An Instant in the Wind*, or *Rumours of Rain*, or *A Dry White Season*, or *A Chain of Voices*, or *The Wall of the Plague*. It was another kind of writer who produced *The Ambassador*, and I have to remain loyal to that young man's agonized and urgent, romantic vision of the world.

It is amusing today to recall the outrage caused by the novel – mainly by its exploration of the link between sex and religion – when it was first published: the sermons directed against it from pulpits, the angry speeches by cabinet ministers, the efforts to ban it. There was even an official inquiry in the Department of Foreign Affairs to establish how and where suspected leaks had occurred: arms negotiations between France and South Africa, which I had used as a fiction because it suited the plot, turned out to have been taking place in reality; a South African ambassador in Europe, as it transpired, had actually been involved in the kind of relationship depicted in the book. Today, more than twenty years later, that turbulence has subsided and *The Ambassador* can be read, quite simply, for what it set out to be: a novel by a young man battling to find or to redefine some values in the wake of the shipwreck of his familiar world.

1985

Third
Secretary

1

I have decided to report the Ambassador to the Department in Pretoria.

No doubt people like Anna Smith, and possibly even Koos Joubert, would read all kinds of personal motives into it: vindictiveness, frustrated ambition, wounded pride, no matter what. Let them. The thing is, Anna's passionate admiration of the Ambassador verges on the scandalous, and Koos is much too obtuse to see what is happening under his very eyes, let alone react to it. I suppose Douglas Masters, in turn, would cite long passages from Satow or Nicholson to argue that a Third Secretary should not stoop to such behaviour. But I really believe I have no choice left. I would be neglecting my duty if I allowed this sordid affair to continue, what with the delicate negotiations with the French Government already in progress.

I'm not saying that my decision is free from all personal considerations. But it is certainly not anything as petty as antagonism or envy, let alone hatred. The only personal motives involved (I must stress this) are disgust, and my deepseated loathing of hypocrisy. If the present Ambassador's predecessor, Jan Theunissen, had been involved – that is, if anybody could imagine old Theunissen in a situation like this – I might have chosen to let a sleeping St Bernard lie. He never tried to hide his essential, flawed humanity. But now it's Ambassador Van Heerden: the great perfectionist, the imposing man-of-influence, and probably the most efficient diplomat to represent South Africa abroad in decades. Not the slightest slip or oversight is tolerated in the Embassy, for the simple reason that he himself never makes a mistake. I have heard diplomats from hostile missions refer to him with nothing but respect, and sometimes with awe. Bonnard of the French Foreign Service recently made it quite clear that Paul van Heerden was the only South African the Quai d'Orsay still cared to listen to.

And then he fools about with that little tart Nicolette, while his wife is away on holiday in Italy. Virtue itself in public, integrity incarnate (although he didn't hesitate, only three days ago, to humiliate me at the Doyen's reception in the Hôtel de Ville). But when the door to Nicolette's little garret is closed and the curtains are drawn so that only shadows can be seen from the street below, it's a different story.

His nights are spent in the rue de Condé. But by day he takes over from God Almighty.

Obviously I've gone through the records to see what happened in similar situations in the past. In 1957 Peter Williams, a mere cadet, accused the chargé d'affaires in Buenos Aires of fraud. Four years earlier Vincent Johnstone accused his Ambassador in Berne of carelessness with classified official documents. There had been a couple of other cases before that, but I needn't go into all of them. It's enough to know that both Williams and Johnstone were summarily transferred back to Pretoria. As a matter of fact, Johnstone is still there. The Department has a highly efficient way of banishing such officials to dingy little offices where they can spend their time drawing up unimportant memoranda or initialling circulars. Williams was transferred to some obscure outpost; he resigned recently. So I am well aware of the implications of my decision. But I happen to know that in both cases I have just referred to there existed considerable suspicion about the motives behind the actions, and *my* conscience is clear. I know I can give such convincing reasons for doing what I'm going to do that no shadow can possibly fall on my future career as a diplomat. And that future is important to me. I'd promised that to myself even before I joined the Corps. I've seen enough of the frustration of careers ending up in culs-de-sac. Even my father will have

14

to admit, one day, that I have made it to the top – in spite of all his snide remarks in the past whenever my future was discussed.

Perhaps it's easy now to rationalize that past. But I prefer not to think too much about my youth. It is of no importance in the present situation. A shrink may find in it some psychological significance in explaining why I am what I am, but I resent picking at my entrails the way Anna Smith does (preferably when she knows that His Excellency is close enough to overhear). Besides, psychology so easily degenerates into a mere formula. I can remember, for example, how at the age of fifteen I had a long series of interviews with a psychologist in Pretoria hired to establish why I was such a 'difficult' child. I quite enjoyed the diagnostic tests. But I still remember very acutely the shock, the disgust, with which I accidentally discovered his final report reducing me to a glib case history. (*Case 325: Keyter, Stephen Wilhelm.*) The particulars about my father (*51; teacher; dominating personality; regards son as weakling*) and my mother (*38; gentle and somewhat reticent; tends to be moody*); all the clever references to '*intelligence above average,*' to '*neurosis*', '*impulsiveness*', '*emotional repression*', '*mother-fixation*', '*tendency towards morbid introspection*'; the revolting phrase, '*masturbation since early puberty*'; and finally the prosaic revelation of everything he'd so slyly cajoled out of me: how, as a small boy, I'd been terrified to sleep alone; how I'd often crept into my mother's bed at night; how my father had reluctantly come to accept this – except on Sunday nights, which I could never understand, until one Sunday night I'd slipped to their room to find out for myself. (*Primal Scene*.) QED.

As diagnoses go it's as much of a gamble as any other. How about this one? – Nicolette curled up in an armchair here in my apartment in the rue Jacques-Dulud, shoes kicked off, feet tucked under her, her darkish blonde hair over her shoulders, as she reads from a woman's journal:

'*People born under the sign of Gemini possess a double personality, so that they are continually at war with themselves. Of all people they are the most difficult to understand. On the one hand they are extremely amiable, on the other hand they can be hypercritical. They usually make excellent diplomats.'* (She smiles – the funny little curl at the left corner of her mouth – then resumes without looking up:) *'They are always active, yearning for what they cannot find. Therefore one should never try to bind them to their promises, or expect them to act consistently: not because they are dishonest, but because to them every moment exists as a separate entity in time, and because they continually switch from impulsiveness to rationalization.'*

'What about yourself?' I challenge her.

'Scorpio. October 21 to November 20.' Her hair forms untidy wisps across her eyes as she leans forward: *'Until their twentieth birthday these people are usually chaste and religious. Then they may suddenly change to the opposite extreme. Some of the greatest saints were born under this sign, as were some of the most notorious criminals. They are good fighters, yet they abhor violence, therefore they often assume the role of pacifists. Sex plays a decisive part in their lives.'*

'You really believe all that shit?'

'That's what the stars say.'

If I think back now, there is only one day from my youth that returns to me uncluttered by thoughts or doubts or the distortions of time. It must have been a Monday morning, because I felt ill. (I used to get headaches every Sunday night.) So I was mad at Mum for calling me back from the front door to put on a clean shirt. Mine – a white one with fine blue stripes – had a dirty rim round the collar. I snapped at her. We had an unpleasant argument. When at last I left for school I slammed the door behind me. And when I came back that afternoon, she was dead. My father explained that she'd somehow tried to clean his revolver.

2

Winter has set in early this year. Autumn was hardly a separate season; merely a morbid prelude to the coming cold, with something sinister and oppressive about it, as if the city found itself on the edge of a winter which would inevitably make it hard and narrow and bitter. Perhaps we will not even be allowed the compassion of snow: everything is just gradually reduced to rigidity, to the nakedness of black tree skeletons in the Bois de Boulogne just beyond these grey rooftops of the boulevard des Sablons.

Among the monotonous buildings one sees the exposed veins and nerves of the city in all its shameless anatomy, an X-ray photograph stripped of illusion. Paris. Perhaps that has been, from the very outset, the most unnerving experience of all: never to escape from an elemental awareness of the city. It is so much more than a backdrop or a random conglomeration of buildings. I have always sensed in it a life of its own which is larger and more elusive than the sum of all the smaller destinies acted out within it. Sometimes I have the impression that the city has served as a catalyst for all that has happened and is still happening. I think of it as a law of nature, of heredity, a parental body; and of us, existing inside it, as its turbulent chromosomes alive with genes. Even my standing here at the window (the panes opaque because of the excessive heating inside), sorting out arguments and motivations for the report I have to draw up, could never have taken place without this deep awareness of the city organism surrounding me. I may appear isolated, remote from that life outside and under my window – it is always easier to stare at darkness from behind the protection of a glass pane – yet it is always *there*, louring and inhuman. The

17

few people who risk it outside, belong to another species – and yet they, too, are fatefully part of me.

There are hardly any pedestrians under the bare trees. The men who, a little while ago, came back from playing *boules* in the parks (it is Sunday), squat and plump in their overcoats and berets, are now standing against the counter of the bistro on the corner, talking, gesticulating, drinking their beer and *vin chaud*. From time to time one of them ducks out into the drizzle and disappears in the direction of the Métro station in the avenue de Neuilly. An old clochard is leaning against the railing of the narrow strip of garden directly under my window, shivering and pathetic in the cold. Nobody else, except for the cars. There are no prostitutes in this smart suburb. Just as well. I can't stand them. Nowadays, when I come across one of them in a back street, I make sure that I address her before her cajoling voice can disarm me. 'How much will you pay me if I come along?' I ask her. It usually works. In the beginning, when I arrived here two years ago, still a virgin and living in the impossibly expensive hotel in the avenue Wagram where the Embassy had booked a room for me, I was much more interested in them and even made special excursions to the boulevard Sebastopol, Montparnasse, and the environs of Pigalle.

It was Koos Joubert who saw to my rites of passage. Koos should have become a farmer, not a diplomat. He is incongruous in any sophisticated surroundings. 'I'll open your eyes for you,' he said (promise or threat?). 'It's high time you saw a bit of life.' That was my first Sunday in Paris, and I actually felt grateful towards him for dragging me from my anonymous hotel room. We had dinner together, in the avenue des Ternes if I remember correctly: he and his timid little wife and myself. Afterwards, 'we men' set out on our own expedition (announced with a wink and a burst of bawdy laughter); Marlene had to take a taxi home – Koos couldn't be bothered.

A few streets away from the place Pigalle we entered a small, dimly lit night club: Koos seemed to know exactly

18

where he wanted to take me. Not a club with a very select clientele. Inside it was smoky and rather tatty; and the naked girls on the stage looked inexperienced and clumsy, a few of them were actually trembling, but whether from the cold or from fear was hard to tell.

'This is just a little appetizer,' Koos said after the second bottle of cheap sweet bubbly. 'Come along. Now I'm taking you to the real thing. Fucking expensive, but guaranteed to break the zip of your fly.'

He negotiated some kind of esoteric deal with a porter at the red velvet entrance to another club, turning round to wink broadly in my direction; and without appearing to move a finger the stranger conjured up two women on the pavement beside us. At first sight, and in that semi-darkness, they didn't look too bad. But once we were bundled into the drab little hotel room above the club, with their furs removed and their scars and flabbiness exposed, it was as if everything – they, us, the bed, the room with its faded and torn pattern-ed wallpaper – had suddenly become weary and unbearably old. I have only a very confused recollection of their wrest-ling, of the dull green bedspread covered with old stains, of the convulsions of etiolated flesh and what seemed like ludicrous patches of moss – and, finally, of the cool, smooth rim of the washbasin under my hands as I stood retching behind a screen bedecked with large pink roses. I heard a crow squawk. The bare bulb on the ceiling became a cyclops eye mocking my burning gaze. Afterwards all possible shades of emotion broke loose inside me: humiliation, anger, resent-ment, shame. But at that moment, standing there, con-vulsed, there was only one senseless thought turning over and over in my mind: *It's Sunday night. It's bloody well Sunday night again. Paris or Pretoria, no matter, it's Sunday night!*

Of course Koos would never allow me to forget it. It was no use trying to fight him. After all, he was Second Secretary while I was – at that stage – a mere cadet. I would just have to learn to live with it.

After that I set out in search of 'entertainment' on my own, but I never entered any of the special little 'private hotels', preferring to remain outside in the dark streets, fascinated in spite of myself by the rhythmic dance of shadows on drawn curtains; until, one night, a redhead with an evil glint in her eyes planted herself in front of me and started shouting insults while a throng of curious, amused spectators formed a circle round us. I broke away from them, blindly and in horror. On the next corner a harpy approached me from a dark niche and grasped my arm, whispering hoarsely. For a moment I stood frozen. Leaned back against the dirty wall she just stared at me through drooping eyelids, no expression whatsoever on her face. Above her red head, in high, uneven letters a fanatic had written: *Love thy neighbour as thys* – The rest was a whitish, dirty smudge. Underneath was an obscene drawing and the word *merde*. And behind her forbidding black letters proclaimed: *Défense d'afficher. Loi du 29 juillet 1881*. Three yards away, on the edge of the pavement, was a round disc fixed to a pole, with the inscription: *Défense de stationner*. The entire city, like my distant youth, had suddenly become a jungle of prohibitions.

'*Alors?*' she said.

I clenched my teeth and murmured: 'OK. Why not?'

She took my hand as if to lead a child to the circus (or to the bathroom, for a hiding?). In this blatant, if false, show of intimacy we passed some staring strollers, entered one of the numerous shady hotels of the quarter and went up to a bleak little room where someone had obviously tried to straighten the crumpled bedspread just before our arrival. I just stood there, watching her as she squatted over the bidet. All the time I tried fiercely to persuade myself that I really *wanted* to do it; that there was nothing else I *could* do. In spite of all the disgust and possibly even fear this kind of situation had always inspired in me, it also held me in a morbid spell as if, quite unexpectedly, this was my chance to avenge something. And it could not be avoided any longer.

With a great show of passion (though her eyes remained

unchanged), she came to me and rubbed her tits against me; then casually stepped back and demanded her fee. After carefully counting the notes she slipped them under her dirty suspenders (which she never took off) and said: 'Well, hurry up, *chéri*. I'm going off duty after this.'

It was a flop, of course. She didn't even bother to sneer. Humming an idiotic little tune, she went to the door where she struck up a conversation with someone in the passage, blurting out all the humiliating details of our encounter while I was still fumbling with my clothes.

Later that night I found myself sitting on the edge of the bath in my apartment, staring into the mirror at my own skinny white body, thinking: God, I'm revolting. I come from a past of Sunday nights and I'm still caught in that spell. Nothing will ever set me free. And I *want* to be free! No I don't. Why not try to be philosophical and conclude that the Tree of Knowledge bears shrivelled fruit; and sometime or other one *has* to taste it? It brings no revelation either of angels or of devils, and there is no god who nowadays rounds up offenders in the evening breeze. Perhaps this is the greatest letdown of all. Adam and Eve could at least count on punishment, which gave them something against which to measure, as it were, the extent of their achievement. But if there is no punishment because there has never been any sin to start with, one can only feel duped.

On a somewhat different level there was the New Year's Eve party in Douglas Masters's apartment in the boulevard Malesherbes: the refined decadence of the 'cultured'. The only memory I really have of that night is Jill. I never heard her surname. I think she was a model in London or somewhere, and she probably came with one of the British diplomats – Masters has many friends from their set. She had make-up plastered all over her; and she was sophisticated, suave, and on heat, wearing a black velvet dress which, in front, reached chastely up to her throat but, at the back, was cut down to her hips. With a much too long cigarette-holder in one hand and an olive between the thumb and forefinger of the other, she moved from one group to the other, alternating conversation with dancing – wild rock'n'roll motions which she could only execute by pulling up her dress to her waist, exposing a wisp of black panties. At one stage I was refilling her glass while she hung round my neck, whispering moistly into my left ear. We danced. Later she just disappeared. I went to look for her. When I opened one door I found myself in a bedroom dominated by a huge French double bed against the far wall, next to a tall ornament – a horrendous vase representing a man with an open skull from which monstrous birds were pecking the brains; on one side was a screaming cross-eyed devil half hidden by fig leaves. On the bed were bits and pieces of clothing, blankets, shapeless movements, a stranger, and Jill. I closed the door and left. A few hours later it was discovered that the vase had inexplicably been broken.

And then, Nicolette. It is neither by chance nor through any bitterness on my part that this discussion of tarts and teases has to wind up with her. How else can one describe her? Oh I know: the surface was something else. But what was she *really*? Scheming and deliberate in everything she did; entirely unscrupulous; self-sufficient, and much too sure of herself, and loose; with a certain hint of passion which could, it seemed, be turned on or off on demand. To Nicolette eating, or talking, or copulating seemed to be equivalent, all of them equally boring, if equally indispensable. (But even that was a mere pretence, for under the surface there was a complete lack of passion, almost an antipathy to passion, a sort of cynicism designed to wound whoever dared to probe her secret.) If there did exist any causal relation between these actions, it led from talking to sex, and from sex to eating (or buying clothes, or any of the other components of what she thought of as 'life'). That was her only hierarchy.

In the beginning, of course, I was not aware of this. In the beginning she was only a fairly attractive if somewhat angular, almost gawky girl who came into my office in the Embassy basement in connection with a lost passport. She wore huge dark sunglasses, a scarf round her darkish-blonde hair, a blouse with one button missing, a skirt and open sandals. Strange, that almost professorial air about her, especially when she removed the sunglasses: something myopic about the way she blinked against the light. Apart from that – although the mere thought is ridiculous – something prudish? And at the same time, unquestionably, something rather vulgar, although I'm not quite happy with the word.

How can I adequately convey the impression she made? I'm so stuck in officialese. Words are too formal, too smug, to record primary impressions. Perhaps I should illustrate this with what may seem a silly example: while I was at university the men students one night caught a bucketful of frogs which were taken to a women's dining hall where a frog was shoved under each white cup. These wild, wet, bewildered, amphibious creatures so completely out of their element under the demure, prim porcelain cups – that is the sort of thing I would like to express. And then, of course, the shrieks the next morning when the cups were turned over – because of these *things*, and their sliminess, their jumpiness – that is what I would like to achieve: but in the end one is left with only the cup in one's hands, all appetite for breakfast gone.

As for Nicolette, then, not only on that first morning but afterwards too, I shall have to rely on approximations, on possibilities, on 'impressions' – the impression, for instance, one gets with some women: of a bare body under the clothes.

She had no perfect figure. There was something boyish about her, a certain awkwardness about her elbows and knees, and her breasts were too small for my liking. And then there was this nonchalance, as if the loss of a passport really wasn't worth so much bother at all. To my consternation it appeared that she had, in fact, lost it several months before and that she would never even have taken the trouble of reporting it had she not needed it to have her *Carte de séjour* renewed by the police.

'You have been here for some time then?' I asked, per-
functorily.

The corner of her mouth barely moved. It was only after
some time, it seemed, that she decided the question might be
worth a reply. Removing the tip of her sunglasses from her
mouth, she smiled, and said: 'What was that?'

'I asked whether you've been in Paris for a long time.'

'*Bien sûr.*' The French came so spontaneously, I doubt that
she herself had even noticed the switch.

'How long?'

'Must you really know all this to give me a new passport?'

'I was only asking.' I felt annoyed. The rest of the interview was very formal. She'd have to make a statement to
the *mairie* in her quarter and bring back a receipt before I
could do anything about the matter. When she left, there was
no guarantee at all that she would in fact come back.

I suppose, thinking back to it now, that it was this very
uncertainty, as well as the touch of friction between us at our
first meeting which made me think of her so often during the
week that followed; implied in that trivial incident was a
challenge of some sort. I must add that I would have been
extremely susceptible to any sexual provocation at that stage.
It was July, eight months after my arrival in Paris, and the
muggy heat was enough to drive one crazy. At four o'clock in
the morning the streets were ablaze with light; it was nine in
the evening before the sunset finally quivered in the thick
green water of the Seine. There was a restlessness in the
blood which urgently needed an outlet. My bachelor life was
becoming too much for me. It was really most disturbing.
And then, suddenly, Nicolette was there. During the week
following her first visit she gradually assumed a very definite
shape in my mind, the memory of her *gamine* body an answer
to my aggressive need.

But when at last she turned up again – just as nonchalantly
as before, casual, almost unkempt, her hair damp with perspiration, a waif – it came as a shock. For all of a sudden she
was so different from the teasing woman of my week's fever-

24

ish thoughts. In fact, she was almost too nondescript in appearance, too *je m'en fous*. And, oh, too direct, too blatant, without the element of suggestion and mystery I appreciate in a woman: she made the impression, not of a girl, but of a *femina*, a positive and disturbing affirmation of body and limbs – yet apparently unaware of it herself.

She sat down before I could invite her to do so, opened her straw bag and started fiddling around in it while I waited with outstretched hand for the slip of paper. But when her hand finally emerged, it held only an empty blue box of Gitanes.

'Oh,' she said. 'Empty.' But I was quite sure she'd known that long before she said it. 'Would you like to offer me one?'

I picked up my own box from the desk and held it out to her. She took one, glanced at the South African trade mark, and said with the merest hint of a sneer: 'How patriotic. Thanks.' She unceremoniously bit off the filter end and spat it out, took some time to pick the bits of tobacco from the moist tip of her tongue, then leaned over towards the lighter I was still, stiffly, holding out to her. 'Ah, good.' She blew out the smoke. One of her open sandals was dangling loosely from a big toe. She sat watching it intently as if it was some acrobatic performance. There was no bra under her blouse.

She seemed to have no intention of breaking the silence at all.

I cleared my throat. There was still no reaction as she sat watching her wiggling toe.

'Well – uh – did you bring the receipt from the *mairie*?' I asked.

'Receipt? Of course.' She fumbled in the straw bag again, brought out a crumpled bit of paper which she carefully straightened out on her bare knee before giving it to me. 'Here you are.'

While I was filling out the form, I became conscious of her watching me. I quickly looked up with the express purpose of embarrassing her, but her eyes (strange eyes, intensely green) continued to stare at me without the slightest wavering.

'What do you do for a living?' I asked to conceal my own embarrassment.

'Model.' And, almost as an afterthought: 'At Dior's.'

I hadn't expected that.

'That's really classy!'

'I suppose so.' She carefully stamped out her cigarette on the sole of a sandal. 'I used to attend classes at the Beaux Arts.'

'And when are you going back to South Africa?'

Once again that peculiar little curling of her lip. 'Let's cut out the questions. I must go.'

I felt like a scolded child. 'I'll get in touch with you when the passport is ready,' I said quickly. 'Shall I phone you at Dior's?'

'Don't bother. I'll call for it.'

She went to the door. Something like panic surged up in me. Suppose she left – and never came back? There was such an elusive quality about her. And I could no longer bear the summer on my own.

'By the way –' I began.

She had just put on her sunglasses again and now moved them to her forehead to look at me, waiting.

'How about having dinner with me sometime?' How atrociously formal!

'Why not?' she said quite calmly.

'Tonight?'

'If you like.'

'Shall I come to pick you up? Where do you live?'

A brief hesitation. 'Neuilly. Near the Étoile.'

'I have a place in Neuilly too. So I'll –'

'But I must come in to town first,' she added quickly. 'A singing lesson. Why don't you meet me in the Champs-Elysées, at the Café Étoile? I'll wait at a table on the terrace.'

'Eightish?'

'Fine.' And then she was out, with a swirl of her green skirt, passing through the typists' office to the reading room. There she probably sat down to page through the papers, because it was fully half an hour before I saw her legs pass my window as she walked across the cobbled courtyard. (From my basement office all I usually see of visitors is from the waist downwards.) I liked her narrow hips; there was a hint of calf muscles on her slim tanned legs. Somehow it felt like a momentous – a very private – discovery.

In the shadow of the opposite wall where the courtyard narrows into the short driveway leading past the Ambassador's residence to the front door in the avenue Hoche, the concierge stood staring after her for a long time after she had disappeared from my range of vision. Only after the front door had banged, did Lebon touch his tie, wink to himself and go to unlock the garage door for the chauffeur, Farnham, to pull out the official Austin. I picked up my telephone and asked the switchboard girl to reserve a table in an exclusive little restaurant in the rue Boissy d'Anglas. Then I returned to the particulars on the form in front of me. VAN/ SURNAME: *Alford*. VOORNAME/CHRISTIAN NAMES: *Nicolette*. OUDERDOM/AGE: *23*. Meaningless statistics. Even the photographs she'd brought with her for the new passport looked impersonal and stern. What did she really mean to me? Nothing, surely. Except that it was summer; she was young; she had immediately said 'Yes' to my invitation – and to whatever had been left unuttered behind my formal words. (The frog in the porcelain cup?)

For a moment I felt aversion. After all, I was so unprepared. Most of my sexual experience had been vicarious, via Henry Miller, Frank Harris, de Sade, Apollinaire, and all the anonymous little books in the green or beige covers of the Olympia Press. But I pulled myself together. What was there to be scared of? I had everything neatly catalogued on paper, and in my mind. And at eight o'clock all the disparate details would, for the first time, be assembled in a coherent pattern.

By half-past eight there was still no sign of her at the Étoile. I could feel the first stirrings of a dangerous mood: the hell if I was going to be on the losing end again. The aperitif on my little round table had been replaced several times already. I

27

sat staring at the crowds streaming past. The city on promenade. Or rather, the whole bloody world, for there were more Germans, English, Americans and Scandinavians about than French; and there in the midst of them all, slightly drunk by now, more rejected than ever before, was I, clinging desperately to the small red island of my top-heavy table. I'd often sat on that terrace, and I used to enjoy it, but now it had become unbearable, as if I suddenly found myself naked in front of all those people with all my threadbare intentions exposed like an exhibit in some seedy criminal case. I never saw her coming, although I kept looking for her. The first I knew of her presence was when she said next to me: 'Oh, here you are.'

'Where the hell have you been?' My relief was greater than my annoyance.

'Am I late?'

'Almost an hour.'

'Oh.'

And that was all she said about the whole thing. Not that she was ill-mannered; actually I think it just never occurred to her that anything like an apology or an explanation might be expected.

She wanted a drink (a martini) but I refused, not without some deliberate stubbornness. We had to move on to the restaurant. If we waited any longer, we might lose our booking.

A little way lower down, on the opposite side of the street, near the Métro, we found a taxi and swerved into the stream of traffic down towards the Concorde, and turned left into the little street where the restaurant awaited us with open glass doors. I had no expectations of the next few hours, and I suppose I concealed my apprehension under a slightly resentful reserve. But while we were still in the taxi she already started talking as if we'd been going out for years. She told me about her singing lessons; commented endlessly on all the latest creations of fashion she had tried on that day and on the prospects of the coming autumn parade – small-talk which would normally irritate me but to which I unexpectedly found myself listening, both amused and grateful, and almost with joy, because it made everything so much easier. It was only when the *maître d'* ceremoniously handed us the large handwritten menus that she became quiet for a few moments; looking up, she flashed him a generous smile and offered him a sensuous '*Merci*' which melted every bit of his professional dignity. That was only the beginning of what, in the course of that long evening, would develop into a shameless flirtation: no harm intended, I'm sure, but none the less embarrassing to me.

'What a dish,' she said after I had given our order, looking back at him over her shoulder.

'Who?'

'The waiter.'

'He's too old for you,' I said coldly.

'I adore older men. Younger ones are so –' She gave me a sly look. For a few moments we stared very hard at each other; then she just shrugged and laughed. 'Well, I still like him. And he's got beautiful hands. Show me yours? I think a man's hands are tremendously important. Even more important than his eyes. You know, I just *love* this sort of menu with all its curls and things. Do you think they write each one separately? Quite impossible to make out a word, of course, but they're gorgeous. And as expensive as hell, but I suppose you Embassy people get a packet. If I earned as much as that, I'd get up at half-past four in the morning – in summer, of course – to see the sun rise (at what time *does* it rise?) and then go back to bed and sleep till noon and lie in a bath for hours. And I'd buy all the clothes I saw, all the stuff I'm now showing off to other people. Jesus, there was one heavenly dress today: all golden, made of straw, you know, raffia, it looked like it was handwoven, just one long sheath, with a wide brown belt and an antique buckle, and then amber earrings and another large chunk of amber on a thin gold chain round my neck, but I think turquoise would also go well with it. D'you like the earrings I'm wearing tonight? Want to know a secret? They come from the Monoprix but I think they look terribly expensive if one doesn't know. Look here's the *melon glacé*. Now just watch his hands when he puts it down. I hope it really is *glacé*. But I suppose it will be, in a place like this. D'you come here very often? I noticed that the *mec* at the door recognized you. And you should have seen the shoes that went with it. You'd never think any human foot except Cinderella's could get in there. Just as well mine are quite narrow –' She glanced down, round the corner of the table, and for one moment I was afraid that she might take off her shoe to show me her foot. 'Now did you look at his hands? I wonder whether he's really French-French? You can line up the whole United Nations, I'll always go for a Frenchman. *Merci, monsieur.* Pity your knuckles are so bony. You ought to tan a bit, you know, you're much too pale. I often go down to that path along the Seine for a tan in the lunch hour. Masses of people doing it, I suppose everybody from Samaritaine, because they're right up against the river. God, but it makes one lazy! Oh good, it *is* cold, I see, and fresh too. Of course you could do it down by Notre-Dame too, on the Île, but there one is stampeded by tourists and there's so many bloody clochards. Stinking to high heaven. Still, I'm rather fond of them, I must say I think I'll go to live under a bridge myself one day when I'm old and down-and-out. A bridge near Notre-Dame, then I can always hear the booming of the bells, how many tons does the big one weigh? It's like the voice of God the Father. And those crazy little flags on the towers. All one needs is an old tin or something for coals, then one could live quite comfortably. Should be easy to find something like that at Les Halles, if you get up early enough. You ever tried their onion soup? It's got to be in winter. Or you can buy chestnuts and throw them from one hand to the other until they've cooled off. But chestnuts always make me feel sad. Oh well, I suppose if one's a clochard you haven't got much of a choice anyway. Here he comes with the snails. *Formidable, monsieur!* I wonder where he lives. I'd love to live on the Île Saint-Louis, but of course that's only for the rich.

What on earth would rich people be doing on an island? And near the bells too? Not that one can really hear them so well from there. It's usually only the hooting of the cargo boats. Most of them come from Normandy, did you know that? The men always look so fierce and stern. I was in Brittany once. During Holy Week, in Saint-Malo. All I can still remember is the one night on the old city wall when the waves came breaking right over us and properly drenched me. I was soaked to the skin and my teeth chattered so much I couldn't get a word out when we got back to the room at last, long after midnight. And Jean-Paul complained that my whole body tasted of salt. Yes, please, fill up again. What is it?'

'Pouilly-Fuissé. Who's Jean-Paul?'

'An artist, I think. Used to be. I didn't know him very well. Only a week or so.'

There were many more questions I wanted to ask, but she was off on a new tangent. After a while she stopped to gulp down some wine in such a hurry that she choked. At that moment the waiter reappeared. Nicolette emptied her glass, leant back in her chair, watching him intently all the time he was serving the *canard à l'orange*, and then started complimenting him again. This time he lingered round her chair a little longer than was necessary. Her cheeks were flushed and because of the overheated interior there were a few strands of hair clinging to her cheeks. She was talking less now, and eating more, almost as if she was afraid that the plate might be taken away before she'd finished. She made no protest when I refilled her glass. All the time I sat watching her with the feeling that I was staring through a one-way mirror which left her completely unaware of my presence.

'I suppose I'm talking too much,' she mumbled unexpectedly, her mouth still stuffed with food.

'Of course not. I like listening to you. Say whatever you want to.' I was vaguely amazed by my own indulgence.

'Who would have thought, ten years ago, that I'd be sitting in a place like this tonight?' she said in maudlin mood, cupping the wine glass in her two hands as she stared either at her own reflection or at the shivering circles of light on the surface.

'What do you mean?'

'I was a real bumpkin, man,' she said in an unexpected, broad accent. There was a new edge to her voice. Her cheeks were more flushed than before. And then she blurted out a long confession, leaning forward and putting her hand on my wrist. It was all so personal that I felt ill at ease. She only interrupted herself to order an *île flottante*, afterwards two *petits suisses* and coffee. I sensed in her a strange compulsion to unburden herself of everything: a miserable childhood of rejection and rebellion, even physical maltreatment; an orphan youth, bleak and utterly joyless. This, then, was the complement to the lightness she had revealed earlier. And it occurred to me, with a sudden touch of despair, that something had gone wrong; somewhere we had taken the wrong turning; we had to get away from there before the evening turned into a disaster.

I beckoned the waiter and paid the bill. Her head was hanging – she was obviously depressed by the long confession – but I noticed that her eyes were watching very sharply the notes I counted into the plate. And once again there was that little curling corner of her mouth: an expression which caused me to wonder rather uneasily whether she was really sitting there, fretting, a desolate nymph gazing at her reflection in a pool under brooding thunderclouds – or whether she was, in fact, mocking me, playing with me (but what sort of game?).

The waiter brought my change and I counted off his tip. At the last moment she interrupted, saying, 'Wait!', took a few extra pieces from my hand and put them on the plate; then she laughed up at him with the cheapest sort of coquetry. With a very Gallic smile he pulled out her chair. She offered him her hand. He hesitated a moment, then raised it courteously to his lips. A woman in a tight evening dress at a table near ours leant over to whisper something in her companion's ear. Stung, I went to Nicolette, took her arm in a much stronger grip than was necessary and led her to the *vestiaire* for her shawl. She insisted rather loudly that I give the attendant a preposterous tip before, at last, we could walk out through the double glass doors.

'What's the matter with you?' I snarled at her.

'Why?' She was fanning her throat with a folded tissue. 'Hell, it's hot!' There were beads of perspiration on her forehead.

It must have been the wine – among other things. But the whole situation had unexpectedly reached a precarious, thin borderline where everything could easily go wrong and thwart my careful calculations.

'Come,' I said, as gently as possible. 'There should be a taxi at the Madeleine. We can do with some exercise.'

She walked next to me, humming a tune I didn't recognize.

'You shouldn't have told me all those terrible things,' I tried to get through to her. 'Now it makes you feel guilty that I know about it.'

'You mean *you* feel guilty.' She didn't even turn her head.

I knew exactly how clumsy and melodramatic it would sound, but I simply had to say it: 'No. I'm glad you told me, Nicolette. Perhaps it's opened up something between us.'

She began to laugh, not quietly at all but as if convulsed by a joke which she knew was rather off-colour.

I had only one hope left: to get home as soon as possible. There I might have more control over the circumstances and recreate the atmosphere that had seemed possible earlier in the evening.

When we reached the taxi rank she asked over her shoulder: 'Where are we going?'

'I thought –'

'Let's go to Montmartre. The city looks beautiful from up there.'

'But it's late.'

'You can go home if you want to. I'll be all right.'

The taxi driver was watching us in his mirror. I could see his unshaven face and sardonic eyes.

'All right,' I said.

The narrow streets of Montmartre were crammed with people. By the time we reached the last incline of the rue Lepic we had to crawl along at a snail's pace. On the place du Tertre we got out and were carried along to the terrace of the Sacré-Coeur by the steady stream of people. Strollers, tourists, holiday makers, accompanied by hawkers and vendors swarming like flies around the crowd. Gnarled old women with bunches of flowers or dolls or *France-Soir*; lanky boys with nuts and sweets and rattles and other noisy toys; ice-cream sellers; and 'artists' who demanded to draw our portraits. And, of course, Nicolette's vanity could not resist this temptation. For ten minutes I had to wait while she casually posed, with flushed cheeks and intense eyes, surrounded by a loud, admiring circle of spectators. Without any embarrassment at all she stood there until he'd finished, then held the drawing at arm's length and handed it to me over the craning necks between us, so that all eyes turned round to stare at me. I paid five francs for the drawing. It was not a bad resemblance after all, although it certainly wasn't Nicolette – but how could anybody capture her on paper? – and then I took her away from there as quickly as possible.

She insisted on having a beer on the square. By this time her negative mood had passed and she seemed to be revived by the cooler air on the hilltop. She still wasn't as carefree as before. This emotion was something stronger, more difficult to determine: an obscure ecstasy, revealing itself in gusts and spurts.

The whole square was a fairground of parasols, green tables and chairs, scurrying waiters, boisterous teenagers and milling, jostling strollers. From the many cafés came waves of dissonant music. And while we were drinking our beers a rubbery youngster in tight-fitting pants and an open shirt came strutting past the tables with a guitar, pretending to sing as he leered through his long unkempt hair at anything that appeared vaguely female. Nicolette's enthusiasm was, of course, aroused immediately. And within five minutes he was at our table, *on* our table, strutting and prancing, her radiant eyes following every ripple of his young male body. And when he tentatively strummed the notes of one particular hit tune, she immediately started humming to his accompaniment. I still don't know how it happened: inexplicably she was no longer with me but dancing with him; soon they were joined by a few other couples. At first they milled round the tables, then moved farther away to the cobbled street, obstructing the traffic. She had taken off her shoes. Her hair came undone, falling loosely round her shoulders. It was a disconcerting dance, an overt expression of sensuality, an affirmation of youthful sex, with dark invitations and overt responses, with all kinds of parodies and variations. I couldn't move a finger. Soaked with sweat, I could feel my shirt clinging to my back. My unsmoked cigarette burnt my fingers. Angrily I dropped it, and clasped the end of the green table until my fingers went numb. I couldn't – wouldn't – understand what was happening. I know now that all the time (which actually could not have been more than fifteen minutes or so) I sat there petrified in an unbearable state of jealousy.

At last I managed to react; and thank God I could do it without causing a scene. Getting up, I moved past the first dancers, took her arm, and simply said: 'Come.' She obeyed without objection. I sensed the confused emotions provoked in her by the wine and the long confession and the heat and the wild music. And this inevitably stirred up reactions in myself. We had to get back to my apartment!

Dragging her with me, I went in search of a taxi, but there was none to be found. On our way to the terrace of the Sacré-Coeur she said: 'Why don't we go down to the Métro? It's much more fun.'

I have an intense dislike for underground trains, but not wanting to provoke another negative reaction I followed her down the cascades of stairs to the bustle of boulevards, night clubs, sidewalk stalls and cafés below. We were halfway down before she discovered that she was still carrying her shoes in her hand. By the time we reached Pigalle and entered the rancid, sticky atmosphere of the Métro, she was complaining that her feet were aching.

'Are you quite sure we shouldn't take a taxi? We'll easily find one here.'

She merely shook her tousled head and stood waiting for me on the other side of the ticket office while I bought a *carnet*. I handed two to the shapeless blue woman at the little green gate and gave the rest to Nicolette. 'Keep them. I never use the damn things.'

She smiled her thanks as if this little gesture meant more to her than all the premeditated luxury of our expensive meal.

We had to wait a long time before the train burst from its tunnel and came to a standstill at the dirty platform. For the first few stations there were no seats and we had to lean against the sticky chromium poles. There was a fat woman with nodding head and gaping mouth, bobbing up and down on one of the narrow brown benches; workmen in crumpled overalls, with day-old beards and greasy, long-read newspapers, sat staring at Nicolette with lecherous eyes. By the time we reached Villiers where we could at last sit down, the depressing effect of the subterranean atmosphere had already begun. At Étoile we had to change to the Neuilly line. At the entrance to the *correspondance* passage she stopped, apparently surprised, and asked listlessly: 'But where are we going?'

'You're tired,' I said evasively, troubled by my own fatigue. 'So I thought you might like a last cup of coffee at my place.'

She looked at me but I couldn't read the dull expression in her eyes. At last she nodded. She was paler than before.

In the next train a young couple took seats opposite us, weighed down by the sort of tristesse which – I presume – follows the hour of passion, when there's nothing else left to do but continue the languid mime of the game of love. Only the gestures were left, the indolent movement of old brown weeds in a lazy sea. There was something unreal in their behaviour: a grotesque commentary on relationships, and on us. It oppressed me; it made me feel resentful.

When we finally reached Les Sablons the heat and drowsiness had acquired almost physical weight; at the exit, above, one became unpleasantly aware of cold perspiration on one's face.

We walked in silence to the rue Jacques-Dulud and crossed the street to my building.

She was a few yards ahead of me and stood waiting for me at the front door, swinging her handbag behind her back. I pressed the button to open the door's latch, and we went in. Inside it was silent, the city suddenly stripped from us like an old skin shed by a snake. Motionless, the staircase wound its way upward, the narrow strip of carpet like an obscene red tapeworm with shiny stripes marking the segments.

'Smart,' she commented cryptically.

She was in front of me. I noticed, once again, the moving muscles in her smooth calves. It was a tiresome climb, four storeys up, before I could unlock my door, and switch on the light inside, inviting her to enter.

As I closed the door behind me she said, her back still turned to me: 'Satisfied?'

'What do you mean?' I asked, uneasily.

'This is what it was all supposed to lead up to, isn't it?'

'Anything wrong with it?'

'No. But why did you really want me to come?'

'To have some coffee. I told you so –'

'Thanks.' With her narrow back still towards me, she walked into the room to inspect the decorations on the opposite wall: a straw mat, a few odds and ends of African beadwork, a small Pierneef etching.

'Why must you people carry South Africa with you wherever you go?' she asked. 'You scared you may lose it somewhere along the way?'

I decided, perhaps wrongly, to ignore the remark, and

went to my narrow kitchen to put on the percolator, staying there much longer than was necessary, to allow her time to acclimatize. She was only feeling a bit ill at ease, I convinced myself. Everything had been so perfect on the square. I just had to hit the right note –

When I finally returned to the living-room she lay comfortably stretched out on the mohair bedspread covering the divan, her shoes kicked off. I hesitated, then went over to the record-player. 'Shall I put on a record?' I hoped my voice wouldn't betray how shaky I felt.

She turned her head to look at me. After a moment she replied evenly: 'If you want to.'

'Anything in particular?'

'Anything.'

I chose something light and sentimental. She didn't move. After a while I went back to the kitchen. I was busy pouring the coffee when the record-player was abruptly switched off.

'Don't you like it?' I called.

She didn't even bother to answer.

When I took in the coffee, she was half-sitting, half-lying on the divan, propped up against a cushion.

'A load of shit,' she said, helping herself to four teaspoons of sugar. 'All this sighing about love. Slobbering in the moonlight. Why are men so damned dishonest?'

'Dishonest?'

'Why do you choose sweet little songs, why do you invite one for dinner, why do you make coffee, why do you keep on playing your little games? Couldn't you just tell me straight what it was you wanted? You think I'm an easy lay?'

Leaning her head against the wall she suddenly burst out laughing, not without an edge of hysteria, spilling coffee on my precious new bedspread.

I angrily put down the tray. 'Nicolette, for God's sake –!'

She stopped laughing, but her eyes were still smouldering. 'And now he's angry. Someone has promised him a sweetie and taken it away again!'

I grabbed her arm violently.

'Leave me alone!' Swinging her legs from the bed she jumped up. The cup rolled over my Afghan carpet. 'Is *this* the sweetie you wanted –?' In one angry movement she had jerked open the zip down her back and stripped the upper half of her dress from her shoulders. Wordless, trembling, she stood before me. Without her dress, she seemed smaller, younger, thinner. There was even a hint of ribs. And cupped in the shells of her bra were her small breasts, soft and protected and private. I desired her, and hated her, and pitied her, all at the same time. But at the first uneasy step I gave towards her, she swung away from me, zipped up her dress again, put on her shoes, raked her fingers through her hair, took her handbag and left. The door was closed very quietly behind her. I couldn't decide whether I should follow her or let her go. But the decision was soon taken. I was still trying to sort out my confusion when, less than five minutes later, there was a knock on the door.

Although I knew it couldn't be anybody else, it was still a surprise to find her on the doorstep. She was pale, but quite composed.

'I have no money for a taxi,' she said.

I wanted to explain, even to plead with her; but all I could do – numbly – was nod and take a few notes from my pocket. She took the money.

'I'll go down with you,' I said.

'No.'

'Please!'

After a while, with a brief sigh, she nodded.

In the narrow sidelane next to the boulevard I opened a taxi door and helped her to get in.

'You sure you'll be all right?'

'Of course.'

'I'd like to –'

'Please go now.'

I realized it would be wiser to obey; so I said goodbye and walked away. When I reached the corner I heard a door slam and turned round. She'd left the taxi and was on her way to the Métro, fifty yards further. Immediately I started after her, but I soon stopped. It was too late to catch up with her without running and causing a scene. Without glancing back (although she surely must have expected me to follow her!) she went down the Métro steps and disappeared. It was a complete mystery. There is no Métro line to another station in this part of Neuilly where she'd said she lived. ('Near the Étoile –') So where could she be going? And why had she come back for money if she already had eight Métro tickets in her handbag?

Sleep did not come easily that night. I couldn't explain my own feelings. I was humiliated and angry; my most urgent need had been thwarted. And yet this very need had lost its overwhelming urgency in the process.

The next morning I telephoned her at Dior's.

'Alford? Nicolette Alford?' the receptionist repeated. 'We've never had anybody with that name here.'

3

This will never do. I knew I would get lost in Nicolette again as soon as I allowed the memories of her to come back. It was in July of last year that it all started; today is the fourth of December. In the course of eighteen months we have come to know each other pretty well – that, I suppose, is how my colleagues would view it. But what does 'knowing' someone mean? (As for the Biblical meaning of the word – there was that one night. Only one. And that was such a wretched affair that all resemblance to the real thing must have been, as they say, fortuitous.) I could describe each one of our meetings in just as much detail – sometimes in more – as that first evening; and every time it would end with the same question mark, the same sense of incompleteness, of something missing. Not that there was anything 'mysterious' about her as I would have liked to believe in the beginning; she was simply a compulsive liar, telling the most remarkable lies even when the truth would do.

The first time I saw her again after her inexplicable disappearance – it was about ten days later, when she came to collect the passport – I tried pointedly to set a trap for her.

'What have you been doing all this time?'

'Nothing special. Just kept busy by my job.'

'Still at Dior's?'

'Yes.'

'I tried to get in touch with you there,' I said calmly, leaning forward to study her reaction. 'But they didn't even recognize your name.'

'So what?' She didn't bat an eyelid. 'Why do you have to know everything about me?'

'And all the other things you told me?'

'Don't you believe me then?'

It was impossible to carry on a conversation like this. I gradually came to suspect that the whole lengthy confession about her unhappy orphan childhood had also been thought up by her fertile imagination. Sometimes she told me other stories in its place, always equally seriously and confidentially. I still don't know the truth. But I doubt whether it implies anything so melodramatic as an attempt to escape from her past. I suppose the simple explanation is that it just doesn't make any difference to her which of her stories is true, consequently she can't understand that it might matter to anybody else. (Or am I wrong? Why do I really care about her truth? What difference could it possibly make?)

Sometimes we went out; often we spent our evenings in my apartment. Once or twice she even tried to mend my clothes – sewing on white shirt buttons with red cotton – but it didn't quite succeed. A few times she tried to cook for us. She insisted on preparing the most elaborate dishes. Once the chicken was almost edible; more often than not the food had to be deposited, solemnly and without comment, in one of

41

the grey rubbish bins at the bottom of the staircase.

Towards October last year I spent two weeks' holiday in the Loire Valley. She offered to look after the apartment during my absence. When I returned a day earlier than expected, I hardly recognized the place. There was no empty chair to sit on: they were all stacked with make-up, stockings, open suitcases, glossy magazines, underclothes or unwashed cups and glasses. The carpet was rolled up against the wall, the bed was broken and sheets, blankets and pillows lay strewn across the mattress on the floor. It was drizzling outside and the heater was turned on full blast. (The electricity bill at the end of that month amounted to 720 francs.) It was quite obvious that she'd been having a series of extravagant parties during my absence; and this suspicion was soon confirmed by an ill-tempered neighbour and the concierge. Nicolette, of course, denied it point blank. But perhaps she had a more subtle way of admitting her guilt; the extraordinary zeal with which she helped me tidy up the apartment.

My other memories of these eighteen months are rather confused. There were constant quarrels. She could drive me mad by teasing me, inviting me, provoking me – only to evade me, laughing, in the end. But while I was furiously shouting all sorts of insults at her, she would coolly shrug her shoulders and say: 'Oh balls.' Or: 'Did you know there was a button missing from your coat?'

Once she suddenly got it into her head that she had to refine her education. She wanted to get acquainted with the great philosophers. With some kind of perverse amusement I brought her the most bulky and awe-inspiring volume I could find in the whole American Library: a scholarly review of philosophy from Socrates to Albert Camus. For three weeks I hardly ever saw her. She studiously worked through every page of that impossible book – and then mislaid it, so that I had to buy the library a new copy. She never referred to it with a single word, not even when I pointedly asked her about it.

Sometimes she would just disappear, evaporate. It was different from the first time, when I had merely lost track of her because she had lied about where she lived and worked, since by then I often visited her in her tiny apartments – first near the Porte d'Auteuil, afterwards a few streets away from the place des Vosges, and eventually in the rue de Condé. On these occasions even her concierge knew nothing of her whereabouts. Afterwards it would transpire that she'd either been 'busy' in another part of Paris, or roamed somewhere in the country, usually all by herself. Once, I know, she went on a pilgrimage to Chartres, with thousands of students, because she often referred to it. (Unless that, too, was a lie. Cathedrals seemed to hold a peculiar fascination for her: that, at least, was what she pretended.)

Why didn't I cut her out of my life earlier? That is one of those impossible questions which touch on a whole submerged web of nerve-ends and motives and evasions. The main reason why I held on to her, I think, was that I believed (or hoped) that sometime or other I would still manage to have my way with her, to succeed with her where, with others, I had so often failed. And at last it did happen, as I have already intimated. It was an evening towards the end of September this year, when the first ominous signs of autumn had already become visible. She came to my apartment to have a bath. (There was nothing strange about that, except that she usually came during office hours, when I was away, once a week or so. Her own little apartment in the rue de Condé has no bathroom.) She arrived early, with her things in a string bag which she casually threw down on the divan. We started talking: the kind of rabbit-warren conversation we so often had, full of dead ends. And, as usual, it soon touched on our 'relationship'. I accused her of being obstinate and petulant. Why should she always keep me on a string, playing an inscrutable little game, always staying out of reach? After all, I knew exactly who and what she was – that she never tried to hide her numerous flirtations with other men. 'Or perhaps they pay you enough? Is that it?' It was the first time I'd dared to taunt her like that.

She flew into a rage.

'I bloody well do what I want,' she said. 'Nobody has ever paid me to do anything I didn't *want* to do.'

Beside myself, I pulled a few notes from my pocket (there was at least one of a hundred francs among them) and threw them in her lap.

'Well, how about this?!'

She said nothing. She picked up the notes, straightened them, arranged them in a neat little pile and put them on the tea table, with an ashtray on top. Then she got up and went to the bathroom. I heard her opening the taps and waited for her to come back, because she'd left the door open. But before I realized what was happening, she was already in the bath.

Then followed one of those silly, childish scenes which seem great fun while they last, but later leave one with a nasty aftertaste. I stood on the living room side of the open door, threatening, playfully and with a touch of bravado, to come in.

'Well, why don't you?'

'You'd sing a different tune if I did.'

'You're just scared.'

Should I? Dare I? Suppose she meant it? Suppose she *didn't* mean it – ? On the other side of the door the water was splashing over the sides of the bath. Taking a deep breath I pressed my burning face against the slit on the side of the hinges trying feverishly to see something inside.

I was still standing there, leaning forward, when she jumped out of the bath and came skipping past me, naked and glistening, to collect her soap and towel from the string bag on the divan. Her wet hair formed dark strings down her shoulders. Before I could react properly, she was back in the bathroom; this time she closed the door. Foolish and miserable, I turned away and went to light a cigarette. Before I had finished smoking it she opened the door and came back: fully clothed, but her hair still wet. She squatted cross-legged on the bed and started rubbing her hair with the damp towel. I stood looking at her, then stubbed out my cigarette very slowly and emphatically and went over to her. For a short while she went on drying her hair with quick, nervous movements, then gave it up and, with the wet towel still in her hands, looked up at me: anxious? mocking? sneering? She must have known that this time it would be useless to resist.

It was over very quickly. She lay without moving a finger all the time I went about the business of making love, her eyes closed, passive, altogether passionless. I should have expected it. I've read that women of her kind are often frigid.

But at least she should do *something*! Silence would be unbearable.

'Well?' I said when I finally got up. 'You can't say you didn't ask for it.' I felt aggressive.

'No,' she answered quietly, pulling down her dress over her knees. I noticed, incidentally, a tiny pair of scarlet panties dangling from one of her ankles, something cheap and vulgar, a bad joke that emphasized the cheapness of what had just happened.

'Why don't you say something?' I insisted.

'What is there to say? D'you expect me to compliment you on your performance?' She laughed quietly and started rubbing her hair as if nothing had happened. 'Lover boy!' Her breathing was slightly irregular.

I clenched my fists, then turned round to fasten my buttons with my back to her, fully aware of how ludicrous it must all seem. And very soon she did burst out laughing, exactly as I'd foreseen and feared.

'You haven't got very much to boast about either!' I snarled.

'No.' She got up from the crumpled bedspread and went to the bathroom. 'How about making us some coffee? We're cold, both of us.'

The bathroom door was locked. The taps were opened as before. And there were thin skins on the coffee cups by the time she finally came back, composed, clean, her hair tidily brushed into the customary pony-tail. We sat in silence while we drank. Afterwards she got up, took her string bag, glanced at me, lifted the ashtray from the table and picked up the notes. She folded them into a tiny square and slipped them under her bra.

'Nicolette –'

'Good-night, Stephen.'

I saw her going down the spiral staircase, each storey narrower than the one above, until, small and distant, she went past the row of rubbish bins and disappeared into the street.

4

Some fortunate cadets are sent overseas very soon. But I was in Pretoria for fully two and a half years before I was finally transferred to Paris. Not that I regret it. It gave me the opportunity of acquiring a very thorough training in more than one section of the Service, passing all the necessary exams, and – which is important in my career – getting to know several men in senior positions. After only one month in Paris I was promoted to Third Secretary – six weeks before Peter Marais in Berne, who is really my senior, but who took longer to pass his exams. My main disadvantage was that after the time in Pretoria, where I'd become used to a predictable, secure way of life, I felt completely stranded in this bustling city with the Embassy the only island where one could still enjoy the sense of security created by the presence of compatriots.

It is not a very imposing building. Seen from the avenue Hoche it is nothing but a large brown door with a shiny copper plaque inscribed in three languages; apart from public holidays there is not even a South African flag to distinguish it from all the other equally large, equally brown doors in the same avenue. Immediately inside the main entrance a few stairs on the left lead downwards to the quarters of the concierge, Lebon, followed a few yards further on by the broad staircase to the front door of the official residence; then the short driveway widens into the small cobbled courtyard on the opposite side of which one enters the double glass doors of the office building. From the reading room, which also serves as foyer, a door on the left gives access to the typists' office in the basement, followed by my own; on the right a dark staircase leads up to the Registry Department and the offices of the other Third Secretary, the Second Secretary, and the First; the last door is that of the Ambassador's own sumptuous office. On the top floor are the three Attachés (Military, Cultural, and Commercial), their respective secretaries and the official translator. Everything is rather cramped, the narrow corridors are ill-lit, and one is eternally surrounded by the smell of old books.

Naturally, I became acquainted with the other staff members very soon: in the Embassy, at a few informal receptions, and especially at a cocktail party Jaap Mouton had organized to welcome me to Paris. At that time he was still the other Third Secretary, an amiable fellow who has since been transferred to Cologne. He was succeeded by Theo Harrington, something of a windbag who is much too conscious of his attraction for women despite the fact that he is already married to a strikingly beautiful but very reserved young girl; but he undoubtedly has a flair for his work. Koos Joubert, the Second Secretary, I already mentioned: an archetypal 'Boer' and a fanatical supporter of Government policy. As a matter of fact, we've had quite a few brushes on this very subject. 'How the hell can a man represent a government he doesn't support?' he argued. 'I'm an Afrikaner, man. If ever my Government goes, I go too. In the meantime I'm a Boer diplomat: if anybody gets in my way, I just step on him.' In reply, I could only counter with the time-honoured statement: 'I serve each successive government with equal fidelity and equal contempt.' But this is not altogether true, of course. It would be more accurate to apply this philosphy to

47

Douglas Masters, the First Secretary, who is correctness itself: to him, everything in diplomatic life forms part of an elaborate game, a never-ending battle of wits and calculation. Yet I doubt whether he'll ever become a great diplomat. His personality is really that of a brilliant administrator as fastidious as any old woman. Compared to his philosophy mine would rather be: my career is a means to an end, not an end in itself. That end? – it is, quite simply, the top. I doubt whether this is just a reaction to my father's attitude. It's something in its own right, something positive, a firm conviction that the only person who 'means' something is the one who proves himself master of every single situation, including the decisive test. Survival of the fittest? Perhaps. Zarathustra? In the final analysis, yes. I've spent many hours of my life with Nietzsche. And I think it is a sad mistake to see in Hitler only the demon of the gas camps: the Third Reich will be rediscovered one day, revalued for what it really was. Not that I ever discuss it with my colleagues – especially not with Koos, who is congenitally incapable of abstract thought.

Koo's colourless, mousey little wife usually stays at home to look after her numerous children. But Sylvia Masters is the exact opposite. She loves to talk about 'fabulous Paree', in spite of the fact that she doesn't know the first thing about the city, or about French. Her mornings are spent in bed: she seldom rises before noon. In the afternoon she goes out to 'tea'. Two Spanish servants take care of the household. Her son is at a private school in England. Sylvia is attractive, I suppose, but spiritually she is anaemic, and sexually as exciting as a wet newspaper. It would be in the interests of my career to get married sooner or later, but God forbid that I choose a wife like Sylvia.

The three Attachés I meet very seldom. Two of them, anyway. I doubt whether Colonel Kotzé has any close friends: he is much too caught up in his military past and the pathos of his present paperwork. As for the Commercial Attaché, Verster, he usually hides behind his thick glasses and has no existence outside his family and his work. Victor le Roux, however, soon became a close friend of mine, probably because he's the only other bachelor on the staff. Victor is a closet writer, although he is something of a dilettante and rather effeminate; but in a small company he can be a delightful raconteur. We spend many long nights arguing about philosophy, art, religion, sex, or whatever.

Then there is Anna Smith. She used to be a teacher, but then she got married and after two years her husband ran off with another woman – who would blame him? – and she ended up in the Foreign Service. Anna is tall, severely plain and lean; and she regards herself as 'a connoisseur of the stage'. Paris went straight to her head. She has her hair done at Alexandre's, she dines in Maxim's, she mixes only with the 'right' people. She likes to regard herself as one of the 'younger set', although her ideas tend to move in an extremely narrow circle. (Move? They stand very firmly, in the tradition of Luther.) She has 'unseverable bonds' with her People, her Language, and her Church – Dutch Reformed. All new South Africans in Paris are sheltered under her wings – a fate I myself could not escape. But we quarrelled on my very first Sunday when she wanted to take me to her church and I made it very clear that I had no intention of using every irrelevant little mystery or feeling of guilt to lift mine eyes unto the hills and trade on the comfort of a convenient fiction.

'But how on earth can you live without God?' she gasped.

'I get along very well. I decided, once and for all, that I was going to have my life here and now and that I'd never rely on the illusion of heaven or hell.'

She still promised to pray for me.

And there were Their Excellencies, at that time Jan Theunissen and his wife. He was a relic from a previous order and, as often happens, had been moved higher and higher by the inscrutable turning of the diplomatic wheel simply because no single mission could bear his general inefficiency for very long; and so, at last, his huge amiable backside had come to rest on this plush chair. He took a liking to me from

49

the very beginning, prompted, I think, by two motives: first, I was prepared to listen sympathetically (!) to his detailed daily exposition of his main concern – that he was not adequately appreciated by the Government because he had been a supporter of its predecessor; and second, I shared a box of South African grapes with him which I received from friends back home shortly after my arrival in Paris. He blatantly favoured me, much to the indignation of Masters' predecessor, Prinsloo. A lot of important and highly confidential work, which normally would never be entrusted to a Third Secretary, was left entirely to my own discretion. Towards the end of his career in Paris it often happened that I was responsible for correspondence on extremely delicate subjects while he never even glanced at the letters I wrote or received. And when protocol demanded his personal signature he would barely scan the typewritten sheets before signing his name at the bottom in his grand, antiquated handwriting.

'There's only one way for a young diplomat to learn the ropes,' he used to say. 'He must do the work himself.' Both of us knew that it was a euphemism; the truth was that his suspicion about the Government's attitude towards him had long ago paralysed all his energy and enthusiasm.

As far as official conduct was concerned, I felt nothing but contempt for him. The same applied to his wife, who would make her appearance at the most solemn occasions wearing an idiotic hat covered with frills and flowers and lace and gilt hatpins. But judged solely as *people* they were one of the most charming and sincere couples I have ever come across.

It is not without reason that I reminisce about the Theunissens, in spite of the fact that they left Paris over a year ago when, evidently to the heartfelt relief of the Government, he could finally be pensioned. I do so because I want to emphasize the enormous difference between them and their successors. Or, more accurately, between old Jan Theunissen and Ambassador Van Heerden.

At first we were all impressed by the new man's appearance. By that time we'd already heard about his reputation at the missions in Vienna, where he'd been Ambassador, and New York, where he'd represented South Africa at the UN. When the doors of the Boeing were opened at Orly and the passengers came down the gangway, anybody would have recognized him immediately, even if he hadn't waited until the very last in order to be escorted to the VIP reception lounge. He was not taller than the average, but broad-shouldered and powerfully built, with greying hair, a strong nose, unwavering eyes, remarkably healthy white teeth – in fact, inviting all the clichés usually employed to describe such a person.

On his third day in the Embassy he telephoned me from his office and asked me to come up to him. I finished the file on which I was working – as I'd been accustomed to do in Theunissen's time – and then mounted the stairs to the first floor. He barely glanced up as I entered, and continued writing. I waited for two whole minutes, following the leisurely circle of the red second hand on the large clock opposite his desk.

'Have I kept you waiting, Keyter?' he asked suddenly, without looking up.

'I beg your pardon, Mr Ambassador?' I was taken by surprise. 'No. Of course not.'

He smiled faintly. 'Of course I have. For exactly two minutes. On the other hand it took you seven minutes to climb one flight of stairs.'

I opened my mouth to answer, but he stopped me with a brief gesture of his right hand which was still resting on the paper. Neither of us has ever referred to that incident since. It has never been necessary. And I suppose I deserved it.

He took a letter from a pile at his elbow, weighted down by a small bronze statuette, and asked: 'Did you write this?'

I recognized it immediately. It was my latest letter to the Minister's secretary in Pretoria in connection with certain negotiations with the Banque de France.

'Yes, Mr Ambassador,' I answered readily, 'I sent it up in your basket to be signed.'

He was holding my letter in both hands, looking at me quite kindly. 'Don't you think you should consult either Mr Masters or myself before entering into correspondence on such delicate matters?'

I could feel blood surging into my face. 'But, Mr Ambassador, I've been working on this business for more than a month now –'

'Then perhaps it's time to set the record straight. In future no letters on confidential negotiations will be written on behalf of any of your seniors without his, or my, specific instruction and approval. As far as this particular matter is concerned, I shall deal with it personally.' He folded my letter, calmly tore it up, crumpled the bits in his strong hand and dropped them into the wastepaper basket. Then he said: 'That will be all, thank you, Keyter.'

There were other, similar, incidents in the course of the first month. I was left in no doubt that all the initiative Theunissen had allowed me was now being firmly curtailed. Even trivialities like using official paper for private correspondence were prohibited. I suppose all these things would fall under the heading of minor irregularities, yet they happen, as a matter of course, in practically all Embassies, as in all State Departments. The result was that a disturbing and unnecessary impression of authority was created. And as could be expected it affected me much more than the others who hadn't enjoyed old Theunissen's confidence to the same extent. To crown everything, I was, at the end of the first month, transferred from my previous duties in the political section to ordinary consular affairs, which are obviously much more tedious than composing and deciphering code telegrams, summarizing confidential memoranda, or being involved in correspondence on delicate and intricate matters of state.

What made it so hard to stomach was that the Ambassador evidently had every right to do as he did and that he was really much more than just a competent administrator. In diplomatic circles he was generally regarded as a man of considerable stature; and within two months of his arrival in Paris there was an appreciable change in the attitude of members of other delegations towards us. But whereas Theunissen had never been a diplomat, only a human being, it is practically impossible to imagine Van Heerden – His Excellency – reduced to the state of 'merely' a man. Unlike other diplomats he does not appear to lead two lives – official, and private – but only one. Oh, he can be affable and suave at receptions, but one soon discovers that even his charm and warmth are devices of a human robot who knows exactly what he wants and – more important – how to get it. I don't mean that he 'acts like' a robot, hiding his personality behind a public face: what makes it so disturbing is that he really *is* the mask he appears to wear. For instance, I cannot picture him in any intimate situation with a woman, not even with his own wife, let alone Nicolette – but I'll come to that in due course.

The Ambassador's wife, Erika, arrived a week after His Excellency, accompanied by their daughter. She must be a few years younger than her husband, probably in her late forties, and it is evident that she must once have possessed what is termed 'classical beauty'. Even now she still reveals the sort of grace which is improved rather than diminished by age. And yet, if one comes upon her unexpectedly, one is sometimes startled by the weariness in her eyes.

She immediately organized a dinner party to meet all the members of staff, even the typists; and she is, without doubt, the best hostess I've ever come across. The way in which her daughter, Annette, mingled with the guests, starting up brilliant, superficial conversations as she went, suggested that she, too, had from an early age been primed for just such a life.

After that first dinner the staff members were often invited, in twos or fours, to the official residence. On these occasions the atmosphere was always formal, yet pleasant and stimulating.

Initially at least, I didn't suspect any ulterior motive in these soirées, but it soon became obvious that Victor le Roux and I were invited over rather more often than the others; and invariably Her Excellency contacted us personally. Victor was the first to say openly, one evening on the pavement of the Avenue Hoche, just after the big door had clicked shut behind us: 'Do you also get the impression that someone's trying to find a husband for Annette?'

'I'm sure she's perfectly capable of making up her own mind. She's quite pretty and after all, she's got lots of time. How old d'you think she is – nineteen?'

'Eighteen.'

'I see. So already you know more than I do.'

He bowed, laughing. '*Après vous*. I'm perfectly happy to remain a bachelor. Anyway, I'm past the crucial age. You're the one who should get married before you're thirty, if your career means anything to you.'

'That still gives me almost four years to fish around.' I didn't tell him about Nicolette, of course, she was my private concern. But, partly because our relationship had once again landed in the doldrums, Victor's casual remarks did strike a chord. Moreover, if something did develop between Annette and me it might compensate for the position of inferiority to which her father had relegated me. It was an idea worth exploring. And certainly, at eighteen, she appeared eminently seducible. Before the week was out I took her to a concert in the Pleyel; it was soon followed by other dates.

I must confess that she surprised me. The moment she was away from her mother she revealed impulses of independence, will-power and enthusiasm I would never have expected in that well-rehearsed little social animal.

In fact, on that first evening, before we'd even reached the Pleyel, she announced very calmly, quite out of the blue: 'Look, in spite of anything my mother may have suggested I'm *not* available.'

I was nonplussed. 'How do you mean, "not available"?'

'For marriage. Especially with a diplomat.'

'But I never –'

'That's why I'm warning you well in time. I'd love to go to this concert and I've really enjoyed our conversations in the past. But I have absolutely no intention of marrying you.'

'I see. You have immortal longings. So get thee to a nunnery: is that it?'

'It may not be such a bad idea after all,' she laughed.

It was difficult to handle the curious mixture of adolescent oversimplification and a disconcertingly mature cynicism in her; but it was a fascinating combination, and the evening was a success. So were the others during the next few weeks. In a way if I was irritated by her brand of innocence – the innocence of a sheltered existence – in other ways I felt challenged by it. But her virginal resistance soon became maddening. Whenever anything more intimate than a kiss was at stake, she became as vicious as a cornered ferret. All right, I decided, then it was up to me to break her in. And one night I took her to a night club in Pigalle, one of the seedier dives, like the one Koos Joubert had taken me to.

She remained perfectly composed throughout the performance, obviously too well-bred to make a scene. But when we came out and I suggested a drink at home, she hissed: 'Just take me home. And please don't bother ever to ask me out again.'

'Now look –,' I said, taking her by the arm.

'Don't touch me!' There was a small, sharp edge of fury in her voice. And suddenly I felt sick: suppose, just suppose, she decided to inform her father about it.

We were silent all the way to the Embassy. I wanted to plead with her, to grasp her hands and beg her not to tell anybody about it. But I couldn't. And at the same time I was furious about yet another failure.

I didn't sleep that night. For days I lived in agony. But nothing happened. Gradually I began to relax. So she hadn't told them. She wouldn't. And everything returned to normal. But deep inside me, behind the tidy surface, there remained a scar and the cancer of fear.

I never thought the mother would try to take matters in hand again. But late in February – a month after the night club episode – she unexpectedly telephoned me at my office and invited me to accompany her and Annette to an Anouilh play in the Gaîté-Montparnasse: they'd received complimentary tickets but her husband would be occupied that night and they didn't feel like going on their own.

Obviously I couldn't refuse, although I'd already seen the play. The whole situation was much too delicate for any rashness. And I suppose I should have felt 'honoured'. I had no idea what to expect and frankly, I was intrigued to see what manoeuvres the mother might try to get Annette and me together again. But the evening was most successful, without a hitch, and Annette didn't show the slightest trace of resentment or antagonism. After the performance Her Excellency insisted that I have a cup of coffee with them at home. *So here we go*, I thought. But the moment we entered the official residence Annette excused herself, with the shallow pretext of a headache. (I must admit that she *was* looking rather pale.)

Her mother hesitated, frowned, then said: 'I'm sorry. I hope my company won't be too much of a burden for you.'

'On the contrary,' I assured her.

She gave no answer, but it was evident that she could see through my superficial courtesy.

The servant brought a tray with cups which my hostess rearranged herself before pouring the coffee. Under the impersonal white lamplight I could see the fatigue she no longer cared to hide behind her make-up, an expression almost of sadness, of emptiness and of experiences beyond my horizon. (But was that what I saw then – or is it what I think in retrospect?)

For a while we carried on the usual polite little conversation about our impressions of Paris, about South Africa, French customs, the latest gossip in the newspapers.

Then right in the middle of a sentence – we were talking about the prospects of an early spring, I think – she suddenly put down her cup and asked: 'Why are we doing this?'

I didn't realize what she meant and sat waiting for an explanation.

'Are we really interested in the weather, Stephen? Is it really so tremendously important that we can't find *anything* else to talk about?' I'd noticed before that she would sometimes become very tense, but it was much more obvious now than on any previous occasion, probably because there was nobody else present. It also struck me how she, just like Annette, became a totally different person when she was alone, as if they were two lovely but poisonous plants which had never been meant to grow together, but which now, fatally, found themselves in a situation where there was nothing else they could rely on. (And how did the Ambassador fit into this?)

'We could talk about anything you wish,' I said obligingly.

'Yes. I could tell you about the clothes I ordered for Annette and myself. Or you could tell me about the latest film you have seen.' She no longer tried to hide her bitterness. 'God, how bored you must feel, Stephen!' Leaning back, she pulled open the curtain behind her with a quick, jerky movement. I noticed the shape of her breasts in the light, surprised by their persistent youthfulness. 'Just look at it,' she said – a sob in her voice? – motioning towards the window. 'There's the city, the whole city throbbing with life. Five million people, behind their light or dark windows, all caught up in the act of living. Does it matter whether they do it gracefully or sordidly? Even the clochards sleeping on Métro grilles have their own way of doing it. They can feel the heat coming up from below, and the cold night wind above them. They can *feel*. They're out there. They're part of something. And here we are – look at us – shut in by our four walls, protected from this strange spectacle, life, of which we've heard, but which we hardly know at all.' For a moment she rested her head on her shoulder. Her hands were clutched, one of them on her knee, the other still holding the half-opened curtain. Then she turned her head back to me and there was a hint of a smile round her mouth. 'You must forgive me. I didn't mean to talk about "us". It's only an illusion, making it easier to bear. Shall we say a royal "we"? But you mustn't stay, Stephen. I'm boring you to death.' Was there something else she really wanted to say? She seemed to be waiting for a signal from me. It confused me.

'What makes you think I'm bored?' I asked.

'I know you are.' She allowed her head to fall back and for a moment the shadows softened her weariness and suggested the beauty of her youth: the delicate nose, and the full mouth, and the firm, stubborn line of her jaw, and the challenge in her eyes. Then she moved her head back into the light. She was no longer speaking directly to me: 'You are young; one of these days you'll be getting married. And then? Then you'll become a true diplomat. You'll be promoted and promoted. For how long? And then, one day? – one day you'll suddenly discover that only one thing has happened – you're no longer young.' She got up and went to a graceful antique cabinet. Opening the door she asked: 'Would you like a night-cap?'

I wasn't feeling like it but I didn't want to let her down. She poured whisky for us both.

'Santé.'

She emptied hers very quickly.

'Why do you pretend to be old?' I asked after a while. 'That's not true. Not you.'

She smiled. 'You shouldn't be so ready with compliments, Stephen. It becomes a habit. So many things become habits. Staying alive, for instance.' She went back to the cabinet, refilled her glass, then walked across to the window and with a firm, decisive movement, closed the curtain. 'And then there's Annette,' she said – but it sounded more like a question.

For a moment I was paralysed with shock. Then I asked, as neutrally as possible: 'What do you mean?'

'Oh my God, Stephen.' She quickly emptied her glass and put it down. 'Look, I don't know what happened between the two of you that night –'

'Nothing!' I protested, much too emphatically. 'Did she –?'

'She didn't say anything. And you needn't apologize. You don't understand what I mean. I suppose you tried to 'teach' her something. Perhaps it's a good thing. And it's inevitable – sooner or later. Isn't it? I don't know. Only, she's so very young.'

Relieved, I said nothing. And she went on: 'I was still awake when she came back. She knew that, but she went past to her own room and never said a word. Before that she used to confide in me. You see, we've always tried to be friends rather than mother and daughter. And it's rather disconcerting to discover quite suddenly that as she's growing up and coming nearer to me in age, she's really moving further and further away from me.'

She turned to the cabinet again.

'You shouldn't drink any more,' I said. I had no idea what on earth prompted me to say that.

But she only looked at me and nodded. 'No, I shouldn't. You're quite right. But what the hell?' She sniffed derisively. Then, quickly: 'I'm not old yet, Stephen. I don't want to be old.'

'Please. You mustn't exaggerate what happened.' It took an effort to sound normal and composed. 'Perhaps you should just let her find her feet on her own.'

'Do you blame me for wanting to protect her?'

'No. But one forgets so easily that everybody has a right to his own life. Annette. And you yourself.'

She didn't react immediately. I realized that we'd reached a critical moment. After a while she said: 'You have answers for everything, don't you?' There was a tartness in her voice, but also something complaisant, which reassured me. Very soon after that I rose to leave. She accompanied me to the front door, once again the immaculate hostess. But as I prepared to step outside she suddenly laid a hand on my arm and said: 'I'm glad you came here tonight, Stephen.'

And once again I realized, acutely, that she was not only

Her Excellency, but also, and very significantly, a woman. I wanted to assure her of that, but it would sound either pretentious or clumsy. And, to tell the truth, I was unnerved by my own discovery. It was too new, too dangerous. Yet I have a suspicion that she could guess my thoughts.

During the next few months we often saw each other at receptions, parties and other social functions; two or three times I was even invited to the official residence, but on these occasions she made sure that I would be accompanied by one of my colleagues, which nicely prevented any possibility of embarrassment. On the surface our relationship was completely formal. This, however, was nothing but a courteous camouflage for what the French would term *sympathie*. It was safer for both of us that way. But I think we both had a presentiment that it must sooner or later come to a head – however little either of us might have wished it.

In May the Ambassador had to attend a conference in Brussels. Victor had home leave and was back in South Africa so that I was the only bachelor on the staff. Consequently, I suppose, it was quite natural for him casually to ask me one morning, as I was passing through the reading room to my office, whether I would care to sleep in the official residence during his absence 'to keep an eye on everything'. Yet I couldn't help wondering whether it had been his own idea or hers. And if it was hers: what were her motives? I would have preferred not to accept, but it was impossible to refuse. And the next afternoon after work I rather reluctantly bundled a few of my things into a suitcase and took up my abode in the official residence.

But my apprehension, it appeared, had been groundless. I was treated like a royal guest; Annette was always in our company; once or twice other people were invited. Erika seemed to be doing her utmost not only to save me from any embarrassment but to make my visit as pleasant and natural as possible. That, at least, was the case until the very last night.

Using the pretext of a 'date' I had dinner at Valentin's in the rue Marbeuf and afterwards went to the rue de Condé. Nicolette was at home, but the evening soon proved to be a repetition of the now customary pattern of trivialities leading up to the inevitable refusal and the equally inevitable quarrel. It was, if anything, even more violent than usual because in spite of all the precautions the preceding week had inevitably taxed my nerves. At eleven o'clock I was back at the Embassy, irritated, depressed and resentful. I pressed Lebon's bell and was let into the official residence. Everything seemed quiet. But as I went past the large reception hall downstairs, she called softly: 'Is that you, Stephen?'

She was sitting at the head of the long empty table, smoking. I don't know whether she had staged the scene intentionally to create an impression of forlornness (she has a remarkable, intuitive – but somewhat melodramatic? – sense of the theatrical).

'Did you have a good time?' It was the obvious question to ask, but I suspected a deeper meaning to her words.

'Not much.' I was in no mood for a conversation.

'A girl? Or do I sound like a nosy old woman?' She must have known very well that she was looking even younger than usual.

'It's no secret,' I answered coolly. 'And nothing unusual either, I think.'

'Of course not. There must be many girls –' She (intentionally?) left the sentence incomplete.

'Unfortunately not.' Against my will I was being drawn into the situation. 'I seem to have a special talent for scaring off people rather than attracting them.'

'You're bitter, Stephen.'

'I suppose I have reason to be.'

It is very difficult to reconstruct the rest of the scene. I can remember how one part of me felt cool, cerebral resentment towards her uninvited meddling. At the same time, I suspect, I also felt a masochistic desire to lick my wounds in public. (Is it an innate urge that drives one to confession? Is this the true substance of religion?) Added to my other feelings was the awareness of being alone with her in that huge baroque hall; of the empty semi-darkness around us; and of her warmth, maturity, sympathy, which made me feel unreasonably young and wronged and yearning, but without the self-consciousness which so often overcomes me in the presence of younger women. I sat down next to her and told her everything about Nicolette, a wandering, incoherent confession of the most intimate details of our relationship. I told her about all the disillusionments I'd experienced in Paris; and then I went right back to my youth, my parents, and the endless row of Sunday nights following my father's long, solemn prayer at the supper table, with darkness surrounding our single illuminated room: the whole paradox of disgust and desire, of revulsion and need. The evening dissolved into night over us. And then it all ended in an unexpected, unavoidable embrace in which there was nothing of mother and child: there was too much despair in it, and desire, and fulfilment and physical awareness.

There was, immediately, a silent agreement between us about the incident, of which we were conscious even while we were still sipping our cognac from exquisite crystal glasses: neither of us would ever, in word or gesture, refer again to what had happened. Because that would define and reduce it. Its true value, its only value, after all, was the very fact that we dared not formulate it, for fear that it would then destroy itself. And therefore, after we'd finished our cognac, we merely put down our glasses and got up to go to our bedrooms; and I said: 'Good-night, Erika.'

I lay awake for a long time. There was no question of anything as easy as 'guilt'. I simply tried to sort out what had happened; and I was aware of the irony of it all – the humiliating episode with the daughter, followed, unexpectedly, by this discovery of the mother. It was all so confusing. All the more so because of the one question looming behind it all: *What would happen if the Ambassador were to find out?*

From that moment, I knew, his very existence was a threat

to mine. Whatever I, or we, might choose to do or leave undone, my fate was now in his hands.

This phase of my relationship with Erika lasted for quite some time without in itself causing either anxiety or particular happiness. There was no attempt to rationalize anything; yet (or perhaps *because* of this) it was a period – if it is not too limp a phrase – of inner peace. And there was only one further episode of any importance, drawing its meaning from the very fact that it marked the end of this period of relative contentment, and made everything infinitely more complex.

It happened seven weeks ago, towards the middle of October, on a bleak, windy evening. At about ten o'clock there was a knock on my door. Nicolette? It would be her first visit since our miserable, memorable evening of bath and bed, three weeks before. I hurried to the door. It was Erika, leaning against the doorpost. She wasn't drunk, but she'd evidently had too much to drink. It was quite a shock to see her outside the Embassy in this state. I was aware of this weakness in her, of course, but usually it was strictly confined to the official residence.

'Are you – occupied?'

I shook my head and allowed her to come in.

'Awful evening,' I said.

'Awful? Yes, indeed. Oh damn, I've forgotten my cigarettes at home. Can you offer me one?' She was trembling while I lit it for her. At last she said: 'I suppose I was just feeling lonesome. Paul is at the British Embassy. Annette's gone out with someone. A student, I think.'

The conversation sagged. We were both irritated by its superficiality, but it was one of those occasions when one gets caught in a whirlpool and can't get out again. She smoked four or five cigarettes. The last one, almost untouched, was left lying on the edge of an ashtray while she absently sat watching its lazy line of smoke.

'Aren't you going to offer me a drink?' she suddenly asked.

'Should you?'

She uttered a short, rough laugh: 'I know. I'm smoking too much. I'm drinking too much. But I can assure you there's nothing else I'm overdoing.'

The cigarette on the ashtray was still smoking.

Suddenly: 'I went to see the doctor. At long last.'

'The doctor? But why? I didn't realize –'

'I only wanted to make sure. It's so easy to start imagining things. And I'm not like Anna Smith who goes to a doctor every month because it's the only opportunity she has of being legitimately touched by a man.'

'What's wrong then?' I dutifully asked.

'Nothing tangible. I just couldn't go on like this. I get upset by everything. I suppose I only wanted him to set my mind at rest.'

'Well –?'

'It seems an operation is necessary. Quite urgently too.'

'But why?'

Her eyes never looked away from mine. 'I won't be a woman any more, that's all,' she said cruelly. And then she added (it was the only time I'd ever seen her lose her self-control): 'Spayed like a cat.'

'Erika, for God's sake –!'

Then, for the first time, she gave way to the hysteria which must have been building up for so long. She cried herself out in my arms. There was nothing I could say or think which would make it easier for either of us; I could only stroke her hair and shoulders. After a long time she calmed down, but she still didn't move. That was the closest I'd ever been to any woman: that monologue which followed. It was very confused, troubled by the after-effects of the shock which still had to be absorbed. Loneliness. Frustration. The loss of contact with Annette.

'– I don't *know* her any more. She's always going out with men I've never even met. I know she's desperately unhappy, but she refuses to come to me for help. It can't go on like this. It's becoming unbearable for both of us.'

And later: 'It's easy for *you* to be here, away from your

country and your people. One becomes blasé. But there's something in me, these days, which drives me back. I know there's nothing to keep me there. But there's nothing here either. I have no ties with anything, I'm drifting, I don't know where I'm going or what's happening to me. I doubt whether you would understand this, Stephen. And yet you're the only one I could come to.'

'But how can I help you? It's so impossible – in our position. Think of –'

'I know,' she said, almost rudely, and got up.

That was the very first time either of us had touched upon it. And immediately, as I'd foreseen all along, everything became very small and hard and circumscribed: an almost cheap little affair.

She didn't reproach me; but I know that in that instant I failed her. (Is this a fate I have to carry with me like a germ? Must it always come to this?)

'I must be looking a sight,' she said, trying to sound nonchalant, even playful. 'Do you think there's anything that can still be salvaged?' And with that she went to the bathroom.

When she returned she said almost casually: 'I've decided – just now – to take a holiday. Annette must come with me. Perhaps that will clear up something. I don't think so, mind you. But at least we can give it a try.'

'Where will you be going?'

'Italy,' she answered, as if it had been decided long ago. 'It's warm there. I've always hated the cold and winter seems to be early this year. Everything is getting cold, I just can't take it any more.'

(Three weeks before, in this very room: 'We're cold, both of us.')

On our way to the door I asked: 'How long will you be away?'

'I don't know. I hate to tie myself to a programme. Let's call it a pilgrimage.' And then, mocking from the open door: 'You see: I'm becoming sentimental. In my old age.'

I kissed her, or she me. It was like a question which had to be left unanswered. And then she went away.

5

I must return to my report. And I must emphasize that I need not rely on conjecture – which would, after all, carry no weight with the Minister – but solely on verifiable facts.

Unfortunately there is no means of determining exactly when the Ambassador's affair with Nicolette started. There are various indications, I think, that it had been going on for quite a while before I first became aware of it – so it would seem to date from some time before Erika's departure. However, since I intend to confine myself strictly to facts, I shall begin with my discovery on the afternoon of 6 November. Of this date I am quite sure, because it was the day just after the party in my apartment when I'd finally split up with Nicolette.

The party. It was her very first visit to me since our wretched little scene. I'd been to her place a few times but it hadn't achieved much. Actually I'd been quite surprised when she'd accepted the invitation, but by that time I'd become used to her unpredictable changes of mood; moreover, in all the time I'd known her she had never missed a party.

Even though there were far too many people in my cramped little apartment the evening was a success. I suppose we were all in a mood for extravagant eating, drinking, and making merry, not knowing what the morrow would bring. Because it was a bad time for South Africa after the unexpected turn the strike in Johannesburg had taken the previous day. The strike itself had been threatening for a long time, starting, as usual, with something quite trivial that got blown up out of all proportion. But it was different from similar incidents in the past in that, this time, it was not confined to threats and counter-threats; very soon dangerous tensions were building up between the strikers in their township and the police cordon drawn around it. At one stage it had very nearly resulted in an open clash. There were rumours that the inhabitants of neighbouring townships would also go on strike in solidarity with the original group. Troops were sent to reinforce the police. The most trifling incident – an arrest for contravening the pass laws; picking up a noisy drunk – could have devastating consequences. And when the threatening situation had nearly reached its climax some of the leaders of the resistance movement had dispatched telegrams to the representatives of various Afro-Asian countries at the UN asking for their intervention. The whole affair had suddenly become a dangerous international dispute.

We had to rely on reports in the Paris newspapers, and on the ominous news flashes transmitted irregularly by the Hellschreiber of our own Information Service. For twenty-four hours a day somebody was stationed at the Embassy in case the Post Office telephoned with news about an urgent telegram from HQ. The Ambassador himself was in his office for almost sixteen hours a day. The previous night it had been my turn. All the more reason for wanting to enjoy my party that evening. It might, even, who knows, get Nicolette in the kind of mood which could make a new start possible for us.

But she managed very adroitly to stay out of my way for most of the night, which was not very difficult among so many people. At the same time she was extremely provocative in her flimsy, tight-fitting, jersey dress. (Didn't she feel the cold, I wondered? Outside it was rainy, and there was a chilly wind.) It was almost eleven o'clock before I found her alone for the first time. She was in the small kitchen, looking for crisps, when I came in to rinse a few glasses.

'Why are you running away from me?'

'Don't flatter yourself.' But she was already on her way to the door.

Angrily I caught her by the arm.

'Let me go, Stephen!' she cried. 'You're drunk.' (Which was a lie.) And then she slapped me.

If we'd been alone in the apartment I swear I would have hit her back. But any moment some of my guests might enter the kitchen and I couldn't risk a scene.

She took advantage of my indecision to wrench her arm from my grip and rushed to the front door. It slammed very loudly behind her. I was standing in the kitchen, my fists clenched, forcing myself to keep calm. Uppermost in my mind was one single thought: This was the last straw; this was the end.

Although none of my guests mentioned Nicolette's theatrical departure, it had a marked effect on the atmosphere. Though we all tried very hard to pretend that nothing had happened, our very efforts made things even worse. By midnight I was left alone among the filled ashtrays and the dirty glasses. The room was grey with smoke; outside the cold rain was streaking against the panes.

That was the night of 5 November. And it was at three o'clock the next afternoon that I saw Nicolette in the Embassy. I was on my way down to my own office from an interview with the Ambassador when she passed me near the bottom of the stairs. I greeted her stiffly. She ignored me. But that was not the reason why I stopped. It was the Ambassador's jacket which she was carrying, carelessly draped over a shoulder. There could be no doubt: anyone on the staff would immediately have recognized that dark blue material with its thin grey stripes. I stood motionless on the bottom step watching her go up to the first floor, where she went past the Registry Office straight to the Ambassador's.

It was not until I was back at my own desk that I was struck by the full implications of the incident. I thought of Erika. Perhaps the scene I'd just witnessed suggested one of the reasons for her hypertension during the last few weeks before her departure? I was dismayed by the cold-bloodedness of it all. While she was travelling in Italy in her state of nervous depression he apparently had no qualms – To think that *he* could act like that, this great pillar of correctness! And with Nicolette of all people! Would that explain her behaviour of the night before?

However difficult it was, I decided to shut the whole incident out of my mind. It would be most unwise to become involved in it.

But less than a week later, on Monday 12 November – I made a note of the date – I was in the reading room discussing a new procedure with the messengers, when she came in through the double glass doors. She hesitated for a moment, then gave a small haughty smile and came past me towards the staircase, a self-consciously defiant air about her. I watched the teasing movement of her dress round her legs until she disappeared out of sight. Generally, even the most important visitors have to be screened by the receptionist. Not Nicolette. She simply went up to his office – and she did it quite openly. Having given the messengers their last few instructions I went back to my own office.

Needless to say, I didn't get much work done during the rest of that day. And by closing time the only thing I'd decided was that I had to make it my business to discover the whole truth. I had no particular aim in mind. Not yet. But it was imperative, I felt, to *know*.

Throughout the next four days I kept as close a watch on Nicolette's movements as I could – but without success. When I arrived in the rue de Condé on the first evening, after work, she wasn't home. (From the rue de l'Odéon, at the back of her building, one can see her window high up on the fifth floor.) I had dinner nearby, then hung around until eleven, but there was no sign of her. I was too tired to wait any longer. For although the tension in South Africa had eased after talks between the strike leaders and the Government, we were still flooded with work caused by the episode – interviews with the media and with industrialists who'd invested in South Africa; negotiations with the Quai d'Orsay for support on the Security Council against efforts by the Afro-Asians to impose sanctions, etc.

69

On the second evening I had been waiting near the front door of her building for about half an hour before she came out and headed for the boulevard Saint-Germain. I followed her to the Métro, but in the bustle of the peak hour I soon lost her. All I did see was that she caught a train in the direction of the Porte d'Orléans, which didn't mean anything, since she might change to a different line at another station. All I could be reasonably sure of was that that line wouldn't take her anywhere near the Embassy. I went home, but towards eleven o'clock a sudden inspiration took me back to the rue de l'Odéon. There was light in her window. I mounted the dilapidated old staircase and went to her door. There were voices inside, but it was impossible to recognize them as the middle door, between the tiny entrance lobby and her room, was probably closed. I went down again to resume my vigil. After about an hour her light went out, but nobody left the building. I was still no nearer to a discovery. It was hard not to go upstairs and knock on her door. The mere thought of what might be going on made me feel sick. But I had to remain uninvolved. So I left her building and came back to my apartment to sleep(!). The next day the Ambassador told me that he'd telephoned me several times during the previous evening in connection with an urgent Hellschreiber message. Which meant that I'd been on the wrong scent anyway.

The third night brought an unexpected discovery, deeply disconcerting in its own way, even if it had nothing to do with the matter I was investigating. At about seven o'clock I followed her at a safe distance as she was threading her way through the labyrinth of streets in the Latin quarter. In the rue Hautefeuille she was joined by a young stranger. They evidently had a date; it was just as evident that she was late. (Damned well served him right.) From his rather unsavoury appearance I took him to be a student, and I doubt whether I would recognize him if I ever met him again. They had dinner in a cheap restaurant (the Acropole in the rue de l'École de Médicine) and afterwards returned to her apartment together. I was prepared for a repetition of the previous night but somewhat to my surprise it was barely ten o'clock before the young man left on his own and walked off in the direction of the Luxembourg Gardens. I quickly went round to the rue de l'Odéon; her light was still on. What could that mean? That she was expecting a second visitor? That they'd quarrelled? Or simply that she was going to stay at home for the rest of the night? After a while I became convinced that the latter was the most likely. But just after half-past ten she came out by the front door and made her way briskly towards the Métro. This time I made sure that I wouldn't lose her again, although I remained fatalistically prepared for a hitch: the ticket woman might shut the little green gate between us if a train happened to arrive at the wrong moment; or Nicolette might recognize me, crouching behind an open *France-Soir*. It was rather risky to travel with her in the same coach, but it would be too easy to lose her if I didn't. Fortunately she didn't seem to be in the least interested in her fellow travellers. It was an endless journey. Cité, Châtelet, and onwards. We passed every possible *correspondance* station as far as Barbès-Rochechouart. There, a few seconds before the doors slammed shut, she quickly jumped up from the seat on which she'd been half-dozing and stepped out on the platform. I followed just in time. She was walking towards the Porte Dauphine platform. For the first time it dawned on me where we might be going. A numb, paralysing lump settled in my stomach. My God, I thought, not this. Sleep around if you must, Nicolette, be unscrupulous, be a bitch, be whatever you wish; but not *this*.

Once we'd passed Pigalle a flicker of hope returned. But even before we reached place Blanche I could see that we were nearing our destination. She got up and waited at the door, her narrow hands holding the handle, her forehead pressed against the glass so that she could stare at the dizzy wall beyond: a child peering at a shop window. (But what was there to be seen in that dark tunnel?)

After the sticky heat and the heavy smell of garlic in the Métro, the cold outside came almost as a shock. It had started to rain while we were inside. People were scurrying past, hunched under umbrellas or in thick coat collars. There was the monotonous swishing sound of car tyres on slippery tar. But Nicolette didn't hesitate for a moment. She obviously knew her way. We went down the rue Blanche, then turned into a narrow side-street; and suddenly, in the darkness between two lamp-posts, she was just – gone. I stopped in my tracks. Cold raindrops were trickling down my collar into my neck. Then, in the shadows next to me, something moved and a husky voice whispered: '*Chéri* –?' Disgusted, I shook the white claw from my arm and hurried on. Between two buildings I noticed a narrow alley. That explained her disappearance. I looked around. It didn't seem very safe to venture in there alone. Ten yards further on there was an entrance to some seedy strip-joint with a thick-set doorman in a faded red uniform standing next to it, watching me like a vulture. On either side of the entrance were the customary illuminated frames with photographs of girls in various stages of undress.

'Wonderful show, sir,' the man said without much conviction. 'The best in Paris. Come in and have a look for yourself. Real value for your money.'

I hesitated, then hurriedly paid him his fee and entered the dingy little hole, feeling my way to one of the empty tables. It was no bigger than a smallish living-room. Everything was musty, and decorated as cheaply and tastelessly as possible. A waiter brought me some champagne I didn't want and which cost the earth. A loudspeaker was blaring forth earsplitting music. It lasted for ten minutes, while five or six other clients were ushered in – all of them male, and all middle-aged. At the bar counter against the back wall a cluster of plump prostitutes were sitting like hens on a perch, cackling and whispering, and consuming large glasses of alcohol. Just before midnight the 'show' started. Clumsy, vulgar capers; second-hand costumes, probably bought for next to nothing on the fleamarket; a complete lack of rhythm and co-ordination in what passed for dancing; hoary chestnuts in the 'sketches'. After about half an hour the greasy master of ceremonies announced the 'star' of the performance. The fabulous, spectacular, unique, sexy Lulu – or something to that effect.

A bundle of gaudy ostrich feathers erupted on the stage. And in the middle of the bundle, like the heart of a flower, was Nicolette, with sensual red lips, heavily painted eyelids and a red wig. The rest of her performance was predictable: the feathers disappeared one by one until she moved about wearing nothing but a tiny, glittering *cache-sexe*. She didn't dance too badly, although it was by no means remarkable. The light changed from red to blue to green to yellow, covering the spectrum with maddening monotony. The music grew louder and wilder. Nicolette was breathing heavily as if unaccustomed to so much exertion. For the first time I could look at her in complete detachment, impersonally, judging her as nothing but a body: her thin arms, her small, firm breasts, pointed upwards as if two bees were perched on them, her slightly angular hips and long legs. Was it possible that she could really be no more than this? But if so, why should it depress me so unbearably? It was unwarranted; *she* revealed no trace of shame or embarrassment. On the contrary: her whole attitude suggested nothing but contempt for that assortment of middle-aged men staring at her; an almost total disregard for that poky room and above all, the disconcerting liberty of one who knows that she belongs to nobody but herself. Yet *they* were still believing the illusion, I thought with bitter amusement: they were adding up her limbs and what was concealed by the little sequinned triangle, calculating the measure of ecstasy she could offer. But I – I had already found the solution to her little mathematical equation; I knew all too well the coldness of her answer.

So why did I get up then, why did I feel the need to run for cover the moment she jumped from the stage and came dancing towards the tables? It was not that I could no longer bear it; and certainly not because I wanted to save *her* any embarrassment. Perhaps it was, I must confess, because I couldn't face the thought that she might find out about *me*. I couldn't handle the idea of knowing that she knew.

In the taxi on my way back to where I had left my car, I tried not to think of anything immediately connected with what I'd just seen. The only question in my mind (and how irrelevant can one be?) was: *How much would they pay her for the performance?*

There was, of course, the possibility that her duties might not end with the show –

But was that really my concern? Perhaps she even enjoyed the work. And then, after all, there was nothing between us. The only thing that really mattered was: if it were to become known that the Ambassador was associating with that kind of person, the situation would be even worse than I'd thought in the beginning.

And so four evenings had, in fact, been fruitless.

At that stage it occurred to me that I might have been approaching the whole matter from the wrong end: it wasn't Nicolette who had to be followed, but the Ambassador himself. This would naturally be more dangerous; it was also, potentially, much more humiliating. If Nicolette found out about my activities, *tant pis*. Confronted with the Ambassador, I would be down the drain.

Yet even my new *modus operandi* seemed to lead me nowhere. On the first evening the Ambassador stayed at home. The next evening he attended an official dinner and went home directly afterwards; the third evening he once again went straight back to the avenue Hoche after a visit to the Australian Ambassador.

But late on Sunday afternoon, 18 November, he took the first suspicious step. From where I'd parked on the opposite side of the avenue I saw him leave through the main entrance of the Embassy. Without looking left or right he started walking towards the Étoile. I turned the ignition key and waited until I could see him get into a taxi. Following a taxi-driver through the streets of Paris would be risky, if not impossible. I could only hope that my assumption had been correct, and try to reach the rue de Condé as quickly as I could. The traffic was not very heavy, but the street lights were already burning in the falling dusk, making it difficult to see. Once across the pont de la Concorde it became easier because one could almost blindly follow the bright yellow lights of the boulevard Saint-Germain.

I first went round to the back of her building to check whether the light was on. But the window was dark. That in itself didn't prove anything. Neither did the sudden appearance of her light five minutes later. I took up my position on the corner of the rue Saint-Sulpice, leaning against a wall, waiting. Every five minutes I checked from the rue de l'Odéon that her light was still on. It was almost an hour later, just as I was returning from one of these brief expeditions, when I suddenly saw her approaching from the direction of the boulevard, strolling leisurely, eating *frites* from a greasy paper bag. Had I been watching the wrong window all the time? I quickly darted back to the rue de l'Odéon. Impossible. Did that mean that the Ambassador had all this time been waiting in her room? But how did he get in – supposing it was he – unless he had a key of his own? It would seem that my bit of detective work was at last leading to something worth while. But it gave me no particular feeling of pleasure: only a wave of nausea at the thought of being found out: for I knew very well that from now on there was very little hope of not being drawn into their intrigue. Perhaps, at the moment, I could still back out. Even that seemed dubious. The mere fact of knowing what I already suspected would not allow me any peace of mind again. I *was* involved. There was no way out – either for them or me.

It was almost seven o'clock before the front door of the building was opened. I slipped round the corner and pressed myself against the wall. It was only when they reached the far side of the carrefour de l'Odéon that I dared to look. There was no doubt at all. It was indeed the Ambassador, walking gravely beside her girlish figure.

If it was just a matter of collecting 'evidence' that would have been more than enough. But it wasn't enough for *me*. I needed to know more. I needed to know – well, everything. It was a purely private necessity. (And I must emphasize again that at that stage I still had no conscious intention of drawing up a report.)

On Friday 23 November, he visited her again. It was about 8 p.m. Like the previous time I had been waiting on the corner of the rue Saint-Sulpice. It was raining; and this might have contributed to the fact that at a given moment (without having come to anything as clearly formulated as a 'decision') I crossed the street and pressed the button at the main entrance. It was a beautiful if somewhat decayed old door, decorated with designs which must have been the work of an outstanding woodcraftsman, centuries ago: apples, grapes, a faun, a nymph. Once inside in the musty entrance-hall I realized, and acknowledged, for the first time that I was actually on my way to her apartment. I mounted the crumbling staircase very slowly, because only every second landing was dimly illuminated by a bare bulb hanging from the ceiling. Besides, the time switch didn't function properly so that the light regularly went out when one was just halfway between two landings. Then it was a matter of feeling one's way, groping along the walls with their loose shreds of plaster, until one found the next switch. Here and there I stumbled over broken steps; but by that time I knew how to avoid most of them.

I must have waited outside her door for at least five minutes. One couldn't hear anything inside. I could feel the skin tighten on my temples and cheeks. (Were they –?) Then I knocked. There was no answer. I knocked again.

After a while I heard a shuffling sound. And then, barefoot, and in her underclothes, she appeared on the doorstep. She had closed the middle door behind her. Her hair was hanging loose. She drew her breath in sharply when she recognized me.

'Stephen! What do you want?'

'I just thought I'd drop in.'

'It's no *use*, Stephen!'

'Are you entertaining another visitor?'

'No.'

'Well, why can't I come in then?'

'Because I don't want you to.'

I suppose I could have forced the door open, but why should I? I had already discovered enough. But there was one thing I could not resist: just before I turned away, looking her straight in the eyes, I said: 'You're playing with fire, Nicolette.' She came out after me as I was going down, and stopped at the railing of her landing. I suspected that she was upset by what I'd said, but I didn't look up at her. Yet it was hard to tell whether I'd scored a victory or suffered a defeat.

I went back to my post. And just as I'd expected the Ambassador left the building soon afterwards. He remained standing in front of the large door for quite some time, looking up as if expecting to see her somewhere above him; then, probably remembering that her window was on the other side of the building, he started walking in my direction. (I had stepped back round the corner.) On the carrefour he stopped again, hesitated, and changing direction, walked briskly towards the boulevard Saint-Michel. Ten minutes later I stepped up behind him where he was sitting inside the glass partition of a café terrace, and said:

'Good evening, Mr Ambassador. I wasn't expecting to find you here.'

He was obviously surprised by my sudden appearance, but he nevertheless invited me to sit down. During the next fifteen minutes, while he was drinking his coffee and I my grog, I casually asked all my meticulously loaded questions: 'Do you often come to this part of the city?' 'Isn't it a nasty night to be outside?' Et cetera. I derived great satisfaction from this game of hide-and-seek. It may not have been very 'noble' of me but at least I'm honest enough to admit it; and how much of what we do is noble anyway? We are not a noble species. That was the first time in all our close contact that I was holding the whip-hand, and it gave me a strange feeling of elation, even of freedom. Not that he gave the slightest hint of having been caught on the wrong foot. He was too much of a diplomat for that. And to my sticky questions he replied, without batting an eyelid, that he was trying systematically to explore the whole city and that yes, it was a nasty night, but he didn't mind being outside in the rain, in fact he rather enjoyed·it. ('One gets so cooped up in the office.') At last we caught a taxi home. Except that, after dropping him at the Embassy, I asked the driver to take me back to the rue Monsieur-le-Prince where I'd parked my car.

And still I did nothing with all the information I had acquired, and which was lying so heavily on my mind. As I had feared, I found myself sucked into a whirlpool, unable to get out, even if I wanted to. And less than a week later (on Wednesday night, the 28th) the next bit of evidence was added to my growing file. There was a reception at the Embassy that night, given by the Military Attaché. The usual boring small-talk and shop over cocktail glasses. But among the guests, to my amazement, I suddenly recognized – you guessed it – Miss Nicolette Alford. I'd never before seen her at any diplomatic reception. That in itself, of course, meant nothing. But I was positive that her sudden interest – after she had so often expressed quite bluntly what she thought of official functions – could not be innocent. And where would the Embassy all of a sudden have found her address to send her an invitation after she'd always steered clear of such things? I decided to keep my eyes peeled. But halfway through the evening I was cornered by the wife of a French general – why do bloody middle-aged women get so interested in me? – and when at last she moved on to her next victim, Nicolette had disappeared. I looked everywhere, hoping that she might still be somewhere in the crowd. But there was no trace of her. As soon as protocol allowed, I left.

The concierge, Lebon, was at his post at the main entrance, looking slightly crumpled, as usual. Whenever one sees him, night or day, he gives the impression of having just been to bed with a woman. I stepped into the street, when suddenly a thought struck me and I turned back to him.

'Have you seen Miss Alford leave, Lebon?'

'Alford?'

I described her briefly.

He gave a knowing smile, suggesting that he knew much more than I might have suspected, but denied that he had seen her. Perhaps she'd left with a group of other guests, he suggested, but he wasn't sure.

The next morning just before tea he came to my office. I was in no mood for gossip. (He knows everything about everybody.)

'Yes, Lebon?' I asked curtly. 'What's the matter?'

'You asked about Mademoiselle Alford last night.' His small black eyes were glittering behind his glasses.

'Well, what about her?'

'She didn't leave until much later, Monsieur.'

'Really?' I made no effort to hide my feelings.

'Very much later.' He leaned over the desk towards me, clearly pleased with himself. 'Just after three o'clock, to be exact.'

I immediately started questioning him more closely, but he had nothing of substance to add. Not that I needed anything more. 'Information', 'evidence', 'proof' – I had more than enough of everything; too much, really. But enough or too much *for what*? Even at that late stage I still had no definite aim in mind. Gathering the facts had been something of an end in itself. The only difference Lebon's new information made, was that I now became very disturbingly aware of the sheer weight, the burden, the ballast of everything that had come to light. No feeling of guilt – why should I? – but merely a heaviness in me, an uneasiness, a weariness which depressed me; and I knew I couldn't bear it much longer. I wondered pointedly: where was the Ambassador heading for? What was still in store for me? Where, and how, could I unburden myself of it all? Because suddenly – too late – I wished for ignorance again; there was nothing I would have wanted more urgently than to have it all obliterated from my mind.

Under ordinary ('normal') circumstances the incident at the reception of the doyen of the Diplomatic Corps, held in the Hôtel de Ville on Friday night, 30 November, would have caused a mere ripple on the surface. But happening, as it did, at that specific moment, it became a strait through which a quiet river was churned into unmanageable rapids. It was a miserable day. The city's many centuries were resting heavily on her. In the early morning, walking along the pavement towards the Embassy through the fog, I saw an undertaker's bus drive past, with rows of mourning people inside. Because of the fog the traffic moved along almost soundlessly, which made everything seem unreal: a macabre journey across the waters of death, with the greyish-black buildings on either side of the street turned into the steep charred banks of the Styx. An inexplicable *misère*, a *cafard*, that sickness-of-a-thousand-names lay aching inside me. As the day wore on my state of mind was aggravated by a hundred minor pinpricks. There was a typist who made a few mistakes in the final copy of a report the Ambassador was waiting for, and for which I got the blame. There was Anna Smith who came downstairs and for almost an hour shared *her* miseries with me. There was the visiting wife of a South African MP who took up another hour of my time with a sarcastic tirade about the inefficiency of 'certain' officials, which she promised to bring to the Minister's attention. And added to all this: a ceaseless, dull sinus ache throbbing in my nose and eyes and forehead.

In the afternoon an important file was mislaid and as I scrambled through my desk and cabinets in search of it I came upon the sheet of paper on which, the very first day, I'd jotted down the particulars of Nicolette's lost passport. Eighteen months lay between me and that distant day. And what had happened in all that time, what had I done, what had I achieved? It was like a blow in the guts: the futility of it all. It was as if, for one awful moment, looking into the most secret corner of myself, I saw a nightmare, the most shattering vision of my life: what I saw was a stuffy little cubbyhole of a room, windowless, and with no light, and the door locked; and inside it a small, grotesque, completely colourless creature whose body is almost totally wasted away, except for his long bony hands and a penis of disproportionate size, eternally erect, standing up like a medieval warrior's club; while in the middle of his oversized head flames a single large red eye. His whole life is spent keeping that feverish eye pressed to the keyhole in the door: but all he can see on the other side is a bedroom, a bed. All he ever does, all he can hope to do, as he masturbates away in unabated frenzy, is to stare at a neverending series of intimate, perverse encounters on the bed beyond his reach, all of them variations of the same basic act of copulation. The little voyeur keeps on shouting abuse at the anonymous couples on the bed, but they pay no attention at all as if, somehow, no sound gets through to them. The only alternative would be to plug the hole and banish all sight, but then the creature would have no air to breathe and besides, he is scared of the dark.

I was aware of a new, deep need in me to be with Nicolette; for a moment I even made up my mind to go to her immediately after work. But then I analysed my motives and tried to guess, beforehand, the outcome of such a visit – and decided against it. What would I say to her? That I wanted her? She would laugh at me, make fun of my desire. More important, I suddenly wondered whether it really was true: *did* I want her? Or did I merely want to hurt her, perhaps to taunt her that I 'knew everything'? I could almost hear her saying: 'So what?' and then inevitably, she would discover how I had come to find out, and I could just imagine how she would react to this variation on the keyhole theme. Perhaps it might still have some effect if I could tell her to her face: 'Now I know what you are. An ordinary little striptease dancer in a tenth-rate joint!' But would that really hurt or upset her? And why should I *want* to upset her? And so on . . . The only outcome was that my headache got worse.

When I left the Embassy at half-past five it was dark already. I came straight home, poured myself a stiff brandy and sat down on a corner of the divan. Stephen Keyter, Third Secretary, budding young diplomat, miserable bloody failure: *prosit*. There was little traffic outside. It's a quiet street I live in. In this neighbourhood people withdraw themselves behind their walls, lock their doors, close their windows. Floor upon floor, building upon building, block upon block – it suddenly became a terrifying thought – all those similar doors, similar windows. And God, all those people inside, teeming, squirming, breeding. In Imperial Rome, in long-lost Babylon, there had already been buildings and cities like this. And still it was going on: people moving and talking and eating and copulating. Generation after generation, sex, sex. And *homo sum* – I refilled my glass and arranged the pillows against the wall so that I could lean back. I was drinking too much, I thought. Those had been Erika's words too – or something similar, anyway. And now she was gone, in search of some place where it would be warm, where she could escape the cold. A 'pilgrimage' she'd called it, cynically. Was there any essential difference between her flight and Nicolette's game of ring-a-rosy round a bed? Both boiled down to self-deception, a bit of make-believe in order to keep on moving, keep the circulation going, warding off the final cold, a pathetic dance of incantation to the long dead gods. One of them off on a little cavale; the other marking time as one of Aphrodite's perfunctory hetaerae. (And how long could it go on? Until the heart stopped all by itself, or until, some day, one decided to 'clean' a revolver?) And somewhere between them (or remote, apart?) was I. What about my own little pilgramage, not towards 'eternity' but towards ambassadorial status in twenty years or so? At least I was living within reasonable, and calculable, limits; I wasn't trying to exorcize anything; I was existing beyond illusion. Was that any more, or less, senseless than any other way of living? Did it really matter?

I put down my empty glass, got up and went to dress for

the doyen's reception. If I could have thought of some excuse I would have stayed away. But since it was impossible without having to explain to the Ambassador afterwards, I dressed in the way expected of me, swallowed a few tablets which I knew would make no difference to my headache, put on an overcoat and went down to my car.

There were several hundred guests in the imposing hall with its crystal candelabras and baroque tapestries. A 'festive occasion'; only, one soon discovers that it is just a camouflage for collective boredom. The next day the Press would trot out all the adjectives expected of it, with photographs of the most dazzling women and the most *outré* dresses; but few would really be fooled by it. Not that it does not have a fascination of its own, sometimes. There is a certain satisfaction in learning to play the game: more, it requires all the wit of Scrabble, the calculation and premeditation of chess, the refinement of *Go* – and the stakes are higher, the rewards can ensure survival. At times the effect of the game can become almost narcotic. Few other experiences impress me so deeply with the awareness of functioning as part of an immensely intricate organism in which all meaning is derived from interaction and from the relation between the whole and its components. It's more than a reduction of individuality: it utterly *dissolves* individuality, makes it superfluous compared to this symbiosis which excludes all 'lower' forms of life, all 'baser instincts'. But on that evening it only irritated me, as a result of either the morose introspection that had preceded it, or the alcohol which accompanied it. I performed all the necessary actions and duly contributed to the conversation, but I remained isolated from the whole. There was no way out of my misery: I would have to stay until the Ambassador left. And since it was the first important diplomatic gathering after the recent trouble in South Africa four weeks before, he could be expected to talk to as many people as possible to set the record straight. Fortunately I managed to steer clear of political conversations during the first half of the evening. But then a conceited young secretary from the Indian Embassy, with whom I'd often argued for hours on end in the past, said something like: 'Of course, this is the beginning of the end for the South Africans.' Then he turned round as if he hadn't been aware of my presence until that moment, and added smoothly, 'Or doesn't our friend Mr Keyter agree?'

On any other occasion I would have either tactfully side-stepped the issue or discussed the matter with professional patience and diligence. But that night I was in no mood for his little game.

'I don't care a damn what you think,' I said. 'Do you think your prejudiced opinion could make any difference to the real state of affairs?'

He reacted very smoothly. After my initial outburst I also stayed within the bounds of courtesy; but I suppose I spoke rather more loudly than I should have. And I forgot, temporarily, that it was my duty as the youngest member of the staff (Harrington being away on home leave) to attend to the Ambassador's needs.

So I was caught unawares when His Excellency suddenly appeared next to me, nodding briefly to the other people in the group, and said very calmly: 'I'm sorry to interrupt, Keyter, but there may be a telegram tonight about the Prime Minister's statement in Cape Town. Would you mind going to the Embassy to hold the fort until I come?' He spoke in English so that the bystanders who were either curious or ill-mannered enough to listen would understand what he said. But neither they nor I could have any doubt as to what the true reason for his intervention had been. What His Excellency really meant was: 'Get out of here as soon as possible.'

Keeping my pose, I replied: 'Certainly, Mr Ambassador', said good-night to the circle of younger diplomats, offered my apologies to the host, and left as unobtrusively as I could.

The strange thing about it all was that I felt no anger on the way back to the Embassy. My mind was, in fact, quite blank. And even while for three long hours I sat in my office waiting for a telegram I knew would never come, I felt no resentment. I tried my best not to think about anything at all.

So I could greet him almost with detachment when he arrived very late that evening and asked, quite unruffled: 'No telegram?'

'No, Mr Ambassador.' I looked straight at him.

'You realize you were guilty of unprofessional conduct tonight, don't you?' he said calmly.

I made no answer.

'I have no idea of what you actually said,' he went on. 'I trust you had enough responsibility not to say anything which could harm us. But your very tone was something I will not tolerate again.'

'I'm sorry, Mr Ambassador.' It was what was expected of me.

'Under normal circumstances your behaviour would warrant a report to Headquarters.' His grey eyes were unyielding. 'I won't do it this time. But in future you must realize that your conduct will be very closely watched.'

That was the end of the interview, except for the words he added at the front door: 'I have a high opinion of your abilities, Keyter. If it hadn't been for that I would not have taken such a serious view of what happened tonight.'

A few minutes later I was back in my own apartment. I made no effort to rationalize the matter. And yet, quite illogically, I knew: this was the point to which everything had been moving all along. Perhaps it was a good thing to have reached it at last. I couldn't have gone on drifting for much longer.

Had I started working on my report that night, or even the following day, formally to accuse the Ambassador of misconduct, my judgement might well have been clouded by personal feelings. But now I've had enough time to reflect and to sort out everything very meticulously. I can see it all with what romantics term terrifying clarity. Only yesterday there arrived a telegram from the Minister of Foreign Affairs with instructions that our earlier, tentative negotiations with the French Government in connection with the purchase of arms must be stepped up. The recent troubles in South Africa will naturally complicate the issue. And should the Ambassador's personal conduct, at this stage, cast any reflection on his integrity, everything could end in failure. That is the crux of the matter. That, and the necessity of bringing to an end the hypocrisy of his double life.

There is really nothing else I can or dare do. I considered discussing the matter with Masters, but I knew beforehand what the outcome would be: either everything would be hushed up, leaving a sword suspended above my future, or he would take the matter in his own hands, keeping me in the dark. Both options are unthinkable. For the first time in my life I have a chance of doing something meaningful on my own. I cannot afford to let it pass.

The Apostle could rely on faith, hope and love to illuminate the darkness of his night. I have no faith in faith, and little hope of hope. And of love I seem to know nothing. All I have is my report. I may have failed in everything else: but not in this.

Chronicle

1

It was at the end of a working day that she came to him.

From all corners of Europe, it seemed, and from the distant country in the south, invisible rays were converging on that solid stinkwood desk, that telephone, that memorandum block, that firm, neat hand. The previous day, 4 November, had brought the news of the unexpected turn in the Johannesburg strike. The Hellschreiber's reports were, necessarily, brief, sometimes cryptic. The evening papers splashed it on their front pages, exactly like the previous occasion in 1960, illustrated with sensational photographs of the strike leaders and the police cordon round the township. The situation was said to be 'under control', but as far as the Press was concerned, it was still only the beginning. There was much talk of 'imminent clash', 'blood bath', 'racism', 'second Sharpeville'.

Special representatives of all the leading French papers received orders to leave for South Africa within the shortest possible time. All these journalists had to be closely screened before visas could be issued to them. Because of the delicacy of the situation each case had to be investigated by the Ambassador personally so that recommendations could be made to the Department of Internal Affairs in Pretoria. Even before the Embassy was opened to the public on the morning of the 5th representatives of both rightist and leftist groups had gathered in front of the main entrance: the leftists to protest, the others to express their solidarity. There were rumours of a full-scale demonstration by students from African countries in the avenue Hoçhe that afternoon. A protective cordon round the block had to be requested.

Urgent cables had to go off to London and Pretoria: the

first to co-ordinate procedures and responses, the latter to request full particulars and instructions. (Twenty-four hours after the beginning of the strike the South African Government, still too busy studying the situation, had not yet transmitted its official viewpoint to foreign missions.) During the course of that day there were visits from representatives of the Quai d'Orsay and other French Government departments; a personal inquiry from the British Ambassador; telegrams from Rome and The Hague; deputations from firms with considerable investments in South Africa. Each one insisted on the importance of his own business. Each required personal attention.

The Ambassador showed no outward signs of either irritation or stress. He did all his work systematically, gave audience to all his visitors, calmed the nervousness of some and the belligerence of others. He had the advantage of thirty years' experience in the Service, which enabled him to cut through superficialities to the essence of matters as he formulated his opinions. Yet it was impossible to rely indefinitely on intuition or habit, as he waited for official clarification from Pretoria. Moreover, he was not the type of person to be satisfied by being on the defensive: he believed in positive, convincing action. But for such action he needed the facts. This had become even more urgent after an announcement of telegrams sent by the strike leaders to the UN.

Shortly after lunch the first telegram arrived. It was decoded without delay and brought to him. Judging from the pompous verbiage of the message it was the Minister's own work: the Ambassador had on several occasions in the past made it clear, in no uncertain terms, that the Minister should rely more on his diplomatic advisers and less on his emotions. The present telegram confirmed his worst expectations: it was a rambling, confused assessment of the situation, followed by vague and sometimes contradictory instructions about the general lines of action to be adopted by the heads of delegations abroad.

The second telegram reached the Embassy at half-past three. This one, drawn up by the Minister's secretary, was short and to the point: *Request immediate interview with French Foreign Minister in effort to keep Afro-Asian proposal out of Security Council.* Half an hour later, after the Ambassador had already instructed Masters to make an appointment with the French Minister, a third telegram was received, with extensive guidelines for the interview. The Ambassador withdrew into his office and immediately set to work on a memorandum.

Even though the Afro-Asian reaction might have been anticipated from the very beginning, it added considerable danger to an already precarious situation. Should these countries succeed with their drastic resolution in the Council – and the circumstances seemed to favour such a result – the consequences for South Africa could be disastrous.

At seven o'clock, while the Ambassador was putting the final touches to his notes, Masters entered with a telegram from London which had just been decoded:

Trafalgar Square flooded by demonstrators. Public opinion so roused that British PM cannot weaken his already shaky position by supporting South Africa at UN. Cable from Washington announces that State Secretary declined our Embassy's first request for interview.

For a moment the Ambassador brooded over the transcript, then looked up at the First Secretary, the shadow of a smile on his face. 'Well?' he said.

The Secretary nodded anxiously. 'So everything depends upon your visit to the Quai d'Orsay tomorrow.'

The Ambassador made no answer. He got up and locked away his documents. 'I doubt whether there'll be any more messages tonight, Masters,' he said, putting his keys into his pocket. 'You may as well go home.'

They went downstairs together. At the entrance to the official residence Masters said goodbye and left. The Ambassador went inside for dinner.

But before eight o'clock he was back in his office, alone in the deserted Embassy, to work out more details for the next day's interview. Nothing could be left to chance. And in spite of the deep sense of futility he had to overcome – there seemed to be so little chance of success – he was conscious of a feeling of power, of being, somehow, indispensable. A kind of passion, dark and muted, channelled into argument after argument, paragraph after paragraph. It was a test, a challenge: himself against the world – an almost heroic struggle, alone in his isolated, illuminated office in that dark building. Each word that took shape in black letters on the white paper under his hand was a small creative act against meaninglessness. He wasn't thinking of his country as he sat there working, nor of a remote, almost unreal Minister in Pretoria. These things so soon faded into abstractions, were so soon reduced to captions in newspapers, to Hellschreiber messages that made their appearance out of the invisible ether, to telegrams decoded in good faith; 'government', 'country', 'nation' so soon became components of a god manifested only in official instructions which could neither be traced back to any origin, nor be used as evidence of its existence. And he found it impossible to react to such a fiction – except inasmuch as all reactions tended to become reflexive. What he did was done because he could not conceive of any other form of existence, because that had become his only way of expression, of finding meaning.

He was oblivious of the passing time. It could have been anywhere between ten o'clock and midnight when he heard the light sound outside his office. He looked up, annoyed. Who could be disturbing him at that time of the night? One of his staff? Not very likely. Lebon? But the concierge never set foot in his office unless he was expressly summoned, and even then he would be hesitant. For a moment he felt perturbed. But he had too much confidence in himself to be upset for long. He shut away his memorandum in a drawer and leaned back against the padded back of his heavy chair, closing his eyes briefly. It had been a long day, and he had been in the centre of everything. Now he was conscious only of a vague, throbbing headache and burning eyes.

A sound at the door. No doubt about it this time. He opened his eyes but made no other movement.

Out of the dark passage she appeared, like a fish surging up from muddy water, blinking her eyes in the light: a strange girl with loose, wet, blonde hair, her clothes dripping wet, her hands – slim hands with short nails, like a boy's – pale against the lapel of her expensive, soaked overcoat.

When she saw him, she quickly wiped the loose strands of hair from her forehead and eyes and said: 'Would you mind taking me home, please?'

He got up, courteously, from habit, but said nothing, clearly expecting an explanation.

'I know you're terribly busy,' she continued. 'But I was – well, I was with a friend on the other side of the Porte Maillot, and he threw me out, and I have no money to go home.'

'Where do you live?'

'Rue de Condé.' She must have noticed his questioning eyes, for she quickly added: 'In the Latin Quarter, near the Odéon.'

'I see. It's quite a way.'

'When the weather's fine –' She moved her narrow shoulders, her teeth lightly chattering. 'But now it's raining.'

'Of course.' In spite of himself he smiled, if very briefly, amused no doubt by her unexpected, incongruous presence in his important world.

'It isn't usually part of my duties,' he said gravely but his eyes were not unfriendly.

'I'm not asking for any favour!' she answered sharply. 'I can pay you back – later.' A brief twitching of her lips, was she desperate? Or just cynical? 'Or tonight, if you insist.' For a moment he was unaware of any hidden meaning in her words, because it was so entirely unexpected. Already her cold fingers were fumbling with the buttons in the much too small button-holes of her wet coat. She glanced at him. For a moment neither of them moved. Behind her he could see the darkness in the passage. She tried to wrench loose the first button.

'Don't!' he said laconically.

Her hands stopped. With a shock he realized how her wet clothes were clinging to her.

'Come,' he said calmly, with an effort. 'We'll find you a taxi.'

Shaking back her hair with a quick, decisive movement, she went out into the darkness, ahead of him.

'And who's your heartless friend?' he asked, trying to sound cheerful, or at least less serious.

'Why do you want to know?' There was no resentment in her voice: it was a mere question.

'I didn't mean to pry. Actually I suppose it was a stupid question. There are five million Frenchmen in Paris.'

'He's not French.' As they reached the reading room at the bottom of the stairs, dimly illuminated by a single light, she said casually. 'It's Stephen Keyter.'

'I see.' His voice was still calm and unwavering, but his next words revealed the change inside him: 'If you'll wait here in the reading room I'll get the car.'

'But –'

'It's safer and cheaper than a taxi.' He even managed a smile. She sat down on the arm of an upholstered chair. He went out to Lebon's quarters, his head bent to ward off the rain. The concierge was in his kitchen, reading.

'Please open the front door, Lebon,' he said. 'I'm going out in my car.'

'Yes, sir.' Lebon was the only person who ever called him 'sir', instead of 'Mr Ambassador'.

While the concierge was unbolting the large door the Ambassador pulled out the car. As soon as the concierge had disappeared downstairs again he opened the door for the bedraggled girl; she got in with sophisticated grace, pulling down her dress to cover her knees. They reversed into the narrow side-lane outside, waited for an opening in the traffic and then steered to the opposite side of the avenue Hoche.

'You'll have to show me the way,' said the Ambassador,

94

almost kindly. 'I'm not quite sure I'll find your street on my own.'

She nodded. Alternating segments of light and shade slid across her face. There was something about her which touched almost forgotten memories in him: an unconscious gesture, a little curl at the corner of her mouth, something indeterminable. It worried him. But she was looking straight ahead, apparently unaware of his searching glances.

'I hope Keyter didn't cause you any embarrassment,' he said as they turned down the Champs-Élysées from the Étoile. 'I'll certainly speak to him.'

'Why?' she asked. 'All men are like that. Weren't you?' She was looking at him now, leisurely studying his face.

'Perhaps,' he answered, his expression inscrutable, wisely refraining from any further remarks.

Halfway round the Concorde she suddenly called out: 'Stop!'

He slammed on the brakes. There was an angry chorus of hooting behind them.

'Must we turn back?' he asked.

'No, it's OK. We can go straight on. Just turn right at Châtelet and drive across the island.'

'You seem to know the city very well.'

'I've been here long enough.'

'All on your own?'

'I'm over twenty-one.' She said it with a hint of bravado which made him smile.

The wipers were buzzing monotonously, sweeping away the steady rain. The sound became an almost obtrusive presence while they waited for the traffic lights opposite the pont du Caroussel, as if both were trying to find something irrelevant on which to concentrate. What was there to talk about, after all? There were so many years and worlds dividing them.

When the lights changed to green, he said: 'Things are looking bad in South Africa.'

'Why?'

'Don't you know about the strike?' He glanced at her sharply.

'No.'

'But all the papers –'

'I don't read newspapers. Besides, does it really matter? We aren't there now.'

'I'm afraid *I* can't shrug it off so easily,' he said sternly, yet not without a touch of wryness.

She reflected. 'I suppose such things are important to you, aren't they?'

He tried to weigh her words, wondering why she'd said them almost as if she felt sorry for him. But all he could find in her was a neutral coolness which belied the suggestion of naïvety he'd suspected in her remarks.

'Turn right here,' she reminded him – just in time.

The river was a lazy, oily presence in the darkness somewhere below the lights of the bridge. Leaning against a lamppost, surrounded by a thin, glowing filigree of rain, a woman stood staring into the night.

'Tomorrow they'll be fishing her body from the water,' said the strange girl beside him. Her hands were fidgeting in her lap.

'What makes you think so?'

'Somehow the river just does it to one, especially at night. She's much too alone there. And it's raining.'

'You're too young to be so morbid,' he rebuked her, glancing into his rear view mirror to try and catch sight of the woman again. But she'd disappeared in the dark rain beyond the headlights following them. 'How do you know she's not just waiting for somebody?'

'You don't know Paris very well, do you?'

That was true. Immediately after his arrival, a year before, he'd spent a week on daily trips through the city with Masters, visiting all the major monuments and landmarks, in order to form a general idea of the whole. But, with the exception of a few Sunday afternoons in the Louvre, there had been very little time for that since then, so that apart from his set routes to other Embassies he knew very little of the city. It remained confined to a continuous low noise behind buildings, an awareness of people and traffic, and – sometimes – a view of the Eiffel Tower's tentacles of light moving in the night sky.

They had to wait for another set of lights on the opposite side of the pont Saint-Michel. Ahead of them, like a broad channel, stretched the wet, shimmering boulevard. He knew it by sight. But on either side there was only a vague suggestion of innumerable streets and alleys, straight or crooked, bewildering, caught among the high buildings, a latter-day *Cour des Miracles* of which he knew nothing. On one of his trips with Masters he had briefly visited the Latin Quarter, but now it was just a confused memory; moreover his visit had taken place in bright autumn sun. Now it was night, and almost frightening, with all the jumbled lines of light reflected in the wet streets. And yet this was her habitat, these very streets where he felt so ill at ease. For the first time since his arrival in Paris he experienced the city as something strange, an organism with its own uncontrollable existence beyond the confines of his daily horizon.

While his own assurance waned, hers was growing. She was talking more easily and freely than before, she was less elusive, less cynical.

'You're cold,' he said once, when his eyes caught her unawares.

'It's all right. I like the cold. Turn here. Oh, sorry, it's a one way. Try the next street.' Her words came more and more effortlessly. 'It's a pity we don't have more snow in Paris. Last year there wasn't a single flake. But the first year I was here it started early in December. I can remember one afternoon when I was sitting on a bench in the Luxembourg Gardens – it was quite late already, just before the gates were closed. The trees were pitch-black, with white lines of snow on all the branches, clean, clear lines, just like those Japanese drawings, you know, on rice paper. I just sat there without moving, with the snow quietly drifting down on me until I was all white. I almost forgot I was there. An old clochard came to sit next to me – I don't think he even noticed me, I was sitting so quietly – and he opened a bag and took out a bottle of wine. Red wine, just plonk, heavy and dark red, beautiful in the snow. He pushed off the cork with his thumb and drank with slow, long gulps, breathing little white clouds. And I suddenly felt this terrible urge to drink with him, so I asked him for a swig from his bottle. Jesus, he got a real fright when he discovered me sitting there next to him. '*Salope!*' he said, and went on drinking. Like he was having Mass all by himself while the whole world, and he, and I, were getting whiter and whiter. And then I left and went to a bistro in the rue Vavin, where I stood at the counter and drank my own glass of cheap, red, heavy wine, but somehow it was different. And when I came outside again, the gates of the Luxembourg were closed and so I had to walk all the way round to get back to my place. The snow was no longer falling, and the world looked different, dark and unfriendly, and I was feeling like that poor bastard in the Bible, you know, the one who got thrown out because he had no wedding garment, so he had to lie outside in the dark, weeping and gnashing his teeth. Hell, can you imagine? – always out there in the dark, whimpering and gnashing your teeth. Oh shit, we've gone too far now. I forgot to tell you. You'd better turn here.'

They swerved into dark, narrow sidestreets. She seemed to know every turning; but she evidently hadn't thought of one way streets so they had to make endless detours. But nothing seemed to upset her.

'I suppose it's crazy,' she said after a while – and he could only guess that she was referring to what she'd spoken of earlier. 'But I think what really frightened me was that ever since I was very small I've always had one particular nightmare: I dream I'm standing outside a large garden or a dark building, with all the gates and doors closed, so that I have to go on walking round and round it, crying, without ever finding a place to go in. Right, now you just follow the rue Saint-Sulpice down to the carrefour de l'Odéon. Look how it's raining! It's getting worse, I think. Do you think it means anything if one keeps on having the same dream over and over again?'

'They probably tried to frighten you with that story when you were a child,' he said soothingly.

She sat staring out in front of her, pensive. After a while she asked: 'Did you know they always use white wine for Mass, not red? I wonder why?'

'Why would that bother you?'

'I think it should be red. After all, it's supposed to change into blood. You think it *really* does?' In a strangely sensual, sing-song voice she began to recite to herself: *'Da nobis per huius aquae et vini mysterium* – I don't know the rest. But it sounds beautiful. Don't you think so? *Per huius aquae et vini mysterium* –'

'Are you a Catholic?' he asked, surprised.

'Jesus, no!' she answered quickly. 'Here we are. It's my entrance over there, the one with the things cut out on it.' She opened the car door.

'You can't cross the street in this rain,' he said sternly. 'You'll catch a cold. Take my jacket.' Without waiting for an answer he peeled it off.

'It's not necessary.'

'Take it.' He opened his door.

'Don't,' she said. 'Why should both of us get wet?' She lingered for a moment to take off her shoes, then jumped out, and darted across the slippery street, barefoot, her head covered with his jacket. At the entrance she pressed the latch button, leaned with the full weight of her slight body against the heavy door to force it open, then turned round to him, shouting 'Thank you!' and blowing him an impulsive, playful kiss. The door closed behind her with a heavy bang.

2

With a wry, wan smile the Ambassador remained waiting in the car for a few minutes, watching the windows of the façade above the door. But no light went on.

Then he shifted the gear-lever into position and carefully started to find his way back. More than once he ended up against one-way streets or culs-de-sac, but at last he reached a broad stream of traffic along the left bank of the Seine, which he followed until he could cross the river on a bridge that looked familiar.

And with that, he thought, the little episode, the little intermezzo in his busy day, had come to an end. There was not even a sign that it had ever taken place. What had it been to him? A brief escape, perhaps; a respite from the day's extraordinary bustle. Nothing more. And yet there was a faint echo lingering in his mind, an ancient memory he couldn't trace. And all the time the feeling persisted that she was not really a stranger, although he didn't even know her name. (Most negligent of him. And she'd taken his jacket too!)

He must have been very near the Trocadéro when he suddenly found a name for his vague, uneasy memory:

Gillian.

And now that he'd found it, he couldn't understand what resemblance there was between her and this night's stranger. Gillian had been dark. Gillian had been shorter. He could think of a hundred differences between them – much to his surprise, because there were so many years between him and that past to which Gillian had belonged. It was the first time in all those years that he had recalled anything specific about her, although it had inevitably happened (less and less frequently) that he would suddenly recognize a swinging dress in a crowd, or a laugh, or the way a girl stopped in front of a shop mirror to touch her hair – absurd little nothings which could cause him to know, or wonder, suddenly: *Gillian –?* But it had never been more than fleeting moments. He had never allowed it to be more. He had shut it out of his mind so firmly and deliberately that at last it stayed away by itself.

But now it had returned: that distant Cape Town night, tired with old wind, the streets desolate, the mountain a heavy, inert mass, the sea an invisible threat in the dark. He was on his way back to his flat in his car, it was late, almost midnight; and he was in a hurry because he felt exhausted. Suddenly, in one of the higher streets, he saw a shadow moving from a dark pavement right across his way, driven on by the wind, drawn sideways by a heavy suitcase. His brakes screeched among the silent buildings; fortunately there was no other traffic at that hour. When he came to a standstill almost on the opposite side of the street and furiously turned down his window, the shadow caught in his headlights changed into a woman. A girl, rather, with windswept hair and a large overcoat.

She stood panic-stricken next to her suitcase.

'I – I'm sorry. I honestly didn't hear the car –'

He got out. There was something diffident in her attitude when he approached her, but he ignored it. Afterwards he realized that she must have been crying, which would explain her sullenness.

'Where on earth are you going this time of the night?' he asked, still a bit shaky. 'Aren't you afraid, walking about on your own?'

She shrugged. Her hair kept on flowing in the wind.

He offered her a lift. She shook her head almost angrily. But ignoring her, he bent over and picked up the suitcase. For a moment it seemed as if she would resist, then she resigned herself to the inevitable and followed him to the car.

'If you could just drop me at the station –'

'Of course. Hop in.' At the moment it didn't strike him as unusual.

They drove on in silence. She was sitting in a tight little bundle against the door on her side, as far away from him as possible, sucking a few strands of hair. Once or twice he looked in her direction, but he couldn't make up his mind and turned his head away again without saying a word.

It was only after he'd dropped her and her trunk at the station and noticed the suspicious stare of a railway constable that he asked her: 'On what train are you leaving this time of the night?'

'I can wait here until tomorrow.'

'But where are you *going*?' He felt annoyed, remembering the important case he had to defend the next morning: he was still a lawyer at the time. He needed a good rest.

'Does it matter?' she asked. 'I just want to go away, that's all.'

'Do your people know about it?' he insisted, uncomfortably aware of how very young she was.

'My father died yesterday. There's no one else.'

He was taken aback by the offhand way in which she'd said it. 'I'm sorry,' he mumbled. 'I didn't realize –' But she wasn't even listening to him.

'Could you find me a place to stay, then?' she interrupted him.

He sighed. 'I'll try. Come, get in again.'

But the hotels were all dark.

'Do you really have nowhere to go?' he asked in despair when his third effort proved useless.

'I don't want to be at home alone.'

'I didn't mean to –' He was groping for words to calm her. 'I'm terribly sorry. I realize how miserable you must be feeling.'

'Oh for God's sake stop it!' she flared up. 'If it's him you're thinking about, well, I'm *glad* he died.'

He didn't even try to answer. He drove to another hotel. There was no reaction to his ringing.

'Couldn't you give me a bed for the night?' she asked, exhausted and irritated. 'I don't take up so much space.'

He hesitated.

He could see the expression in her eyes. 'You scared?' She gave a short laugh. 'Of course, it's "not done".' And then, almost with disgust: 'My God, I'm not asking you to sleep with me!'

She pushed open the door and tried to get out. He quickly made up his mind. Walking round to her side of the car he ordered sternly: 'Get in.'

'I didn't *ask* you for a lift. It was you who insisted.'

He kept calm as he pushed her back into the car. Wrenching herself free from his hands she suddenly started to cry; but she made no attempt to resist when he closed the door.

And while she was lying back against the seat, sobbing unrestrainedly, he swung the car round to Sea Point and took her to his flat. There was nothing he could offer her, except a cup of strong black coffee. She took it in both her hands and emptied it slowly without once looking up at him. Then she swept back her dark hair with an irritated, tired gesture, wiped her eyes with her hands, got up and asked politely: 'Where can I sleep?'

He gave up his bed for her and took his own bedclothes to the couch in the living-room. But sleep eluded him, and for hours he lay staring into the darkness listening to her occasional movements in the bedroom next door. Once he heard her sigh. And he kept on wondering about her, and about where she had come from, about her smouldering eyes and her nervous gestures, about her frailness, about her future; theirs.

For he had foreseen correctly: it had not been an insignificant encounter which would end the next morning. It was only the beginning of a storm which was to break down all his firm convictions, all his certainties. It was the first, the *only*, reckless act of his entire exemplary life.

He reached the place de l'Étoile and went round to the avenue Hoche.

His momentary confusion was past. There could not possibly be any sequel to this night's episode. And Gillian's return to his thoughts could, at the utmost, cause a short period of anxiety and then pass. He was no longer twenty-five, but fifty-six; no longer a young lawyer but an Ambassador; and he was engaged in important work. This night's strange girl was only one of the countless waifs of her kind in Paris. In herself, she was of no consequence; even among others of her generation she was probably unmemorable. How much more so in the context of *his* life filled with important people, important decisions, important circles within circles.

Immediately beyond the BBC building he stopped in front of the Embassy and got out to press the bell. There were hasty shuffling footsteps, and then Lebon was standing in the doorway with his creased jacket, the fine purple veins around his eyes and nose outlined mercilessly in the harsh light.

3

The Ambassador left his car in the courtyard and while the concierge drove it into the garage and locked up for the night, he hurried back to the office building, shivering without his jacket. At two o'clock the light was still shining from his window through the delicate web of rain outside. Gradually all noises faded from his immediate surroundings, but he remained conscious of a dull drone in the background: like the sea, only more insistent. And it disturbed his concentration, because he had never been aware of it before. It was an awareness not only of sound, but of the light and darkness of the entire city, of alleys and avenues, brilliant shop-windows and crumbled walls, of strangers and natives, of people like himself – and people like the stray girl who'd appeared so uncalled-for from the dark; he was aware, above all, of the memory she'd stirred up in him, the way a ripple in a pond might cause a bubble to rise upwards from some submerged root. It was time he, too, went to bed. There was an ache of weariness behind his eyes. He got up, arranged his papers on the desk, locked up the others, put off the light and went slowly downstairs in the dark. There, having locked the front door behind him, he stepped out in the light drizzle and swiftly crossed the courtyard to the official residence.

Inside it was all empty, very silent. The servants had gone to bed long ago. On his way to the staircase he passed formal arched doorways, antique wall ornaments, and the dull glimmering of candelabras surrounded by darkness. When he reached the top he stood still for a moment, from habit, wondering: Erika –? But then he realized: Erika was far away, she was in Italy. Unsmiling, he proceeded to his room. Erika would be far away even if she had been here. Why should he find the silence so disturbing tonight? She'd had her own bedroom for many years. He couldn't even recall what had prompted her to move out of his, or how long ago it had been. In the end an incident like that lost all intrinsic value to become merely another inevitable step in a journey that had no remembered beginning. First there would be the decline of love into habit, a brief frenzy followed by an hour's lying awake wondering: Why all the fuss? Wasn't the whole business really a let-down, even slightly humiliating? Then, gradually, the intensity would subside into cohabitation without the bother of sex. It would be a consolation if he could convince himself that it had really been different once, perhaps before Annette's birth. But it was hardly more than formal assurance. Could it be that their marriage had become a habit even before it had been consummated, for the simple reason that everybody had always taken it for granted that they would choose each other? That was what had been expected of them. It would satisfy their parents. It promoted the Afrikaner cause. His father: a school principal in Johannesburg, an energetic cultural leader in a time before concepts like 'language' and 'nation' had become mere slogans. Hers: one of the first Afrikaners to make his mark in big business, at a time when industry was dominated by Jews and English. What could be more obvious than that this boy and this girl had been 'meant' for each other? It was as much divine providence as was the future of the nation.

Only once had anything ever come between them and this ideal. Gillian. But Erika, and her parents, and his, had never known about her. Erika might have suspected it. How else would she have explained his sudden departure to Europe only six months before their planned wedding? He'd stayed away for eighteen months; for eighteen months he'd *lived*. And then he had returned to take up, once again, all the ties he had so readily shaken off: he married Erika; he entered the diplomatic service.

And now, at last, he was here, in Paris. This was the summit. He had fulfilled everybody's expectations: his relatives', his Government's, Erika's, even his own.

But, as usual, there was no time to abandon himself to the free flow of his thoughts. The few hours of sleep ahead of him were much too precious. He undressed, got into the bed, and put off the light. As he was gradually submerged in sleep, he watched as if from a distance a lazy interplay of water images. The white circle of light on his desk. A face framed in blonde hair, with raindrops on the cheeks – but before he could recognize it properly it changed into other faces, they faded away. A garden – it was like a memory, but not his own – and somebody wandering round and round it in the dark. A station scene. A city; cities; people –

Just before six o'clock he woke up. Outside it was still dark, but a darkness alive with sound and movement. He turned on the light, took a bath, shaved, dressed and went outside. The sky was still overcast but the rain had stopped. His footsteps echoed from the walls of the courtyard as he walked to the office building. For a moment he stopped to enjoy the cool darkness; then he unlocked the front door, went up to his office and started arranging his papers in the impersonal light. At eight o'clock he went down for breakfast. Immediately afterwards, before the staff arrived, he was back at his desk, working on the documents he'd put aside the previous day to draw up the memorandum.

Anna Smith was the first to arrive. Still wearing her coat and hat she appeared in his doorway, irritatingly apologetic, to ask whether there had been any new reports. He reassured her.

'I get so upset when I see what people are saying about our country, Mr Ambassador. If only one could *do* something –'

He nodded briefly. 'Is there anything else, Mrs Smith?'

'Actually there is, Mr Ambassador. But I don't know whether I ought to bother you with it. You see, it's a rather, well, delicate matter. But I *do* think you ought to know.'

'Well?' he asked patiently.

'It's one of the messengers, Mr Ambassador. The younger one who was appointed last month. Pierre.'

'Shouldn't you discuss staffing matters with Mr Masters?' he asked quietly.

'Yes, Mr Ambassador. But it's not an ordinary matter. It's rather difficult to explain. You see, I heard that Pierre – how shall I put it? – that he – that's what I *heard* anyway – with *men*, you understand, Mr Ambassador? Unlike other boys who go out with girls. I mean –'

'Do you think it affects his work as a messenger?' he interrupted her.

'Oh no, not at all, it's just –'

'So you have no complaint about his work?'

'No, Mr Ambassador.'

He folded his hands on the desk. 'In that case, Mrs Smith, I suggest we allow him to lead the kind of private life he prefers, don't you think so?'

She blushed. 'Of course,' she said precipitately. 'Please, Mr Ambassador, I don't want you to think that –'

'I can assure you I'm not thinking that at all, Mrs Smith.'

She went to the Registry Department. He resumed his

own work. At five past nine, as always, he went downstairs to make sure that nobody was late for work. Just as he reached the reading room on his way to the basement offices, Keyter opened the front door, hesitated, mumbled a quick 'Good morning' and an apology – but from the expression in the dark eyes burning in his pale face it was evident that he didn't mean a word he said.

The Ambassador turned round and went upstairs again, aware of Keyter's stare following him. Ambition, he thought. In itself it was commendable. But in Keyter it was something unhealthy, he had too much of it, it verged on the fanatical. There was only one remedy: it had to be channelled properly, it had to be tempered all the time. That was the only way to become a diplomat; he knew that from his own experience. Keyter often reminded him of himself in his youth. Only, he'd been balanced, more systematic, more consistent, knowing that the fulfilment of the smallest duties eventually added up to success. Keyter was more impulsive, plagued by a restlessness which seemed to have no outlet. He should find himself a good, doting wife. This thought suddenly reminded the Ambassador of his visitor the previous night. Keyter had thrown her out, she'd said. He frowned. Could it be that the Third Secretary was leading a secret life? He might well be the type of person who existed only in terms of extremes: asceticism or debauchery. A wasteland in between.

He set to work again, summoning the First Secretary for more particulars on recent negotiations with the French Ministry of Industry, knowing that Masters would know everything by heart. If only the man could learn to handle large wholes the way he dealt with intricate details he would have a brilliant diplomatic career ahead of him.

At twenty minutes to eleven he got up; and almost as if embarking on just another of his day's countless ordinary duties, he put his memorandum in a briefcase and went downstairs to where the chauffeur, Farnham, had already parked the official car. Farnham touched his cap when the

Ambassador got in and received a short 'Good morning' for an answer. Nothing else was exchanged between them on their way to the Quai d'Orsay. At the Minstry of Foreign Affairs, the Ambassador ordered laconically: 'Please wait here.' Then he went up the broad steps to the front door.

The interview started formally, an almost purely intellectual exercise. The Minister sat listening, his cheekbone supported by an immaculate hand with a narrow gold ring on one finger; his eyes were expressionless. When it was his turn to speak, he calmly reminded the Ambassador of France's considerable international responsibilities which might override a concern for matters that did not directly involve the Government.

That marked the transition to the more subtle game: references to relations and actions in the past and the implications of these for the future; then, as he had done so often before, the Ambassador offered, in his inimitable way, an exposé both clear in outline and crisp in detail of the delicate situation in his country within the context of Government policy, of race relations, of history and motives and goals. At the end of the interview there was no perceptible hint of any positive result. Except for a thin smile round the Minister's mouth and a cryptic goodbye: 'I appreciate your explanation. I shall discuss it with my Government. If necessary, I'll contact you again.'

But this in itself suggested a possibility of success, and the Ambassador knew exactly how to react to such nuances. When he got back into the black Austin his face was almost relaxed.

Shortly after he'd returned to the office, Koos Joubert came in with a few letters. But without much beating about the bush he stated the real cause for his visit: 'I take it you did a thorough job on the Minister, Mr Ambassador?'

'He has to consult with his Government first.'

'Well, I hope they've got more sense in them than the blarry English and Americans. It's high time those damn blacks at the UN get a trouncing they won't forget quickly.'

'We hope they can be checked, Mr Joubert,' said the Ambassador.

A few minutes after Joubert had left, he locked away his documents and left in the official car to have lunch with the British Ambassador.

When he returned at about half past two the day's press cuttings, prepared by Victor le Roux, were waiting on his desk. He was still looking through them when Keyter entered with a draft letter.

The Ambassador scanned it, nodded, and said: 'Thank you, Keyter.' Then, almost pleasantly, he added: 'Well done.'

Keyter showed no reaction. As often in the past, the Ambassador became aware of the young man's exceptionally long thin hands and bony knuckles.

Then he was left alone again. But it lasted for barely five minutes, when there was a soft knock on his door. Before he could answer, it was opened and suddenly, just like the first time, she was standing in his office with her curiously mocking smile and her green eyes (he hadn't noticed their colour before) and the shape of her small breasts against the large jersey. She seemed taller than he'd remembered from the previous night. All this he noticed in passing, as he waited for her to explain the reason for her visit.

'You busy again?' she said, as if surprised by it.

'We can't all loaf about.'

'Pity,' said the girl. 'You really ought to be out in the streets today. The city's like one great merry-go-round.' She came nearer. 'I just brought back your jacket.' She took it from her left shoulder and hung it over the back of the nearest chair.

He could feel his hands pressing hard against the dark wood in front of him.

'Why did you bring it back?' he asked with sudden anger.

'Why shouldn't I?'

Could she really be so naïve, or was it a pose? Not that he cared about her motives. All that mattered was that she'd acted most irresponsibly.

'I would have sent for the jacket,' he said sternly. 'It was quite unnecessary for you to bring it back.'

'But I *wanted* to,' she answered simply. 'I had to come and thank you for last night – for not throwing me out like he did. One can't sleep on a Métro grille when it's raining. Besides, it's not very safe for a girl.'

'It's a ridiculous idea anyway.' He was scolding her like his own daughter. But remembering how she'd seemed quite willing to 'pay' him for the favour last night, he felt a twinge of uneasiness. Trying to change the subject, he asked: 'Why didn't you ask one of the messengers downstairs to announce you?'

She laughed. 'Jesus, but you're in a foul mood today, aren't you?' Coming past him to the window she peered curiously at the scene outside. 'What a depressing view you have from here,' she said, her back to him. 'Only the little courtyard and the high walls. Looks like a prison. And d'you know how stuffy it is in here when one comes in from outside?'

'Usually I have too much to do to worry about such little inconveniences.'

'Oh.' She looked round. 'Am I disturbing you? I suppose it's very important work you're doing?'

'It is.'

She came past his desk again, stopping in front of a calendar with a colourful South African scene and said: 'How lovely!' Her green eyes looked up at him. 'It must be nice working in such a smart office?'

He made no answer.

She turned to the door, lingering for a while at the chair to smooth a crease in his jacket, and looked back at him: 'You're a very good man,' she said. '*Au 'voir.*'

He moved from behind the desk to open the door for her, but she was out already. He could hear no footsteps. How lightly a girl can move, he thought, how weightless she is, like a bird, how free – She was gone; and here he was left with

111

no more than the sober knowledge that she had been here with him a minute ago, shrugging off his reprimands, his irritation, his work, the whole weight of his existence.

A sudden impulse sent him back to the window. Through the glass he stared into an ambiguous world: what she'd called the depressing view of the courtyard and, super-imposed upon it, the reflection of his linear office interior with its one burning light. And which of these two, he suddenly wondered, was real? Or were they both no more than schematic representations of other worlds, other contents, other dimensions, endless possibilities? The door to the reading room slammed below and a moment later she crossed the slippery cobbled courtyard outside, skipping blithely through his thoughts and through both scenes in the window pane. Just before she disappeared from sight Lebon appeared at the corner of the driveway. The Ambassador saw him lift his beret as he said something. She replied, and laughed, and went away.

The Ambassador returned to the orderly security of his office. The large Persian carpet which obediently absorbed all sounds. The paintings on the white walls, all South African: a Pierneef; a Maggie Laubscher, a Wenning water-colour. The solid, imposing desk with a small Van Wouw bronze on the corner. The rows of books behind glass doors. The heavy chairs upholstered in dark leather (a jacket draped casually over the back of one). Impressive simplicity; the practical elegance of unchallenged authority.

He picked up the calendar which had caught her eye, star-ing absently at the rows of dates, down and across, each one an adequate sign encoding the day's experience, arranged in the reassuring chain of chronology. Time suddenly checked, caught in figures: the expression, in black (and sometimes red) on white, of what was happening, of what was past, and of what was still in the future, to be relegated to the past in due course.

Here and there a date had been ringed in pencil.

*

22 October: Erika and Annette at the Gare de Lyon, half an hour early for their train to the south. It is only about eight o'clock, but the cloudy autumn weather creates the impression of an hour lost in the deep of the night.

'You needn't wait,' Erika insists. 'We can manage quite easily.'

'I have time.'

They stroll up and down the dirty platform; neither can think of anything to say. A train packed with soldiers is preparing to leave. Here and there boisterous groups are leaning through windows, singing, shouting, whistling at passing women. Others sit passively among their bundles in the narrow corridors, staring into the void. Leaning against a lamppost a young couple are saying goodbye, their bodies passionately, shamelessly pressed together.

Annette giggles nervously as she keeps on glancing back at them. With an unnecessary edge to her voice Erika says something scathing about the 'disgusting public spectacle'.

'They're young,' he objects patiently without knowing why he should find it necessary to defend them.

'Does that make any difference?' she asks, piqued.

'I suppose not.'

Then a bell rings. In the distance a loudspeaker voice starts crackling; raucous and inhuman. The young soldier scrambles into the already moving train, forcing his way through the bodies. The girl remains on the platform, sobbing her heart out. On the station clock the minute hand continues its short, jerky jumps from one line to the next.

Shortly afterwards the Italy train pulls in.

'I hope you'll have good weather,' he says.

'I'm sure we will. At least we'll have a rest.' A brief pause. 'If only we were going home.'

'Home?'

'South Africa, of course.' She glances at him, then looks away. 'I'm tired of living among strangers, Paul.'

'After twenty-five years you should be used to our kind of life.'

113

'After twenty-five years all I know is that I'll *never* get used to it. And it came as a rather unpleasant shock.'

'What are you trying to tell me, Erika?'

She shakes her head. 'I don't know. It's just – I keep on waiting for something to happen. I don't know if Italy will help. We've reached a dead end, Paul.'

'It was you who always wanted this life.'

'Blame it on me, then.'

Perhaps he has never before realized so acutely how much of a stranger she is to him, how impossible it has become to get through to her. And yet theirs is supposed to have been a 'happy' marriage.

The train will be leaving at any moment.

'Is there anything we should still discuss before you go?' he asks.

'Is there anything we've ever had to discuss?'

'What on earth is the matter, Erika?' He grasps her hand.

The train jerks. He kisses her hastily, presses his lips to Annette's cheek, and is left behind as they disappear to the south, into the night.

The Ambassador put the calendar back on the desk. There was no time for these memories. He still had to send a telegram to Pretoria, and compile his report on the morning's interview.

As he sat down again he remembered that strange exit line: '*You're a very good man* –' He wondered what she could have meant, and why she'd said it: this uninvited footloose girl whose name he did not even know.

4

He never thought she would come back again. There was no reason to expect it, nor, in a weaker moment, to hope for it. During the week after her second visit, he occasionally remembered her (it was unavoidable), usually in the form of a question or a smile, at most as an episode. Perhaps he sometimes felt vaguely regretful that it had been so inconclusive, but then: what else could possibly have come of it? And when he did think of her – usually when he was alone in the large house, late at night – it was confined to: *I should have asked her name. How does a girl like that survive in Paris?*

On Sunday 11 November he was unexpectedly summoned to the French Ministry of Foreign Affairs. It was a short interview, but gratifying in its way. France did not see its way open to veto the matter in the Security Council, but the Government was prepared to intervene behind the scenes to temper the Afro-Asian proposal, mainly because a dangerous outburst in the Johannesburg troubles had been averted.

The next morning, as he was working on his new report – having given special instructions to be left undisturbed – there was a knock on his door and somebody entered. The girl.

He immediately got up, furious about the interruption. At the same time he'd been caught so unawares, after a week in which she had so insidiously troubled his mind, that he found it hard not to show the sudden flash of joy he felt.

'*Salut,*' she said. (Was she deliberately teasing him again?) And when she reached the chair on which she'd draped his jacket the previous time, she asked: 'May I sit down?' Without waiting to be invited she chose the most comfortable chair, and with that curious prudish gesture of hers arranged

115

her dress. 'I know you're up to your ears as always,' she said. 'But I'm here on business.'

She needed money, she explained with disarming frankness. In that case she should talk to the consular secretary, he answered. Besides, the Embassy could only offer assistance in the most urgent cases, usually to send destitute South Africans back home. But, she insisted, her landlady had threatened to throw her out unless she paid part of her overdue rent before tomorrow. And she couldn't get any money before Friday. Where did she work? he enquired. At a night club. He scowled, but she quickly explained that she was a singer, and that it was a very respectable place, even though they paid her a miserable salary.

'Go to the consul's office anyway,' he said firmly. 'They'll consider your case on its merits. And for the last time, please! – if you ever come back again, you must ask a messenger to announce you. Understand?'

She ignored his last words. 'If I go to the consul he'll only give me a new lot of forms to fill in. And I hate forms. That's why I came to you. I thought –'

'Look, young lady,' he said severely, coming round the desk. 'This is not the sort of thing I wish to encourage. But for this once I'll give you a hundred francs.'

'I didn't come here to beg!' she said with unexpected vehemence.

'I didn't mean to insult you,' he answered, refusing to relent. 'But if I lent it to you it would just give you an excuse to come back again.'

'Do I embarrass you then?'

He went to her, irritated, but somewhat chastened as well. 'My dear girl –'

'Don't treat me like a child.' Her voice was dark, but no longer biting.

'What's your name?'

Her first reaction was to look at him suspiciously, on the defence. When she finally answered, it was so quickly that she had to repeat her name before he could catch it.

116

Paternally he tried to overcome her resentment, doing his best to explain that without rules and regulations everything would subside into anarchy. Her only response was a short, derisive laugh. And, very reluctantly, he had to admit to himself that she wouldn't understand the first thing about his disciplined form of life. (Like Gillian – ?) He nevertheless tried to present it as persuasively as he could. But right in the middle of his explanation she interrupted him (clearly without any intention of being rude) saying: 'You shouldn't wear that tie with your suit. It's much too old for you.'

'I won't do it again,' he answered with the hint of a smile, but sighing.

'And now may I have my money, please?'

He handed her the note. 'Will it be enough?'

She nodded, undid the top button of her jersey and slipped it under her bra.

'I'll come to your night club one evening,' he promised, trying not to sound patronizing.

Her green eyes were mocking.

'Where is the club?' he asked.

'Oh, you'll never find it,' she said lightly, on her way to the door. '*Au 'voir*. And thanks ever so much.'

'Goodbye, Nicolette.'

Once again he was left with the impression that she had – perhaps – just been playing another game in which he could not but be the loser. Nobody else had ever done him out of a hundred francs so easily. And now he had to return to the report which would, once again, prove his worth and weight as a diplomat. Hopefully, he thought wryly, the Government would never instruct him to enter into negotiations with Miss Nicolette Alford.

These twenty minutes had wrought a subtle change in his attitude to the whole affair. He was forced to admit this, even though it wasn't possible to define it to himself. There was only a suggestion that a breach had been opened in the walls of his fortress. But why? Because she'd succeeded in making him feel guilty about his attitude? But surely that was ridiculous. And he had expressly warned her not to come again; he had no doubt that, this time, she would obey.

Perhaps, however, it was not even necessary for her to return in the flesh. She had left her name; and an impression; and an open door – into the unknown.

It vexed him to admit this vulnerability in himself; and he tried to compensate by acting brusquely towards his staff, even towards Masters with whom he'd always got along well. But Masters ascribed his attitude to a natural reaction after the exceptional success of his negotiations and refused to be upset by it.

5

That night he deliberately tried to sort it all out. For it was annoying, it was unthinkable, that an unknown young waif should really make any difference to himself and his way of life. Why should it bother him that, unlike anyone he'd encountered in years, she hadn't been impressed – not in the least! – either by his personality or his status, or that she couldn't care less about his express orders or the rules of the Embassy? That was still no reason why she should be anything more than a brief disquieting episode. He had to conclude that what really upset him, might have very little to do with her personally. The only reason why she had disturbed to some extent the regular flow of his life was that she had revived his memory of Gillian. And even that was senseless. Gillian belonged to the past, she'd been the sole folly of his life. But then: the sort of folly which gradually, whether one wanted it or not, grew into the very fibre of one's existence. A growth, a tumour: but whether malignant or benign was difficult to say.

The whole episode had lasted for less than two months:

from the windy night she'd accepted his lift, first to the station, then to his flat, until the day he'd left by boat with all the money he'd been saving for his wedding. Her father, whose death had led to their first meeting, turned out to have been a pastor of some sect or other. She'd consistently refused to talk about him. Never before had he come across such intense hatred in any person. From the few bitter remarks that sometimes escaped her, he concluded that she'd had a very turbulent childhood. The pastor's religion had consisted mainly of fire and brimstone, so that as a child her dreams at night had been a never-ending foretaste of hell. Her whole life had become a maelstrom of terror and hate and there was no mother to offer her comfort or sanctuary (whether the woman had died, or left her husband and child soon after the birth of the child, he'd never been able to establish). Once Gillian had tried to run away. Her father, suddenly driven to despair, promised that he would never force his will on her again, or punish her in his idiosyncratic, shocking, highly efficacious way. (For the most trivial offence or hint of 'vanity' she would first be thrashed – his religious fanaticism clearly included a marked streak of sadism – and then subjected to hours of Scripture reading and passionate prayer on behalf of her 'sinful, damned soul'.) And then he died, without any warning, before his fiftieth year. A heart attack, it seemed. And suddenly she was free, terrifyingly free, a freedom she directed against everything and everybody. 'I want to live, live, live, live, *live*!' she cried one night. 'Don't you understand? No, you won't. Not you with your obedient little bourgeois soul. But you can't keep *me* from doing it. Nothing can. I'll do everything, anything. Even if I have to go to hell for it. At least I'll make sure I deserve it!'

It was a fanatic, fantastic existence, inflamed by this burning desire to live, an urge so ferocious that it seemed to turn everything into its own paradox: thus her passion for life, the need to say '*Yes*' to life, expressed itself in practice, in a destructive iconoclasm, a head-on attack on all conventional

119

values – which, turned against herself, made her the victim of her own anarchy.

This was the girl he'd fallen in love with. For forty days. The duration of the Flood. The time between Resurrection and Ascension. Everything in which he had ever believed, everything he'd taken for granted, she took away from him, leaving him in despair. And then she, the succubus, jeered at him, taunted him that he lacked what she called the guts to follow her on her way to destruction.

Yet, at the same time she was astonishing in her ignorance, her innocence of 'life'. Often she was dismayed by her own discoveries; but she could never turn away, because she was too proud and too passionate. She had to try everything.

The Ambassador tried to stop the flow of his thoughts. There could be no sense, no use, in recalling that past, not after all these years.

– In between her outbursts there would be islands of serenity and happiness. She would cry over a sad story. She would nurse a wounded bird; she would bring little plants from the mountain and nurture them at home; she would knit a tea-cosy for an old man who lived alone. She could be infinitely patient with children; and she often went to the Gardens to play with them – and with the squirrels. She could sit at the piano and play for hours on end, Chopin or Mozart or nursery songs, lullabies, hymns.

But after *All things bright and beautiful* she could, without warning, start thundering away in a total cacophony of random chords until at last she would slam down the lid, sobbing hysterically. There were moments when he believed she must be mentally unbalanced; not mad – simply unable to contain so much rage in her frail body. And he just couldn't offer her whatever it was she needed most desperately.

After those forty days, he left. For eighteen months he lived in Europe, trying to squander all the pent-up emotions she'd provoked in him. Then, one day, he received a letter from an acquaintance, not even a friend, containing the casual sentence: '*I suppose you've heard that the girl you went out with, Gillian, I think, died in Durban recently?'* He went to a travel agent and booked his passage back to South Africa.

6

The whole next week the Embassy was like a broken anthill, day and night. Until, one evening, sitting in his office, remembering her first appearance from the dark, listening for her footsteps as if expecting her again, he knew it was impossible to go on like that. He would *have* to go to her, just once, to find out more, to have a quiet conversation, to rid himself of the hallucinations she'd awakened in him. Because he wanted to be free of Gillian – and of her, this stranger, Nicolette; even if it meant treating her, deliberately, as a child. His mind made up, he felt strangely composed, as if a burden had been finally removed from him.

But the Friday night there was a dinner party at the Dutch Embassy. Saturday evening he had an important interview with the Canadian chargé d'affaires. So it was late on Sunday before, with a feeling of sudden freedom, he could finally walk up to the avenue Hoche, take a taxi in the avenue Wagram and go to the rue de Condé. There he paid the driver, allowing him to keep the change from the ten franc note, and went to the door where she had entered the first night. For a moment he studied it closely, almost with amusement: that dilapidated entrance to a long-lost paradise. As he pushed open the solid door, he was aware, not of excitement or of expectation but – curiously – of a feeling of resignation, as if at last he knew exactly where he was, and what he was doing; as if, in that movement, he was abandoning many things, including hope; thinking, almost fatalistically: Come what may –

He turned on the light in the lobby. There were five or six

121

grey, dented rubbish bins in a row underneath the rickety post boxes on the wall. Only one of these had no name on it, so he assumed it should be Nicolette's, on the fifth floor. He looked up at the crooked old staircase. The light went out. Scowling, he felt his way along the wall until he found the time switch again, then knocked on the concierge's glass door. But there was no answer, so he began to climb the stairs. The second landing had no bulb, and he stumbled over broken steps. An old, heavy odour pervaded the place, of food and cats and dry rot and centuries of human activity. It was the Ambassador's first experience of one of these old buildings and he almost decided to turn back. When the light failed for the second time, he actually stopped for a moment, considering retreat; but then he took out his cigarette lighter and made up his mind to continue, after all. On the fifth landing he pressed the time switch again. There were two doors, the one on the right bearing a dirty name card: *Mme Cosson*. The one on the left was anonymous. He went to it, hesitated, then pressed the button. To his surprise the bell rang both inside and on Mme Cosson's side. And it was she who eventually opened, a slovenly old hag in a loose dressing gown, with dishevelled hair.

'What do you want?' she asked.

'Is Miss Alford at home?' enquired the Ambassador coolly.

The old woman giggled. 'No,' she said. 'But I don't think she'll be away long. Not that one can really tell, of course. Not with *her*.'

'Thank you.' He turned back.

'I'll unlock for you,' she offered, taking a bunch of keys from her gown pocket.

'It's not necessary,' said the Ambassador. 'I can come back later.'

Ignoring his protest she shuffled across the landing and unlocked the grey door. 'There,' she said. 'Now you can wait inside.'

He was still unsure whether he shouldn't rather leave,

offended by the old hag's presumption. But where would he go? Home?

'Thank you,' he said briefly and went inside. There was a very small entrance hall with two doors, the first leading to a kitchenette with slanting walls and ceiling. He noticed a chair in front of the stove, but it seemed uninviting and cold. The second door took him into her bedroom. He stopped on the threshold, feeling guilty, an intruder, and yet it intrigued him. The room was in an incredible mess. The narrow, uncomfortable single bed (coir mattress from the look of it, worn out and lumpy) was unmade, a pyjama top lay on the pillow, the trousers on the threadbare mat next to the bed. A nylon washing-line with a number of knots tied in it was strung between the open wardrobe and the window, with two pairs of stockings, a petticoat, a bra, three diminutive panties and a man's shirt hanging from it. Over the back of the chair was a wet towel. There was a table with a bright red-and-white checked cloth, strewn with illustrated magazines (back numbers, probably bought second-hand from a *bouquiniste*), a portable radio, one shoe, a stack of unwashed dishes and plates, lipstick and a pretty little reading lamp with a frilly shade. On top of the open wardrobe was a large suitcase; on the floor was another, open, filled with crumpled clothes, as if this were only a temporary residence. On the walls were a few pictures cut from calendars or magazines. Above the bed he noticed, with some surprise, a small cross, rather worn, but beautifully carved. On the floor, next to a large wicker chair, was a cheap record player and some records, most of them without sleeves. On the chair lay a flute.

He went from one thing to another; and, suppressing the uneasy feeling of being an imposter, he began to scrutinize everything with great care, hoping perhaps to find in this confusion a key to the strange girl who lived here. But everything remained anonymous, disconnected, without life or special meaning. There was by now an almost passionate urge in him to get beyond the surface of these things, to use them as clues which would reveal to him the meaning of this girl-life so alien to his own orderly existence. And at the same time he felt guilty, as if he were paging through a stranger's diary. Among the magazines he found a dilapidated soft-cover copy of Baudelaire. On the flyleaf someone had scribbled an illegible name. *Marc* something –? As he flicked through the yellowing pages phrases and lines seemed to leap at him, not from the book but from some submerged layer of himself: *Tu mettrais l'univers entier dans ta ruelle, Femme impure – Elle endort les plus cruels maux Et contient toutes les extases – vert paradis des amours enfantines – Tes deux beaux seins, radieux Comme des yeux – coeur plein de choses funèbres – Plonger au fond du gouffre –* Slightly dizzy, he had the curious feeling of being transported from this little room to another time, another place. Those eighteen months in Europe, after Gillian, travelling, living, writing, reading, reading. Troubled by an emotion almost too violent to contain he closed the book and thrust it back among the magazines, and turned away as if he'd been caught red-handed in some shameful act.

As he was trying to coax some heat from the heater which seemed broken, he heard a key turning in the lock of the front door. A moment later she entered, her hair loose over her shoulders.

'Oh,' she said, not at all surprised. 'It's you. *Salut*.' She crumpled up a paper bag, wiped her greasy fingers on it and dropped it into a cardboard box in the corner next to the table. 'You been waiting for a long time?' She carefully licked her fingers, one by one.

'It doesn't matter,' he said. 'I wasn't busy tonight.'

'Ouch.' Shivering, she came over to the heater. 'It's hell-of-a-cold, isn't it? I don't know what I'm going to do this winter. These things never warm a room up properly. One really needs a fireplace.' She turned the knob and gave it a kick. 'Why didn't you switch it on?'

'I couldn't get it going.'

She stood there until a faint suggestion of warmth began to radiate through the room. Then she casually straightened the crumpled blankets over the bed.

'Did old Cochon open the door for you?'

He nodded, unable to suppress a smile.

She sat down on the bed, pulled in her legs under her and drew a blanket round her shoulders.

'Why did you come here?'

At a loss for words he could only shrug. 'I – I just felt like it.'

There was a little twitch at the corner of her mouth.

'You shouldn't live in a room like this,' he changed the subject.

'Why not?' she asked, surprised.

'It looks awful. Falling to pieces. Surely you can't be happy in a place like this!'

'Depends on what you're used to, I suppose,' she said soberly.

He felt crestfallen, clumsy. 'Can't I help you?' It didn't sound the way he meant it.

'With what?'

'Anything. Money –'

'I'm not for sale.'

There was a throbbing in his temples. 'I never suggested that you were. What makes you think –'

'You're a man.' She smiled. 'Men always want to help. Of course they believe they're being quite unselfish about it. Then, just when they've got you all tied up, they suddenly want their reward.'

Her words deepened his fatigue and made him more painfully aware of the distance between them.

'Don't you realize that I want to help you because I believe you *need* it, because I feel sorry for you?'

'Sorry?' She didn't seem taken aback, only genuinely surprised, intrigued. 'Why on earth would anybody feel sorry for me?'

'I don't think you have a very easy life.'

Resting her chin on her drawn-up knees, and with that familiar little twitch of her lips, staring blankly at the window, she said: 'I was born on a Wednesday, you know.'

'What on earth has that got to do with it?'

Looking past him, she recited, to herself, the old jingle:

> *Monday's child is fair of face.*
> *Tuesday's child is full of grace.*
> *Wednesday's child is full of woe –*

He made no answer. Warmth was breathing silently through the room, a lazy, almost imperceptible presence, but undeniably *there*. And gradually he began to relax as he abandoned himself to it, and she too, easy in the reassurance that it was now warmer inside than outside, beyond the window, and that there was a precious if vulnerable awareness of consolation and compassion in the light. And their conversation was flowing more easily now, with no more hidden meanings behind every sentence, without asking too many questions or expecting too many answers. There was no need for that any more. Later, in the cold outside, it would return; but now, here, together, he sitting at the foot-end of the bed and she beside him, they were content. In the growing warmth she shook the blanket from her; later she even unbuttoned her jersey; but she made no other movement and remained sitting with her head on her knees and her hands clutching her slim bare feet. Unusual hands, he noticed, with a slight unevenness in her fingers, and with very short nails; and her feet were small, narrow for their length, but not bony. She was young, more than child, not yet woman. Never in his life had he been so close to the strange world inhabited by females of the species. But was it really *she*, he wondered, who'd stirred up these thoughts in him, or would the same have happened to him in the presence of any other person of her sex and age? This sudden doubt caused him to withdraw a little.

'What do you really *do* in Paris?' he asked.

'Nothing much.' For a moment she was distant again, looking attentively at her toes. 'In the beginning, four years

126

ago, I did all sorts of things, here, there, everywhere, just to stay alive. Then it became winter. I had no money left. One morning I sold my overcoat. It was as cold as hell. I thought I'd get at least five or six thousand francs for it, but the bloody swindler paid me only fifteen hundred. Old francs, of course. I bought me a *baguette*. And then somebody stole my purse and ran away. I tried to catch him, but no use. So I went on, just eating my bread, and walking, walking, walking, trying to keep warm. In the end I was so tired I couldn't care any more. I sat down in the Luxembourg Gardens among the winter trees, feeling my body grow colder and colder. At first it was awful, but later I got quite drowsy and I thought if only I could fall asleep I'd never wake up again. Then somebody came to sit down next to me. A student. His clothes were pretty threadbare but at least he wasn't cold. He started talking to me. I can't even remember all the things I told him. Then he proposed something. You know –? At first I shook my head, Jesus, I was too cold for anything. But he kept on. So I said: "All right, if you buy me something to eat and let me stay with you all night." He laughed and helped me up and took me home with him. I never even asked his name.' She clasped her hands round her feet again. He felt pinpricks of perspiration on his forehead, cold against the warmth of the room. She laughed softly. Started to hum something. Then stopped, as if she had forgotten the tune. Unable to do anything else, he listened to her as she quietly recited: '*Agnus Dei, qui tollis peccata mundi, miserere nobis.*' She drew back her hands, and folded her arms round her knees to support her head, turning herself into a praying embryo. '*Agnus Dei, qui tollis peccata mundi, dona nobis pacem.*'

'Nicolette!' he said, almost sternly.

She lifted her tousled blonde head and looked at him with large, innocent eyes. 'What?'

'What are you doing?'

'Nothing.' She swung her legs over the side of the bed, rubbed the numbness from her thigh muscles, then drew up her dress to just above her knees, looking critically first at her legs and then at him as if she expected a comment. But when he remained silent, she merely laughed, wriggled her feet into her shoes, rearranged her dress and said in a matter-of-fact voice: 'Would you like some coffee?'

He nodded absently, trying to decide which of her quicksilver attitudes had been serious, and which play; or was he too old ever to understand those changing moods?

From the kitchenette he could hear the hissing of the gas stove and the sound of running water, a clicking of teaspoons and cups. And all the time he remained where he was, staring passively at the chaos in the little room which now seemed to form a harmonious whole, as if a catalyst had appeared to assemble all the disparate elements.

'Oh, fuck!' he heard her exclaim. The sounds stopped.

She appeared in the doorway. 'There's no more coffee.'

'Shall we go to a café?' he suggested with a smile.

'Oh yes! But I'll have to brush up a bit first.' A minute later she called from the kitchen: 'Will you bring me my lipstick, please?'

He found it on the table, picked it up and took it to where she was leaning over the washbasin in front of a small cracked mirror, then stayed to watch the flowing movements of her young arms as, with raised elbows, she arranged her hair. He had to wait for some time before she took the lipstick and started pulling faces in the mirror. But when he turned round, meaning to be considerate, she uttered a sound which seemed to mean: 'Stay!' With a mixture of embarrassment and fascination he obeyed, and watched the strange spectacle as if he'd never seen it before. (When *had* he, in fact? Annette and Erika always locked the bathroom.) She attended to her toilet as if it were a dance she performed, not without vanity: it was lighthearted, it was fun – but at the same time tremendously serious; enthralled, he found in it a magic quality: not just a series of gestures, but a ritual.

At last she turned round to him, ready.

'You look beautiful,' he said with the courtesy that had

become a habit; but this time there was a new meaning in his formal compliment.

She smiled, with mocking eyes. Then they went out together; and he watched almost with admiration the graceful way in which she went down those crumbled steps.

'Where shall we go?' he asked when they came outside. 'You'll have to show me the way.'

She chose a street into the labyrinth.

'Have you had dinner already?' he suddenly asked.

'*Frites*.'

'Then we'll go to a restaurant,' he decided firmly.

Afterwards he would never again have found his way to the little place where she'd taken him that night. All the time he was conscious only of strange, narrow streets and the high lines of the rooftops. The restaurant had room for no more than four tables, covered with sheets of paper on which, afterwards, the *patron* scribbled their bill. There were only a few other clients, probably students, arguing in a corner. All that really mattered was Nicolette; and he sat watching her as if she were a strange, amusing little animal which he could study with scientific impartiality as she consumed incredible quantities of food – talking non-stop all the time.

At the same time he was strangely conscious of *himself* sitting there opposite her in the quaint little restaurant. What had brought him there? What was he doing there? What would happen if someone he knew found him there with her? Everything had an air of unreality. At one stage, overcome by something like claustrophobia, he almost got up to escape, back to his familiar world. But in the growing drowsiness brought on by the warmth and the heavy, cheap wine he stayed on, staring at her, listening to her, as she buzzed on and on like an insect, eating, occasionally greeting somebody who entered or went out. Just keep on talking, he thought vaguely: keep on talking, talking, keep on all night, never stop, allow this moment to *last*. Don't break the spell.

But in spite of all his attempts to persuade her to order more dessert, more cheese, more coffee, so that they could stay longer, she finally leant back and, with an expression of complete satisfaction, said: 'If I had another crumb I'd burst!' And without waiting for him to call the waiter she did it herself, and asked for the bill, and leaned over to watch very closely while the Ambassador counted off the money.

Five minutes later they were back in the cold streets in the dark. She was walking next to him, holding his arm, singing the old, melancholy, roguish little song:

> *Au clair de la lune, mon ami Pierrot,*
> *Prête-moi ta plume, pour écrire un mot.*
> *Ma chandelle est morte, je n'ai plus de feu;*
> *Ouvre-moi ta porte, pour l'amour de Dieu –*

He listened absently, only partly aware of it all, conscious of the paralysing weight of the coming parting.

As they approached her front door, she darted ahead of him and pressed the latch button, laughing. He opened the heavy door for her, almost hoping that she would invite him in – knowing very well that he would have to refuse if she did.

'Thank you,' she said, slightly out of breath. 'It was a wonderful dinner.'

'I should thank *you*.' In spite of the annoying formality of his words he meant it very sincerely. 'You know, I've suddenly discovered that I've been living in Paris blindfold.'

'Oh, I'll show you the city,' she promised. Then rising to her toes, she touched his mouth with cool, soft, moist lips, and went inside. One hand on the railing of the old staircase, she waved at him and went upstairs. Without moving he remained where he was, straining to listen to her voice as it became fainter:

> *Au clair de la lune, Pierrot répondit:*
> *Je n'ai pas de plume, je suis dans mon lit.*
> *Va chez la voisine, je crois qu'elle y est,*
> *Car dans sa cuisine on bat le briquet.*

The rest was inaudible.

7

'Oh, I'm so glad to see you, Mr Ambassador!' Sylvia Masters approached him with outstretched, limp right hand, a large carbuncle of a ring gleaming on one finger, a heavy bracelet on her wrist. 'We feel so guilty about luring you away from your work, but it's such a *special* occasion.'

She was acting as hostess at Victor le Roux's party, turning on all her anaemic charm to welcome the guests at the front door of the luxury apartment in the boulevard Haussman.

The Ambassador greeted her politely, overconscious of her bare, white arms. She was wearing a light pink dress which did not go very well with her reddish hair. Why should he find it so particularly offensive tonight? That, and the gaudy necklace round her thin white neck, and the large earrings flickering with every movement of her head.

'Mr le Roux was rather secretive about tonight,' he said, feigning interest. 'Is there anything up his sleeve?' (What he really thought was: *Couldn't she wear a tighter bra?*)

'It's still a secret,' she giggled. 'A big surprise. Come, you *must* have something to drink. What would you like?'

He followed her into the large, imposing apartment with its high walls, decorated ceiling and Empire furniture; one wall in the living-room was covered with two luxurious tapestries. On the far side of the room was a large ornate overmantel crowned with a dry arrangement of proteas and other South African flowers – Victor le Roux's own work.

There were not too many people, about eighteen or twenty. The Ambassador found his way among them, stopping occasionally for a short conversation. More than once he noticed Sylvia again. Excellent hostess after all. He'd seen her a few times at the Embassy during office hours – something of which he strongly disapproved – and had noticed how very different she looked in the daytime: usually wearing tweeds, with a greyish listlessness in her eyes. But on evenings like this she seemed to revive. This was her only true element, he thought. He had often noticed something similar in Erika. Yet Erika was altogether different. She had an innate charm, and immaculate taste. Perhaps even too immaculate. He smiled absently into his glass as he continued mechanically the conversation in which he was involved. He remembered how, during the first years of their married life, he'd sometimes noticed a hint of uncertainty in her. But she had soon acquired the polish her role demanded of her, so much so that he often had to admire her self-assurance, her quiet sophistication. At home, withdrawn from the public eye, she would often be untidy. She tended to smoke too much. And drink too, he suspected. Although nobody would ever notice it at a party. He sighed, wondering where she was tonight.

(And: *she*? In her dilapidated old building, in her drab little room, with her young eyes, light years removed from this apartment with its faded luxury.)

As he stood listening – apparently with intense interest – to the wife of the British Cultural Attaché, somebody (Masters) clapped his hands and the hubbub died down, except for Anna Smith who was still finishing a sentence, followed by a howl of laughter.

'Ladies and gentlemen –!' Masters was a polished speaker, his humour admirably dry.

'– Mr le Roux has indulged in a bit of poetic licence – or would it be licentiousness?' (They laughed.) He held a slim green volume above his head and revealed the secret: Victor had published a collection of prose impressions of Paris, illustrated by himself.

Everybody duly oohed and aahed, pressing nearer to see and to congratulate. Sylvia flung the etiolated tubers of her arms round Victor's neck, and kissed him. He was grinning with embarrassment, his longish hair plastered to his

132

perspiring forehead, his glasses large and dusty in the light.

And then, the inevitable: *For he's a jolly good fellow* (which Anna Smith and Koos Joubert sang in Afrikaans).

The Ambassador did not immediately join the cheerful bustle. Only afterwards, unobtrusively, he approached Le Roux to congratulate him. And then he returned to the Embassy.

Victor's book. The severe line of his mouth slackened into an almost wry smile. Thirty years ago he, too, had been entertaining such hopes: during the eighteen months before his wedding, here in Europe. He'd filled hundreds of pages, typing away like a man possessed in cramped little rooms in Chelsea, or Arles, or Salzburg, or Florence, until the neighbours would start hammering on the walls in the early hours. Perhaps it had been a way of clearing his system of all that had remained of Gillian. He hadn't spent much time analysing his motives; all he'd really cared about was the need to give expression to the emotions inside him. Writing and writing; reading like a man obsessed – three months in Florence reading nothing but Dante – then returning to writing. He'd published a few articles in magazines to stay alive; but his real work, an uncompleted novel, remained in his drawer.

Eighteen months of creative excess. It included women, of course. But after Gillian he'd steered clear of involvement. Most of his energy had gone into the growing pile of typewritten pages on his table. In the occasional breaks he allowed himself he travelled extensively, usually on his own. It was all part of a ritual of purification.

As the novel neared completion he started making plans for the future. If it succeeded – and he was confident it would – he would make writing his life. He would keep on *living*.

But it turned out differently.

After his marriage he still wrote something from time to time, but the novel was left untouched. He was so involved in his new career that he could no longer withdraw from it. Gradually it became his sole form of living and expression. Just as well, perhaps. He doubted, now, whether he'd ever had any real talent. It had been nothing but a temporary urge.

Why did he allow these memories to come back to him tonight? A sign of dotage? He sniffed. He should concentrate more on his work and allow himself less time for irrelevant images from a detour in his past.

8

Erika wrote —

Here in Rome the weather is cool, but it is still sunny. For a few days Annette insisted on exploring the ruins – I ask you! – but most of the time we are shopping in the Via Veneto and the streets near the Piazza d'Espagna. Not much else to do – even though we seldom get up before eleven in the morning. Last night we had dinner in a restaurant in the Via Marche with the Kriges. Remember? – we met them on our last home leave. The night before that there was a party at the Embassy. Tonight we're going to a night club. And tomorrow there's another party at one of the Italian Ministries. I'm not sure yet whether I want to go. Annette has met a young man in the Italian Foreign Service and seems to be with him wherever he goes, preferably without me. I suppose I should let her be. There's a strange gap between us. It seems to me she's desperately looking for something: what it is, I don't know; neither does she, I think. Is it something peculiar to a young girl, or does everybody experience it at some stage or another? I can still remember how I rebelled against my life during those eighteen months before our wedding when you were in Europe and it seemed as if our relationship had gone to pieces. One's demands are so absolute when one is young. I even, melodramatically, considered suicide. (My God, what does a mere child know of life and death? It seems to me it is only now that I'm gradually beginning to grope towards the meaning of these things.) Alternatively, I

134

thought I'd marry the first man who turned up, preferably an alliance to shock my parents. They were so prim and proper. (So 'comme il faut', I suppose I should say nowadays, to be in vogue.) But every time it looked as though there was a chance of escape, I shrank back. I was too scared. How bourgeois of me! It's so easy to make believe, to play the little game. Yet it becomes more and more difficult to play at 'people'. Perhaps one's imagination wanes as one grows up. Anything, as long as it takes away the need to think.

My thoughts are wandering, I'm sorry. It is time for my bath. Tonight I'll be wearing one of my new, rather décolleté dresses; just an experiment to see whether I could still shock myself. Annette has been in the bathroom for over an hour now. Have you ever noticed how beautiful she really is? But what does it matter, in the end? One of these days she'll get married – to her Italian or to one of his successors – and then? Is that the only thing being beautiful can conceivably lead to?

You mustn't work too hard. Still, what else would you do if you weren't working? Has it always been like this, Paul? I cannot remember that it was ever different. Love, Erika.

9

It was a lonely week. The evenings following Le Roux's party were miraculously free. Usually the Ambassador welcomed these opportunities for finishing work that had fallen into arrears, or for reading the latest publications on international politics. But this time there was an unsettling awareness of silence, of isolation, a feeling of being lost in immense space. When he was working in his office he turned on the lights in the passage and the reading room as well to create an illusion of life, whereas normally he was strongly against a waste of electricity.

135

On the Friday night, immersed in a book on Anglo-French relations, he suddenly heard a woman's laugh somewhere in the basement. It was so vague that he wasn't even sure he'd really heard it. Lebon's wife perhaps? But he had seen her go out earlier in the evening. Probably a mistress then. The thought was curiously painful to him. He closed the book and got up: tonight he would permit himself the extravagance of going to one of the luxury cinemas in the Champs-Élysées. He put on his coat and went out. It was raining, pleasantly cool after the overheated residence. Because he so seldom walked he forgot to take the short cut along the rue de Tilsitt and landed at the l'Étoile. The rain was coming down steadily. He pulled his hat over his forehead, measuring the distance to the nearest cinema. He would be drenched before he was anywhere near it. Almost blindly he ran the few yards to the avenue Wagram, opened a taxi door and jumped in. A few raindrops trickled down his neck.

'Rue de Condé,' he said. Could it really be as easy as this—?

When he reached the fifth floor of her building, out of breath because he'd mounted too quickly, the light on that landing was also missing. Fortunately he'd taken the precaution of using his cigarette lighter to guide him up the old staircase. For a few minutes he stood outside her door to regain his breath, then knocked, realizing the finality of his gesture, but aware, also, of the challenge in it: as if the contact of his knuckles with the scaly wood affirmed his rebellion against loneliness, silence, protocol and fate.

For a long time all was silent, and he was just wondering whether he should turn back or ring the bell for the old landlady to let him into Nicolette's little garret like the last time, when – without any sound of footsteps – the bolt clicked inside and the door was opened. She was barefoot. Her hair fell over her shoulders, a loose blonde mass; and she was wearing only a halfslip and a bra. There was neither surprise nor embarrassment in her attitude as she stepped aside, quite matter-of-factly, to let him in.

136

The Ambassador hesitated. 'You shouldn't open the door if you're not dressed.'

'Why not? Come in. I was just going to wash my hair.'

'Even so. It's not decent.' Irritated by his own clumsiness he asked, accusingly: 'Were you expecting someone?' (Why did he say that? He hadn't come here to quarrel!)

'Would you like to sit on the chair in the kitchen while I'm washing?'

'No. Take your time.' He went to her bedroom.

Shrugging her smooth shoulders she darted into the kitchen with a gay swing of her halfslip. He could hear water running. She was humming a tune he didn't know.

Gingerly pushing away junk on the table he sat down on one corner. In spite of himself he strained his ears for the sounds coming from the kitchen, then took out a cigarette and lit it. As he sat smoking, his thoughts seemed to become clearer. More relaxed, his eyes inspected the room. There was the same carefree mess on the bed, chair, table and wardrobe as before. On the bed lay a pile of newly ironed clothes.

Had he detected something deliberately provocative in her attitude towards him? Hardly: she couldn't have expected him here tonight. And yet – her singing grew louder, interfering with his thoughts. A thinnish, unformed voice. It couldn't be a very distinguished night club she sang in. He stubbed out his cigarette in the lid of a drinking-chocolate tin.

She stopped between two bars, calling: 'Hell, it's raining, isn't it?'

'Yes.'

The song went on.

A minute later: 'Why did you come over?'

'To visit you.'

'Oh.'

It was more than half an hour before she came from the kitchen, vigorously rubbing her hair with a blood-red towel. Without any attempt to tidy up first she flopped down on the heap of clothes on the bed, folding her feet under her.

Question, answer; question, answer.

He was waiting for some magic sesame to change it all, to bring an end to the futility of this little game, but she seemed to derive a perverse pleasure from it. He found it hard to fathom her mood: cynical at times, remote; and yet her words were belied by what he perceived as a mixture of conscious and unconscious sensual invitation in her attitude – her words part of one game, her body of another.

Then came the knock. They both heard it. She shook her damp hair from her face, and unfolded her long legs. He made no movement, but his whole body was tense.

When she reached the middle door he said sternly: 'Put on your clothes first.'

'Why?'

He went to the bed, picked up a crumpled dress and pressed it in her hands. 'I insist that you dress properly before you open that door.'

She was standing right in front of him, almost touching him, her eyes shallow and smouldering. Then, with a quick movement, she flung the dress from her and swept through the middle door, kicking it shut behind her with one bare foot, and went to open the front door. Furious, he started out after her. But when his hand touched the knob of the middle door he realized in what a compromising situation he would be trapped if her visitor saw him there, and his hand dropped. He could hear her talking to someone at the front door – a man's voice – but it was impossible to make out anything. For a moment he looked about, then hurried to the window, hoping it would offer some means of escape; but below the railings of the tiny balcony there was only the perpendicular, wet, grey wall of her building, five storeys high. The Ambassador turned back. The voices at the front door were silent now, but Nicolette stayed away. He waited for another minute, listening tensely, his hand trembling slightly on the door knob; then he quickly flung it open. The front door was ajar. At the rails of the staircase her slight figure stood leaning over, looking down into the stairwell.

'Nicolette.'

She turned round.

'Come back.'

She came towards him, dancing coquettishly on the tips of her toes. Grabbing her arm more brusquely than he'd meant to, he pulled her inside and slammed the door behind them. In the middle of her small room she turned round to face him, folding her arms across her small breasts so that her chin could rest in a cupped hand.

'Who was it?' he asked.

'Wouldn't you like to know!' she mocked.

'Who was it?'

She went past him and sat down on a corner of the bed. 'Somebody who loves me very much,' she said theatrically. 'He wanted to make love to me.'

His head was throbbing. 'How long do you intend going on with this kind of life?'

'Just as long as I like.' There was a dangerous edge in her voice.

'Put on your clothes,' he ordered. 'You've been prancing around naked long enough!'

'I don't dress in front of strange men.'

For a moment he had to struggle very hard not to slap her. Then he turned his back and remained standing, unmoving, waiting, seething.

She uttered a short derisive laugh. But after a tense silence she relented, chose a jersey and a skirt from the mess on the bed, and started dressing.

'Naked!' She spat out the word. 'You think I'm naked just because I haven't got clothes on?' Her voice became deeper. 'That's not naked. You're naked when the man you love holds you against him and turns you round with your back to him, and puts his arms under yours and holds you, and talks to you, and lets his hands stray, talking all the time, very softly, talking, caressing you and talking to you. *Then* you're naked even if you're wearing a thick overcoat.'

'Have you finished?' he asked. He was breathing heavily.

'Long ago.'

He turned back. She was leaning over to reach under the bed, coming up with two nylons. Slowly, almost lazily, she started putting one on, taking her time, pointing her toes at him. Then the other. Sitting back at last, she stretched out both her legs, looking at them critically, and asked: 'Do you like my legs? Or are they too thin?'

He didn't answer.

She shrugged, got up, arranged her skirt, and moved her expressionless green eyes to his. 'You must be impotent,' she said, with a derisive pout of her lower lip.

He looked at her; then away. 'You're very young,' he said.

He walked past her, outside, closing the door behind him. In the darkness of the top landing he hesitated, half turned back to reach for the door knob, knowing she was inside, waiting. He shut his eyes. Then, slowly, he went to the staircase and started feeling his way down very cautiously.

When he came outside, there was a short lull in the rain. He began to walk towards the nearest taxi rank, but the thought of his home, empty and formal, made him change his mind and he turned right, in the direction of the boulevard Saint-Michel. Feeling a need to be with other people, even strangers – *preferably* strangers – he chose the brightest, busiest café, where a large crowd huddled on a steaming terrace. For ten minutes he waited patiently for an empty seat; then he sat down at a small round table and ordered coffee from an irritable perspiring waiter. It soon became unbearably hot in his thick overcoat but there was no room to take it off.

Suddenly Keyter was standing beside him. It caused a momentary tingling of shock, followed by inexplicable, profound relief.

'Have a seat,' he said.

The Third Secretary, he noticed, was clearly surprised to find him there; and it gave the Ambassador a feeling of satisfaction, indeed of amusement. (If only Keyter knew –!)

'Do you often come to this part of the city?' the young man asked.

'Sometimes.' His expression remained unchanged, but inwardly he was smiling. 'I'm trying to explore the whole city systematically.' (*Actually, I've been visiting a girl. A real bitch. A beautiful young bitch.*)

'But it's such a nasty evening to be outside, isn't it?'

There was something mephistophelean about the pale young man, thought the Ambassador: one might almost think he was trying to make the most ordinary questions and remarks sound sinister.

'One gets stifled in the office. The rain is quite a pleasant change.' (*She said I was impotent. She thinks her legs are too thin. Do you know how lovely they are, Keyter? What would your reaction be if I suddenly told you –? But of course you know her: you threw her out that night when she first came to me. You may be a cynic, Keyter, and you're trying desperately to look sophisticated, but you're really so very young –*)

At last they went back together in a taxi. The Ambassador got out in the avenue Hoche; Keyter proceeded to Neuilly. But instead of pressing Lebon's bell, the Ambassador turned back and, in spite of the rain, went to the Champs-Élysées where once more he entered a crowded café.

10

It was final, it was the end, and he resigned himself to the inevitable, forcing himself not to think about it again. Going back to her was impossible, quite impossible. Even so he couldn't resist the adolescent impulse personally to send her an invitation to the Military Attaché's reception in the official residence. Not that he expected for a moment that she'd accept it! So he was really caught off guard when, that

Wednesday evening, he saw her enter the door of the reception hall. With calm dignity she handed her card to the porter who announced her, then formally greeted the Military Attaché and his wife, and disappeared into the crowd. He was involved in a conversation with a member of the French General Staff when she came past him, and murmured: 'Good evening, Your Excellency.'

He nodded stiffly and, noticing the General's knowing expression, explained: 'Some student or other, I presume.'

'I see.' The Frenchman cast a long appreciative glance in her direction, from her slim back down to her ankles, and resumed the conversation.

The Ambassador could neither avoid nor deny a new feeling of elation, even if it wasn't free of danger. (Or was it because of it?) Although he kept it under control very effectively the evening seemed suddenly to glow with a new warmth that made him feel almost light-headed. And behind the flow of his conversation with the General he was trying to puzzle out *why* she had come, after all. Could it be a subtle counter-challenge? A new offensive?

An hour later, however, she was gone. He had not seen her leave, but there were so many guests that she could easily have slipped out unnoticed.

From that moment the reception seemed destined. Even after most of the guests had left a few conversations dragged on and on – perversely, he was convinced. To round it off, the Ambassador dutifully invited the Military Attaché and his wife for a last drink in a smaller lounge.

It was quite late by the time he finally took leave of them at the front door, tired, his head aching dully. But there was still work to be done and he crossed the courtyard to the office building. Until past midnight he worked methodically and with forced concentration on a report requested by the French Foreign Minister. Returning through the cool courtyard he lingered for a few minutes to look up at the glow of the city lights reflected by the low clouds; then he entered the house, locked up, and went upstairs to his room.

It was almost imperceptible, yet the moment he reached the landing on top of the stairs he became aware of a scent, warmth, a presence. He stood quite still, trying to find an explanation for it. Erika's door was ajar. He crossed the thick carpet and switched on the light in her room. It was empty. But the scent was more obvious here than on the landing. Perhaps one of the servants had been here. To make quite sure he also went to Annette's room. (The three bears – ?) Everything appeared impersonal and tidy; yet there was the same intangible impression that everything was not quite as it should be. With a weary shrug he closed Annette's door behind him and went to his own room.

Her tousled head stirred on the pillow when he put on the light. One shoe was lying on the edge of the bed; the other had fallen on the floor. Except for that she was fully clothed, her dress crumpled as she lay curled up like a hedgehog on the expensive damask spread.

He stood on the threshold, his hand frozen on the button. She moaned in her sleep and stirred again. Then she raised her head, blinking at the light and at him, mumbling something, only to fall back against the pillow.

The Ambassador went to the bed, removed the shoe and put it very fastidiously beside the one on the floor.

'I'm cold,' she sighed.

He took a warm dressing-gown from behind the door, covered her with it, made sure that she was tucked in properly, and then put off the light. There was only a faint glow from the landing visible through the open door. He heard her heave a deep sigh; then she relaxed and her breathing became deep and even again. He sat down on the uncomfortable straight-backed chair at the bedside. She was merely a vague shadow on the blue bedspread, her hair a dark mass on the white pillow. And there was her breath, her sweet breath, and a scent, and warmth. A mere child, he thought. God, he was getting sentimental. Soon he would have tears in his eyes. But it was dark, and that was a good thing. And it was silent. Only she was breathing, alive on his bed, sleeping, a shadow in the shadows. He'd sat with his daughter just like this, once when she'd been very small, and ill, and Erika had been exhausted. And in the night he'd given her water, and sat next to her, and tucked in the blankets round her small shoulders, and looked at her little blonde head moving restlessly on the pillow, and he'd tried to hum to her without much melody: Sleep, sleep, my little one; sleep, sleep, my little one. Outside had been the wind and the restless trees. Outside, tonight, was the city, the wintry city, with late pedestrians and cars and the never-ending convulsions of its tired grey heart. And once with Gillian, after they'd been in the sea, that one solitary occasion when they'd made love, a cold, rainy night, and she had always been so frail, but she would never listen; he was half frozen, but she kept on, naked into the waves, through light white foam and blue-grey hills of water under the rain; she was possessed by something, a savage ecstasy, singularly alive in the sea, with her white limbs and the wet strands of hair on her cheeks; and at last he forcibly brought her back to the empty beach under the heavy hulk of the mountain and the green port jackson trees, she was shivering, blue with cold, but laughing, laughing, her head thrown back, as she stood in front of him glistening like a pearl; it was the first time, it was the *only* time, there on the beach among the wet green shrubs; and there was fine white sand clinging to her shoulders and buttocks when they got up, and in his mouth was the salt taste of tears and the sea; they rubbed each other dry, shivering, laughing, and then they ran back for something hot, brandy or red wine; but the doctor had to be called, it was pneumonia, and nobody thought she'd ever come out of it alive, but she did; and he was sitting at her bedside, aware of her nearness and her frailty, and once she put out her hand and laughed softly and whispered: 'I'm glad, I'm not sorry. I'm glad.' And then she fell asleep and did not die.

And so the night grew old and young around them, marked off in neat segments by the mute, melodious chimes of a clock somewhere in the large house: from outside in the

144

boulevards and the streets and alleys under the cloudy sky came long lines of sound caused by the traffic, but all the time he remained conscious only of her, and of her hair, and of her breathing; and once or twice he got up when she stirred, to tuck in the gown round her shoulders again.

It was past two when he realized that she was awake, lying without moving, her body tense: trying in the dark to find out where she was.

'Nicolette?' he asked.

She quickly sat up, the gown clutched to her throat like a blanket.

He got up and put on the light. She blinked, shook her hair back over her shoulders, then smiled slowly, as if she meant to apologize but first wanted to gauge his mood.

'I was so tired,' she said at last. 'It must be very late?'

He went to the door. 'I'll go and make us some coffee. The bathroom is next door, if you want to straighten yourself up a bit.'

She smiled, and nodded. Ten minutes later he heard her coming down the stairs. Neither spoke. But when she was finally seated in one of the large armchairs, holding her cup in both hands (Gillian!), she remarked quite casually: 'You and your wife sleep in separate rooms.'

'Yes.'

Her eyes gazed quietly at him over the edge of her cup, but she made no comment.

'The third room is my daughter's.'

'I know.'

He frowned, questioningly.

'I saw her clothes in her cupboard,' she explained, without a hint of shame.

'They're away on holiday, in Italy.'

'And now you're all alone in this big house?'

With a single nod he admitted it all.

'I must go home,' she said. 'What time is it?'

'Almost three o'clock. Must you?'

It was an unnecessary question, and her only response was

145

to get up, arrange her shawl round her shoulders and pick up her evening bag from the chair.

'It's a lovely dress,' he remarked quietly.

'Yes, it is.' There was a quick little smile on her tired lips.

'I'll take you home.'

'Don't bother.'

'You can't be outside alone at this time of the night.'

'It won't be the first time.'

He shook his head firmly and went out with her, opened the front door himself and pulled out the car. It was very quiet as they drove along the deserted streets with their rows of yellow lights, back to where she lived.

'Good-night,' she said, as he opened her heavy door for her.

'Good-night.'

They didn't touch.

He stood waiting in the lobby until she reached the first floor. Then he went back to his car and returned to the Embassy. As he bolted the front door the sleepy, dazed concierge made his appearance. Behind him there was shallow, yellowish light in one of the windows. Without looking at him directly, the Ambassador said good-night, entered the official residence and went up to his room where his bed still bore the imprint of her body.

11

The following weeks were exceptionally busy, even more so because of the new series of negotiations in connection with the South African arms deal. To begin with the Ambassador had several private interviews with the French Foreign Minister; then, during the subsequent discussions with the Defence Minister, he was assisted by the Military Attaché,

Colonel Kotzé. Convincing arguments had to be found and adequate security offered. The recent troubles in South Africa had ended peacefully, the French Ministers insisted, but what would happen in case of new clashes? Apart from this, the UN situation still required attention; there was a confidential report in connection with a Communist congress in Paris that had been attended by some prominent black South Africans; there were negotiations with a group of influential French politicians who wanted to visit the Republic.

Only once could he get away from his urgent business to visit Nicolette, and then she was not at home. Having no desire to talk to the landlady, he returned disappointed – and yet, in a way, relieved because of what had happened, or because of what had *not* happened. A few days later he nevertheless repeated the visit. She was out again, but on his way down he met her on the stairs and went to a bistro with her for a cup of hot chocolate.

And that was the meagre balance sheet of almost three weeks. Yet all the time the Ambassador could sense that he had become drawn into a strange, fascinating process which had begun, unnoticed, somewhere in the past and was now moving into the future. Its destination was unpredictable; and to resist it seemed unwise. Everything was tentative, a whole out-of-focus constellation of possibilities caught in an equilibrium so delicate that the slightest imprudent word or gesture might disturb it. That state had finally been reached the night she'd slept in his bed – in itself the result of everything that had preceded it – and it seemed to be determined by something beyond themselves: they could not enhance it; they could only, if impatient, disturb it. And so he was doing his work, and she was going her secret way through the Minoan labyrinth of the old city. He was continually aware of her; and she, presumably, of him. But it was all dormant in a layer of hopes and imaginings provisionally beyond the conscious.

It lasted until Tuesday 18 December.

12

It was an ordinary long white official envelope with the embossed coat-of-arms of the Republic on the back.

It was addressed simply to *The Ambassador* and marked: *Strictly Personal and Confidential*.

Inside was another envelope with the legend: *Top Secret*.

It contained a letter from the Foreign Minister on a foolscap page, and eight typed quarto sheets.

His Honour explained, with almost offensive correctness, that the report (attached thereto) was intended for scrutiny and comment by the Ambassador as soon as possible. He felt convinced that the Ambassador would be able to furnish an explanation which would speedily bring this unpleasant and presumably unwarranted matter to a satisfactory close. He would like to emphasize that the Department was regarding the conduct of the Third Secretary in an extremely serious light; and it could be anticipated that as soon as the Ambassador's expected commentary was received immediate steps would be taken accordingly.

The hands holding the white sheet did not move. The Ambassador's only reaction was an almost imperceptible pursing of his lips. Calmly and deliberately he removed the paper clip, put the letter on the desk and leisurely read through the report. There was no expression on his face. Merely a slight movement of the eyebrows when, for the first time, he came across the phrase: *Miss Nicolette Alford, a South African girl of questionable morality*.

Finally he replaced the letter, locked the document in his safe, and went through his other mail. Then he summoned Anna Smith to dictate a few letters. After she had left, he asked Masters to come to his office for a discussion of the

First Secretary's report on proposed extensions to the Embassy building. He suggested a few minor changes in Masters' text before handing back the report for its final editing. At half-past twelve he left in the official car for a business lunch in the rue du Faubourg Saint-Honoré. Shortly after two o'clock he was back in his office to give audience to the editor of *Le Figaro*. Then he signed the letters Anna Smith had typed, drafted another of his own, gave her a few new instructions, and at exactly half-past three he picked up the telephone and asked Keyter to come up to his office.

A few minutes later the young secretary was standing in front of the stinkwood desk, unsuspecting, one hand on the back of a chair.

That was where she'd left the jacket. *Corpus delicti* number one. For a moment everything inside him threatened to break out so that he had to clench his hands. Then, composed again, he said: 'I've received a report from the Minister.'

'Mr Ambassador?'

'Or rather, a copy of a report. With your signature on it.'

Now he was quite calm, watching attentively, with almost scientific interest, the two red spots gradually appearing on the young man's pale cheeks. On the wall opposite the window the clock was meticulously ticking off the seconds.

'Mr Ambassador, I – you must realize that I merely did what I regarded as my duty. I have a great respect for you. It was just that I thought the reputation of the entire –'

'I have already studied your motivation in the report, Keyter. I'm gratified that the reputation of our service is so important to you.' He moved into a more comfortable position, leaning slightly backwards, his fingers pressed together. 'Now perhaps we can dispense with the official trappings. Do you care to tell me why you *really* did it?'

'But Mr Ambassador, I assure you –'

So this, the Ambassador thought, this was hate; this was what it looked like face to face.

'In other words you acted according to your sincere conviction. What a pity you didn't consider discussing the matter with me first, or with Mr Masters, before you acted. Was it necessary to disregard protocol?'

'It was urgent.'

'I appreciate that. I'm sure nothing else would have persuaded you to lay your whole career on the line.' He nodded, almost gently. 'That will be all, thank you, Keyter.'

'Mr Ambassador –' He remained standing, the two red blotches of anger on his cheeks and something smouldering in his almost colourless eyes, and – perhaps? – a hint of doubt as well. But he left his sentence incomplete. Turning round abruptly he opened the door to leave.

'Keyter.'

Clearly struggling to maintain his composure the Third Secretary looked round.

'Why did you throw Nicolette out of your apartment that night?'

Suddenly there were tears behind the young man's eyelashes. His lips were twitching; then he quickly went out and closed the door with a short, furious click.

It was silent in the big office.

The Ambassador got up and went to the heavy safe against the wall next to the glass book case. Only then, his hands clutching the smooth, cold corner of the safe, did he abandon his pose. It had been a last, formidable show of strength. To what end? To deliver a final blow to a man already driven to despair, while he himself was cringing?

But God, God: not *this*!

He was perspiring. He turned round to face the office, *his* office, half-raising his arms as if trying to protect it all; then they fell limply to his sides.

'Bloody irresponsible fool –!'

He restrained himself. The whole situation was disgusting enough as it was. He could only make it more humiliating, more vulgar by losing his temper. It was all so childish really. Surely he had enough confidence in his own ability to crush the matter quickly and efficiently.

He unlocked the safe and took the report back to his desk.

For an hour he forced himself to work on a draft commentary. Then he crumpled all the written pages and burnt them to ashes in his waste-paper basket. What explanation did they expect of him? – *Your Honour, she was tired and she was sleeping, untouched, on my bed and I covered her with my dressing-gown and sat up next to her until she awakened – Your Honour, I was waiting in her room while she was washing her hair and afterwards she said I was impotent and I left – Your Honour –*

It made him feel sick to think of everything reduced to statements, self-defence, apologies.

But what was the alternative?

He started again, but with the same result. Long after the rest of the staff had left, he burnt the last few pages, locked up the document again and went out. The cold darkness was burning his overheated face and body. He went to the main entrance, nodded at Lebon, crossed the street and proceeded to a restaurant in the avenue Wagram.

But before the dessert which he'd already ordered could be served, he called the waiter, paid his bill, leaving an exorbitant tip, and went out. A fine drizzle had started.

And now: 'home'?

No. When he reached the main entrance he turned away again, towards the Champs-Élysées, unable to face the isolation of his sanctuary. At the same time he was irritated by people; he felt cornered among them. He went on walking until the drizzle sent him scurrying to the middle of the street, where he got into a taxi and ordered the driver to take him to the Latin Quarter. At the Odéon he got out, not wanting the driver to discover his real destination (why not?), and from there he walked to the old, carved door in the rue de Condé, which, even though he'd been there only a few times, suddenly seemed more hospitable to him than the forbidding entrance to his own residence.

There was no answer to his knock on her door. He waited for five minutes. She *had* to be there! How could she *not* be there? But she wasn't.

He slowly went downstairs, and round to the rue de l'Odéon, his eyes searching for her bedroom window high up under the line of the roof. It was dark. He started walking towards the Luxembourg Gardens, then back again, and up the stairs to her door. There was still no answer; and under her door there was still no line of light.

It was imperative for him to see her. For this was the point – he saw it all now with astonishing clarity – everything had been leading up to. It would be easy to say, with hindsight, that he should have foreseen it; but it had caught him unawares. And now there was only one thing he could do; he must find her, talk to her, bring it all into the open. The whole report was based on a ridiculous misrepresentation. He was innocent. Before the next morning every suspicion, the merest hint of guilt had to be cleared up, even if it meant waiting here for the rest of the night.

He pressed the bell. Almost immediately the landlady's door was opened behind him and a segment of her sallow face appeared in the slit. She must have been standing there, waiting.

'I'm looking for Miss Alford,' he said. 'I must see her. It is a matter of urgency.'

The door was opened wider. No, she had no idea where the young lady was. If she had to ask every time she went out there would not be time for anything else. But she could unlock the door again if Monsieur would care to wait –

He shook his head, but as she closed the door he changed his mind and said: 'All right. If you please.'

In the small bedroom he wandered about aimlessly, restlessly, trapped, no longer sure that he'd done the right thing. Hesitant, he returned to the pile of records and magazines on the floor, pretending to himself that he was just browsing. There was no sign of the Baudelaire. Abruptly he stood up again, strangely annoyed, not so much because he couldn't find it as because he now had to admit that he'd been looking for it. As he went over to the window he noticed a movement in the building opposite, one floor down from Nicolette's. At first it was just the movement itself that caught his attention – the relief of having something, *anything*, to focus on, even the random motions of a stranger in a strange room: it suddenly seemed immeasurably significant to be standing there, half hidden by the curtain, observing without being observed. A man in a red dressing-gown, sitting on a bed reading a newspaper; getting up to fetch some cigarettes across the room; returning; resuming his reading. A woman appearing from the mysterious interior of the building, wearing a short black tunic; undressing right in front of the window. She was pregnant. The man put down his paper and came to her. She undid his gown. They embraced. And because of the distance it was all happening in total silence, without words, a Punch and Judy show with unselfconscious exhibitionism; life on a very basic level, a relationship that could be expressed and satisfied by the most elementary movements and gestures.

The Ambassador turned away. He wished he could shrug off the banality of the scene; in spite of himself it had unsettled him. Somehow he couldn't face the idea of staying in that little room, unable to banish from his mind the couple making love across the street. And so he hurried out, closing the door behind him. Lifeless, in alternate light and darkness, the five flights of stairs stretched down into the deep well. When, at last, he reached the carrefour, he deliberately chose the smallest, darkest streets. Soon he found himself in sinister little alleys which, a month ago, had not even existed in his mind. Narrow lanes with the odour of waste water, urine and rotten vegetables; disintegrating, crooked buildings supported, here and there, by ugly buttresses; stray cats; a tattered old clochard, tired and drunk, pushing a child's pram containing all his earthly possessions; groups of students in dirty doorways, arguing and gesticulating, surrealist figures with burning eyes, pale faces, dark beards; the noise of laughter, dancing and arguments from Chinese or North African caves and bistros dark with smoke; the wailing of a child being scolded somewhere in the dark. And all this was *her* world. An unreal, grotesque, fantastic world where pedestrians came shuffling past in the rain, shadows without substance; where lampposts were crowned by round spheres of light which didn't seem to penetrate the dark; a world which made him wonder whether he himself was real, had ever been real. He walked on slowly, trying unconsciously to select from all those unrelated things elements of her, explanations for her. A middle-aged traveller lost in a dark wood. And he thought, incredulously, how until recently Paris had been nothing to him but a name printed on top of a sheet of official paper, a set routine, particular routes, a definite assortment of people.

After many detours, which more than once caused him to lose his way, he arrived back in the little street at the back of her building. Her window was still dark. This time he was not alarmed. The city itself had caught him in its grip. He resumed his wandering along another half-dark street, turned left, and strayed into a new labyrinth, until a broad stream of traffic suddenly opened up in front of him, with the dark, soundless Seine beyond. He crossed over to the pavement on the riverside, went up the steps of an old wooden bridge and stopped at the rails. Twenty yards away from him, invisible in the dark, someone was playing on an asthmatic accordion. Now and then, in a raucous voice, the musician would sing a few loose snatches of the melancholy tunes he was trying to play, but after a while the singing and the music stopped; perhaps he'd fallen asleep, perhaps he'd left. Perhaps, who knows, he'd plunged into the river. Only the dark, slow motion movement of the water continued far below, its leaden ripples reflecting distant lights. All sounds were muted in the drizzle.

He stood there thinking, remembering an impossible, distant night, and her words: '– *That's what the river does to one* –' But the memory was incomplete, merely a vague feeling of unrest. '*Tomorrow they'll be fishing her body from the river.*' What drives one to do it, he wondered? What would drive *her* to it? The thought came as a shock to him. For it

154

didn't seem out of character for her one day to attempt it. There was that inexplicable melancholy in her. She was a total stranger to him. But who wasn't? His wife, his own daughter? He kept staring out across the river. Would it mean that, against his own volition, he had become so conditioned by his work, his way of life, that nothing else was real? Whatever wasn't useful, practical, immediately relevant, had to be banished from consciousness, repressed, merely because there had never been either the time or the inclination to ponder on private experience. All that mattered, was the Pattern, order, predictability, protocol: everything that had always been so secure, so reliable. And why not? With complete detachment he decided: he had simply lost the faculty to *feel*. But was that so much of a loss? It was his sudden isolation here in the darkness, in the rain, above the moving water, that had prompted these gloomy thoughts. Perhaps he was not leading anything like a 'full' or a 'complete' life: but it was all he *had*. He could not give it up and start anew. He had no wish to. He was content with what he had, wasn't he? – and determined to retain it, come what may.

He resumed his journey, wandering from street to street; but now he regularly returned to the river as if mesmerized by its presence.

Content? He was Ambassador. He was fifty-six. He had reached the summit. He could go no further. But suddenly he found the thought as oppressive as the dark streets through which he'd been wandering. Yet why should it disturb him? He had always known that such a day would come. Sooner or later one inevitably reached a point where all possibilities were at last fulfilled. All that remained was to accept it, to mark time, to continue. But for how long? He might be transferred, one day, to London or Washington, but that was hardly relevant. A slight change of scenery, no more. Instructions. Negotiations. Reports. Receptions. Conversations. Official functions. Letters and telegrams from a remote, invisible Government. It was his chosen way

155

of life. He'd entered into it with open eyes. – *A remote, invisible Government*. Was that it? A Minister who existed exclusively in terms of coded telegrams, instructions, memos; an official letterhead, the copy of a rambling report, *For your scrutiny and comment*. No flesh and blood, nothing concrete, material, tangible, present, real. Riots and strikes reported in newspapers, in Hellscreiber summaries, in top-secret communications. Laws, regulations, emergency measures: nothing of all this had any immediacy. It was all remote, transformed into language, codes, officialese. Everything had to be accepted in good faith, taken for granted; his whole life depended on some magic *if*: the assumption of a Government, a Head Office in Pretoria, thousands of kilometres away. As if he were some toy operated by remote control. Was there anything he knew for certain, anything he could place his life at stake for? Those distant riots and emergencies, government decisions: *what was it all about*? Did he really care enough, believe enough? All those delicate negotiations to win French support in the Security Council, to clinch secret arms deals: what did they really amount to? A feather in his cap, proof that he was indispensable – to what? A system abhorred by the whole world –? That really was beside the point, beyond his framework of reference. Why *should* he care, if it had never assumed a shape apart from that of words? The system itself operated and existed only to the extent in which it was *remote*, invisible. It was present only in its absence – like God, he thought, in the mind of a good Christian who might commit the most atrocious acts in the pious conviction that it was sanctioned by a Being whose existence was, per definition, unprovable.

On a little square near the river, below a dark statue, a windblown couple was trying to repair their broken-down scooter. The girl – light hair, large coat, narrow jeans – was holding a torch while the boy was working on the carburettor. There was a tense frown on her face, and her teeth were chattering. They seemed oblivious of everything around them: completely isolated from the whole world in their unimportant little crisis. But they were *together*. And here he was wandering through the streets, alone. Where was Nicolette? Where Erika and Annette, where Gillian, where anybody in the wide world? His bewilderment drove him past restaurants and bistros where invisible people had taken refuge behind steaming windows, until he reached the island, and the heavy blunt towers of Notre-Dame. In his thoughts were words and random phrases from Erika's last letter, three days ago. She would not be home for Christmas. Perhaps she would stay in Italy for another month, or longer. ('*What does it matter whether I am here or there? What does it matter whether I* am, *or not?*')

Was it inevitable, then, was it something fatal, this solitude both he and Erika seemed to have succumbed to? Was it impossible to escape being caught in the mere *process* of living – moving, eating, working – reducing steadily and grimly all contact with other people?

He followed the little street beside Notre-Dame and crossed over to the Île Saint-Louis.

Keep walking, he thought. Keep moving your arms; talk aloud if you must. He was playing a part; that of a voyager; an ambassador, delegated from death into this foreign country, life – and all the time he was *aware* that he was playing. How could he get out of it? By reliving the few confused, insane, fanatic weeks with Gillian? The mere thought was absurd. It did not rest with people or time, present or past; it concerned only himself.

He went to lean over the stone wall bordering the river, staring towards the back of the cathedral. And he felt almost resigned as he thought: once in his life, in the battle against Gillian, there had been an experience of agony, which made him think that things could never become any worse; then there had been another kind of agony during his eighteen months of self-imposed exile; and another, when he had to accept the fact that his child would never be to him what he had hoped she would become. Each time he had thought:

157

This is terrible, this is unbearable, this must be the final crisis. But tonight's agony was more subtle, worse than ever before: the discovery that one can be *satisfied* with a life like his – the acquiescence in a pattern, the acceptance of a system, the resignation to a predestined existence. In reality he had long ago ceased to *be*, not only for himself, but for his Minister, his Government, his country. He could be cast aside and replaced and the work would go on as usual; perhaps, at times, less smoothly, and not always quite so spectacularly; but the brute force of the great machine had enough momentum to carry on.

But what could he do about it? Reject the system? – he *had* nothing else!

It was very late. He had to go back to Nicolette. Finding her had become even more urgent than before. It was she who, that first night, had stepped from the outer darkness into his life to set everything in motion.

On his way he came past an office building in which a few windows were still illuminated. At one desk a grey-haired man was sitting, leaning forward, writing, isolated in the sterile circle of his reading lamp. And to the Ambassador the man at the desk was no stranger, but himself, sitting there, remote from the rain and the night, working, hour after hour, night after night, day after day, caught in a monotonous eternity; and he felt the urge to shout: 'Come outside!' But he knew that the man would not even hear him, so he bent his shoulders and continued on his way.

The moisture was penetrating his thick overcoat. He was walking more slowly than before; weary; saddened by memories. It was not even a moment of choice, he thought – it was much more final. It was, very simply, a confrontation with his own hollowness.

She wasn't home yet. Where in this wild city could she be? He was much too tired to resume his aimless wandering. On the floor of her landing, in the dark, he sat down, resting his back against the dirty wall. He would wait. Perhaps she'd come home any minute now. Perhaps she'd never come. No matter. He just *had* to wait, whatever happened; it was the only thing he had left to do.

He had to break away. From her. From their few precious hours together. But was it possible to disentangle oneself from anything, ever? His whole life had been an accumulation of ties, links, responsibilities. A wife; a child; a household; and all the manifold links of his career. Nothing had ever happened accidentally, nothing had ever been forced on him; and there was nothing he would willingly discard. It was this very fact, that he had *wanted* these ties, and still needed them, which held him, irremediably trapped. For what was there beyond the framework of his life? Gillian had desperately tried to break loose, to break out, to become free, to *be*. Nicolette was free already, but her liberty bewildered him; she was dancing too lightly through this dangerous world; she was too elusive, and too untouched, too ephemeral.

He must have dozed for a while. But his burning thoughts continued in his dreams: he was wandering through unfamiliar streets, round and round a closed park, and all his efforts to enter were in vain. Then he awakened and thought, angrily, that it had been *her* dream, not his. Unless, at this moment, she was dreaming of him. She – or someone else. And if the sleeper were to wake up the dream would end, and he with it, like Tweedledum and Tweedledee.

At half-past one he heard the front door slam downstairs, far away; and the few landings with electric bulbs were illuminated. He heard voices. Someone laughed. She. A man answered. He could hear them coming up the stairs, singing. At first it was nothing but a tune whose words had been lost somewhere in his memory:

Au clair de la lune –

Then a burst of helpless laughter, and the little song started all over again. When they reached the third floor, the song continued:

159

> *Au clair de la lune, Pierrot répondit:*
> *Je n'ai pas de plume, je suis dans mon lit —*

By the time they approached the fourth floor their mirth was becoming boisterous:

> *Au clair de la lune, l'aimable Lubin*
> *Frappe chez la brune; elle repond soudain:*
> *Qui frappe de la sorte? Il dit à son tour:*
> *Ouvrez votre porte, pour le Dieu d'amour.*

At the beginning of the fifth flight of stairs they struck up the last verse. Somewhere a door was opened and a sleepy voice shouted at them to shut up. But they only laughed, and went on singing:

> *Au clair de la lune, on n'y voit qu'un peu.*
> *On chercha la plume, on chercha du feu.*
> *En cherchant d'la sorte, je n'sais c'qu'on trouva,*
> *Mais j'sais que la porte sur eux se ferma.*

Her companion – young, tall, thin, probably a student – reached the landing first and stood waiting, leaning drunkenly against the wall, while she was fumbling with her keys. At last the door swung open. She turned round, laughing. Theatrically, gaily, with slow emphasis, they repeated the last line as they went in:

> *Mais j'sais que la porte sur eux se ferma.*

The Ambassador remained sitting on the dark landing opposite her door without moving. Why had his headache become so unbearable? She had every right to come and go as she wished, with whom she wished.

After a long time he got up and went to her door. There he stopped, helpless. He looked back at the staircase. It was a dark void. He thought he could hear her laughing inside, far away. He had to go. What was he doing here? But he made no movement. From time to time he still heard – or imagined? – her distant laugh. His head was throbbing. He was wet with perspiration.

It was almost three o'clock when at last he turned away from her door. From inside, from the deep, secret world of her room, he could hear the sound of lazy voices. He took out his cigarette lighter and set out on the long journey to the lobby downstairs, thinking, for no apparent reason, of the scene he'd witnessed earlier that night, in the window across the street. In a sudden, fierce flare of anger he shook his head, as if that would help to expel the memory.

Exhausted, he arrived downstairs and sat down on one of the rubbish bins near the entrance. Now only a limitless desolation was left in him, all thoughts gone. He looked up. From the skylight, very high up, came a faint glow of light. The rest of the building was dark. For fifteen minutes he remained sitting, simply because he had no courage to leave, to face the finality of the front door slamming behind him.

Then, suddenly, voices erupted from her room upstairs and a minute later he heard her visitor's footsteps coming down towards him. He did not move. The young stranger passed within a few feet of him, a tired, relaxed smile on his face, his hair untidy. Without even glancing at the Ambassador he went to the door, struggled with the latch for a moment, cursed, and disappeared.

The Ambassador got up. Once again using his cigarette lighter, he went upstairs, very slowly. There was no thought left in him.

He knocked on her door. There was a slight movement inside, but no answer.

He knocked again.

'Who is it?' she asked in a worried, childlike voice.

'Open the door, Nicolette!'

The latch clicked and she peeped out. 'What do you want?' she asked sleepily. 'It's late already.' She yawned, covering her mouth with her hand. The blanket she'd draped round

161

her, slipped from one of her shoulders.

He forced his way past her and went straight to her room. It was warm inside. More than the warmth of the radiator: it had a physical, human quality about it. The bed was crumpled, the pillow deeply indented. Her coat and dress were on a chair, her underclothes on the floor.

His hands were clenched.

'What time is it?' she asked, dazed with sleep. 'Why did you come so late?'

'I've been waiting for hours.'

She pouted, shaking her head. 'I've been asleep for ages.'

'You've been – making love.' He found it hard to pronounce the phrase.

'What makes you think so?'

His jaws were tense. 'I was outside all the time.'

'Oh.' She looked neither guilty nor surprised.

He took a step nearer. There were spots in front of his tired eyes. He grabbed a corner of the blanket she was still clutching and jerked it away from her. She was naked. She made no attempt to cover up.

'Little slut!'

She seemed to be waiting very patiently, resigned to the inevitable.

His anger, his hours of waiting, his confusion, his disillusionment, everything that was crumbling around him – it all suddenly broke loose in him; and it was all directed against *her*, this girl standing so calmly in front of him, unashamed of her nakedness. His hands fumbled with his clothes; he caught her right arm in an angry grip, threw her on the bed, forcibly took possession of her. But force was not necessary, for she offered no resistance. With her eyes closed she let him have his way, a small twitch of pain round her mouth, her teeth biting into her lower lip.

Immediately after it was done he was overcome by shame. Brusquely he moved away from her, slumped on the edge of the bed. Now there was nothing left. He had made a mess of everything. In the window he was mercilessly revealed to

162

himself against a background of nocturnal darkness: a middle-aged man with greying hair and a hint of flabbiness round his middle, a naked blob of protoplasm ridiculously posed on the edge of a bed in an ugly, chaotic little room, his face contorted. He pressed his head into his hands, as if to obliterate his own image.

She made no movement behind him. After a very long time he felt the touch of her hand on his shoulder, her hair against his back.

'Why are you so unhappy?' she whispered.

She propped her back up against the wall, moved a pillow in behind her and drew him back, his head on her lap. His eyes were still closed, in humiliation and despair. Her cool hand was stroking his glowing face.

'What's the matter then?'

He shook his head. 'Nothing.'

She leaned over and with a corner of the sheet wiped the perspiration from his face and shoulders.

'I wanted to hurt you,' he said, his eyes still pressed tightly shut. 'I lost my way somewhere and I wanted to take it out on you. I'm no better than any ordinary thug.'

'Thug. Vagabond. *Clochard*.' She seemed to enjoy repeating the words, a child playing with pebbles. 'It's such a friendly word: *clochard*, don't you think? I'd love to be one.'

'You don't know what you're talking about.' But there was no harshness left in his voice. Something new was spreading through him, not resignation but a curious feeling of rest, a serenity he hadn't known for years.

'I know very well,' she insisted. 'I've often watched them under the bridges with their drums filled with red coals. Once, it was late one autumn afternoon, I was lying on a bench in the little garden below Notre-Dame, far away from the city, staring up at all the transparent green and yellow and brown leaves above me. I was lying with my head on my arms, and I was half asleep, I could vaguely hear the children shouting and playing. I pretended I was a clochard and it was such a wonderful feeling of, you know, being at peace with

163

myself, in my little circle of sunlight, for that one hour. I knew it would soon be dark and I wasn't sure if I'd have anything to eat – I was very poor then – but I didn't care. Because, at that moment, for that hour, I was *there*, lying in the sun, with the leaves and the sky above me, and now and then, very faintly, I could hear the organ in the cathedral. Perhaps it was just my imagination. But even that didn't matter.'

That's right, he thought. You were *there*. You're here now. I've been living among ghosts and illusions for years: nothing has been real. *Remote, invisible.* But *you* are real. You're real. You're the only *presence* in my world of shadows.

'What are you thinking?' she asked.

He looked away, embarrassed. 'I was envying you your hour in the sun. But you're so young, you see. It's easy for you.'

'It's easy for anybody.'

'I'm caught in a web, Nicolette. *I* can no longer lie in the sun. I have my work to do. Such important work. Oh, God –!'

'Do you really have to?'

'You know.' He managed a cynical smile. 'All my life I've been preparing myself for "something", for "one day". At first I wanted to get past my cadet period. If only I could be Third Secretary, I thought. Or: if only I could be sent overseas. Or: wait till I have a child. And all the time, behind everything else, there was one thought: when I reach the top one day –'

'What then?'

He opened his eyes. 'That's exactly what I am trying to find out now,' he said. 'Every time I got what I'd wanted. And now I've reached the goal I've always been working for. So what? Everything is still the same, exactly the same. A little more responsibility, a little more power, a little less freedom. And what else –?'

'Isn't that enough?'

164

'But what have I got?' he asked. 'What am I doing that is really worthwhile?'

'You're lying with your head on my lap,' she said.

He looked up at her narrow face with the provocative mouth, and the smooth line of her cheekbones and jaws, and her wide, impossible eyes. Her small, high breasts, wide apart like a Renaissance madonna's, firm and round, and tilted upwards, with light-brown haloes. Raising himself on an elbow he examined her whole body as if he'd never seen a girl before. (How many years had it been –?) The tips of her hipbones, and the smooth, taut belly in between. The tiny birth mark high up on her right thigh. Her slim, long legs with almost boyish knees. And all the time her eyes were watching him, sure of herself, smiling at him, inviting him; and this time it was gentle and with much tenderness: at first with dark undertones, tentative and almost tragic, but gradually becoming both freer and more intense, as her hands and feet, her arms and legs and breath came alive, until her whole body was moving against his. In him, too, elementary reflexes took over, excluding all memory, hopes and fears, everything except this ecstasy. Until the moment arrived when he was flung into a void, a small universe lost in himself, and in her – the paradoxical moment of aloneness and togetherness. He became aware of her small teeth against his shoulder, and her fingers clawing into his back, and through her tears and her small bird-like sounds he heard her moan: 'Oh God, oh God – !' And long after all movement had stopped he knew, from the almost desperate way she was clutching him to her, that she needed him, that there was *someone* who needed him; perhaps for a few minutes only, but she needed him, now, and maybe in the future.

He moved his fingers in her hair.

'I love you,' he said.

'No, don't.' She shook her head, looking at him with her bright, sad eyes. 'Don't. It's enough for us to be together. Love is unbearable. I want something I can bear.'

'I want to be with you, care for you, protect you, always,' he said.

She shook her head again. Her eyes were anxious, even though her mouth was smiling. Almost sadly he moved away from her. She got up, went to the door to put off the light, and returned to him, snuggling into his arm like a small animal, with her back to him and her hair against his cheek; and in the narrow, uncomfortable bed, on the moist mattress with the hard buttons, she was soon serenely asleep while he still lay awake.

The dark glow of the city came filtering through the wet panes of the window, marking a dull rectangle above the bed. And caught in this uncertain frame was the shadow of her little cross suspended from its nail. For no reason at all he repeated the words she had said the other day: *Agnus Dei qui tollis peccata mundi, miserere nobis. Agnus Dei qui tollis peccata mundi, dona nobis pacem.*' And more softly, pensively, once again: '*Dona nobis pacem* –' He could hear her breathing against the pillow. Such a small bed, he thought. Such a small litany. And all around them loomed the night. But this he had; this *they* had, and it could not be taken from them.

Without questions, without any thoughts, he lay beside her, allowing the tranquil osmosis of their bodies to go on and on. And at last the early light stole through the window and the low murmur of the city was splintered into all the separate sounds of day.

He had to get up, and dress, and go.

Outside it was clear and cold as he hurried to the nearest taxi rank. It was deserted. He hesitated. Then, for the first time since he'd arrived in Paris, he went down into a Métro station.

In the course of the day he returned Keyter's report to the Minister, accompanied by a laconic note: *No comment.*

Ambassador

1

How can I give a chronological account of her if she has no chronology? She is a continuous present tense, a book one starts reading in the middle and which has no cover, title page, beginning or end. What I have of her is a jumble of loose impressions: shreds of conversation, incoherent dream images, fantasies, superstitions, desires, delightful pagan innocence, lies, small gestures, passions, long pauses, unreasonable fears and questions, an attitude of the head, a curling of the lip, a laugh, an obscene word. Memories of her are never thoughts but sensuous experiences. The sadness of a crumpled towel. An open laundry bag with dirty clothes. The scent of shampoo. Or an apple – often an apple – on a corner of the table, half eaten, with a fresh, clean, sensual white shell-pattern of toothmarks and tiny, glistening speckles of saliva round the bite. I see her emerging from the narrow bed on cold weekend mornings, screwing her eyes against the colourless light, wandering through the room naked and aimless, not knowing what she's looking for, picking up a shoe, pulling out a drawer, stopping for a moment with a stocking draped over an arm, bending over to pack away her records (the small tight globes of her bottom, the devilish little goatee), then suddenly discovering herself in the new mirror with the gaudy gilt frame: scrutinizing every square inch of her body, piling her hair on her head or letting it fall over one shoulder, until, at last, she comes to her fingernails and examines them one by one – only then, perhaps, shivering with cold, she may drape an old blue gown loosely round her. I see her lying in my arms, her head against my shoulder in the legendary innocence of a girl lost in sleep as in water, a sleep deeper than water, a soundless, still, inorganic layer of existence, beyond dreams. And I smell her hair, and her cheap or expensive perfume, and herself: the ageless *odor di femina*. She walks through the darkness inside Notre-Dame in a sober dress, a scarf round her hair. She laughs in a third-rate music-hall, her head thrown back, lips and teeth glistening and moist. She stands with a handful of snow in a limitless white park lined with black trees. She leans against a rail in the Métro and – a puppy – makes friends with some stranger who leers lasciviously at her. She cries over a bird nest fallen from a chestnut tree in a storm. I taste her tears. On her mouth I taste cheap sticky sweets or salty *frites*. Oranges. I taste her tongue. In the small of my back I feel her drawn-up knees. On my arms the grasp of her greedy fingers. My cheek remembers the playful touch of her lips. And in my hand sleeps the memory of a small breast. I shape the syllables of her name as if the sound would bring her to life. But at last my tongue stops on the final consonant, unpronounced; all thoughts come to rest on what remains ungraspable in her. She has the transparency of true mystery – glass one stares through without being aware of it. Self-sufficient? Yes: yet she does not exist in isolation, because through her I return to the past and call up all the possibilities left unfulfilled; through her I explore all my relations with those around me; through her I am forced back into myself, ever more deeply, in the hopeless hope that in the end it will lead me to *her*. When I think of her, she is a myth, a fairytale; she is Héloïse, Francesca da Rimini, Pasiphaë. All the names revived from those months of furious random reading I'd spent in Europe before returning to the fold, to Erika and the rest. All this I must add up, trying to solve her equation, to find a solution for her x. But when all is said and done, what remains is, simply, *she* – known, unknown, unknowable.

2

Lying on her back on the narrow bed, one knee drawn up to support the other foot, she is absorbed in the delicate task of painting her toenails green.

I'm standing at the window, satiated with looking at her, watching the room opposite where the young pregnant woman I first saw a month ago is removing her necklace and earrings in front of the open curtains. She has already noticed me; yet, without any hesitation, she proceeds with the strange metamorphosis that transforms her from a sophisticated creature in a coat and tailored two-piece to a vulnerable mother animal with protruding breasts and belly. And all this is taking place without any selfconsciousness or mystery or perversity: a sober fact. Her husband, who entered a moment ago, leads her away from the window to the bed. It is like a silent movie; but no comedy, because, throughout the pantomime – only, of course, it is *not* a pantomime, and that makes all the difference – I get the disconcerting impression that what she is desperately trying to convey to me, in the coded language of her banal striptease, is not just passion, not even despair, but the simple terrifying need to communicate. Her code *is* its message. There is nothing beyond itself.

'Are they at it again?' Nicolette asks, wiggling her big toe in front of her eyes.

'Who?'

'The people across the street.'

'What do you know about them?' I turn round, not without a touch of guilt.

'Nothing.' She sets to work on the second foot.

'They should at least have the decency to draw the curtains.'

She laughs, without looking up.

'How long have they been living there like that?' I enquire. 'So – exposed.'

'For quite some time. At first they did draw the curtains. It's only lately, since they got married, that they don't care any more. She used to live there on her own. From time to time she had a different man with her. Then this one man kept coming back. She got pregnant. And then they got married – at least, that's what I think, for I've seen a ring on her finger.'

'That's no reason to offer free *expositions* to the whole street.'

'I suppose she feels trapped somehow.'

Her attitude suggests that she might like to say more, that she knows more than she has revealed. But she leaves me with the riddle, continuing her pedicure.

'This is really not a good place for you to live.'

Two green eyes look up at me through loose, blonde strands of hair. 'Why not? People fuck everywhere – even in Neuilly or the avenue Wagram.' Adding, deliberately: 'I've done it there myself'.

Does she realize what she's doing to me with those constant allusions to her secret life? Sometimes I wonder, almost dazed: What's the matter with me? What am I doing here with her? What could she – or anyone like her – offer me? Sometimes I feel an urge to treat her like a child, to give her a proper thrashing, so that she'd realize *what* she's doing. Above all, there is this despair in me: Here I am with her, but this is not all there is to her, it isn't the whole *she*. There are others in this city with a stake in her. More agonizing still: every single male inhabitant of the city carries her memory in his conscious or subconscious mind, whether he has slept with her, or sold her a pair of nylons, or brushed against her in the Métro, or merely stared at her legs. She is not confined to these four walls huddled so closely together under the roof. Like a single cheap grain of bath salts pervading a whole tub of water, she has permeated Paris: every alley and crumbled

172

wall, every juke-box or pinball machine in cheap little cafés, every old newspaper wrapped round greasy *frites*, every dark church, every clochard, every dented rubbish bin, every stained glass window, every moist black stone along the dirty Seine contains something of her – a glance, a footstep, a single hair, a tear, a drop of spittle, the sound of her laugh. And what fraction of her life belongs to me? Is it not presumptuous even to think that I possess anything of her, as if anything about her could ever be 'had'?

She screws the pointed cap back on the varnish bottle and comes over to the window, pressing her nose against the pane. Deliberately refusing to stare, with her, at the convulsions behind the window opposite I watch her instead. But when she suddenly utters a short laugh I risk a glance: the man is standing at his window shaking his penis at her. While anger tightens my jaws, she reacts nonchalantly, smilingly, by pressing the *fica* sign against the window. Then, with one easy sweep, she draws the curtains.

'Why do you look at them if it upsets you so?' she asks.

For a moment I'm at a loss for an answer.

Then, out of the blue, she remarks: 'You don't get along very well with your wife, do you?'

'On the contrary, we get along extremely well.'

'But you don't need each other.'

'What makes you think so?'

'I don't think you really need, or *want*, each other.' Without warning the conversation has reached this point of precarious balance where an answer, however casual, may assume tremendous importance. And suddenly I'm tired. Tired of fencing, pretending, playing. It's senseless anyway; I don't want another of our 'clever' conversations where the only aim is to avoid the truth.

'I want *you*, Nicolette.'

For a moment she seems ready to deflect the remark. Then, unexpectedly demure, she says: 'Yes.' And she presses herself against me to kiss and to be kissed, repeating, more emphatically: 'Yes', as if trying to convince, not me,

173

but something inside herself. And the moment I know or believe, or hope, that she has surrendered, she remarks neutrally: 'She'll come back. And then you will forget all about me. I wish you wouldn't. I wish you'd stay with me for ever, and never leave me alone again.'

'My love –'

Taking my handkerchief from my pocket she wipes her rouge from my lips.

After a while she says: 'Come. It's not too cold outside tonight. We're going out.'

'Why can't we stay here?'

'No.' Her eyes are anxious. 'It's – stuffy inside.' And without waiting for an answer she goes to the cupboard, peels off her dress and changes into slacks and several jerseys.

'Why do you always want to go out the moment we are together?' I protest. 'You're not afraid of me, are you?'

'I want to show you the city like I promised.'

It always happens like this and I dare not resist; perhaps she really wants to show me the place. But even so I'm sure there must be a hidden motive. Rebellion? – but against what? Or a challenge? – but to whom?

'OK, I'm ready.' She flings the ends of a long red scarf over her shoulders. In spite of the meticulous attention to her toes her feet are now buried in black fur-lined boots. 'Am I all right?'

I smile, and ask: 'All right for what?'

'For the night.'

'You're more than all right for the night.' Middle-aged, I turn to the door and open it for her. 'You'll have to show me the way.'

She begins to descend the staircase winding down into the dark, circle after circle.

Hesitant, still undecided whether we should leave, I stop after the first few steps.

'Come on!' she calls up to me. 'We have a long way to go!'

I have little hope that it will lead to anything. But if I turn back, she will no doubt continue without me. And so, with a

174

sigh, I follow her down. Reaching the circle of light on the landing below, isolated between darkness and darkness, she glances back briefly, then she moves on with the unself-conscious knowledge of her youth. Desire stirs in me again. Everything, these days, depends upon such minute, fleeting gestures, ephemeral foam drifting on a dark wind; and yet, for that very reason, immensely significant.

She has already reached the third flight of stairs, which has no light. A small dog is barking behind a closed door. 'Poor little thing,' she says. 'He recognizes my footsteps. You see, he never gets enough to eat. His owners are too bloody greedy – so I have to smuggle him food.'

I make no comment.

On the edge of the next circle she stops for a moment to ask: 'Do you have any money on you?'

I nod, surprised.

'I feel like spending a lot tonight.'

She goes frisking down the next flight. Following her, I feel both amused and perplexed by the readiness with which I yield to all her whims. And I remember Erika's regular complaint about my stinginess.

'Watch out!' she calls from the lobby below the last flight of stairs. 'The door was open all afternoon and the rain came in. It's a proper swamp!'

In spite of her warning I lose my balance in a slippery puddle, and stumble against one of the rubbish bins. With an infernal clattering the lid rolls over the floor, echoing through the whole building. Nicolette bursts into laughter.

There is an angry shout from the concierge's door, followed by a stream of invective. Still laughing, Nicolette takes me by the arm, and we leave the angry old man behind in the dark.

She leads me past a dilapidated little bistro – closed down and boarded up a long time ago, it seems; the tattered canvas awning still sporting the barely legible name Café Alighieri – into an obscure, narrow, silent alley. The noise of the traffic is shut off behind the high buildings. Our footsteps echo

175

against the walls. The small shops and boutiques are all lugubriously shuttered and padlocked. Here and there a lamppost stands caught in its own circle of light. It is very cold, but there is no wind, and the sky is open, although no stars are visible. The high buildings create the impression that one is walking along deep, subterranean passages in a doleful city.

As we pass a dimly lit bistro there is a sudden outburst of noise and violence inside: two drunken, tattered women are fighting like furies. One of them is pushed through the open door and stumbles against us. Hysterical, she staggers to her feet again, swings round and aims a blow at Nicolette. But before the quarrel can turn into a serious brawl – it is obvious that Nicolette is ready to hit back – an apologetic *patron* hurries outside and drags the hag away. I grasp Nicolette's hand in mine and, ignoring her protest, persuade her to resume our exploration of the night.

'If that man hadn't stopped us –!' she pants, looking back.

'I'm sure he was sent by heaven,' I reply, not quite re-covered from the shock myself.

To my surprise she begins to laugh.

We follow the gradually widening streets until the parallel lines of the buildings on either side suddenly open on the place Saint-Germain-des-Prés, ablaze with light, swarming with people like a thing possessed of its own life. The whole city seems to be converging on the square. Ascetic young men with hollow eyes; girls with stark white bony faces, tousled hair and black clothes, like resurrected corpses; tourists; strollers. And all round the teeming square the lights seem to be burning like fires: pale lights that enhance the unworldly atmosphere of the scene; the crowd a swarm of beetles scuttling about the open graves of existentialists, living and dead.

It becomes hallucinating, terrifying: this milling motion without direction, movement without reason; heresy against sense and coherence; a meaningless, aimless rebellion under

176

a heaven without stars, against the large closed doors of the morose church.

She strolls through it all with ease and grace, crossing the boulevard against a red light while walls of traffic are dammed on either side, hooting and shouting; students, going berserk, are frolicking among the cars, climbing on bonnets, shouting wisecracks and abuse. Police are scurrying to and fro to control the traffic, their black cloaks fluttering.

'Where are we going?' I shout against the nerve-racking noise.

'Nowhere,' she laughs. 'Just walking. Don't you like it?'

I look at her hair, which has as always come loose round her shoulders; and the easy swinging rhythm of her long legs and her big warm coat; and the little clouds of mist escaping from her mouth with every word or laugh.

We reach the small garden under the church where a thin circle of people lost from the crowds sit shivering on hard benches round a cluster of bare black shrubs; from the high branches of the trees badly concealed floodlights illuminate the massive tower.

'Last night someone committed suicide by jumping from up there,' I hear her say. 'Long after everybody had left. Awful, isn't it?'

As always, I suspect a secret meaning in her words, but her face is expressionless, half hidden by the thick scarf.

There is a scream in the branches above our heads. Nicolette cries out, frightened, catching hold of my arm with both hands. All the heads turn upwards.

'An owl,' murmurs one shapeless coat.

'I thought it was another crank trying to —' She laughs nervously. 'Or a ghost. It gives me the creeps. Come, let's go.'

Once again we cross the crowded street, pick our way through the throng, and find a table in the corner of a café terrace.

'Like it?' I ask, wryly, when the large glasses of hot red wine are placed before us.

'Delicious.'

'I was referring to the racket outside.'

'It's always like that,' she says, emptying four or five packets of sugar into her steaming glass. And the happiness kindled in me by her spontaneous enjoyment of the wine, together with the warmth that gradually invades my frozen body, change my sullen fatigue to a relaxed glow of pleasure. At one stage I even laugh with her at a bundle of bewildered strangers outside, gawking like fowls with protruding necks at the turbulent crowd.

'Saint-Germain-des-Prés: done,' says Nicolette.

Laughing, I banish the memory of how, until recently, I was exactly like those strangers, forever on the verge, outside it all, unable to understand.

When I look back at Nicolette there is a slovenly old man in a brown coat standing beside her chair. Everything about him is tattered and tired; yet his beady eyes are wrinkled with laughter above cheeks covered by a web of red and purple veins.

She leans back, smiling; then turns to me and introduces him: 'This is old Brunetto.'

The old man grins through his unkempt beard and raises his hand – whether in greeting or blessing I cannot tell.

I answer with a formal nod, reluctant to encourage him, questioning her with my eyes.

'Old Brunetto is Italian,' she explains. 'He's a *péd*. He used to live in Florence, but after the war he came to Paris. Now he's telling people's fortunes in the cafés.' She turns to him and repeats something in rapid argot.

He answers in what sounds like a mixture of French and Italian, which she obviously understands, for she leans across the table to translate: 'No ordinary fortune-teller, he says. He's really a prophet.'

'I see. Not honoured in his own country: is that why he's here?'

She ignores the remark. Turning back to him, she offers him her right hand, palm upward. The old man bows to our

178

neighbours, mumbling: '*Permette*?', removes a chair from their table to ours, sits down heavily and takes her small white hand in both his dirty paws. For a few minutes he sits mumbling to himself before breaking into what I take to be his 'prophecies'. Occasionally she translates a few phrases for my benefit. There is great happiness in store for her. A good man. Middle-aged? (He glances in my direction, winking.) He can see a church. And darkness. And an easter egg.

'But what does it *mean*?' she insists. Then, to me: 'Every time he sees new things.'

'He has to, if he wants to keep on making money out of you.'

Ignoring me, they proceed to discuss his esoteric symbols.

'Now it's your turn,' she announces at last.

'No. It's nonsense.'

'But you *must*! Brunetto isn't a quack! Oh please do.'

Grinning patiently, he sits waiting, realizing – I suppose – that sooner or later, for the sake of peace, I must concede. When, at last, I reluctantly surrender my hand to his claws I wonder with some amusement: What would happen if one of my staff suddenly looked through a window – ?

He begins to 'read'.

'He says you're a very important man,' Nicolette interprets.

'Thank him for the compliment. But it won't make any difference to his tip.'

'He says you're engaged in difficult work.'

I merely sniff.

'He says there's much happiness in store for you.'

'Thank you.'

'But he says your own people are going to reject you because they don't understand you.'

'I'll take the warning to heart.'

'He says he can see a goat walking towards a hill, but without reaching the green grass.'

'Is he quite sure it isn't simply an old goat looking for a tender leaf?' Somehow it doesn't sound like a joke.

'And now he please wants his money.'

'Tell him he is a wise master speaking immortal words.' I hand him a ten franc note. 'Thank you, Brunetto,' I add in French, with exaggerated politeness.

He thrusts the note into his pocket, then raises both hands in blessing – and to my embarrassment I see two tears trickle over his flabby cheeks into his beard.

'Brunetto always tells the truth,' says Nicolette very solemnly as the old Italian disappears into the night. 'I wonder what he could have meant with 'darkness'? Do you think it has anything to do with my dream? Remember, I told you –'

'Come,' I interrupt her, disturbed by the old fortune-teller who has made his appearance like a conscience in beggar's clothes among the strangers.

And then she leads me into the lanes of another labyrinth in the direction of the Seine, as far as I can make out. In front of what seems to be an ordinary bistro she stops, and gestures towards a staircase against the inside back wall, leading to a basement from where a muffled din of voices and music can be heard.

'Haven't we seen enough for one night?' I ask wearily.

Her only answer is to take my arm and lead me inside. She seems to know the place, for with a slight nod in the direction of the waiters behind the counter she proceeds straight to the staircase. On the landing is a huge poster representing an upside-down clown.

As we descend lower the noise increases. From a bend in the staircase one has a view of a long, narrow room, lit by only two bare bulbs, far apart in the ceiling; inside is an assortment of phantom-like creatures moving through a whorl of smoke to the accompaniment of monotonous, oppressing drum and trumpet music. Occasionally dancing couples appear from the cloud of smoke, closer to us than the dim figures in the background; shabbily dressed, with white faces and long hair; some of them performing the slow lazy movements of algae, joined at the pelvis like Siamese twins; others moving more jerkily, with groping arms and spastic heads; and as they come dancing past, they turn their heads back wordlessly to stare at us with hypnotic, expressionless, red- or black-rimmed eyes.

We find two empty chairs at the end of a long table, sur- rounded by billowing smoke; visible and invisible surrealist creatures are talking and laughing, sometimes screaming, moving past us, and disappearing again; and in the corner the disembodied drum continues its compulsive beat, working up to regular climaxes and then fading away, without ever falling altogether silent. We are drawn into a witches' sabbath, temporarily undisturbed in our corner – but not for long.

'Let's dance,' says Nicolette. Her eyes are large and excited, with a strange, terrifying expression in them, as if she's in a trance.

At first I decline, but she lays an urgent hand on my arm and makes it impossible not to yield. Tentatively we move into the outer circle of dancers, but as I become more and more aware of her shameless youth so close to me, and of her abandonment to the disturbing, evil heart-throb of the music, I shed my reluctance; and soon we are sucked into the whirlpool by the magical motions of the dance. All thoughts, all customary relations, lose their significance and disappear; we too, Nicolette and I, disappear; pure motion takes over – determined by the rhythms of the invisible drum. And it is only when at last we drift loose from the throng and return to our seats at the long table that I become aware of my fatigue again. Her hair is damp, but she shows no weariness; I am wet with perspiration, my legs almost numb.

A young demon with hair curling round his ears appears at our table and greets Nicolette. She laughs up at him, and I notice that she is breathing more rapidly than before. They seem to be old acquaintances (but where did they meet?) and go on talking for some time without paying any attention to me. Until he suddenly stops in the middle of a sentence to enquire, with a glance in my direction: 'And the old chap?' ('*Le vieux*' are his words.)

'My father,' she replies without hesitation.

He extends a bony white hand which I accept. But he seems to be speaking a language infinitely more foreign than French, as if we belong to different worlds. And after a short moment of feigned interest in me he returns to Nicolette.

'Come,' he says; it sounds more like an order than an invitation.

She looks at me.

Raising his hand he pretends to pronounce a magic formula over her: '*Rafel mai amech zabi almi!*' Then, taking her hands in his, he insists: 'Now you have no choice.'

She gets up with a laugh, leans over to press a playful kiss to one of my moist temples; then they dissolve into the cloud. The drum is moving towards another climax, accompanied by a hysterical saxophone – or can it be a distorted human voice? It is difficult to tell – the whirlpool is turning faster, the whole infernal movement is spinning on and on. And somewhere in that cloud, I know, is Nicolette, lost in the semi-darkness among the possessed. Sometimes I catch a glimpse of her with her head thrown back, her hair loose and free, her mouth open, laughing, screaming, or panting; otherwise I suddenly catch a glimpse of her, subdued, quiet, her head nestled on a shoulder against the pale smudge of an unknown cheek. And the only thought I am aware of is that I have lost her, for a few minutes or an hour perhaps, but irrevocably, because her present is everlasting; and I know that she is young, devastatingly young, wonderfully young; and that I am old, *le vieux*, her father, a stake from which she had to untie herself before, like the others of her generation, she could lose herself, convulsing in this ecstasy of the void. And it takes place with so much seriousness, even the laughing and cavorting, as if they are all caught in a ritual: a primordial pattern to which one cannot react in any conventional way, with any ordinary emotions. So I am left only with a feeling of dazed anguish, isolated at the far end of the table against the bare-brick wall; and yet I remain fatally part of the scene. For half an hour, for an hour, for hours, I remain waiting, in vain, until the drum is no longer beating in the corner but in my own breast, throbbing convulsively, desperately, orgiastically, so that I have to lean back, nauseous, gasping for breath.

Almost panic-stricken I get up and shuffle along the wall through the smoke while people, chairs, tables, floor, walls continue to dance to the tempo of my raging heart. In a far corner I notice a red arrow pointing to a few steps leading further downstairs. Stumbling, I follow the arrow, close a door behind me, and remain standing for a few moments to allow the dizziness to pass, only vaguely conscious of the now distant noise. A narrow passage takes me to the inevitable doors marked *Messieurs* and *Dames*. I open the first. Inside it is almost dark, with only the light from the corridor coming through the fanlight. In one of the four or five similar cubicles in the washroom I hear voices: laughing, panting, groaning. Resigned – nothing can surprise me any more – I pass the row of brown doors to the urinals against the opposite wall. The third door is wide open and in passing I catch a glimpse of a young man and a girl inside standing pressed together, both half-naked, pumping away like dogs. On the floor, propped up against a little heap of the clothes they've shed, is a torch, which casts their grotesque shadows against the back wall, resembling giants with writhing torsos frantically trying to escape from a well.

A few minutes later, when the toilet door swings shut behind me, the giants are still dancing on the wall.

Nicolette is waiting at our table in the *cave*, nonchalantly, as if nothing has happened. Only her paleness and the beads of perspiration on her forehead and round her mouth suggest the contrary.

'Shall we go?' I ask.

She obeys without protest. From the staircase I cast a final look back. At one of the nearest tables a girl is pouring a glass of wine into her open upturned mouth. Even before she has swallowed it the man next to her leans over and starts kissing her greedily. Then they are shrouded in a cloud of smoke. In the far corner the saxophone resumes its agonizing wail.

Nicolette is already waiting outside in the sudden, crisp cold. Above her, inclined over the dark line of the buildings, is the thin sliver of the moon.

We are silent on our way back. There is so little one can say. The steets are almost deserted. Under a lonely lamppost my watch hands reveal an unemotional V – ten to two – but it has stopped: a minute or hours ago? Timeless, we surrender ourselves to the dark streets.

Once she takes a short cut along a narrow passage without any street-light. And in this utter, final darkness, without any apparent reason, I think of Keyter. 'Do you often come to this part of the city?' he asked his Judas question, weeks ago. I smile wryly in the dark. And yet: would I have been here tonight – 'in this part of the city' – if it hadn't been for him?

But her hand which touches mine because she is afraid of the dark, banishes all thoughts. Empty, we wander through the city's emptiness.

At last her entrance with its weather-beaten scenes from a pagan paradise appears before us.

'Shall I come in?' I sigh.

She nods.

'Come to think of it,' I say, 'it hasn't been –'

'We're tired,' she says, as if that summarizes and concludes everything. 'Come.'

Upstairs, circle after circle, up to the little moon shining faintly through the window in the roof. Her step still confirms her invincible youth; at the same time there is something infinitely more wise in her than I have ever noticed before.

And then: the light of her small room; and our little bed.

3

– and then Naples and Pompeii. Dolce far niente. *See Naples
and die. The great illusion. Naples is a lavatory with a view on
the sea. but I very conscientiously 'did' it all: in Italy one does as
the other tourists do. So I dutifully strolled past tumbled walls and
loose stones in Pompeii and, like a good tourist, implicitly
believed whatever the guide reeled off as rapidly and with as
much conviction as one recites the Lord's Prayer.*

*Will you sneer, or smile, if I told you that I have also explored
Neapolitan museums which are usually only whispered about in
polite company? And that in Pompeii all the doors usually
unlocked by a lewd old guide for men only were opened for me? I
had to use my 'influence' of course. Our Embassy had too much
red tape (the wretched Third Secretary, Immelman, is, like
Shelley, an 'ineffectual angel'), so Annette's Italian in the
Foreign Service arranged everything. He probably regarded me
as a frigid, frustrated woman in her menopause in search of
'kicks'. (Perhaps he was right, although my last few grains of
self-respect would not allow me to admit it.)*

*I know I'm avoiding the issue. For how can I write about it?
How can I force myself to confess all the uninvited, forgotten
things this excursion has brought back? It was not so much the
stones or the lava of Pompeii that moved me: mine was a different
kind of pilgrimage.*

*Twenty-five years of our way of life tends to make one blasé.
But I must confess that suddenly seeing those statues and symbols
and frescoes with their shameless affirmation of sexual delight
gave me a sort of spiritual concussion. At first I tried to shrug it off
with polite scorn. But, Paul!, one cannot remain immune from
these things for long. At first I tried to dismiss it with the obvious
reaction: 'What an immoral lot these old Romans were. No*

185

wonder Pompeii shared the fate of Sodom and Gomorrah!' But if you live on the slope of a volcano, Paul, knowing – even if it's only subconsciously – that the mushroom cloud of death is hovering lazily above your rooftop day and night – you, too, may feel inspired to scribble on a wall: Carpe diem . . . Ergo vivamus, dum licet esse, bene! But I think even this is a much too simple explanation for Pompeii. These people of the frescoes and statues, those calcified corpses still excavated from their beds or streets or dining-rooms or baths, those people were not indulging themselves in one never-ending orgy. If they adorned their walls with the fica and the phallus it wasn't because each house was a bordello, but because that must have been their way of exorcizing the Evil Eye, warding off Invidia. How could they resist the Unknown except by using the most basic symbols of life? This wasn't just their response to Evil, but to death itself. Every grave bears the insignia of Priapus and Venus. There was nothing vulgar or crude about their attitude to sex. It was the miracle through which men and women could live openly, purely, in the full freedom of their senses, the only way in which they could share the pleasure of the immortal gods. I see it almost as a sort of Mass, a transubstantiation, through which death was transformed into life and life into death.

Et cetera.

Do you see how well I've digested everything the guide told me? I made copious notes while he was talking. Point one: sex and Evil Eye; point two: sex and Death –

And now they are dead, all of them, all those beautiful people of Pompeii. Did you know that in a prostitute's little room in a bordello they found a basket with charred onions and beans? Take your choice: the immortal delight of the gods – or a basket of onions and beans. And what have I got? I am nearly fifty. (Annette's Italian insists – of course! – that I'm looking younger than forty. Mirror, mirror on the wall –!) I am not even whole any more. I can hardly remember a time when I was whole; and you, I suppose, have forgotten it altogether. Before Annette was born I'd never been very pleased with the prospect of having a child (after all these years one may as well phrase it politely) but at least I had hoped that I would give birth in the normal way, like other women. And then it was a caesarean. Everyone deeply grateful to doctor and staff. Nobody realized that, suddenly, I was no longer I – bourgeois, if you wish, insignificant in my own right, but at least living in a whole body; perhaps even a beautiful body. And now there was this scar, thick and swollen under my fingers at night, a hideous purple scar, a reminder of my own inadequacy. I'd never been able to 'make' anything, to create anything. The only bit of creative talent I'd ever had, had gone into the making of this child – and even that I couldn't do in the normal way. After a while I resigned myself to it, of course. With the years the mark has faded. But it has never disappeared completely, it is still there. And one day, when they lay out my body, it will still be there; whitish, a line of leprosy.

I can remember the first night, three months after her birth, when you came to me again. How your fingers moved across my belly and suddenly grew tense. You didn't say anything. You went through the whole process, step by step according to the prescribed rules, as methodically as you did all your work in the office. But I knew your hands were afraid of that long, swollen scar. I knew, because I, too, was afraid. I tried to resolve my fear in you, but then I felt your hands move away from the wound and I knew there was something which could never again be said between us. From that moment neither of us would ever know me any more: this stranger bearing the mark of Cain – not even on my forehead but, how humiliating, on my belly. What has become of me, the 'I' who used to inhabit my unscarred body? You will have forgotten that night long ago; our nights together were never very memorable. But I couldn't, it has been branded into me, a scar of the mind much more than of the flesh.

I am not blaming you. It is I who never knew, or never accepted, that there was so much one could give or receive, so much to be shared, in that act we relegated to the dark. I could find many plausible reasons for this: my obedient, carefully planned childhood; the strict discipline; boarding school; the holidays at home when I had to be initiated into my mother's social obligations. But one reaches a stage where plausible reasons *are no longer adequate, and then one has nothing left but oneself.*

All this soul-searching merely because some Italian has given me a series of lectures on the role of sex in the life of the old Romans – as if he were explaining the respiratory system of the frog!

Annette accompanied me on these excursions although I suppose she would have preferred to go about on her own. (Do I see a frown of disapproval on your face? I'm sure this isn't your idea of educating a girl of eighteen!) Sometimes I reproach myself about it. More often I think: That'll teach her. But teach what? What is it in me that drives me to shock her, to shake her awake, to force some response from her?

But it is unfair of me to use this letter as an attempt to come to grips with what I really need to sort out on my own.

I suppose it is time we should think of coming home. It is January already. But the thought chills me. There is too much I must come to terms with first.

Love, Erika.

4

On the last day that chronology mattered, Wednesday 19 December, early in the morning, when I left her after the first night we'd spent together, I set out quite mechanically for the boulevard Saint-Germain, chilly after the warmth of her little room. It did not even surprise me to find the taxi rank deserted and as I went down into the Métro and walked along the corridor to the ticket office my only thought (if indeed I had any thoughts) was: So this is my new dimension. I can no longer expect preferential treatment, or special consideration. I must learn to adapt. And it almost seemed like a challenge, a new adventure. I joined the queue and bought my ticket. To the annoyance of the people behind me I first stopped in front of the nearest wall-map to trace my route; then I flung myself into the crowd and was swept through echoing corridors. Despite the early hour it was stuffy inside, with a heavy smell of old garlic and stale bodies. Somewhere ahead of me, where trains came clattering past at short intervals, a pair of green gates regularly swung shut to stem the tide. And all the time new people were converging in the dammed-up crowd, from numerous corridors, down numerous stairs. Sleepy girls with pale faces under their make-up, their hair coming undone in the throng. Businessmen in grey overcoats and black hats, reading their papers held in hands outstretched above their heads. Housewives with string bags. Chattering children on their way to school. Students with hair curling over their collars. Couples in passionate embrace, kissing with open mouths in spite of the jostling crowd. It was as if, suddenly arrived from another planet, I was looking for the first time at the spectacle of humanity.

Usually one is so preoccupied with keeping all the processes of life going that there is no time to observe, let alone to meditate. And what unsettled me, was the sudden thought that whatever was not properly observed or meditated implied not stasis but loss: a form of regression, because one's faculties of interpretation, of *understanding* were blunted. And never – not since Gillian and my eighteen months of liberty – had I lived so much or so deeply as those past twenty-four hours. Or even the last six hours, ever since the door had opened in her dark building and two voices had come up the stairs singing *Au clair de la lune*. Twelve hours ago I'd been in a taxi on my way to the rue de Condé. At that stage everything had still been undecided, brooding, fermenting. And now – ? Life seemed no less complicated than before. I had no more certainty about the future. But at least I was no longer working with mere possibilities or hypotheses. Whether I wanted to or not, I was confronted with a *fait accompli*. Nothing was simple; but everything was lucid.

The green gates swung open once again and this time I was pushed through onto the dirty platform. A minute later a train came bursting from the tunnel. I was bundled into an already overcrowded second class coach (it hadn't occurred to me to buy a first-class ticket). Forced into a corner with some object pressing painfully against my back, I stood staring at the walls of the tunnel outside sweeping past.

Was it really necessary to spend a brief night with a girl in an uncomfortable little bed in order to come to this? But the how and why were scarcely relevant. What mattered was the simple *fact*. And how elementary it really was! Her sort of life had always been there, undetected, on the periphery of my own. The only difference was that, now, I had *discovered* it; I'd become *aware* of that disturbing freedom surrounding the predictability of my own routine. No; even that was simplifying the issue. Of course I'd 'known' about such freedoms: it was just that I'd refused to acknowledge them as options for myself.

The doors slammed on the next station, and we rattled on.

– Could it all be reduced to this? – all the organizations people had devised to bolster their security: state and church, commerce and politics and education, everything: the more laws there were, the more regulations, the more securely one's pattern of existence was predetermined, the easier one could continue without the need to think. And all this to maintain an illusion – the illusion that there *did* exist a cosmic, basic pattern of order, that the universe was functioning according to set laws, and that, consequently, society and the individual should also be governed by laws. For this was the only way one could contain the terror of the freedom that lay at the root of all things: this passionate life which existed without aim or pattern or direction, this essential chaos. Even something as matter of fact, as 'natural' as clothes might be regarded – the obvious practical considerations apart – as a form of protection, not so much against heat or cold, as against the terrifying liberty of sex. (Three hours, one hour ago she had been naked in my arms –)

190

(Châtelet.)

The doors flew open and I stumbled out with the crowd, trying to find my direction, jostled from all sides. The green gates were already closing for the next train before I finally noticed the yellow sign indicating the *correspondance* to Neuilly and hurried along to the right platform. I was wet with perspiration, my clothes crumpled. Yet I was hardly aware of it, moving as if in a trance.

A train stopped. Somehow we all got in. The doors slammed.

– Within a week the Minister should have my answer. Before Christmas. He wouldn't be back at work before the New Year. Then there would be the series of Cabinet meetings prior to the next session of the Assembly. It would probably be February before he could attend to my file. Judging from my past experience of him, his first step would be to approach a senior member of my staff for further information and comments. Only then, and provided the matter appeared serious enough – as I felt sure it would – a commission of inquiry might be appointed. Would they send anybody from Pretoria? Unlikely, I thought. It would be more practical, and more discreet, to appoint a few of my colleagues in Europe. Van Huyssteen in London? – I hoped not. We didn't get along all that well. Perhaps Saunders in The Hague. Some time in March – ? Of course, everything could happen much faster; on the other hand it might drag on much longer, until after the Budget debate in the Assembly. Still, a date towards the end of March seemed the most likely.

(Louvre.)

– It could no longer be denied. I was on the edge of a precipice. A knife-edge of choice, between the established pattern of my life and the new freedom I'd glimpsed; between surrender or revolt. The only real shock, I suppose, was the suspicion that neither possibility was necessarily more 'valid' than the other. In some archive file, a hundred years from now, it would really make no difference whether I had quashed Keyter and continued 'doing my duty' as before

– or whether I'd chosen Nicolette and broken the 'rules' as I'd done once before, with Gillian. And yet: having become aware of the precipice, having acknowledged its existence, how could I ever be at peace again?

(Tuileries.)

– *I had three months left*. It was as if I'd just left a doctor's surgery with the verdict of a terminal disease. Three months between now and –? It didn't leave me with much time. I could barely think any more. Everything which, in the course of my journey so far, had developed in such logical terms, distilled in the alembic of the previous night, became clouded again.

Standing there in my crumpled clothes, leaning against a door, swaying to and fro, the only thing I could think or hear, the only thing of which I was still conscious, was that one figure: *three*. Even when I tried to remind myself that it was mere conjecture, I knew that it had already, in the secret processes of the mind, crystallized into a fact.

Four stations to go. I counted them on the map above the door, then tried to concentrate on the advertisements above the seats. *Santé sobriété*. Do not drink more than one litre of wine per day. *Banania*. *Vichy*. A ski holiday. (Forget your worries; everything organized beforehand.)

The train was jerking, swaying. An old woman leaning against a pole lost her balance for a moment. Nobody bothered to help her. At the nearest door stood a young couple in a passionate embrace.

(Champs-Élysées-Clémenceau.)

– Three stations. Three months. I hadn't 'willed' it to be like that: it had simply happened. It was unavoidable. That night when she'd appeared on the threshold of my office, try-ing to take off her wet coat to bribe me into taking her home – that night had been the beginning. No: by then it had already been under way, as it had been that windy night in Cape Town when I'd stopped to pick up Gillian and her large suitcase. Perhaps it had already been going on for ages at the time of my birth.

Would it have been easier had I *not* known about the three months? Suppose Keyter's report had taken its own course beyond my knowledge until the very last moment? Then I could have lived those three months without knowing. Or was it better to know, and live in agony?

Adam and Eve had lived in their garden in the supreme happiness of ignorance. But the fruit of knowledge had to be picked. Not to rebel against God, not to obey the Serpent, but simply because they couldn't have done anything else. To be human means to desire knowledge. Without knowledge there can be no sin; without sin, no knowledge. And how can we exist without either?

(Franklin-Roosevelt.)

– And so they'd eaten of the Fruit. Which gave them knowledge of themselves, of the simple fact that they were *there*.

(George V.)

– What does a man do who has only three months to live? Does he go on working as usual until they have to carry him off on a stretcher? Does he write his memoirs? Does he go mad? Or does he, quite simply, carry on living? How does one learn to live after so many years of merely passive existence, of 'being lived'?

That I did not know. I only knew that I had those three months left. And I had the choice between mere living and being. I was on the boundary of a limitless, unknown region. It was a country I could explore, a world I could travel through. Nothing compelled me to do it: I could go on as before. But suppose – suppose I slung my rucksack on my shoulders and walked straight into that wilderness: what an adventure! Of course, my equipment might fail me: I might fall into a river, or tumble down a mountain and break my legs; I might wander deliriously across waterless plains. Or the land itself could be disappointing: a mere wilderness, a desert without end, without beauty, without value.

But was that really important? Even then it would remain

the choice between a familiar illusion and an unknown possibility.

(Étoile.)

Almost too late I recognized the name on the blue and white tiles of the concave wall. The train doors were already gliding shut when I quickly jumped out and hurried upstairs towards the exit in the avenue Wagram. The clouds were dispersing above. Light was shimmering on wet roofs and branches.

I could see the amazement in Lebon's eyes as I came in through the main entrance.

I said: 'Good morning, Lebon. Looks like it's going to be a beautiful day, doesn't it?'

Glancing back from the steps to the official residence where I was going to change my clothes I saw him still gaping at me, with stains of light on his glasses and a frozen drop at the tip of his purple nose.

5

I find that I am returning more and more frequently to Gillian. Perhaps it is simply because, nowadays, I allow my thoughts to wander at random; there is nothing I deliberately *exclude* from thinking or remembering any more.

The day she took me to her father's house. She wanted to collect a dress. By that time she'd been living for some weeks in a room I'd found for her near my own flat (fiercely independent, she had refused to move in with me); and she was getting tired of the things in her suitcase.

It was a very ordinary bourgeois house of the type which was then regarded as 'modern', with a red roof and bay windows and a veranda. The garden was in a state of sad neglect: a very formal, very well-planned garden, all the flowerbeds carefully surrounded by pointed bricks, and a rockery with a cement angel in the centre.

I was waiting for her to unlock the front door, when she suddenly said, with that cynical mocking expression of hers: 'I haven't got a key. I threw it away.'

'How are we going to get in, then?'

'Break in.' Without waiting for an answer she went round to the back. Rather reluctantly I followed her, but by the time I reached the kitchen door she'd already broken the window.

'Put your arm through and lift the latch.' She was standing with her arms behind her back, whistling.

'How can you be so irresponsible, Gillian?'

'Oh.'

Knowing it was useless to argue, I opened the window, climbed through and unlocked the kitchen door from the inside; but by that time she was already perched on the window-sill.

'Well,' she said as she landed inside, her face a bit tense. 'Nothing has changed.'

It was slightly musty from standing closed so long.

'Now go and get your clothes,' I said, perturbed by the way she was looking about her.

Ignoring me, she wandered down into the long passage.

'The bathroom. "Only ten minutes, Gillian. That's enough for a bath. We must avoid the temptations of the flesh."' She turned round to me, pale. 'And if Gillian is still inside after ten minutes, he comes to check. *He* is immune to the flesh, of course.'

She opened a door on the left. 'Bedroom. Where my mother died, one night, years ago. With praying and singing and burning of candles.'

'Gillian –'

She seemed to be sleepwalking. Another door. Her hand trembled on the knob before she flung it open. 'Study. Where the man of God retired to be inspired from Above.' She went inside. There was a large bookcase with glass doors against one wall. A smallish desk covered with neat piles of papers, held down by weights. A large Bible. Straight-backed chairs. Framed texts on the walls. *God is love. Bless this house. The Lord is my Shepherd.*

'Can you feel the pious atmosphere?' she asked. Never before had I heard anyone speak with so much hate. 'On this chair I had to learn my passages from the Bible whenever I'd done anything wrong. I was first thrashed, of course. "*I am the Lord thy God, which have brought thee out of the land of Egypt, out of the house of bondage –*" "*It is a fearful thing to fall into the hands of the living God –*" "*Repent ye therefore, and be converted, that your sins may be blotted out –*"' Shaken by a fit of trembling she was unable to continue.

'Come,' I said. 'Let's go.' I took her by the shoulders. But with amazing strength she shook me off.

'And there – that's him!' she cried. On the wall next to the door was a row of photographs: forefathers, parents, a faded young woman; and, the largest of all, a youngish man with an ascetic face and fierce eyes, an uncertain, thin mouth, a high forehead.

'Why do you hate him so much, Gillian?' I asked.

'You'll never understand,' she said, breathing deeply. 'Your father never threw your mother out when she was six months pregnant with you! In the middle of the night. It was raining. She often told me about it, all those years when we had to fend for ourselves. In the end she went mad.'

She fell silent.

'Why haven't you told me these things before?' I asked.

'Why should I? What is it to you?' Her eyes burned in mine, then she looked away. After a moment, suddenly composed, she went on: 'I saw her go mad. At night I could hear her shuffling through the house, moaning and crying. Then she fell ill. I was eight years old. When he heard about it he sent for us and forced us to come back, so that she could die decently at home.'

'And then?' I asked with an effort.

'And then he tried to take it out on me. He used to say there was a devil inside me. I was my mother's child, he said. One day I would go mad like her. Sometimes I almost killed him in his sleep but I was too scared. Can you understand? I was scared.'

She became hysterical. Wildly, desperately, she swung round, and grabbed the large black Bible from the desk. Before I could move a finger she hurled it at the portrait. The glass was smashed, the whole floor covered in splinters, but the portrait was still hanging crookedly from its nail.

Pushing me out of the way, she rushed to it and tore it from the wall. Her hand was cut by a sliver of glass so that a thin red line of blood came trickling down her palm and wrist. She was crying, soundlessly at first, dropping on her knees beside the portrait, tearing it to pieces. Then she buried her face in her hands and burst into violent sobs.

I just stared at her, unable to do anything. After a very long time she looked up, wiping her face with her hands. A streak of blood was smeared across her cheek. Small red drops fell from her wrist on to the Bible which lay open, its pages crumpled. It seemed a long time before, with a brief glance in my direction, she picked up the Bible and wiped her fingers over the bloodstains, as if unable to grasp what had happened.

'He's dead,' she said.

Almost solemnly, she began to pluck out the stained pages, and as she went on her gestures became more violent, more deliberate: Genesis, Law and Prophets, Song of Songs, Gospels, Epistles, to the very last prayer of Revelation.

'Gillian! Are you mad?'

She shook her head. Every muscle in her body was taut. She got up. 'He always said I would go to hell. All right. So I'll go. I don't *want* to be good!' She was swept away by her mounting passion. 'When the last trumpet sounds and God comes to look for me, I want to say NO to Him. I wasn't made to be good and to say yes. You can go to Heaven if you want to. Just leave me here! Leave me here and let me *live*!'

Exhausted, she turned away from me and leaned her head

against the wall. For a long time she made no movement. Then she seemed to straighten up; without looking at me she went out. I heard her open another door in the passage. But I remained there, trying half-heartedly to push the mess aside with one foot.

(Gillian, Gillian, I think now: did you really believe you could rid the world of evil by wiping one obscene word from a wall? Did you think you could destroy the system by breaking *me*?)

After a long time she returned, wearing another dress – presumably the one she'd come for – and with her hair tidied. Her eyes revealed traces of tears, but there was no hysteria left.

'Come,' she said. 'We'd better go.'

6

The evening of 24 December.

Anna Smith: 'What a pity Her Excellency could not be with us. Christmas is the one time of the year one *must* spend with one's family, don't you agree? Oh, to be back in South Africa: Paris is such a terribly *profane* city, so Catholic. What a good thing our little group can be together tonight.'

Our little group. Our little group of strangers in this strange, cold world. (And a mile from here she's waiting in her little room.)

Sylvia Masters: 'Let's all go somewhere and paint the town red! Would somebody care to fill my glass? Oh thank you *so* much.' And she struts about like royalty, in her dress with its frills and lace and little bows. Somebody accidentally spills a few drops of wine on it and offers an exaggerated apology; she shrugs it off with polished charm, but her eyes have the glint of steel. And for the first time it occurs to me that she can be a dangerous woman, a poisonous woman.

Victor le Roux: 'Christmas has lost its meaning. We're left with the trappings – trees and presents and good wishes – but Christ Himself has been reduced to X. We still perform the actions, but nothing more: it's a charade.'

Stephen Keyter: 'Why should the Church complain about Christmas becoming commercialized? That's the greatest guarantee for survival. The church *wants* to be exploited so that it can preach humility: following the example of Christ, who was, above all, a masochist.'

And among them I find myself, Mr Ambassador, moving about, mixing with my staff, carrying on conversations, pretending to be disappointed 'because Her Excellency cannot be here'; and as soon as I can do so without being impolite, I offer my apologies and depart – just as Anna Smith gathers her little group under the glittering Christmas tree to sing 'Silent Night'.

Closing the door of one life behind me I hurry through the cold into the next: the life of streets and things and people; a single person, a girl, Nicolette.

She's been waiting for a long time, in her warm cap, a coat and boots reaching up to the middle of her calves; and she's impatient.

'You *promised* to come early!'

'I did the best I could. Do you still want to go to Mass?'

'Of course!'

I glance at my watch: 'We'd better take a taxi then.'

'No,' she says stubbornly. 'We've *got* to go on foot.'

Here and there, from the bistros and *caves* of the Latin Quarter, one hears jazzy music, but the sounds are woolly, muted by walls and drawn curtains. There are few pedestrians about: some clochards on their way to the Salvation Army's Christmas reception under the bridges of the Seine; a lonely drunk leaning against a lamppost singing unmelodious carols, occasionally interrupted by declamations: 'On earth peace, good will toward men! Hosanna-hic! How about a franc for a poor man?' For the rest, a few tourists looking for something to make their night memorable; and sullen taxi drivers standing about in little groups at their *têtes de station*, rubbing their hands or sharing a bottle. We walk briskly through the deserted streets. And as we proceed the city gradually comes to life around us. The boulevard Saint-Michel is teeming with people. From all directions, they come, heading for the river, the island, Notre-Dame. The entire square under the cathedral is swarming with the thousands who, out of habit, superstition, devotion or curiosity, are drawn to the midnight Mass. All along the rue du Cloître-Notre-Dame the police have constructed barricades to control the surging movement towards the doors. The queue, eight or ten abreast, already stretches the whole length of the cathedral. We have to fall in at the back.

We are silent.

At a quarter to twelve the crowd begins to show signs of impatience. A few barricades are broken down. There is jostling and cursing and shouting. Nicolette uses the opportunity to slip ten or twelve paces forward. I follow her for a yard or so but dare not force my way past a few old women. Far ahead of me I can see her bright red woollen cap, but nothing more. Above us loose clouds are drifting past the pale stars, creating the impression that the cathedral is falling, and we with it, and the entire unfirm earth.

She worms her way further forward. A few people call out angrily after her. Her cap disappears in the throng. She has been looking forward to tonight so much, with that inexplicable passion in her which I have noticed before whenever she speaks about religion. (Perhaps this, and sex, are her only two passions. For the rest, she blithely skims over the surface of things, defiant, or ironical, often oblivious, untouched by it all.)

Another group of people must have been allowed into the cathedral for suddenly we are moving ten, fifteen yards forward. For a fleeting moment I catch sight of her cap again, very far away. Then it disappears and once more the surge comes to a standstill against the grim black walls. We have no hope of getting inside in time now. Yet we all remain in the queue, stubbornly willing a miracle to happen.

The midnight bells begin to peal, loud and jubilant, high above. All over the city it rings out until the whole night is caught in reverberating sound. In the Latin Quarter fireworks are crackling. Through the massive cathedral walls one can feel the vibrations of organ music, the faint gloria of the sopranos.

Slowly the crowd begins to spill across the square. Some are still waiting, but by the time they get in the Mass itself will long be past. I turn away from the barricaded corridor, in search of Nicolette. For five, ten minutes there is no sight of her. Then her hand slides round my arm from behind and she says: 'Come. Let's go back.'

'Nicolette –' I put my arm round her. 'I'm so sorry, my darling. If only I could have made it on time.'

She shakes her head. On the bridge, light falls across her tense, cynical face.

'I suppose it was inevitable,' she says. 'It's like my garden – remember? I must always stay outside.'

'Don't exaggerate!' I scold her, more harshly than I want to. 'It's not *so* important after all. And we can always go to Mass in the morning.'

'Yes.'

It is the sort of acquiescence which infuriates one because it is so entirely disarming.

'Please try to understand, Nicolette!'

'I understand perfectly well. It's not important, like you said.'

'Now you're being childish!'

She lets go of my arm and walks on ahead of me, alone. (Gillian would have exploded, but Nicolette is different. I'm realizing it more and more.)

After a while she stops, waiting for me to catch up with her again – probably because the streets are becoming darker now - and in her characteristic way, *à propos* of nothing, she says: 'Did you know I've never been baptized?'

I don't answer, still feeling both annoyed and guilty, and not knowing what she may be aiming at.

'I've never received *any* sacrament.'

'What do you know about sacraments?'

'"*A sacrament is an outward sign of inward grace.*" I looked it up in one of the booklets on the stand inside Notre-Dame. One is supposed to put the money in a box next to it but I had no change with me so I just took it. Do you think it was sinful?'

'Not venial. You pay far too much attention to the things you read. What difference does baptism really make?'

'A hell of a difference,' she answers firmly. 'If you're not baptized you have only your natural human life. This body.' She strokes her hands down her sides in strange disgust. 'But if you're baptized you have a supernatural, immortal life as well. Don't you think that's important? Unbaptized, you live without grace.'

'What grace?'

She shrugs. 'I'm just telling you what I read in my little book. And it's true. I know.'

I would like to believe that she is being deliberately naïve: her too ready acceptance of any printed word from horoscopes to liturgy; the complete lack of digesting anything. But to do this would in itself be naïve. She can turn anything from a cobblestone to a chalice into a mystery (in that she resembles Gillian; but why are they still so many worlds apart?).

'Are you coming up?' she asks at the main entrance of her building.

'Of course.'

She nods and goes in. I follow, feeling my way.

'Would you like some wine?' she asks, back in her room at last. 'I'm all shivery.' Not waiting for an answer, she goes to the kitchen where numerous empty bottles are stacked in a corner, finds one which is still half full and brings it back to the table in her bedroom. With her head slight bent she pours a little into a tin mug. Then she smiles, very faintly, even with a hint of relief. Almost solemnly she comes to the bed and rummages through a pile of old illustrated journals she bought along the Seine; after a while she extracts a small black missal from the rubbish and begins to page through it. Intrigued, I watch her in silence. She comes back to the table, tidies the cloth and picks up an old crust of bread that must have been lying there for a day or two. The light is reflected in the window above her head. She seems to have forgotten about me, about everything. Her fingers are twitching nervously as she begins to recite something to herself; only the edges of her lips are moving. (But is it a Sanctus, or a rhyme from Mother Goose?) Staring intently at her hands, she carefully breaks the little crust into three equal portions and brushes the crumbs from her fingers. One piece is dropped into the mug.

'*Hoc est enim corpus meum.*'

Her hand begins to form a cross, but she does not complete the gesture.

'*Hoc est enim calix sanguinis meum.*'

She looks in my direction, but past me.

'It remains wine and bread,' she says quietly. 'Do you see?' As if she's trying to prove something. But what – and to whom?

Then she turns round abruptly, opens the bottle again and fills the mug to the brim. A few drops spill over the sides. She wipes it off the tablecloth with her fingers and licks them. Then she gulps down the wine, shudders, refills the mug and hands it to me. In the very corners of her eyes, under the lashes, there is a hint of tears.

7

It is strange, at times impossible, to think that the course of my 'ordinary life' can continue almost unchanged. At first I was, perhaps, more consciously aware of it than before, as if I had to prove to both my staff and myself that one can go on. But because no one, not even myself, seemed to find anything strange in it everything in the office has gradually returned to routine. The mailbag is still delivered on Tuesdays to be opened by a fluttering Anna Smith. Le Roux regularly brings me the French press cuttings for scanning. The secretaries write their reports, deal with the consular problems, receive visitors. There are still telegrams to be decoded and others to be composed. Telephone calls, interviews, negotiations, talks, receptions. (The only difference is that I tend to delegate more routine work to others; that I am more regularly represented at official functions by one of my staff.) There was one week of exceptional pressure when the news of our arms negotiations was suddenly leaked in a French newspaper, causing immediate public protests. For a while the whole transaction was in the balance, which forced the Minister of Defence to pay a quick private visit to Paris. A new round of discussions with the French Government had to be organized. But all these things are mere ripples on the surface of my days. Often I catch myself smiling ironically at the 'importance' of my task, especially as far as the arms deal is concerned. And yet, there is no essential, obvious change in my routine, much to my own surprise. (Why *should* it surprise me?)

Anna Smith still turns up regularly to pour out her heart; once she even burst into tears because Joubert was allegedly maltreating his wife ('such a *dear* woman'). Masters comes in to discuss work; Koos Joubert to fulminate against 'the bloody French'. Keyter, too, comes to my office, but relations between us are strictly formal. Sometimes I try to scrutinize his face, but he's always been an enigma.

Only once, when he brought me a couple of visa applications he lingered on the doorstep for a minute.

'Is there anything else, Keyter?'

'Mr Ambassador –' After a brief pause he continued: 'Haven't you heard anything –?' For that fleeting moment there was unmistakable eagerness in his attitude.

I waited for him to complete his sentence, but he changed his mind, his eyes became expressionless again and he concluded bluntly: 'It's not so important, after all. I beg your pardon, Mr Ambassador.' And he left.

Should I have called him back? But what was there to say? I picked up the visa forms he'd brought and worked my way through them.

But in spite of the apparently unchanged routine there is one very important difference: I am almost constantly *aware* of the fact that I am sitting on this chair, at this desk, occupied with this particular piece of work – almost as if, from an astral plane, I am looking over my own shoulder, an impersonal, detached judge of everything that is done.

I find it impossible to escape from an increasing sense of unreality. Once before, during my eighteen months of wandering, I was sometimes working in my room until very late at night, when I would suddenly look up, for no reason at all, with this same uncanny discovery of myself sitting in that small pool of light, surrounded by the immense, dark world. I would feel like jumping up and rushing into the quiet streets outside, shouting: 'I'm alive! Nobody believes it, but *I am alive*!' What affects me nowadays – like that night beside the Seine – is that everything in this office is done *on behalf of* other people – not even 'people', but on behalf of an organization, a monstrous machine called 'Government', something invisible, something which, perhaps, does not even exist any more (how would I know, isolated in a foreign country?), but is kept going by the sheer momentum of so many years.

Sometimes I go down to the reading room to page through old newspapers. I've read all the news long ago, of course, but now I can judge it not as a daily chronicle of confused events, but as a glimpse of contemporary history: finished, complete, undeniable, and lacking the urgency of something still in the process of happening. Rape. Murder. Contraventions of the Immorality Act. Sabotage and attempted sabotage. Ministerial comments. Political statements. Demonstrations. Mrs A. enjoying a few days' holiday in Cape Town. Mr B. breaking the record for keeping awake. The Rev. C. accused of heresy. Strong southeaster in the Peninusla. Drought in the Free State. Large banana surplus. Readers' letters: 'Keep Our Cities White.' 'Farmers need more subsidies.' 'Nothing wrong with modern youth.' 'Ban Sunday sport.' 'Make adultery punishable by law.' Photos of VIPs; Grape Queens; Springboks; Ministers' wives at a garden party –

So this is South Africa. These are its interests. These are its people – judging from my pile of newspapers on the dark green leather of the table in the reading room. And I know only too well that it *is* the truth, proved by holidays on home leave, once every five years. Each time one sets out with so much enthusiasm; and each time one crawls back, tired and perplexed, disillusioned by visits to colleagues or relatives whose lives have long ago stopped touching one's own; until, at last, one escapes to the coast, among strangers, on a vacation like any other.

And this is the country I have to represent. I must solicit support for a policy in which I cannot believe, because it no longer exists in my personal life. I must handle its affairs, although they mean nothing to me. I must buy arms for it, although apart from the personal prestige involved, I do not care whether I succeed or fail. I am no longer concerned with anything which happens there; it has no meaning for me; I have no sympathy with it. I no longer know the people, no longer understand their motives. When I am visited by compatriots, we discuss business for five minutes, ask a few well-meant questions, and say goodbye. When a delegation arrives and has to stay for a few days, we profess nostalgia for 'real South African food', for 'good old Afrikaners', for 'the splendid Cape'. I doubt whether they believe it any more than I do: but at least they still *have* to believe in its reality, its inevitability. At least they are involved in it; it is their milieu; it is – perhaps – the justification of their existence, their world?

And – *my* world? It is no longer ever there. But it is not here in Paris either. How is it possible? – only six weeks ago I started exploring the streets of this city for the first time, accompanied by a strange, beautiful young girl. So what if I get along very well with various French diplomats, editors, industrialists? – they do not form part of my world. It is impossible to live in a city for two years and then to think one 'belongs' there. I am simply residing here, protected by the thick walls of my Embassy, snugly rolled in the cotton-wool of protocol and bureaucracy. And soon – when my three months of grace have expired – I shall not even have *this* left. But God, God, is there no place for me at all in this world? I am fifty-six years old: I can no longer set out in search of a new place to call my own.

8

Nicolette outstretched on her belly, with delicate brush strokes of light on the fine hairdust between her shoulder blades; the freckles on her shoulders; the smooth tension of her hard round buttocks and the fine peach-down at the bottom of her spine; the threadbare crumpled sheet; the rough blanket with dark shadows in the folds; the silkiness of her hair; the sure modelling of her cheekbones under the skin; the jewels of her eyes.

9

I had been to a meeting, and when I opened the door of my flat I realized immediately that there was something wrong. Switching on the porch light I waited, listening. There was no sound. But as I was on the point of proceeding to my living-room I heard a muffled laugh from the bedroom.

It was Gillian, lying in my bed, shading the light from her eyes with her hands, peeping at me through her fingers.

'Surprised?' she asked.

I took out a cigarette and lit it, trying to regain my composure. 'Not very much,' I finally said. 'Would you care to tell me *why* you are here?'

'I was afraid of sleeping alone.'

'You haven't been afraid for all these weeks.'

She shrugged carelessly, sitting up, naked. 'You're late.'

'And tired.'

She refused to take the hint. (We had never made love, at that stage. It was long before that terrible, wonderful night in the sea.) I waited for a few minutes, then turned round, closed the door behind me and went to the living-room; as I expected she soon made her appearance in the door, casually wrapped in a sheet.

'Aren't you coming to bed?'

'Gillian.' I went up to her and stopped, looking into her eyes. 'What are you up to tonight?'

'Nothing.' There was a hint of warning in her voice. 'Don't you ever take me seriously?'

It was a dangerous moment. I put my hands on her smooth shoulders; the sheet slipped off. I could read in her eyes every-

208

thing she cared to exhibit; virginal bravado; provocation; uncertainty; fear. There was no need for her to say more. I *knew*. It was indeed no new game. It was, like everything else she had ever done, an expression of her rage to be free, to break loose, to try everything – good or bad. There was nothing uncertain or concealed about this urge: like everything else about her, it was frank, direct, uncomplicated; and – dare I say it? – innocent. It was only a few weeks since the windy night of our first meeting, but already I knew I loved her – or what, at that stage, I thought of as love. Already she was engaged in the fatal process of gaining complete possession of me, the way a drowning person gets hold of his rescuer. Why it had to be *me*, I could never explain; nor whether it would have been less fatal had it been someone else.

But here she was standing against me, my hands clutching her shoulders so violently that she had to bite on her teeth, though she made no sound as she stared straight back at me. The initial challenge had changed to invitation, then to suppliance. The sheet lay at her feet like a large white shell. At that moment we were beyond thought or emotion, hate or love. All was fire. I no longer reasoned in terms of thoughts or images; it had become a much more primitive process, a simple series of impulses, like a prism slowly turning against the light.

With a great (and surely uncalled-for?) effort I let go of her shoulders, picked up the sheet and wrapped it round her; then I turned away. I have no idea why I acted like that. It was certainly no moral scruple. Perhaps I merely sensed that making love at that moment would be no liberation for her; or perhaps my motives were much less altruistic – simply the fear that I might disappoint her. (And how could I *not* disappoint her? Her expectations were absolute.) I desired her, I wanted her, but if I took her, it had to be because love itself required it, not because she wanted to use me as an instrument to prove something to herself. It all sounds so terribly cerebral, so unconvincing in words – even more so today,

209

thirty years after the event. I think I am beginning to realize why I could not complete my *magnum opus* in those years: I am much too sceptical about the words I use; I have no 'gift'.

'I thought you loved me,' Gillian said.

I made a half-hearted gesture, but could not answer.

'I thought somewhere deep inside you you would at least have something like warmth, ordinary human feeling. But you're as cold as ice. You're a bloody robot. You've never been able to feel. You're scared of feeling –!'

'No, Gillian!'

But she was already on her way back to the bedroom. Five minutes later I heard her go to the front door. I wanted to speak to her, but she slammed the door and there was nothing I could do but remain where I was. I made no movement. Much later I heard a clock strike twelve. Then I got up and poured myself two or three neat brandies in a row and went to bed. But I could not sleep, alternatively blaming myself for not having taken advantage of the situation, and wondering whether she had been right after all – that I was, indeed, incapable of feeling.

At two o'clock there was a soft knock on my door. At first I thought is was my imagination. But then it was repeated, very softly. I didn't even bother to put on a dressing gown, but went to the door in my pyjamas.

It was she.

'Where have you been, Gillian? What's happened?'

'Nothing.'

She came inside, switched on the living-room light, took my cigarette case from the sideboard and lit one. Her hand was trembling lightly and the first draw resulted in a violent fit of coughing. She said nothing. I was watching her from the door. There was something infinitely weary about her, as if she had wilted. It was visible even in her hair.

I tried to talk to her, but she ignored me. It must have been at least fifteen minutes before she said in a very neutral voice: 'So that's that.'

'What's the matter, Gillian?' I felt like shaking her.

'There's nothing remarkable about it really.' Her voice was still shallow and calm, but deceptively so. And by that time I knew the expression in her eyes.

'To be quite frank, I found it rather sordid. That's all.'

She leant back on the sofa, closing her eyes. After a while she had to press her eyelids very close together, and they were trembling; in spite of her efforts a few teardrops emerged. But there was no sound, no sob.

I sat down next to her and took her hand in mine. It felt cold in spite of the early summer warmth.

'What have you done, Gillian? Why didn't you stay here?'

She was breathing deeply, then opened her eyes and sat upright. With a quick movement she opened her handbag and took out a crumpled pound note.

'Take it,' she said and, after some more rummaging, brought out a few half crowns, shillings and two pennies. 'This too. I had to give the rest to the taxi driver.'

I was mechanically stroking the note on my knee, unable to say anything.

'D'you think two pounds is the usual fee – or was the sailor being mean?'

'My God,' I whispered. 'Shut up. Please shut up.'

She got up. I couldn't tell whether she really meant to go. She got as far as the door and stopped there, pressing her head against the wall, her hands grasping the door-post.

'Don't let me go again, Paul. Whatever you do, don't ever let me go again.'

I think it was at that moment that I first began to understand the truth behind such clichés as 'sin' and 'guilt'.

10

She is standing in front of the ugly mirror, half-kneeling on a chair littered with make-up things, pulling faces at herself as she lines her eyes. Her mouth is half open, the tip of her tongue pressed against her upper lip. I'm sitting on the bed, leaning against the cupboard. The sheet is still warm of us, and my body is still remembering hers. But she, it seems, has already forgotten all about it; what is past – a minute or a year – is immediately absorbed in a free fluid movement deep inside her, secret like a subterranean river.

'Where are we going?' I ask, without much curiosity, even with a touch of resentment.

'*I'm* going out.' She opens her eyes wide and blinks a few times.

'Alone?'

'Mm.'

'Where?'

'Just out.'

'To your night club – to sing?'

She quickly glances at me in the mirror. 'Mm.' Non-committal.

'But why tonight? All last week you stayed at home.'

'I only go there every other week.'

'I *want* to go with you.'

She shakes her head and continues with her ritual.

'But it's New Year's Eve,' I insist. 'I want to spend it with you.'

'No.'

But I have already made up my mind. There's so much I still have to find out about her. I *want* to know so much more. She is a moth playing round a thin ray of light, visible only for

212

a fleeting second when she's caught in the light; often she disappears completely in the dark, leaving neither trace nor promise for the future.

It is not for any sentimental reason – 'our little group'! – that I want to go with her. But there is something so depressing about one year's merging with the next that I feel the need to hide in a crowd. It has nothing to do with celebration or exuberance: that is merely a civilized mark for the ancient, primitive fear of the unknown, and, perhaps, of death. Even an ordinary midnight (surely a phenomenon as regular and natural as high tide) retains something of its ancient terror, reminding one of births that take place in the night, old people who die in the dark, even the act of love which is performed, habitually, in darkness. How much more significant, then, this night, charged by legend and tradition with such deep collective memories that it becomes a sort of spiritual springtide, a culmination of all the terrors of living, camouflaged by outrageous festivity. Usually, of course, one acknowledges nothing but the festivity as such; but having once discovered the deceit inherent in any custom, any 'system', I suppose one tends to look for hidden meanings everywhere.

So I wait patiently, almost enjoying her increasing nervousness.

'What time is it?'

'Nearly half-past ten.'

'Then I must go. Honestly.'

'But not alone.'

'*Please* –!' Her cheeks are flushed. 'Can't you see I don't *want* to take you with me?'

She goes to the door. I follow her. At the top of the stairs she turns round as if to say something, then changes her mind and begins to run downstairs at great speed. But I manage to keep up with her and we reach the entrance lobby together.

While I hold the door for her she makes a visible effort to control herself. 'You can come with me next time,' she says. 'I promise. But not tonight. Please, you don't understand.'

'Why should it upset you? Surely you don't mind singing in front of me?'

'But –' She lifts her hands, then lets them fall back. 'It's such a scruffy little place, you may not like it.'

'If it's all right for you to sing there why can't I go there too?'

'Oh *fuck* it!' There is an angry glare in her eyes. She starts off towards the carrefour, ignoring me. But at the first corner she stops; and the argument is resumed.

Why can't I just let her go? It's obvious that my insistence is distressing her; after all, I have no 'right' to her. I must learn to be content with whatever small segment of her life she shares with me. And yet –

'What time is it now?'

'Twenty to eleven.'

There is panic in her eyes. 'Oh God, *please*! I'm late already!'

I don't answer.

She hesitates. For a moment anything seems possible: she may walk on; or she may turn back; she may even slap me. But at last she only shrugs and with a hint of defiance in her voice, she says: 'All right then. Come along if you must. But you better find us a taxi and see to it that we get there before eleven.'

We hurry to the boulevard. The address she hurriedly gives to the taxi driver is completely unknown to me. (Not that that means anything!) Sitting on the edge of the seat she keeps on urging him to go faster: '*Vite! Vite! Vite!*' Until the driver flares up and snarls something at her. Without any hesitation she counters with a word I would never have expected in her vocabulary. To my amazement the driver's face breaks into a broad grin and the car shoots forward. Relaxed, she leans back. And when we stop at her address – with five minutes to spare – she makes sure that I give him an exorbitant tip.

For a moment we are left on the dark pavement. Then she mysteriously disappears from my side and only after a

214

moment of shock do I notice the narrow doorway behind me. From an illuminated entrance covered by stained red velvet curtains, a seedy doorman beckons at me. It takes some time before I grasp what he is trying to convey to me: I must enter through the front; Mademoiselle has gone round to the stage entrance. Still reluctant, I pay him his entrance fee and find myself ushered to a table where a waiter promptly serves me with champagne I haven't ordered. Nicolette was quite right, I think wryly: I would never have allowed her to come to this little hole if I'd known what it would be like. The loud music and the first few items soon confirm my worst impressions. Strip: solo. Strip: duet. Strip: en masse. All that changes from one depressing act to the next is the faces of the girls. Girls –? There are a few flabby ones who must be nearer to forty than thirty. Some of them actually have dirty feet. One stumbles over the hem of her dress and a man's voice curses her audibly from the wings. The music is deafening. The heavy smoke gives me a headache. Grimly, I try to confine my thoughts to the present, not to anticipate anything; when at last she makes her appearance in a bunch of coloured feathers, I feel no shock – merely sad resignation. There seems to be a stirring of new interest in the audience. A microphone shoots up from the footlights and she starts whining a tuneless song into it while slowly, monotonously her feathers are shed until only one is left. But it is not she. I refuse to admit that it can be she. That is not the hard, sensual body which, a mere two hours ago, was moving against mine. I don't know this stranger. This isn't even a woman. It is nothing but a blatant female sex on stilts; and a voice: a cry of rebellion and desire and hate against the low, smoky ceiling, against the audience at their little tables, against *us* at our little tables, against me at my little table with my cheap expensive champagne. The music, too, goes on screaming, moaning, cursing, mocking, blaspheming. And all the middle-aged and old men lean forward, propped up on their elbows (one of them knocks over his glass without noticing it), their mouths half open and slobbering, their eyes

215

bulging, their moist hands clasping and unclasping on the tables. The music grows louder and louder, the voice stops at the highest piercing note: suddenly all the lights are turned on, and she jumps from the low stage and comes dancing down the rows of tables. It is like a wind blowing across a wheat field, the way all the heads turn to follow her. Unable to look any more, I sit there sipping my champagne as if it were the most precious drink my tongue has ever tasted. It is the only way I can think of to ward her off, to keep her at a distance, to exorcise her like an evil spirit to go her way and leave me unmolested. At the same time I know very deeply that there is no way out. She warned me not to come; she wanted to save me from this; she knew what would happen. But I refused to listen. And now both of us are caught in it, and the unavoidable must happen, *because* of us, *for* us. I do not even consider the possibility of leaving, knowing that if I fail to face this ultimte knowledge, this ultimate agony, everything that has happened until this moment would be senseless; would be undone. Having acquired knowledge, we must now learn to *live* with that knowledge. It is unbearable, but we have passed the stage where we could still claim special consideration. And so she comes dancing to my table, and stops, and turns round, and laughs; and turns back to me, and leans over – one of her breasts touching the tip of the bottle – and kisses me on the forehead. I can feel the moist, sticky lipstick smudging my skin. All the anonymous spectators are applauding, shouting bravo, thumping on the old red carpet with their feet. I realize how they envy me, how some of them will lie awake tonight, peering into the dark with burning eyes, trying to tame their erections as they relive this little scene. But I shall go out with the red smudge on my forehead; and long after it has been washed off it will still be there.

All the time, while they are applauding, she is looking at me, and I am looking at her; and I know that she would like to cry, but that she won't, because this moment is beyond such facile emotions; so her eyes keep taunting and mine keep taunting back; and we go on playing our little act to the slobbering audience; caught, both of us, in this feeling of disgust, this nausea, which at the same time is the most intense communication there has ever been between us. And while we are caught in each other, in this strange moment of timelessness, we hear the sudden outbreak of noise outside, like a dam of sound bursting over us. All the streets, the entire city, come alive with hooting cars, an enormous wave of sound as if, suddenly, there is nothing in the world but sound; as if everything is broken up into neutrons and electrons of sound – not the scream of birth, or the cry of love, or the wail of death, but *mere* sound: the earth and all humanity caught in a roar that reverberates against the dark heavens.

And then, after the first tremor has passed over us, she goes her way with nimble feet, dancing back to the stage, throwing her arms wide open, crucifying herself against the light before she disappears behind the gaudy curtain.

Later a waiter brings me another bottle of champagne. I pay without looking up or counting the change. Outside the streets have gone berserk. Inside the show goes on. She appears a few more times, either alone or with others, in an assortment of costumes. Some of the spectators leave and their places are taken by others. My forehead is burning. There is a red smudge on my handkerchief. I feel glued to my chair, drenched with perspiration. And it is three o'clock before the thickset manager with his shock of greasy black hair appears on the stage among the naked dancers, slapping one playfully on the bottom, to announce the end of the show.

Outside in the cold street I have to wait for a long time before she appears, smelling of cheap soap and cold cream; all her make-up is removed.

'Oh,' she said, as if surprised. 'You waited?'

'Of course.'

'It's cold.'

'Yes.'

'Shall we find a taxi?'

'If you want to.'

217

'There should be some on the place Blanche.'

'All right.'

We go to the square, and get into a car, and drive off.

She sits serenely in her corner, looking out.

Only when we reach the place du Châtelet with its rows of depressing yellow lamps, she says: 'I warned you not to come.'

'Why do you do it?'

'Why not? It's a living.'

This, I think, is the strangest thing of all: not that we have so few words left in this deep, desolate region we've reached, but that the few we have left are so meaningless. Or is it the contrast with the surrounding silence which makes it more conspicuous?

The old, damp smell of her building filters through to us as I open the door for her. I've told the taxi driver to wait; all I know is that I want to get home as soon as I can, tired of words, tired of questions, tired. But she remains standing in the middle of the street and says: 'Stay with me. Please.'

Too weary to argue, I return to pay the driver, close the door after us and go up the stairs with her. As she enters her little room she starts peeling off her coat, and drops it on the floor. I pick it up and hang it over a chair. It is stuffy inside. Almost by instinct she goes over to the window to look out, but it is dark in the room across the street. With a crooked little smile she returns to me.

'Happy New Year,' she says lightly.

I merely nod.

'You're angry with me.'

'No.' It is true: I'm not angry. What I feel is impossible to say.

'Sit down.' she points to the chair at the table; I obey. Without a word she strips a blanket from the unmade bed, drapes it over me and studies it critically for a moment, before she undoes the length of string she uses for a washing-line and ties it round my middle. In the cupboard she finds a rosary which she solemnly places in my lap.

218

'It is half-past three in the morning, Nicolette. What are you up to now?' My limbs are heavy with fatigue.

'Playing a game,' she answers. 'You think I was wicked. I sinned. So now I have to confess. You be the priest.'

'No! There's a time for everything. This is perverse.'

'It's only a game. I often play it by myself. But tonight it's more important. It's the end of a whole year.'

'Leave me out of it. I won't listen to you.'

'You needn't. I'm sure priests don't listen anyway.' And then she kneels down at my feet, her elbows on my knees. 'Father,' she says, 'I hardly know where to begin. I have so many sins.'

I close my eyes. It must be a dream. It is too idiotic to be true.

'What is there to forgive, Nicolette?' I sigh.

'No, no. A priest never calls one by the name. You must say: "My daughter".'

'My daughter.'

'It doesn't matter whether you forgive me or not, Father. It's enough for me to confess.'

'All right. Let us begin then.' In spite of everything I can't help feeling just a little bit amused.

'Tonight I was dancing when I should have gone to Mass.'

'That was very wrong.'

'And I danced naked.'

'That's even worse.'

'And I kissed a man.'

'Unforgivable. My daughter.'

It's like a merry-go-round slowly gathering momentum.

'Is that all?'

'Oh no, Father. It is only the beginning.'

'But why must you confess it all?'

'What will happen if I don't? It's not only for myself, you see. There's all the others too. The other girls on the stage with me. And the *patron*, who fired Jeannine because she tore her dress. And all those who stared at us thinking we were somebody else. And the girls at the door selling their love.

219

And the men who bought it. And all the others in the city, in all the other clubs and places. Those who sing and don't mean it. Anyone doing anything and not meaning it. I know I can't sing. I lied to you. But I told you not to come with me and you wouldn't listen. I know I should have stayed home with you. And I should never have gone to your place that night, because you were busy and I disturbed you. And yesterday morning I stole a bar of soap in the Prisunic when they weren't looking. And I tried to hide in the Luxembourg Gardens at closing time but they found me and chased me out. Why do they always chase one out? I'm not doing any harm in there. But I suppose it *would* scare the shit out of one to be there at night, all alone among those black trees. I was in Versailles once, you know, in the forest, after they'd shut the gates, and it was all dark and locked up, and when I reached the lake, there was a long line of birds flying past overhead with the most awful cries, it sounded like death, and in the end I had to climb over the grille for I was too tired to go all the way back to the far side where the gate is always open, and I was too scared among the trees anyway, and I tore my dress as I jumped down. Why does it happen like that? Why do I want to get in when I'm outside; and if I'm locked in I get scared? Why can I never find rest? I ran away from home to come to Paris, to escape, and I never even wrote back. Except once, to ask for money. There were so many things I've had to do for bloody money, and sometimes people cheated me and threw me out after – you know –'

She goes on and on; and gradually I get the impression that I'm part of a fantastic play without beginning or end, with characters appearing and disappearing without aim, laughing and crying without reason, continually in revolt against something unknown; and because I'm so exhausted and sleepy the scene sometimes reels before me, as if I'm watching it through water. But when I return to my senses and once again see straight, I hear her voice monotonously going on and on, only more and more tired. Her sentences become muddled, sometimes she repeats the same things over and over, and a few times she rests her head on my knees, so exhausted that I can hardly hear what she is mumbling. And when at last she falls silent for several minutes it occurs to me that she may be waiting for an answer.

'*Ego te absolvo*,' I whisper, more for her sake than mine.

'No!' she cries, lifting her head violently. 'Why did you say that? Why are you trying to forgive me? You don't even know *what* to forgive! I don't want to be forgiven if I've done something wrong. I *want* to be guilty, damn it, I *want* to be punished. Otherwise there'd be no *sense* in sinning!'

I try to pull her to her feet, but she stubbornly remains kneeling on the floor.

'You're tired,' I whisper. 'We're both exhausted. You no longer know what you are saying. The game is over.'

'It is never over.' Can she really mean it? I find her unfathomable.

'Come,' I say. 'Let's go to bed. That is your punishment.'

She smiles, shaking her head. 'No.' But this time she allows me to help her up, and she stands quietly before me so that I can undress her. It is the beginning of a new game, a gentle game, a sweet, warm, good game, which continues after we have put off the light, leaving us in the dark. Now all that is visible is the pale rectangle of the window, and the shadow of the little cross in its reflection on the wall.

11

I know I'm not writing regularly enough. But how would you like it if I sat down every Saturday or Sunday to send you a neat little inventory, framed between a loving introduction and a charming conclusion, of all the parties and receptions we have attended in the course of the week, everything we've bought, all the places we've visited either because we felt we should, or because we wanted to, or merely because there was nothing else to do? The alternative, it seems, regrettably, is that each letter becomes an emotional outburst on paper – which is rather unfair to you! What would our friends think of the cool, reserved Erika they used to know? You see, I have too much time for soul-searching. It's like the bottle of bad sherry Anna gave us once, with the sediment at the bottom. If one poured too quickly it was undrinkable. Why did we bother to keep it? Afraid of 'hurting her feelings'? All these ridiculous, polite little fears! Why didn't we invite her for a large glass of her own dregs instead?

But I promise you this will be the last time I pour my sherry over you. We're coming home at last.

The decision came rather unexpectedly. You see, it's all over between Annette and her handsome Italian. By the time I got wind of it, it was already three days after the event. Like a good mother I tried to sympathize with my daughter's broken heart, trying to convince her that it would be for her own good to confide in me. She refused. Soon it degenerated into a free-for-all in which I accused her of no longer trusting me, of deliberately withholding things from me, etc. 'And why shouldn't I?' she asked – our obedient, dutiful little Annette! 'Why can't I lead my own life?' And then it was her turn to tear strips off me, for God knows how long. Accusing me of treating her like a little hothouse plant that has to be protected from the wind. Choosing all her clothes. Making decisions about her diet, her conduct, her thoughts. And, in conclusion, she shouted that she'd now had enough and wouldn't listen to me again. I didn't know what to say. I was too dumbfounded in front of this stranger who was no longer my child. This scene had been coming for a very long time, I suppose, but whenever we'd had a tiff in the past I tried to persuade myself that it was only temporary, that it 'would pass'. There are so many ways of deceiving oneself!

When I finally walked out, she shouted after me: 'I'm sick of your jealousy!'

'Jealousy?' I asked. That was the last accusation I'd expected.

'Yes! You've always been jealous of me. You just want to use me because you've got no life of your own. You've always been

222

afraid that Father might take me away from you. And that's what you called love!'

I went out. Heaven knows through what streets I wandered that night. And all the time I was thinking, thinking. I remembered how I had resented having a child. It has practically been one of the conditions of our marriage. You couldn't understand it. But could I? Was it my way of avenging the humiliation you'd made me suffer? – not by going away for those eighteen months, but by coming back convinced that I was yours for the asking. Why did I so readily say yes? So much for 'free will': I accepted because my mother wanted me to turn you down. And so, because I wanted to rebel against her, we got married after all. Still, I think I loved you. I know I did. But God knows there was so much resentment, so much suspicion in me. How could I give birth to your child before I felt free to give myself, before I wanted to? But she was conceived and born anyway. You were so proud and happy. How could you know that your very elation scared me even more? However ironical it sounds now, I was afraid that the child might make it easier for you to reject me in the end. I'd always felt rejected. A 'second choice'. The two of you could turn against me. What else could I do, Paul? Oh, I know only too well, now, how absurd I was. But I thought the only thing I could do would be to win her as an ally before you could. And that was what I called love: clinging desperately to a child I had not wanted, because she was the only thing I could call my own, and because she could so easily become an opponent. We were never temperamentally suited to each other, she and I. And what will happen now? Is it too late for anything?

Whatever happens, we are coming home. I am coming home, not very proud of myself. I'll have to learn to forgive myself before I can hope for anything else; but is that so easy? And does it make sense? It's not enough to accuse oneself if one wants to be freed from guilt: so how can forgiving oneself be enough? Forgiveness must come from elsewhere, from someone less wretched than oneself. This terrible, primitive need to confess! But whom does one turn to? The Church is no longer fashionable, it has become an equation incapable of *solving x. But one must go somewhere, otherwise this guilt becomes too much, drawing into its whirlpool too many innocent people: it becomes collective guilt, and every generation adds to it, making redemption more impossible.*

You must help me drink my bottle of sherry, Paul. Perhaps, if one closes one's eyes and swallows very hard, one can drain it in one draught.

Love: See if you can decode this word. Erika.

12

Her hair against my neck and her open lips against my shoulder where, a minute ago, she bit deep into my flesh, she asks in her unexpected way:

'How does one say in Afrikaans: *faire l'amour* – to make love?'

'One doesn't. There are two sets of words, but one sounds like a medical text book, and the other like graffiti on a toilet wall.'

She laughs but her eyes remain serious: 'What did *you* say then when you and your wife made love?'

'We never talked about it.'

'Oh.' She is lying quite still, breathing evenly. After a while she adds with a giggle: 'Marc always talks about putting the devil into hell –'

'Who is Marc?'

Her eyes, which have been looking past me, return to mine. Is she a little bit frightened? Did she say something she never meant to say?

'Just a student,' she says, with a shrug.

'How did you come to know him?'

'I know many people in Paris.'

'But *him*?'

'Met him in a café or somewhere. I can't remember. He sometimes looks in for a chat.'

'Just a chat?'

'Does it matter?'

I dare not answer.

'You jealous?'

'No.' I'm not. It's the truth, I swear. All I am aware of is this endless weariness in me. I have never known that *détresse* – this emotion beyond despair – could be so serene.

I move away from her.

After a while she gets up and puts on her clothes. There cannot be many women, I think as I sit watching her, who can be just as sensually provocative in the act of dressing as in that of undressing. A sudden pang: how often has *he* watched her dress like this? Marc: is this the latest name of fate? All these weeks I have had the feeling of moving *towards* something, towards her – yet all the time he's been there too, part of her, as real as I, and perhaps even more real in her eyes.

'Just a student –'

It is possible that I sometimes came to her while his seed was still in her. She never showed any sign of it. How was it possible? Because I belonged to the past, absorbed by her body, and therefore forgotten? Or was it, is it, all part of her never-ending game? And how long is it going to last? There is not much left of my three months. And then –?

She suddenly comes to me, taking my face in her long hands, forcing me to look up at her.

'Why can't you understand?' she asked. 'It makes no difference to *us*.'

'And "we" make no difference to *you*?' When she declines to answer I decide to press on: for the first time I dare to confront her with it: 'Did you know that a commission of enquiry may be sent from Pretoria soon?'

'Why?'

'To investigate our – well, whatever there is to investigate about us.'

At first she looks sceptical; then puzzled. 'And then? Will you have to go away?'

'Not necessarily.' After a moment I add: 'Would *that* make any difference to "us"?'

She shakes her head but she is no longer looking at me. It isn't necessary for her to say anything. I know already.

Yet I insist: 'Will you stay with me whatever happens, Nicolette?'

Impatiently, desperately, she swings her head back: 'I don't know, I don't know, I don't *know*! Why must you go on asking questions? How can I know what is going to happen?'

'Will that be the end for us?'

'Will you be sacked?'

'Does it matter?'

'We're *here* now. Nothing else matters, does it?'

I get up and begin to put on my clothes.

'Don't go away.' She takes me by the arm. 'Stay here. Stay with me, always. You must never, never go away.'

'Do you love me?'

'What does it *mean*?' she asked in despair. 'People say it all the time. It's so easy. A word is nothing.'

'I know. A word is nothing. And to love may be nothing. But I love *you*.'

I take her in my arms. Over her shoulder I can see the snowflakes whirling softly across the street, but the curtains opposite are drawn.

She must be knowing what I am looking at, for with a little laugh she says: 'The woman's shy tonight. Or perhaps it's just to keep out the snow.'

13

I take long walks through the city, more and more often these days, sometimes with her, sometimes alone. It has become a profound need, more urgent than the simple wish to see as much as possible of the place while I am still here, or an attempt to find, beyond the confusion of streets and buildings, a more coherent pattern of things. It is, really, a daily discovery that everything that has happened, everything that may still happen, has been so predestined by the city itself. Paris: it is more than a context for events. It is itself an event, a long process taking place, involving us, part of ourselves. By the same token it is more than a background for her, or a symbol of her: it is, simultaneously, a synthesis of all her elements, and a being with its own existence. The city has its own head, and heart, and belly, and sex. And it seems as though, in the process through which I am robbed of all other convictions, opinions, certainties and possibilities, the city is becoming more and more alive, a more and more persistent presence.

14

In the early evening, while we are waiting for our red wine in a warm, smoky, pleasant little café, she absentmindedly scratches something on the corner of the table with a bent hairpin. A single, innocent word in the old dark wood: *MOI*. When she catches my eyes she covers it with her hand and drops the hairpin in the cheap green ashtray.

15

Random thoughts in the serene courtyard of Saint-Séverin:

It is easy to talk about love. She said so herself. It is thinking about love which is difficult. And it happens so often these days, as I am more and more inextricably caught in the web of Erika, Gillian, Nicolette.

For a long time I have succeeded in keeping away all thoughts of Erika, apart from a dutiful weekly letter. But now that she is coming back, after her confessions, I'll have to come to terms with her reality once again.

Long ago, when I returned to her that time, I did not give it much thought either. I never regarded the relationship with her as a problem. Gillian had died. Something had been rounded off, now was complete, final, without regrets about the past or speculation about the future. It was *obvious* that I should return to Erika. In fact, it actually surprised me that she did not immediately accept to marry me but insisted on first 'thinking it over'. Not that I had any doubts about the outcome; I took it for granted that neither of us had any alternative.

The first moment of unexpected panic came on the wedding day, when after hours of driving through pouring rain, we arrived at our destination and suddenly found ourselves alone in the anonymity of the hotel room. She smiled, nervous, as if trying to convince herself of something. But it was no use. What she needed was the reassurance of *my* certainty. And, suddenly, I had nothing to offer her. We were desperate to establish *some* kind of understanding, of ordinary human contact before we could proceed with what custom and circumstances required of us. But at last we switched off the light to put the seal on our failure. And although we had more success soon afterwards, at least in terms of technical procedures, we were soon gnawing at each other's wholeness and security. Still, we managed to survive without obvious friction, in strict neutrality.

Sometimes, inevitably, I rebelled, wondering what would happen if I tried to appease my frustration elsewhere. But I anticipated the cynical expression in Erika's cool eyes, and the kind of remark she might make ('Go ahead, if you must'). And I desisted.

Yet she'd been so carefree and gay earlier, before our marriage, before Gillian. Not that she'd ever been like Nicolette: Erika was always 'proper'; Erika had never been 'that sort of girl'; Erika always managed to make me feel – I may as well admit it – inadequate.

But how does this tally with the woman who wrote those letters from Italy, the woman who is now coming home to me? How does it tally with 'us' – the people we've been for twenty-five years? How does it tally with *now*? I don't know. Is it not presumptuous to talk of 'love' if it has never been anything but a mere possibility?

And Gillian. Surely what I felt for her was also 'love'. Love? My God: *odi et amo*, a fire meant to purify body and soul and eventually consuming only itself. Or did it, for that very reason, involve something essential to love: the urge to *be*, to affirm oneself in the face of all destruction?

Or is love, simply, the only response to unbearable solitude? A drug to make life easier to bear? But love is no soporific! It's too acute for that, much too painful, too relentless in its exposure of whatever is devious, superfluous, or insincere.

And Nicolette? *Lassata, non satiata*. She can devise, for hours, for whole nights, delightful new games, new positions, intimate little ecstasies: each one of them an act in itself, free from the blemish of thoughts or words. With her, love is a never-ending mystery, a quest for insoluble riddles, for the origin of myths. With her, love is a form of bewilderment, because it confronts one with the chaos inside oneself; her body is, indeed, a wilderness, a labyrinth from which I cannot, and would not, escape.

And there is always this irony: love is supposed to 'last forever', to be based on at least an assumption of duration – but our relationship has always, since the very beginning, been finite, calculable within the days and hours of three months – and consequently doomed to futility; and yet there is nothing else I *can* do, or could have done. In the end even Nicolette will be lost to me; in the end there will be nothing. 'And so, *Amare liceat si non potiri licet* –?) But now, at this moment, while it lasts, she is indispensable: not in any petty, selfish way, but *essentially*.

It seems to me the concept of being 'born again' is merely the Christian equivalent of an experience which is fundamental to every human being: an act of renewal, a dying of the self, in order to become aware, anew, of world and self. And in this sense I have been born again through her. Once born, one cannot crawl back into the womb, however much some may try to do so; once reborn into this new awareness of the world, it is just as impossible to undo or deny it.

Perhaps 'civilization' is responsible for the difficulty one has in coming to terms with it? After all, love is not a civilized thing, but a primitive need. If, indeed, I have unnecessary, unessential 'needs' left in me, I shall have to dispense with them as the time grows shorter and shorter. But can this be done voluntarily? Or must one wait for grace? And where is *that* to be found –?

16

The previous night it had still been winter. I remember it clearly, for I can still see the misty panes through which we were looking at the people of the window opposite. I can still hear her say: 'She can't have very long to go now. It must be eight months already.' And I remember the sudden distress in her eyes as she went on: 'I don't know *what* I'd do if it happened to me. I wouldn't mind having a baby – provided it's a girl – but then she must just *be* there, one day, without this whole business leading up to it. I'm sure giving birth is just like dying; one must feel totally trapped, there's just no way to sidestep it! It would drive me mad –'

The snow had melted weeks ago but it was still bitterly cold; at night – and that night too – we gratefully snuggled in each other's warmth against the thin movement of the wind across the slanted roof.

And then, the very next morning, it was suddenly, inexplicably spring. One knew it from the very way the light came through the window; and from the call of the *brocanteur* in the street below; and it was visible in the first suggestion of green in the chestnut trees of the Luxembourg Gardens when, later that day, I left my work and went out with her and with hundreds of others to enjoy the sun; one could hear it in the laughter of children who'd shed their overcoats to run about in the parks; it was obvious in the cafés which had cast off their terraces overnight, leaving chairs and tables exposed on the sidewalks.

'The cold will come back,' I still hear her warning. 'It's always like this: a false spring in February –'

But it didn't really matter. The touch of despair that had always been part of my attachment to her had suddenly disappeared; everything was pervaded with a new sense of joy. Perhaps that, too, would prove illusory like the too early spring. But it was there all the same; it was there to be relished. Those were serene days, quiet and timeless – perhaps the last peace we would ever know together. But even that did not trouble us. For the first time, perhaps the only time, I learned to exist in a continuous present, like her.

I remember –

We are walking on the promenade along the Seine, or sitting on stone steps, drowsy of the sun, her light dress pulled up high above her boyish knees, her sandals kicked off, her toes in the dirty water. We are strolling hand in hand under the early green chestnut trees, drinking Coke. She sticks peach blossoms in her hair in the path below the Palais de Chaillot. We stand on the open balcony of an old green bus travelling recklessly to the Bois de Vincennes. She skips ahead of me in a flimsy summer dress, her legs and her body outlined against the light like the wick of a candle inside its flame. We are standing together on the Eiffel Tower, on the Arc de Triomphe, on the towers of Notre-Dame: she is scared of heights – another form of ecstasy? – yet she insists on climbing every tower in sight. We are sitting in a cheap cinema where she soaks her handkerchief with tears.

Endless conversations. She tells me all about herself: a different story every time, but I have learnt long ago not to be upset by her lies because each one of them is completely true at the moment of telling. In a few light moments she summarizes a whole past of shadows.

Sometimes, more and more frequently, our conversation turns to Erika. Will it not change the relation between us? she asks quietly, never urgently. And I assure her very sincerely: Nothing can make any difference to us. Nothing can change what exists between us. After all, if Erika's return can affect our love it would mean that our whole relationship depended only on Erika's absence. And it is much, much more complex than that.

Yet all the time I have the secret fear that Erika's return

will indeed make a difference. What it will be, I have no way of knowing yet; perhaps it is not even of immediate importance. But it is inevitable that the large, calm, inexorable movement in which we are caught will accelerate and become more defined when she comes back.

But now, together in this early spring, everything is still caught in timeless bliss.

17

It was on the afternoon of 22 February that she came back. I went out to Orly to meet her. While Farnham was driving smoothly along the autoroute lined by long rows of lampposts with gracefully bent heads, I tried to visualize the meeting at the airport, and its consequences, later. How and when would Nicolette be introduced in our conversation? How would Erika react? What would happen next? But something in me was clogged. I could not even think of any *possible* answers; and much to my confusion I could no longer even visualize Erika's face.

But the moment she stepped from the Boeing and moved away from the other travellers towards the special VIP lounge I knew her well enough again to notice that she had lost weight. Not much, but still. That was the only difference. I felt almost disappointed because I'd expected that what she had written in her letters would somehow also be revealed, however subtly, in her appearance. But even when she allowed me to kiss her, she was the same reserved stranger as before; her hair a few tints lighter than usual; her make-up immaculate; her eyes smiling with calculated friendliness.

'Hello, Paul.'

'Hello, Erika. Enjoyed yourself?'

'Yes, thank you.'

'Glad to be back?'

'Of course.' With a hint of cynicism in the corner of her mouth. 'And how are you?'

'Oh. I'm all right.'

Then Annette was there too, as formal and as mondaine, it seemed, as her mother, who looked more like her sister; but not quite sophisticated enough to hide a touch of uncertainty: a quivering of the mouth, a question in the dark eyes.

'Hello, Father.'

'Hello, Annette.' Our lips touched lightly: was she afraid that I might smudge her lipstick, or that I would feel the trembling of her mouth?

'You're lovely,' I said, and meant it.

While Farnham was taking care of the luggage we went to the official car.

'Donald and Mary sent their regards.'

'Thanks. Did you see them often?'

'Almost daily. No changes in your staff here?'

'No. The Jouberts are going on home leave in two months time.'

Annette lagged behind, watching two amorous pigeons on a ledge. Erika and I reached the car, and suddenly I realized that we were alone.

'Erika –?'

There was a flickering of her eyelids but she made no answer.

'Are you sure you're all right?'

'Of course.' She looked into my eyes, and got into the car. 'Did you miss me?'

My turn to answer: 'Of course.'

Annette was approaching with Farnham and the porter. I watched her, intrigued, almost startled to discover that she was really a young woman. As she reached the door she noticed my gaze, and smiled with a hint of embarrassment.

We didn't talk much on the way back: a few remarks about their holiday, about officials in the Embassy in Rome, a coming fashion show in Paris.

Once Annette said: 'Why are you so thin, Father?'

'It's your imagination,' I answered. Too quickly.

Erika: 'It suits you, you know.'

With that the tone was struck for the next few days. It came almost as a surprise to see how little difference their presence in the official residence made to my life. We saw each other at breakfast, lunch and dinner and talked about obvious, matter-of-fact things. Perhaps it was just as well. It couldn't last indefinitely, of course; sooner or later we would have to face each other, and talk it through. This fencing was too deliberate. And it soon became frustrating to go on finding excuses for going to Nicolette at night. Neither Erika nor Annette ever came to my office, so I used 'working late' as the most obvious explanation; once or twice I had to visit a colleague for 'discussions'. But it still meant that I had to be home by eleven or twelve; and this lay heavily on the hours I spent with Nicolette. We tried not to make any reference to it, but it was obviously beginning to trouble her too. And this disturbed me; the balance was so precarious.

About a week after Erika's return Nicolette, for the first time, refused to make love. And when I insisted she flared up.

'I'm not a street-girl!'

'What on earth makes you think that?'

'That's all you want of me nowadays. And we must always hurry up so you can go home again. I'm nobody's dirty little secret.'

That was the final warning. I could no longer avoid a confrontation with Erika. I felt too tired, too despondent, to face her that same evening; but my mind was made up to get it all out into the open the very next day.

It was with a feeling of relief that I entered the official residence and went upstairs. Erika's door was closed, although there was still a thin line of light underneath. Annette's stood open. For a moment I hesitated on the landing. Then the bathroom door opened and Annette came out, her cheeks glowing, her hair damp. She was wearing a dressing-gown of

235

soft yellow towelling, carrying a small bundle of clothes under her arm. And it came almost as a physical shock to see her like that: vulnerable, young, beautiful.

'Oh – good evening, Father!' She smiled in her slightly hesitant way. 'Have you just come back?'

I nodded. Once again I thought: Can this really be my daughter – this young woman with the subtle, free movement of her limbs inside the dressing-gown?

She came to me.

'You're working much too hard,' she said.

'It's a habit.'

'Would you like a cup of tea?'

'Won't we wake up the household? It's so late.'

'It won't take long.' Still clutching her bundle of clothes she held out her free hand to take mine. A gesture so much like Nicolette's that it actually made me feel guilty.

In the kitchen I sat down on a straight-backed chair, and watched her set out the cups and boil the water.

'You'll be nineteen soon,' I said, more to myself than to her.

She looked at me over her shoulder, surprised. 'Yes. Why?'

'And this is the first time in years you and I have been alone together.'

She went on working, her back turned to me.

She was a stranger to me. How could I love her? Yet that was the discovery I made, perched on my white kitchen chair. She was a girl; she was free. Even if I was confined within the pattern of my life she could be free on my behalf, flesh of my flesh. She was a woman, in touch with absolutes beyond my reach. I abandoned myself to memories. How many times, years ago, I'd watched her through a window, or listened to her laugh? But then, gradually, I'd noticed her shedding that freedom which had been her natural heritage, as she was drawn into her mother's pattern to become a model child, a well-behaved little tame monkey. I'd seen her accept it, without resisting. And so I'd closed my heart to her, withdrawing once again into myself. Which was a passive way of hating.

Yet now, together in the flat light of this white kitchen, I made the unsettling discovery that she was *not* what I had all the time believed her to be. If I'd noticed it earlier –? But earlier, before her Italian holiday, she had indeed been different. She'd been an impersonal statement, now she was a question mark.

She handed me my cup of tea. I took it and touched her, and held her hand. She glanced up, startled.

'What happened in Italy, Annette?'

Her face became tense; for a moment she looked just like Erika. 'Why do you ask?'

'Your mother mentioned something about it.'

'A lot of lies, I suppose.'

'Did it hurt very much?'

She was struggling against the emotion. Suddenly she began to cry, her head buried in her arms on the table. I put my hand on her shoulder but made no attempt to stop her. After a long time, without looking up, she said: 'Why did he have to rush me all the time? Why couldn't he be patient? Pressing me, pushing me. Wanting me to get married. Wanting *me*.'

'And you didn't love him.'

'I did!' She looked up at me passionately. 'And I still do.' For a moment it seemed as if she would begin to sob again, but with a quick, angry gesture she wiped the tears away and continued: 'But I was scared. He made me feel cornered. I don't want to – miss out on life. I don't want to become like you and Mother.'

What could I say?

'I spoke to Mother. She was thrilled. Eager to see me married. Not for one moment did she seem to realize that what I was trying to tell her was, for God's sake, to *help* me!' Her eyes were burning in mine again. 'Why did you always leave me with her? Why did *you* never help me? Didn't you know I needed you?'

237

The clock in the lounge struck half-past twelve, a discreet, civilized sound. She looked up, almost scared; then, without looking at me again, she picked up her clothes and her cup of tea and went to the door.

'Annette.'

She stopped.

'I know we've been living past each other all these years. But perhaps it's not yet too late –?'

I could see her hesitate. Then she took a deep breath and said softly: 'Good-night, Father.' And she went out, through the dark dining-room to the staircase.

The following afternoon, directly after work, Anna Smith 'just popped in', after a few days' illness, to welcome Erika 'back in our midst' and to express the hope that her holiday had been pleasant. 'We all missed you so much,' she said with great conviction. 'And poor Mr Ambassador! He became quite absent-minded lately, the last thing anybody would ever have expected of him, don't you think? Now you know me for a frank person, Mrs Van Heerden, and I want to tell you what an awful admiration we all have for your husband. And he's just not the same person when you're not here. Pining away, you might say. Now please don't misunderstand me: of course we all know you needed a bit of a holiday –'

Erika's sardonic eyes looked at me, then returned to Anna.

When at last we came back from the front door, more than an hour later, she said, with a sharp edge of irony in her voice: 'My poor husband. Have you really been so lonely?'

'It's time you and I had a quiet talk together, Erika.'

'Talk? That's all we've been doing since I came back.'

'No. We've just been fencing all the time. We never seem to get round to anything of real importance.'

She stopped at the entrance to the private lounge, erect, suddenly defensive. 'And what can be so particularly important?' she asked.

'What you wrote me from Italy. Perhaps you found it just as unnerving as I did. All those long confessions in *your* handwriting. You've changed, Erika. Why are you trying to cover it up now?'

'Oh, the letters?' She moved nonchalantly past me to where she'd left her cigarettes on a long low table. 'You should burn them. Incriminating evidence. And entirely false, I suppose. I can hardly remember what I wrote.' But her calm words were contradicted by her hands clutching the packet. 'A little *crise de conscience*. You shouldn't attach too much importance to it.'

'There's no need to be evasive, Erika.'

She shook her head, blowing out smoke. 'You must remember I was away from my familiar surroundings, away from you. I had more time to think than was good for me. That's all. And now it's past.'

'Much of it was true.'

'Was it?' Her eyes became narrower, scrutinizing me through the smoke.

'Except that you accused yourself only, omitting that I have my own share of guilt.'

'Please! Not you too,' she said, much too quickly. 'It was enough that I had to put up with myself. I can't take any more melodrama. It's *past*, I assure you. Don't keep on nagging. We've learnt long ago to live with it.'

'So you won't discuss it?'

'It's just that I don't have much faith in words.' She turned away from me, announcing: 'Please excuse me. I must look after tonight's dinner. The servants have become very unreliable in my absence.'

'I have something to tell *you*.'

'Yes?' She turned back politely, but I knew her well enough to sense her irritation.

'I shall be going out again tonight.'

She shrugged. 'Oh well –'

'I won't be back before tomorrow morning.'

For a moment she frowned. Then there was a slight change in her expression. 'I see.' She fell silent, and nodded. 'I see. I don't suppose it's entirely unexpected.'

'You don't understand, Erika.'

'Please don't try to explain.' She smiled. 'I won't bind you.'

There was nothing else for us to say. Only when I turned round to go did she ask: 'Was it really necessary to tell me?'

I did not answer.

It was only three days later that Erika personally brought me my cup of coffee after work. Her attitude suggested that she had something on her mind, but she evaded my questioning glance and calmly sat paging through a *Marie-Claire* while I was drinking.

Then, almost casually, still flipping over the pages, she said: 'By the way, she was here this afternoon.'

'Who?'

'Your little – what shall we call it? Hetaera? Hierodule?'

'What are you talking about?'

'Your *petite amie*. Your courtesan. Your mistress. Your little tart. Miss Alford.'

'Nicolette?' For a moment I was dumbfounded. And yet that was exactly what I should have expected of her.

'I suppose that would be the name you know her by,' Erika said. Then, with a flickering of her mouth: 'And how does she address *you* "Your Excellency"? Or "Sir"? Or simply "Uncle"?'

'Don't be vulgar, Erika.'

'I'm sorry. On the other hand, I expected *you* to reveal more taste too.' She studied her fashion illustrations. 'Surely someone in your position could have made a better choice?'

'I'm not prepared to discuss her with you. Not like this.'

'Perhaps it would be better not to say anything, I agree. If that's really your taste it isn't much of a compliment for me, is it?'

I put down my empty cup and stood up. 'What did she come for?' I asked stiffly.

'She brought some flowers. I wasn't sure whether they were meant for you or for me, so I gave them to the servants.

Quite expensive; this time of the year everything comes from hot-houses, I presume.'

I paid no attention to her. But as I reached the door she let down her mask, if only for a fleeting second:

'My God, Paul,' she said, 'you're disgusting!'

I blundered through a few rooms. It took some restraint not to start breaking things. Was it Erika who had made me so mad, or Nicolette? I don't know. I only know that it took a long time before I could think coolly again. What else could I have expected? I had made my choice with open eyes. And as I went out to the Métro I knew, once again, that whatever happened, nothing should be allowed to come between Nicolette and myself. This was the only meaning left to my life.

But there was still Annette. It is difficult to tell, now, whether she avoided me on purpose, or whether it was just the normal course of our lives that separated us during the next few days. But one afternoon I was on my way upstairs just as she was coming down. For a moment she seemed to hesitate. Then she merely looked away and came down past me swiftly, without a word. I could feel my heart grow taut. Strange as it might seem, that moment was more painful than the two conversations with Erika.

I called out after her.

She stopped, but didn't look round.

'Where are you going in such a hurry?'

'Just – out.'

'What's the matter?'

She shook her head. Then unexpectedly, she swung round to me, her hand clutching the rail, and the words came jerking loose from deep inside her: 'I thought – in Italy, and the other evening – and you said -' Her voice faltered for a moment but she went on: 'And all the time you were doing this! You deceived me! I thought – and believed, and hoped – that everything would be different now. I've never felt so *dirty* in my life!'

241

Long after the front door had slammed I was still standing there. When, finally, feelings began to filter back into my mind, I tried to console myself with hackneyed phrases: Adolescent. Over-reaction – Give her time – She'll calm down – But it was useless. And I couldn't even trick myself into believing that it might help. I simply had to accept that everything which, up to that moment, had been maintained by make-believe was now beginning to fall away from me. I couldn't tell how long the process would last, or where it would take me. I had no control over it any more. I could only go on.

But to lose my daughter, at the very moment I thought I'd found her –

18

In the early evening, through my office window above the desk with the small calendar and the French submarines, I see a soundless jet gliding through the sky beyond the buildings of the city, writing, like a human hand, its cryptograms on the blank blue wall above.

It was the first time I had ever seen Douglas Masters flustered.

'Mr Ambassador,' he said, 'I know I shouldn't come to you with this, but right now I'm so furious that I can't think of anything else.'

'What is it, Masters?' I was struck by the uncommon paleness of his face.

'I've had a letter from the Minister –' He fluttered a handful of papers.

'What is it about?' It was unnecessary to ask: I already knew what was coming.

An instruction from the Minister to make discreet enquiries about the background to Keyter's report, a copy of which was attached. He was to reply as soon as possible.

'It seems quite clear to me.' I pushed the documents back towards him.

'But – this is preposterous, Mr Ambassador! Why was Keyter not called back to Pretoria immediately? Couldn't the Minister have contacted you personally?' He must have been extraordinarily upset to lose his restraint so completely.

'I already saw the report in December.'

'But why was the matter not quashed on the spot?'

'I preferred not to comment.'

For a moment he gaped at me. At last he asked, almost pathetically: 'But surely the whole thing is just a parcel of lies?'

'The facts are correct, Masters. Only the interpretation was wrong.'

'But in that case –'

'The situation has changed somewhat since then. In the present circumstances the interpretation may also be correct.'

I sat watching him with almost complete detachment, as if the whole matter concerned someone else. He was struggling bravely to master the blow. At last he seemed to make up his mind.

'I can't be disloyal to you, Mr Ambassador,' he said, tight-lipped. 'I won't comment either.'

I shook my head, touched, in spite of myself, by his sincerity. 'Unfortunately the matter is not so simple, Masters. I was given the choice either to defend myself or to let the matter run its course. You have been given instructions which must be obeyed.'

Unable to answer he swallowed, arranging and rearranging his papers in a most irritating way. 'What must I do? he whined.

There was something grotesque in the situation.

'Why don't you talk to Lebon? I'm sure he can report on all

my movements. You are quite free, of course, to tell the Minister that you also discussed it with me and that my attitude remains unchanged.'

'But it would be so easy to stop the whole thing.' He was practically pleading. 'Think of what it can lead to! We need you here. Mr Ambassador, this is no time for flattery, but surely you realize that you're indispensable to the Government, especially at this stage of the arms negotiations!'

Should I have countered with the obvious cliché that 'nobody is indispensable'? I knew only too well what he was offering me. Frankly, if I'd thought that a change of heart could still be useful, I might have reconsidered – if more for his sake than mine. But at that stage, if anything mattered to me, it was the very need for things to run their natural course. To avoid it, or to thwart it, would not be cowardice so much as a denial of any possibility of meaning in what had happened, in what was happening, in what might yet happen.

I shook my head.

'Mr Ambassador –' But the matter was now beyond the reach of words, and he knew it. I felt sorry for him in this crisis where neither Satow nor all his years of experience could help him find a ready answer.

'There is only one little thing, Masters,' I said. 'In Keyter's report you will find the address of the person concerned.' I deliberately refrained from mentioning her name. 'I don't know whether it would be expected of you to approach her for information as well. But if you can do without it, I shall appreciate it very much.'

'Of course!' His eagerness was quite pathetic.

But that was not yet the end of the matter. The same evening, as I came back from one of the rare official functions I had to attend personally, Stephen Keyter was waiting with Lebon at the main entrance of the Embassy. Could he see me for a few minutes? I invited him into the residence, but he was afraid to be disturbed by Erika or Annette, so we went up to my office. He seemed excited, but he didn't speak before the door was closed behind us.

'Well, Keyter?'

'Mr Ambassador.' He fumbled with the cigarette I offered him. 'Mr Masters came to see me tonight.'

'I see. He spoke to me this afternoon.'

He was flabbergasted. 'So – you know –?'

I nodded.

For a moment he seemed to weigh the knowledge in his mind. Was it too heavy to bear? All of a sudden he exploded: 'Why are they doing this, Mr Ambassador? Don't they believe me?' Then, impulsively: 'You yourself have never believed that I had no personal grudge against you.'

'On the contrary. I couldn't agree with the procedure you adopted. For the rest you did your duty.'

'It was more than duty.' For a moment he closed up again. His lips were twitching nervously. Then he continued: 'I know you'll think I'm being idiotic or conceited, but my career is the only thing that really matters to me. And tonight Masters said – he was furious – that my whole future may be – he said he would personally see to it that – Mr Ambassador –!' For a moment he was struggling helplessly for words. 'Don't you understand? Nobody has ever understood. Nothing is ever difficult or ambiguous or obscure to you. You succeed with everything you do. But I – even when I was a child my father wanted a *son*, you see, not a sickly weakling who spent more time in bed than out of it. He wanted to make a man of me; that was his one ideal, because in every other way he was so desperately unhappy and frustrated. And then I turned out his greatest failure. I joined the Service because it promised so much for the future. I wanted to get somewhere. I *had* to get somewhere. And now?' His hands were pressing down on the desk. 'What must I do now?'

'Wait. That's all you can do. It's all we can do.'

He clutched his head between his hands and remained in that position for a long time, his cigarette forgotten on the ashtray, a lazy spiral of smoke whirling up to the ceiling. I was looking at him as if I'd never seen him before. Earlier, I thought, there had been suspicion on his side, perhaps even hate; resentment and scorn on mine. He'd been the hunter, I the hunted. Now, unexpectedly, he was bewildered and had come to me for help; and I could feel a curious compassion for him; this young man who'd always hidden his emotions behind his cerebral cynicism, and who had now discovered that he might well become the victim of his own intrigues.

'What did you say to Masters?' I asked.

'Nothing. I told him I first wanted to think it over.'

'Why did you come to me, then?'

'There is nobody else.'

'You are much too young to withdraw so much into your own shell,' I tried to soothe him, upset by his confession. 'Why don't you lead a more active life: friends, girls –?'

'Don't you think I've tried? And every time –'

We fell silent. And it was only after a long pause that I said, without really knowing why: 'Nicolette?'

He looked up at me, shook his head, cast down his eyes again.

'But you *knew* her.'

He said nothing.

'She told me.' Something was urging me on. 'The very first night she came to see me, last November, after you'd thrown her out.'

That touched him. He looked up. But his answer came as a surprise. 'Was that the first time you had met her?'

'Yes. Why?'

'But I thought –' He didn't complete his sentence. 'She lied to you, anyway,' he said after a while. 'She left, of her own free will. I never threw her out.'

'I suppose I should have guessed as much.'

He didn't answer for some time. Then: 'Of course. You know her.'

I made a movement with my head. What could I say to make him believe me: I did *not* know her, nobody knew her?

'I wanted her,' he continued unexpectedly. 'Perhaps I could have learnt to love her. Perhaps. But it would never have worked out. She always despised me – and she tried to

246

mask it by playing hide-and-seek with me.' With some self-pity he added: 'Perhaps it served me right. I've never inspired much confidence or trust in anyone.'

'Accusing oneself brings one nowhere, Stephen.'

'That's not what I'm trying to do,' he said. 'It's the truth I'm telling you. First there was my mother. She was the only one who ever cared for me. Always took my side. But I didn't want her pity. And so I turned against her too, although she was the one who really deserved to be pitied. My father was a hard man –' He sighed. 'Do you see how mixed-up it all is? But how could I trust her after I'd discovered that she was a hypocrite, a ball of clay in my father's hands –?' And suddenly he plunged into a long, confused narrative about Sunday nights at home, pious prayers followed by a nauseating scene in his parents' bedroom. 'And then she died,' he concluded, exhausted. 'She used my father's revolver. It's something I've never been able to come to terms with. I still see her before me at night, in my sleep. It becomes a sort of poison in one's blood, and it gets worse all the time, until there's nothing else left in one. I can't bear it any more. I don't know what is going to happen. And now I've brought this thing upon *you*.'

He got up, composed again, as if his last words had sent him scuttling back into himself. 'I must go,' he said, almost formally. 'I've already wasted too much of your time.'

'You mustn't brood on it like this,' I said, uneasily. 'I'm sure your report will be accepted. And you can easily convince them of your sincere intentions. I can vouch for it.'

He showed no reaction. But when we reached the small courtyard below he said: 'I'm sorry, Mr Ambassador. About everything. I'm terribly sorry.'

Our hands touched in the dark. Then he left. I remained in the courtyard, thinking: how strange, how strange that Nicolette, who had once been the gulf between us, was now the only thing we had in common: her game, her lies, her never-ending mystery.

19

The endearing way she has, whenever she feels upset or sad, of twirling a little curl on her forehead with one finger, faster and faster, until she is soothed or falls asleep.

20

On Christmas morning she ignores all her expensive presents and puts on a demure warm dress and coat, covered by an ugly plastic raincoat; round her neck she wears her worn-out old brown rosary like a piece of valuable jewellery.

Long before the Mass we are waiting inside Notre-Dame.

At first the interior is merely an expanse of darkness with the distant glittering of candles before the Virgin, and the glowing reds and blues of the stained-glass windows. But gradually one's eyes discover the large, heavy columns motionless in the dark; and chairs; and railings round the central block.

In the dusky light of the entrance a couple of small girls are trying to climb up the font, giggling, sprinkling each other with holy water. Beside me Nicolette draws her breath in sharply at this playful blasphemy. Before I can do anything to stop her, she rushes to the font and slaps the two small bottoms. One of the children, scared out of her wits, escapes through the door; the other lets out an earsplitting yell. Nicolette glances round quickly to make sure that no one sees her; dipping her fingers in the font, she crosses herself.

With a slight gesture of her head she beckons me deeper into the dark interior. Her hands, holding a much-fingered missal, are clasped serenely at her breast. I follow her, past chapels with dull mirrors of light on old paintings brown with smoke, round the back of the choir with its fine railings and woodcarving, and back along the opposite wall.

Next to one of the massive columns she finds a place where one can lean on the balustrade.

'We can't go in,' she explains. 'Those seats are reserved for the baptized.'

'But who would know?'

'I would. So would you.'

Organ music reverberates in the high vaults. The introibo. Her body becomes tense beside mine. Already she has forgotten all about me. And suddenly I feel the need – a need as real as physical thirst or the urge of sex – to be joined with her in that fierce elusive ecstasy she so desperately seems to be reaching for. I don't want to be a mere spectator any more. Through her, with her, I want to be changed, transfigured; I want to break out of myself and leap into freedom, illumination, meaning.

I never had any dramatic 'break' with the Church. In my childhood I regularly attended the Sunday services because that was the done thing: without deep conviction, it is true, but also without any conscious doubt. Then came Gillian who tore up the Bible and jeered at it as she jeered at all my other conventional beliefs. During my eighteen months in Europe I was never inside a church: once again it was not a matter of conviction, and certainly no form of rebellion – it merely seemed irrelevant. It was just as natural, at that stage, for me to discard the habit as it was to resume it after my marriage. Perhaps it was the linear, hygienic nature of Calvinism that never appealed to me: stark, unimaginative, sober, the miracle of bread and wine reduced to a formula which had long ago lost even its symbolic power.

In South Africa going to church was part of the accepted way of life; in Europe it was not. And so, ever since our first transfer abroad, we gave up the custom. Sometimes, of course, I have to attend a service in my offical capacity; and then I go without thinking twice about it. It is part of my duties. Was.

The celebrant, in his ceremonial dress, is sprinkling the congregation with holy water. With that the whole intricate pattern of the Mass begins, slowly at first, almost like a great heavy wheel coming into motion – *In nomine Patris, et Filii, et Spiritus Sancti* – and once again I became aware of her reaction: no discernible movement, barely a gesture, a slight quivering, as if she too is trying to reach out from herself, beyond the balustrade separating us from the faithful, beyond all barriers, to a wider expanse, a purer form of existence, salvation; and I can feel my own urge growing with hers, because I know it will give meaning to so much of the confusion I live in at the moment.

The altar is censed, then the bishop. It is the transition to prayer, the dialogue between heaven and earth, the eternal yearning.

The slow motion of a little while ago is becoming more urgent and more mysterious.

Kyrie eleison.

Christe eleison.

Kyrie eleison.

The bishop spreads his hands across the altar, brings them together again; and then the walls start trembling: *Gloria in excelsis Deo* –

A little flick of her wrist as she turns over a page in her missal.

In the large liturgical movement of prayer, reading, and singing, in the reaction of the congregation – standing up, crossing themselves, sitting down again – I try to determine: is *this* what she has come for, to form part of this rhythm and illusion of certainty, this unchanging pattern – the very things Gillian tried to escape from?

Credo in unum Deum – Everything lucid, fixed in the unequivocal words of the Latin text. Why could all our words and experiences not be so charged with essence –! Where did the watering down begin of everything which had once been vital?

Da nobis per huius aquae et vini mysterium – Once, in another existence, she pronounced these words. I thought, then, that she was being flippant; how mistaken I was!

At the beginning of the Sanctus she closes her eyes. I put my hand on hers in my desperate desire to join her in that unfamiliar dimension she has seemed to attain. She remains unaware of my touch. I have been left behind. In my ears I hear the Hosanna, but it is nothing but sound, superficial melodic joy. And when the bishop commences the same ceremony she performed for me in her little room, last night, I realize that I cannot be drawn into it at all.

Hoc ist enim corpus meum.

It is very silent now. Every word and gesture is in code, pure symbol. And I have lost the key.

Is this the only way in which we can survive – through an endless series of symbols? For things are unique; the smallest event can never be repeated; even last night's emotion is absent today with the repetition of the same ceremony. And because it is impossible for two experiences ever to be similar the only solution is this search for common denominators, symbols to render life intelligible. We cannot go on without them. Yet this very habit keeps us away from essentials, from truth, from the things themselves!

Pater noster qui est in caelis –

I am forced to listen, trying, in my own language, to find the key to the miracle that must change the wine of each separate word into blood.

Et ne nos inducas in tentationem. Sed libera nos a malo.

It comes so unobtrusively, a liturgical necessity; yet the moment the phrase is pronounced by the congregation, and by Nicolette beside me, it becomes the clue to much I've tried to grasp in her. *Sed libera nos a malo*. It is not for the Mass that she has brought me here today, not for the bread and the wine and the burning of incense: the true reason is this phrase.

This is why she is content to stand outside the railing, listening to the words alone. *Libera nos* – God, as such, is hardly important. Surely Nicolette desires no eternal life. All she wants to escape from is the fear that liberty may include evil; and that she may destroy herself by remaining free. And so she takes refuge here, in this beautiful pattern which will, just as surely, destroy her once she gets enmeshed in it.

And I? Is this the reason why I've come with her? *Libera nos* –? 'Salvation'? The beauty of the ritual. Faith manifested in the Church: the enormous organization, the infallible remedy for all troubles, the answer to all questions (*Come to Me* –!) But, surely, that would bring me back to Genesis: the choice between happiness without knowledge, and agony with knowledge. Is not the foundation of all religion the maintenance of the illusion that Paradise still exists? Its image remains alive in us because we cannot otherwise bear the idea of wandering eternally in the land of Nod. We know the angel with the sword is guarding the entrance to the Garden, so we plant our own little garden, trying to persuade ourselves that it is Eden.

Ite, missa est.

21

It was the last time, although I was not yet aware of it, that all the inhabitants of my tidy ordered world had come together. Erika and I at the front entrance (Annette refused to appear in public), she elegantly dressed in one of her new Italian outfits, every little wrinkle removed through hours of conscientious preparation. Third Secretary Harrington, small black moustache trimmed handsomely, accompanied by his attractive wife with her peroxide hair. Koos Joubert, formidable and smiling, a few yards ahead of his wife in the outfit she wears to all formal occasions. Stephen Keyter, thin and polite, and Victor le Roux with his unkempt boyish looks. Douglas Masters, clean-shaven, brushed, oiled, with a little bow to Erika and convincing excuses for the absence of his wife. Anna Smith, draped in purple silk and green beads, a strong aroma of Chanel and a hat trembling with multi-coloured flowers. Colonel Kotzé, the Military Attaché, short and erect beside his plump, motherly wife. Herman Verster, the Commercial Attaché, with his large, soft goat's eyes behind thick lenses, accompanied by his wife who looks like a queen in drag. Acquaintances from other Embassies. A few strangers Erika had met at esoteric social functions.

Then drinks, as the conversation began to flow more smoothly and the customary groups drifted together from the conglomerate crowd. Waiters in white and black moving about with trays. Laughter. Animated discussions.

'You should have seen it. It was absolutely –'

'Did you know that Hutchinson has been transferred to Copenhagen –'

'The bowling at Lord's –'

'Now surely –'

'You must remember it hasn't yet reached the Committee stage –'

'I can't see how Britain could possibly –'

'Do tell us all about Italy –'

Almost without signal, as if everything had been planned in advance, everybody moved to the dining-hall. Anna Smith landed within earshot and, leaning forward, embarked on a detailed description of how she'd made her own hat. On my left a Canadian woman repeatedly told me, each time in different words, how delighted she was that her husband had just been transferred to sunny South Africa. On my right, French policy in Europe was criticized. Someone complimented Erika on the main dish, followed by a general murmur of approval.

Every single guest had his or her predestined role to play. Each came equipped with a well-tried set of opinions and

253

convictions: like information punched on a card, so that each time the correct key was applied the same formula was conjured back.

I didn't know whether anyone there really believed in it any longer, but nobody would even for a moment consider an alternative; this existence was so well established, so harmonious, so successful. If life had lost its power of transubstantiation, we nevertheless went on drinking the wine, eating the bread, making the required gestures. Come fill the cup. Tomorrow, thank God, we die. *Et après nous –*

After the meal the movement flowed back to the reception hall. The ladies sat down in a corner, on chairs and settees; the men formed little standing groups. I had a conversation with Kotzé. Then with a British diplomat. After a while I took my empty cup back to the coffee table which had been placed near the archway to the dining-hall.

Behind the archway there was a small group of men. And I heard Koos Joubert's loud voice: 'But what the hell, let the man have his fling if he wants to! Why not? That's what women are there for –'

They didn't notice me. I carefully placed the empty cup with the rest, and turned round, and went back to the nearest group.

'I've always maintained that the French –'

'But you have to consider –'

In the background: 'What a pity all the good old Afrikaner traditions are disappearing –'

'I still prefer living in Paris to –'

'Such an up-and-coming young man –'

It took an effort to continue; the light amusement with which I'd played the game with them before had evaporated. But it was going on and on: there seemed to be no end to the evening.

'But don't you think –'

'Surely no one in his right mind –'

At half-past ten the first guests left.

'Are you sure you wouldn't like to stay?'

'It was absolutely –'

As we turned back from the front door Stephen appeared in the entrance to the reception hall. In spite of Erika's polite insistence he was adamant that it was time to leave. They exchanged compliments. Then I accompanied him to the front door.

Suddenly I saw in it an opportunity to escape.

'Are you in a hurry?' I asked.

He seemed surprised. 'Not particularly –'

'I wouldn't mind a bit of fresh air. May I walk with you for a little way?'

'Of course,' he said. 'I came by Métro anyway.'

Lebon opened the main entrance and saluted. One side of his collar was turned up.

Silently we walked along the deserted pavement. Perhaps he was waiting for me to speak. Perhaps it had been naïve of me to come along. But the heart pays scant attention to propriety.

'It's been a pleasant evening,' he said after a while.

'No need to be polite, Stephen.'

He made no answer.

'The cat's out of the bag,' I said at last, when we had to wait for a stream of traffic in the rue de Tilsitt.

He glanced at me.

'I overheard Joubert saying something about the report,' I explained.

'I haven't spoken to anyone!'

'I never thought you had, Stephen.'

For a while he was silent. Then he said: 'It's possible that Sylvia Masters may have blurted out something.'

That would explain her absence. I could imagine her affected voice: 'You'll just have to tell them I couldn't come, John. I can't face it. To think that all this time –'

'It must have been upsetting for you,' Stephen said.

'Just unexpected. I suppose I'll have to get used to it.'

At the Métro entrance he stopped: 'Wouldn't you like a night-cap in my apartment?'

'Very much, thank you.'

We spoke very little on our way to Les Sablons. There we went up to his apartment and, still silent, sipped cognac from his large bubble glasses.

'It's a very pleasant place. You have good taste.'

'It's not homely enough.'

'One needs people for that. Not that it always helps, of course.'

He merely nodded. After a while, scowling into his glass, he said: 'Nicolette stayed here once while I was away on holiday. You should have seen the place when I came back.'

I smiled. 'I can imagine it.'

'Sometimes she came here to have a bath, usually during office hours. Then one night –' He took another sip, leaving the sentence unfinished. A minute later he said: 'She came back one evening just before Christmas.'

I looked up, holding the glass very tightly, waiting.

'She pretended that nothing had ever happened. I wasn't very accommodating, I'm afraid. If only she'd said something, made the slightest gesture, to prove that she felt sorry, or upset, or anything. But she'd come merely to tease me again. She was always intrigued to see how far she could go with me – and then she'd laugh at me. She told me very spitefully, that night, that she was having an affair with you –' He looked down at his hands, 'I told her I didn't care a damn. To crown everything, she showed me a tie she'd bought for you and asked me whether I thought you'd like it. I opened the door and told her to go. And she went.'

'I see.' It was almost as if I'd known it for a long time.

Like the previous time she was the main topic of our conversation. Not that we spoke much. And at last, when there was nothing left to say, he went downstairs with me.

'It's beautiful outside,' he said.

'It's a night for walking.'

Slightly cool, with just a breath of wind, and the outline of a crescent moon behind flimsy clouds.

We began to walk away from the Métro, without any

definite direction, along the dark lanes of the Bois de Boulogne. Now and then one of us spoke. But most of the time we walked along in silence, leisurely, each wrapped in his own thoughts, yet gratefully conscious of the other. Fifteen minutes, half an hour, an hour. Time no longer mattered. And when we returned at last the Métro had closed down for the night and I had to take a taxi.

'Good-night, Mr Ambassador.'

'Good-night, Stephen. Thank you.'

There had been something completely natural about the whole evening with him, the promenade, the brief spurts of conversation. And why not? For in the new emptiness he had become the only person I could still talk to.

And I sat thinking gratefully of him in the taxi on my way home, back to Erika's cool displeasure about my 'neglect of duty' and the 'affront' to my guests.

22

In spite of the mystical attraction the Church has for her I often notice, whenever we pass a priest or a nun in the street, that her right hand forms the fica sign against the Evil Eye.

23

We came down Table Mountain together, late in the summer afternoon, hand in hand, with an empty rucksack on my shoulders, Gillian moving beside me with nimble feet, untouchable in her happiness, with sun on her hair and in her eyes, and a rare serenity in her face. All day long there had been nothing to upset her. Early in the morning we'd followed an easy route to the top where we'd made a fire among the speckled rocks; for the rest of the day we'd wandered about, talking, dreaming up impossible plans, lying on our backs high above the sea under the scattered clouds, desiring nothing more.

'Things can be so confused at times,' she said on the way down. 'Tomorrow, perhaps, it will be so again. But on a day like this I know I really love you. And I don't ever want to be without you again.'

I saw the wind playing with her dark hair, and the casual way in which, from time to time, she swept back the loose strands. And I knew that this happiness was too impossible to last – yet that was exactly what she expected of me, *demanded* of me. And if I failed her, not only I, but everything she could believe in would be destroyed for her. She had fastened herself to me like a mussel to a rock, in the desperate faith that I would save her. But I couldn't.

And when I left her that evening with an almost uncanny sense of wholeness, I started calculating how much money I had saved for my wedding with Erika; I had made an inventory of all my possessions; the next day I sold everything I would no longer need, booked my passage on a boat, and a week later, without telling her or anyone else, I left. I was not trying to escape. It was the only thing I could do if I wanted to give her one last chance, however improbable, of finding something, somewhere, to save us both from the precipice. I didn't know whether she would make it. But there was a chance, and I had to let her take it. As for myself: I had to withdraw from everything she'd broken down around me, and try to start again on my own.

24

It is not only for the sake of completeness that I must also relate this, but because it is, indeed, unavoidable. What was strange was not that it happened, for I'd been prepared for it, but that it took such a long time to happen.

Anna Smith came sobbing into my office that morning: 'I don't know *what* to do,' she said. 'I couldn't believe it. Anybody else, perhaps, but not you. And to think how I trusted you with all my personal problems, all my secrets –!'

It was difficult to tell what that had to do with the whole matter, but it would be useless to interrupt. She insisted on knowing what my plans for the future were, whether I intended going on with my work as if nothing had happened.

'I don't think there is any alternative, is there?' I asked.

'Then I'll have to resign,' she sobbed. 'I can't possibly go on like this. I have to consider my reputation. What will my people back home say if they hear that I've been working in the same office with you all the time?'

Comical, melodramatic – undoubtedly. But at the same time I realized that such judgements and condemnations would, in the future, be a constant threat to my relationship with Nicolette.

With the exception of Masters (who came to give me his formal assurance that after serious consideration he felt convinced that our personal relations need not be affected by his disapproval of my unprofessional conduct), none of the others made an attempt to discuss the situation with me personally. But I knew that for a long time it would be the main subject of all their reactions:

Harrington: 'It's normal isn't it? Most men of his age get

an itch. A matter of hormones –'

Colonel Kotzé: 'Shocking. A man in his position should have enough self-restraint –'

The typists, giggling: 'It's naughty but it's nice –'

Once I happened to overhear Victor le Roux warning someone: 'I don't think we should be so ready to judge –' But when we met at the main entrance only a few minutes later, he merely said goodbye, like all the others, and went his way. Not, I presume, because he felt resentful or embarrassed, but simply because there was no earthly reason why he *should* do anything else. We had nothing in common.

25

Oh you girls of Paris –!

With your long hair and slim brown legs and your spring buds of breasts, black eyelashes, sappho lips, with string bags in your hands or books under your arms: joking gaily and self-consciously with the gendarme at the Luxembourg gates in the dusk when the park must be closed –

Leaning, crushed and swaying in the Mètro, against pale young men with fanatic eyes and eager hands, ignoring the crippled old women stumbling to their seats –

Walking across the bridges of the Seine where once there were markets and fairs with acrobats and fortune-tellers, swinging your narrow hips and sometimes, in despair, flinging yourselves into the dark green waters under the high cathedral –

Playing the timeless love-game against the fences of parks, Mètro rails, shop counters, old doors, or dirty walls, with more or less abandon, more or less sincerity, more or less joy –

And each one, each one of you, carries, like her, between your smooth thighs, the *gouffre* of Baudelaire!

26

I knew very well how hard it must be for Erika to continue as if nothing had changed, but after so many years I also knew her formidable willpower and I expected her to keep up appearances until the very last. If ever she referred to the subject again, I thought, it would be in the same sarcastic, condescending terms as before.

So it came as a surprise when, one afternoon when we two were alone at table (Annette was attending an art lecture somewhere), she asked: 'How long are you going to go on like this, Paul?'

I looked up. Her eyes were calm and cold. 'I thought we'd discussed the matter,' I said. 'My life needn't interfere with yours in any way.'

'Somehow it just doesn't work out that way.'

'You first suggested it.'

'There's no sense in blaming each other, Paul. It's just that things aren't as simple as they seemed a week ago.'

'Nothing has changed.'

She shook her head. 'No. It is no longer private. It's not even confined to the Embassy any more. I had tea with the wife of the Dutch Ambassador this morning. There were quite a few people. Nothing was said directly, of course, but enough was implied to make me realize that it's become one of the sauciest little bits of diplomatic gossip at the moment.'

'Sooner or later it had to become known, I suppose.' I spoke as neutrally as possible.

'But don't you understand, Paul? It's no longer a matter of you and me. What about your position? There are responsibilities you have no right to ignore. You have certain obligations.'

'Don't you think I've not thought about all this a long time ago? I know it's not easy, Erika. But I wasn't caught unawares.'

'And what about *us*?'

'Us?' I had no idea what she meant.

'You and I. I'm no longer sentimental or idealistic, Paul. When I came back from Italy I didn't think we'd be able to make a completely new start. But at least I was prepared to *accept* certain things. And now –'

'We've been married for more than twenty-five years. Is there anything we can show for it? Is there one single thing we've ever shared? But it wasn't for lack of trying. Isn't that so?'

'What do you want to *do* then?' She made no effort to maintain her composure.

'Exactly what I'm doing now. It won't last long. What is going to happen afterwards, I don't know. I am trying not to think about it. Even at this moment I have very little, almost nothing. But it's something. And it is more than I've had for years.'

'Yet it was you who came back from Europe that time and insisted that we get married, even though *I* had misgivings.'

'I did what I considered the "right" thing. That is what I've always done. Now I know better and I'm not trying to deny my guilt. But how can it possibly improve matters if I discarded the only valuable thing I have left and tried to convince myself of a new lie – knowing it's a lie?'

'In other words I don't count anymore.'

'There's nothing I would like more than to see you happy, Erika. But that won't happen if we go on playing blind man's buff together.'

She got up. 'So that's that?'

I nodded slowly. If only I could put out my arms to comfort her, but it was no longer possible. The years behind us had been too sterile.

If only I could help her accept it. But there was something new in her, a hopelessness, a lostness I'd never known in her before, a desperation of which I would never have thought her capable. And it led up to an evening I dearly wish I could forget, however necessary it was for what still lay ahead.

When I came into my bedroom from the office to change for the evening, she was sitting on my bed in her dressing-gown. Her hair was tousled, presumably from her bath.

Surprised, I stopped on the threshold.

'Erika! What are you doing here?'

'Is it so unusual to see your wife in your bedroom?' She laughed shrilly.

That, and her way of speaking, sounded a warning: she'd had too much to drink. It was the first time since her return from Italy.

'Are you ill?' I asked, with as much restraint as I could muster.

'No, I'm fine. That's why I'm here.' She tugged at the loose lapels of her gown. 'Or don't you want me here?'

It was like a slap in the face. But I controlled myself, not wanting to lose my temper while she was in that state. 'This is no time for fooling around, Erika. What are you trying to do? You've never given yourself to me willingly. Not even the first time!'

She got up, reeling slightly; but her voice was sober: 'How could I? You never allowed me to give myself. And I wanted to. I *wanted* to, d'you hear me? That first night I lay praying, pleading all the time: "Dear God, please let him succeed. Please let us succeed. Please let something *happen* between us!" But it didn't.' Her words were becoming confused and jumbled. She fell to her knees, sobbing: 'But it's not too late yet. We can still try. We can't just let everything slip away from us!' Exhausted, she lay forward, resting her head and arms against the bed.

'Please stop it, Erika! There's no point in bringing it all up again. You're drunk.'

'Drunk?' Another laugh, her head falling backwards.

'Now I'm drunk! But I *want* you. You are not going away to make love to another woman tonight. You're going to stay here with me, I want you!'

Clenching my jaws, I took her under the arms and picked her up. 'Come to bed, Erika. I'll help you.'

She hit out at me, but stumbled. If I hadn't caught her, she would have fallen.

'Leave me alone!' For a few minutes she stood swaying on her feet, mumbling all the time: 'You're going to stay here tonight. You're going to stay with me –'

I turned round to go out.

'You don't even know about the doctor!' she cried suddenly, almost triumphantly.

'What about the doctor?' I no longer knew what to expect.

'I'm going to have an operation. He told me before I went to Italy. And after the operation it will be too late. You'd better stay here *tonight* –!' She flung open her gown exposing the full length of her body, trembling, very white.

I felt sick. Why couldn't we be left with a little dignity? Was *this* necessary?

She was reeling. I caught her as she fell and took her to her own room. Then I telephoned the doctor. Before he arrived Annette returned from somewhere in the city's secret heart. She didn't greet me.

'Please go up to your mother,' I said.

She went upstairs. A minute later she called from the landing: 'What's happened? What have you done to her?'

'Stay with her,' I ignored her questions. 'The doctor is on his way.'

If only I could say: 'It's not my fault.' But she wouldn't have believed me. Perhaps I could no longer believe myself.

Ten minutes later the doctor arrived and gave her an injection. Hypertension; nothing to be worried about, he said. Symptomatic of her condition. He would advise us not to postpone the operation for much longer.

'I only heard about it tonight,' I said, embarrassed. 'Is it serious?'

'It can become serious. It is, of course, a very common complaint at her age.'

After he had left, I went up to her room. She was sleeping. Annette was sitting at her bedside but she didn't look up.

I went out again. I couldn't go to Nicolette in that state of mind. There was no one else, not even Stephen, I could talk to. So I had dinner in a restaurant nearby and then returned to my office to work until past midnight, as I'd done so often in the past.

The next day she seemed quite composed again, although she was still exhausted.

After lunch (Annette had already gone up to her room) she said in her old, calm way: 'I'm sorry about the scene I made last night.'

'You weren't normal. Don't think about it any longer.'

'Sometimes one is normal when it looks least like it. But it was disgraceful. It won't happen again.'

'Of course it won't.'

'I mean: I'm going away.'

I stared at her.

'Back home. To South Africa. I should have gone there in the first place, instead of to Italy. It's the only thing I can do.'

'But there's nobody in South Africa you can go to.'

'I know. That's why I am going. I'm not trying to escape. On the contrary, I'm trying to act responsibly – I'm sure that's what you expect of me.'

'Must you?'

'What else can I do?' Her eyes had a very wise expression. And I had to admit that it would, indeed, be a solution – for the moment. I would have preferred it not to happen just then, but I had no right to interfere. But her considerations were more important than mine. And why should I try to save face if neither us nor anybody else still believed in our marriage?

Less than a week later I drove her and Annette to Orly. Because everything had been arranged through the Embassy there was no delay at the customs. In a small, formal VIP lounge we sat together for the last few minutes.

We talked about the magnificent airport building. The infallible flight schedule. The friends she would meet in London before proceeding to South Africa in three days' time. Annette didn't take part in the conversation.

Then their flight was announced by the loudspeaker. I accompanied them to the last glass door.

'Goodbye, Erika.'

I kissed her.

At the very last moment her fingers bit deep into my arm. 'My God, Paul –!' she whispered.

'As soon as everything is settled, I'll probably return myself,' I said, simply because something had to be said. 'Then we'll see each other again. Perhaps it will be very soon, a few weeks from now.'

'Do you really think it can be as simple as that, Paul?'

'We'll see. In the meantime – good luck.'

She nodded and started walking towards the illuminated corridor that led to the tarmac.

'Annette –?'

My daughter was standing before me, looking at me, but without kissing me, she turned away. She was crying.

I didn't want to go up to the crowded terrace to see them take off. Blindly I just walked on and on. Somewhere outside, very far from the building, I finally came to a standstill, and leaned over a balustrade. Before me was the vast, dark expanse of the airfield. It had begun to rain. But I remained standing, watching as the steps to the plane were removed. Listening to the deafening scream of the engines. Seeing the monotonous blinking of the wing lights while the tyres screeched on the wet concrete as they moved away in the dark. After a few minutes they disappeared behind other planes. Still I did not move. The rain was pouring down. At last, in the distance, I heard the roar of the engines. Very far away a tiny red light started moving horizontally past me, then described a graph into the air. It did not remain visible

266

for very long. It was raining too hard. Cold and drenched I returned to the waiting car.

The weather was changing, I thought. Nicolette had been right: one couldn't trust the early spring of February. The cold was setting in again.

Nicolette

How the hell can one bath in a basin? I just had to get used to it, there was nothing else I could do. I bought the little red basin in the Monoprix the very first week I got here and took it with me wherever I went. It's getting rather old and worn by now. Paid too much for it too, but I didn't know any better then and I still had some money, it was before I had to sell my coat. It's not like a *bath* at all. Keeps one's feet warm, and that's that. And the old cripple is always staring through the skylight from his balcony across the street and there's nowhere else for me to put the basin. Perhaps he's got no other place to stand either and it doesn't really matter, I suppose, for I stare at the people of the window opposite, and they stare at the old Hungarian couple sunbathing on their little balcony on the third floor of my building, and I suppose *they* have someone else to stare at, and so we zigzag across the street all the way down to the ground. I wonder whether he ever goes out with his crippled leg. Never seen him on the stairs. Always standing on his balcony whenever I look out. Perhaps he's disappeared by now. It's time I went back to check up. Usually I never stay away from my room for so long, unless I leave Paris, of course. But I seldom do that nowadays. I used to do it very often. I've been here in the Embassy for days now, almost a week, I'm sure. And here I'm lying in warm water in the big white bath, steam against the roof and walls, shiny teardrops trickling down the tiles. Must be more than an hour I've been lying here. Why shouldn't I? I can lie as long as I like, there's nobody to bother me. The one servant who tried to be cheeky left yesterday. Just as well. I don't know why there should be so many of them in an Embassy. I love the green bath salts, except I think I used a bit too much today. His wife must have left it behind. Or his daughter. I keep on forgetting that he has a daughter. She wasn't here when I brought the flowers. Only the wife. Very friendly, except for her eyes, she even invited me in for a cup of tea. Wanted to know all about me. I can't remember what I told her. Why do people always want to know? Stephen too. I used to go to his apartment, to take a bath, mornings when he was away at work. And one evening –

What I like most is to rest my head against the edge, my feet on either side of the taps, all bright and shiny. He never told me whether he liked my legs. Too skinny, I'm sure. But I've got nice feet. Funny things, bodies. And this little curl here. Marc never got tired of playing with it even when he's half asleep. *Nicolette-à-la-houppe* he calls me. And *minette* is what he calls that. *Faire minette*. He can go on all night. Not the Ambassador. He gets tired more quickly, or else he thinks he ought to stop. I wonder if he's shocked by the games I sometimes make him play. He's so serious. I know he thinks I'm just a sort of little circus animal doing tricks and things. I amuse him. And one of these days he'll get tired of me and drop me, what am I to someone like him? Sometimes he talks about trouble coming, but I know it's only to make me used to the idea so it won't hurt so much when it happens. Why should he really care about me? My hair is getting all wet, lying like this, but so what? Mum was always at me. Daddy didn't mind a bit. Used to wash my feet. He *had* to, else I kicked up a row. Sometimes the Ambassador comes to sit on the edge of the bath, especially when I'm having a shower, I love a shower even more than a bath, the thin jets stinging your shoulders as you stand there, your hair getting soaked, until your whole body seems to turn to water. I love having an apple to eat under the shower. Yesterday there were no apples so I tried to smoke a cigarette but it got all soggy. I used to have apples in the garage too, those days. The dark garage always smelling of fresh straw, and other smells too, of tar or oil or something. The boys whispering as

I lay munching my apple. Bloody ridiculous, lying like that with one's dress pulled up so that they can take a look. I never did it for free. They did all my homework for me, and brought me apples, and sweets, and pocket-money, whatever I asked for. Pigeons too, commons and pedigree homers, they built me a whole big cage for them. But I never liked pigeons in a cage, so I let them all fly away in the end. It's like two small pigeons breathing in his hands, the Ambassador says. He likes them that way, he says. Too small, I think. I can remember how I once stuffed cottonwool in there and how shy and proud it made me feel. He's got beautiful hands, the Ambassador, perhaps a bit too broad, but they're kind and gentle. Daddy's were thinner and not so strong. We always went for a walk at night and on the first corner there was the honeysuckle growing wild in the hedge of the vacant lot. The smells of those evenings. And when it rained on the hot tar. Sometimes he stuck flowers in my hair. And Mum got so mad if we stayed away too long. It always happened that way. She scolding the two of us, or him. Until he couldn't take it any longer and went away. I wonder whether she also likes lying in the bath for so long. I don't think so, mind you. She doesn't look the kind. I like pretending it's really my home, and that I'm living here now that she has gone away. That's why Francine left, said I ordered her around too much. I ask you. All these rooms, and the carpets, and the tapestries on the walls. It's like a bloody museum. But I suppose they have to make do with what they get. Stephen's place is much more pleasant and homely, I wonder whether he planned it all himself –

This bathroom must be as big as my whole bedroom. I really should go back. Wonder what's happening to the people opposite? It can't be long now, a couple of weeks, or days. I never knew one could get as big and blown up as that. I once saw a cow that blew up, must have been on a walk with Daddy. They had to cut a hole into her belly, just like that, with a knife. Green lucerne, they said it was. But it was no use, she died anyway. They're not fucking so regularly these days. She cries a lot. I can't stand tears. I'd rather jump into the Seine than let that happen to me. I wonder what it would feel like? The water, so green and deep. Better not to struggle. Just give up, let the stream take you away, slowly, very slowly drifting along, until you remember less and less, and care less and less, and feel death taking you, not in a hurry, but slowly, passing under all the bridges of the city, under the misty sky which grows darker and darker until you can see no more, a singing sound in your ears, singing everywhere, dying, dying splendidly, just like when there's someone inside you and the small feeling grows bigger and bigger, at first it's only there, deep inside you, his voice in your ears, gentle, saying words you cannot understand, his hands round your shoulders or in your hair, then it spreads all through you, your belly and legs, your breasts, your arms, your fingers and toes, a throbbing in your head, and your eyes pressed shut, your own voice crying in your ears, crying and pleading and sobbing and praying, not praying in words, but turning into prayer all by itself, sort of, all of you, the you which is so much more than the ordinary you, until way beyond the last darkness you wake up in blinding light and slowly drift back again, first to darkness, then to dusk, to quiet light, and you open your eyes and you smile, wearily, your mouth still against his shoulder, but the kind of smile that's neither happy nor sad. I've died that way so many times. But every time it's only my own voice praying. Never a priest's. *Dies irae, dies illa*. I love going to funerals. Sometimes I ride with the relatives in the black municipal bus. They all think I'm one of them. Otherwise I wander through Père Lachaise, especially in summer when one can get away from the sun under the heavy green trees among the tombs. Sometimes I take flowers with me. There are so many graves without flowers. But I have no wish to *be* dead. Dying is different. You know you're going. But once you're dead you don't even know you're dead. You just lie there under your tombstone, boring as hell. *Pie Jesu Domine, dona eis requiem*. It sounds like the fairytales he used to tell me on our walks at night, all those magic words and rhymes. Strange to think of him and Mum. In bed, I mean. Still, they must have done it, else I wouldn't have been here. And the Ambassador and his wife. But they had separate rooms. One can understand that, I don't think she really knows what it's like to *feel*. And I'm sure she's the kind who feels all ashamed to look at herself. I suppose if she looks at her down there she gets the idea that it's a wound or something, a mistake, the way they leave a slit in a doll or a bunny where they stuff in the cottonwool. No wonder he's really like a boy who's not seen a girl before. I bet she never allowed him to take a proper look. And he says thank you each time. Marc is different. Violent. He hurts me if he wants to, I hate him for it, and yet it's wonderful. He's so sure of himself one can go to him to be safe from the world, and from loneliness and everything. Yet, when I am with the Ambassador, when he's so gentle, he's like Daddy, I think, then I want to be everything for him he wants me to be; and for me he is hands, and a voice, and sometimes a face. With Marc I go mad, everything starts tumbling around me. It's like the building is falling in, and the earth, falling, falling through the night. He tears me open and lets me out of myself, sure of myself, and of everything, of all the world. And yet, with the Ambassador, somehow, I really *feel* more. And when it's over and we're lying together, it's almost unbearable. It also makes me feel free, but at the same time I'm alone in the night, with nothing familiar near me, and all I know is that we are there, together, alone and that I need him more and more because I can no longer find my way in the dark. I mustn't allow him to use me like this, as a toy. But in the beginning it was I who wanted to play with *him*. And now there's nothing else I can do. I wonder it it's sinful? Why do I always know about sin when I'm with him? It is nothing I *am*, nothing I *do*. I don't know. Neither does he. On New Year's Eve he didn't know why I wanted to confess. He thought it was just another game. And what I really wanted to ask was simply: Dear God, forgive me for loving him, but it's like my father, and what we are doing is like the flowers he used to stick in my hair at the corner of the vacant lot in the evenings, and like the washing of my feet when I had my bath. Forgive me for *knowing* that he'll leave me and for pretending not to care, forgive me for not knowing what I did wrong and for only knowing that he *thinks* I've done something wrong. It isn't my fault; forgive me for that also. One gets so damn confused when one is praying. Sometimes I don't pray, when it doesn't feel like when we're making love, like with Stephen. With him it was like going to the dentist. Or like the last time in the garage when the neighbour's boy said *that* word and I got up and pulled up my knickers and dusted my dress and left. I never let them have another look, not one, not even when they put all their pocket-money together and brought it to me. For Stephen I was just an adventure, a hill he could climb, a body. Not even a body, just an organ to spill his seed in. He wasn't trying to find anything when he was with me, so he found nothing either, and then he thought it was my fault. If only he knew –

What a pity they put the mirror on that wall, and such a small one too. In a bathroom one should have mirrors all over the place – walls, ceiling, the lot. Why are some people so ashamed of their bodies? They say the nuns in convents don't even allow the children to bath without clothes. If I had a house of my own I'd have mirrors everywhere. Especially round the bed. Every time you move your head, you should be able to see yourself a hundred or a thousand times, from all angles. When I was small I used to lock myself up in my room and unhook the tall mirror of the dressing-table and parade in front of it for hours, wearing all sorts of clothes, or naked. I'd pull faces, and stand up, and sit down, and bend to the left and to the right, and look over my shoulder, and go down on all fours, and even squat on the mirror. The day after my eleventh birthday the mirror slipped from my hands just as I was putting it back on its hooks. Never seen a thing break like that. Suddenly I was scattered on the floor all round me: here a nose and two eyes, there a leg, there a hand, there a part of my body, and eyes, and eyes, and eyes, eyes every-

276

where. As I tried to pick up the bits I cut my hand, and got scared and ran away, and only came back when it got dark. If it hadn't been for Daddy I would have got a hell of a hiding. He just took me in his arms and comforted me, and then I *really* started crying. Not because of the mirror and the eyes, but because of the seven years of misfortune ahead of me. And it worked out exactly like that. Only a week or so after that he left us and never came back. Mum didn't want to keep me with her and sent me to boarding-school. I ran away. Then another school. Later she sold the house. We never lived in the same place for more than a year, often for only six months. Usually in hotels. Our suitcases were always packed. We never settled down anywhere. It went on like that until the day after my eighteenth birthday. Then I knew the spell was broken, the seven years was over. I could start living again. Mum was having an affair with someone, as usual. Charles, I think his name was. Or Kevin. Imagine anyone with a name like that. Or Eddie. There were so many of them. But this one she wanted to marry and I was in the way. So I went to him and borrowed money from him to come to Europe. Never paid it back. The trouble is, I honestly never have enough. I don't know how it is. Sometimes I lose it. Or I give it away to clochards. So every so often I'm in the shit. The Ambassador can't understand it, he's so careful with everything. He gives me a lot, whenever I ask for it, just like Daddy did; but it's no use. It lasts for a day or so, then I'm broke again. That's why I took the strip job in the club, but now he's forbidden me to go back. What's it to him? It's only every other week, not later than two or three in the morning. So what's the fuss? I take off my clothes in front of *him*. Why not in front of others? I don't belong to him, I belong to nobody, I wasn't made of anybody's rib. But men always want to *possess* you. As if they haven't got enough as it is. But in a way I suppose it's all right. For now it means it's a kind of sacrifice really, whether you want to or not. And that gives one a good feeling, I find. It's *necessary*. It's not superstition, it's the truth. When I was small there was a terrible storm one night. I was sure it was the end of the world. Next morning I decided to make a sacrifice so there wouldn't be another storm. I found a frog in the garden and put it on top of a lot of old papers on a pile of stones and cut off its head. Jesus, it was awful, blood and the frog kicking and wriggling in my hand. I don't think I've ever been so bloody terrified in my life. By the time the frog was dead I was quite hysterical. But I knew I *had* to do it. I lit the papers and ran away and for weeks I never came near the place again. It was years before there was another storm like that. And once Daddy got ill: I was lying in my bed listening to the footsteps in the house, and the doctor's voice, and there was light under my door. That was the first time I got scared to death. And again I knew that only a sacrifice would help. I couldn't face a live thing again, but I took my prettiest doll and chopped off her head and burnt her. It almost broke my heart. Mum took strips off my backside for it and I deserved it, of course. She would never understand that I didn't do it because I hated the doll but because I loved her. Anyway, Daddy got well again, so it just proved how right I was. Later, with the boys in the garage, I sometimes asked them to tie my hands. Then I'd lie there with shivers running down my spine, just because I felt so helpless, like being sacrificed. And that was the same feeling I had the first time it happened here, in Paris. I can't remember the room or the man. I haven't the faintest idea in which part of the city it was. Some stupid little room with a bare bulb. And it hurt. But in a way that reassured me, I knew I was being sacrificed again – to something. I didn't know who, or what, or even why. I only knew it *had* to be that way, sooner or later, and I was glad it happened. It's always been like that ever since. Sometimes a useless little Cain offering, all smoke and no fire. But sometimes it was good. I suppose Abel must have felt like that, with the wide blue sky and the smoke almost invisible, not a breath of wind, straight up to heaven, a transparent little tree growing before his eyes. Some sacrifices I brought willingly. Others were taken with force. But each time I felt relieved afterwards. Not that I can remember any separate occasions, really – they all seem to merge, to blur. Except that one night. The only man, I think, I've ever *loved*: so much, that when he was inside me, I begged him to put his hands round my throat and throttle me, I wanted him to kill me, I loved him so much. It was on the way to Chartres, in the early spring, soon after I first got here, a sort of pilgrimage of thousands of young people from Paris. It took a few days to get there, I can't exactly remember how many. We were on foot. A strange, wonderful feeling: this big surging movement of a whole crowd of strangers, and I among them, going somewhere. Mealtimes, we broke up into smaller groups and ate food from our rucksacks. At night we slept in the open, the sky was cloudless. Chilly, but cold. And I thought about the cathedral at the end of our pilgrimage. Nothing has ever meant so much to me as that unknown cathedral to which all of us were going. It was like walking in a trance, alone among all the others. We were singing. Some had guitars. At night there was sweet, sad music in the distance. I didn't know a soul and I was glad I didn't, because now there was no one I *had* to talk to, except if I really felt like it. And I was free to say whatever I felt like, because they were strangers who wouldn't remember me, and even if they did it wouldn't matter. It was just one streaming movement like a river in flood, further and further. And then, that night. It was late, past midnight I think, and it was very quiet, except for one little guitar very far away. There was a sliver of a moon and one could barely see one's own hand in the dark. I was awake, lying with my arms under my head, looking up. Then there was a sound. Vaguely I could make out this figure standing against the sky, next to me. He squatted down. I asked him why he wasn't sleeping. He started when he heard my voice. Why wasn't *I* asleep, he asked. We began to talk, whispering so as not to disturb the others. About all sorts of things, our pilgrimage, and the cathedral which he knew well, and the weather, and the wonderful night. And then we talked about Easter and Holy Week, anything, everything. Except about ourselves. We weren't important. Later he lay down beside me and his voice became even softer and his hands moved to the buttons on my breast, leisurely, the most natural thing in the world. And then his voice stopped and only his hands went on whispering, and mine began to wander across him, shyly at first. His body was smooth and young. And he was so unhurried. There was no need to hurry, for I knew it had all been predestined, and the night was long and kind. I think I even fell asleep once, and started dreaming. But at last I could feel him on me, and inside me, and everywhere, and then, I think, there was nothing but the dream. When he got up at last I just lay there, unmoving, empty and filled, thinking over and over: *Hic est enim corpus meum*. His hand touched my cheek ever so softly. And then he was gone. I began to recite the paternoster but I fell asleep before I could finish. I don't think there is any other man I've ever known better, although I never even asked his name or saw his face, I loved him so much because these other things were so irrelevant. Nothing else *mattered*. He wanted nothing. So I could give him everything, and he to me. Why can't it always be like that? Why couldn't Stephen be like that? Why was he always so impatient? Why did he always want to *force* me? Didn't he know –

This is very special soap he gave me, smells like expensive perfume. I think I'll remember the soap best of all when I go back to my room, once he's got tired of me and thrown me out. It's always like this. The smells. The tastes. I can no longer remember the neighbour's boy, even though it was he who started the game. But I remember the smell of the garage. I can still smell it, every time. And the apples, half sweet, half sour. They say it wasn't an apple Eve gave Adam, so I wonder what the hell it was, and why they lied to me. And the honeysuckle of the vacant lot. Daddy's face, too, has disappeared; the little photograph I had of him was in one of the pockets of the coat I had to sell, I could never find it again. Odd, isn't it, that something that once meant so much to one can disappear so completely. But I can still remember the vague, sad smell of his jackets. And his hands after one of our long walks. Like those of the man in the night, but it's really the grass I remember, and the damp ground. That, too, is a kind of sad smell. The Ambassador's office clothes are dry-cleaned too often, they only smell of benzine. But in his wardrobe I found a few old jackets which I go to smell every day when he's away. Tobacco. Shaving cream. Something else besides, sweat perhaps, something of himself. I know if he finds out about it, he'll laugh at me again, and perhaps run his fingers through my hair as if I'm just a funny child. He never knows *how* worried I feel about him when he is away, or how scared I am that there may be something about me he doesn't like. I *want* him to like me. Everything about me. I don't want him to think I'm too thin or my legs are too long or my breasts are too small. I don't want him to think I'm bad or ungrateful. I want him to *understand*. To believe everything I say, and trust me, and never to laugh at me. I wasn't sure what would happen the night I rang the bell outside and told the concierge a lie and went up to his office. All the way from Neuilly I was merely thinking about how I could get my own back at Stephen. I wanted to hurt him, to land him in trouble. I was so bloody *mad* at him. When I got to the Étoile I suddenly remembered the Embassy was very near there, and I thought about the Ambassador. So I decided to go to him and tell him all sorts of things about Stephen. But when I got to his office door, the only one that had light underneath, I saw him sitting in the light, writing, the way Daddy used to sit with his poems at night. I always sat curled up in the big green armchair that smelled of cats, watching him while he worked. So I decided just to ask him to take me home. He looked so tired. I think it gave him a fright to see me standing there. And I was scared he'd turn me out and let me go home alone. All the way in the avenue de la Grande Armée I hadn't been scared at all. Why should I? I've been *everywhere* in Paris at night. But then, there, I was suddenly scared of going on alone, in the rain and the dark. And I *was* tired. He frowned, and I thought he was going to give me blue hell. Then, suddenly, I wondered what he'd do

281

if I started taking off my clothes. Perhaps he'd come for me right there, in his office. Men are strange creatures. Well, I thought, so what if he did? Afterwards he could take me home, or give me money for a taxi. But he didn't do anything. He felt sorry for me. If he'd taken me the way I thought he would, I'd never have come back to bother him. But because he was kind to me when there was no need for him to be kind, there was nothing I could do except come back. And I had to do so every time, again and again, so he could start *liking* me. Jesus, I didn't want charity. When he stopped at my building he wanted to come with me. I said no, of course, I was sure he wouldn't listen to me. What man would have? But sure's hell, he did. I suppose he thought it would scare me if he came along. And I stood in the rain with his jacket over my head, wanting to plead with him to come inside to my room and sleep with me. For then it would have been *done*. Then I would no longer owe him anything for his goodness. But he kept on believing me when I said no again. I didn't want him to be kind to me. It's just as bad as being a bastard. René was like that. It went on for months. He beat me and shouted at me and hurt me. He was often drunk and then he didn't care what he did to me. Many times he threw me out of his room after he'd screwed the daylights out of me. He couldn't care less if it was cold or raining outside. Some nights I thought I'd die of exposure. But every time I went back to him to be shouted at and beaten up. In the end he got scared that someone else might take me away from him and he started treating me better. This set me free again, so I left him. They've got no right to bind one like that. Every time I tried to provoke the Ambassador, to dare him to do something, I *wanted* him to take me. Yet, if he *had* taken me that first time he came to my room, I would have hated him for it. It's all so confused, I mean, in a way I *wanted* him to do it but if he did, he'd no longer have been kind to me and then I could no longer stay with him, and if he did, he would have done so just because I'd provoked him or something, and then he'd have thought that I was a slut, and I couldn't stand that. Jesus, can anyone make sense out of that? All I know is that I'd have jumped into the Seine then. I don't want to be tied to him, yet I can't bear being free from him either, unless he could let me go without being less kind to me, and surely that is impossible. Oh, I don't know. I really don't. And then, at last, he did come to my room that one night and took me. He tore the blanket from me and threw me on the bed. And *took* me. But that, too, he did because he was good, not because I'd tricked him into it or anything. And with that he really tied me faster to him than ever, because before that there hadn't been *this* between us. 'Two and two who once have lain together are forever almost one.' Who said that? That was the night Marc was with me. In the *cave*, first, and then in his room, and then he brought me home and it started all over again. He was drunk. We woke up everybody with our singing, our voices echoing through the whole building as we came up the stairs, and people shouting at us from their bedrooms *Au clair de la lune*. We always sing it. But it isn't 'our' song. It's *mine*. It became mine on my very first day in Paris when I heard an old clochard sing it in the garden of Saint Julien le Pauvre. He was just like the poor old Lubin of the song himself, wandering through the streets in the dark, asking Pierrot to open his door and to bring a light and a pen to write with. What on earth would he want to write in the night? And Pierrot refuses to open, he's too snug in his bed. It's like the bridegroom shouting at the poor girls with the empty lamps to stay outside, they can't come in to the party. And so old Lubin goes to the girl next door. But all this wandering in the dark has made him crafty. He no longer says: *Open, for the love of God*. He says: *Open, for the God of love*. And together they start looking for a candle and a pen, and as they go on searching, the door closes behind them and then it doesn't matter any longer whether they find something or not. It's different from my dream, for the dream never ends happily. It never ends. It's like after Daddy had gone away and I started sleepwalking. Usually it was in the house, but one night I went outside, and by the time I came to my senses, I was in a strange street. It was dark as anything. I had no idea where I was and I just started running this way and that, not knowing where to go. I heard a clock strike twelve and got terribly scared, for I knew that was the time the ghosts came out, gnashing their teeth and crying like the wind or screeching like owls. There was a park with a tall hedge. Trees swaying in the wind. Behind every tree something was hiding, waiting to jump on me as soon as I came past. I began to cry, running, running all the time, and hurting my feet on the hard asphalt. I couldn't get out of the dark. I couldn't go on any longer. And then a car stopped. It *had* to, for I was right in the middle of the street. I heard the brakes and I thought: *Now they've got me*. And when I woke up again I was at home in a hot bath and then in bed. I must have given them my address. That was the only time my sleepwalking took me so far from home. But the dream remained, and it's still with me, except when he is with me, holding me in his arms. He also likes my song and sometimes he hums it with me. He doesn't know why I sing it, of course, to him it's just a little song, and perhaps, if one thinks about it, *everything* is just a little song, with a bit of sadness in it, and a bit of joy, not that it really matters, but I suppose it's better if it could end happily. Stephen just got annoyed when I sang it and one night he said: 'I wish you'd stop wailing this idiotic little tune!' I wish I could have explained to him, but Stephen is so impatient. He can't stand me. He can't stand any woman. Sometimes I wonder whether he's a *pédé*. But I don't think so. I *hope* not –

It has begun to rain against the window. Now I can lie a little longer. It's so snug and quiet and protected here in the warm water. Not that I don't like the rain; I adore walking in it. Such a wonderful feeling of sadness and aloneness, like my first days in Paris when I didn't know a soul and had nowhere to go. I can walk through these streets for days on end. I love the Champs-Éysées and the boulevards around the Opéra and of course the fashion centre around the rue François I. But if I really have to choose I think I'll take the dirty little streets near Les Halles and the rue Saint-Denis and all those culs-de-sac, especially at night when the trucks unload their vegetables and meat carcasses and stuff. Or the streets between the rue Monge and the rue Claude Bernard, of course. And around the place des Vosges. Perhaps I like it because it makes me feel scared. Nobody pays attention to you when you're walking along those streets, but there are always invisible eyes peering at you through the dark doors and windows and from the nooks and niches of the old buildings. Voices whispering in the dark. And stray cats. I can't stand cats. The old buildings all propped up by scaffolding else they'll fall in. Like some of the old clochards who can't stand on their feet any more. They spend their days sitting under their bridges. Talking to themselves, their hands trembling. The DTs, I suppose, or old age, or illness. I wonder what happens to them when they die. Perhaps they have a special cemetery somewhere, like the dogs; at the back of Montmartre. Or else they're cremated. I'd hate that, it's like going to hell. Much rather throw them into the river. They spend all their lives on its banks anyway. If I were a clochard I'd love to be carried away by the river when I'm dead. And if I knew they were going to burn me, I'd lie on the edge of the water and roll in just when I'm going to die, in the night, so that they won't find me. I told Stephen I'd love to be a *clochard*. But that wasn't quite true. In a way I'm one already. I don't stink like them, and I'm not old or ugly, and I don't drink so much, and my clothes aren't so worn, but I don't think it depends on what one looks like to be a *clochard*. I don't think one could really *become a clochard*. One is born like that, the way some kittens are alley cats even if they're born in a beautiful house. Stephen is a *clochard*. He doesn't know it, of course. He'll never know it, because he keeps on fighting against it. But he *is* one, all the same. So he and I should really –

I was here in the bath that night, using his wife's green bath salts, or his daughter's, when he came back from Orly. It was later than I thought. I'd just begun to wonder whether he would be coming home at all. Perhaps he'd gone to my room first. But somehow I *knew* he wouldn't. Perhaps I shouldn't have come here to wait for him, I knew he'd be feeling miserable. But I also knew he needed me. He never said so, of course, but I'd known it even before he took his wife to the airport. He was so mad when he came in and found me here. Ordered me out of the bath and everything, said he wanted to be alone, I pulled faces at him and clowned around in the bath, a whole performance, even though I ached for him inside. He didn't think it was funny, he was just getting madder and madder, and I didn't think it was funny either, but the show just had to go on, else we'd both start to cry or something. I had to make him forget about his wife, that's all. I'm not jealous of her. Why should I be? But if I hadn't come here that night, he'd have started missing her and blaming himself, thinking all sorts of impossible thoughts. So I damned well *had* to help him. Men are like that. He's even more clumsy than most. Sometimes I feel a hell of a lot older than him. He thought it was just another of my games when I asked him for an apple, and lay here in the bath eating it. I splashed about in the water, and soaped myself before him, and asked him to wash me, and whistled as I dried myself, and then asked him to keep me warm because I'd left my clothes in his room. He was sort of at a loss: first picked up the towel I'd dropped, then stared more or less helplessly at the rim in the spotless bath: I bet it was the first time this bathroom had ever been in such a mess. And then he had to pick me up, for my teeth were chattering, and he took me to his room. He left the light on, for he wanted me to dress. Even at that moment he thought I'd get dressed and go. Instead, I took off his jacket. And then he knew there was nothing else he could do if he wanted to get rid of his loneliness. He took me into his bed and made love to me. After a while his body suddenly began to jerk. I thought he was coming, but it wasn't that. He was *crying*. And all the time he stayed inside me. It was the most passionate he'd ever been with me. And when he fell asleep at last, it was already getting light outside, it felt as if we were dead together, and we were happy together. And after we'd slept for a while he moved and whispered against my cheek: 'Stay with me, Nicolette.' And I smiled and tried to answer, but I was too tired, and we slept on. He's forgotten all about it now. I'm sure. Of course, he meant it when he said it: but by the time the sun woke us up he was no longer my lover of the night, but the Ambassador, and I was just someone he'd picked up to have a bit of fun with. Sooner or later he'll get tired of me, what have I got to keep a man like him interested in me? If only it would last until Easter. I don't know why I wish it so badly, but I *do*. I want him to go to High Mass with me. It doesn't matter what happens afterwards. Why did Jesus ever allow them to crucify Him? He should never have become a man. Bloody stupid of God to allow it. Why should it always be necessary to bring sacrifices? It makes one guilty. If only I were sure that the bread really changed into His body, and the wine into blood. It would make everything so much easier. It would make everything worthwhile, I think. But now I don't know. And I'm scared. I don't want to go to High Mass alone on Good Friday when all is black and the altar bare. I can't face it again. Not another year. And yet I can't stay away either. So he's *got* to come with me. We can stand beside the column again. It'll be so much easier if he comes with me. Stephen never wanted to. He jeered at me and said I was pretending to be a fucking nun. He thinks I'm a hypocrite. He never even wanted to go inside to look around. He doesn't believe in anything. But I don't think he really means it. I think he's afraid. He got so mad when I said so! Yelled at me like anything. I had to cross my fingers. Why didn't he come with me? Perhaps he was just too timid. Perhaps he'll still come with me one day. If only he could learn to believe in me –

Jesus, my hair is absolutely soaked, but so what? There's a big fire downstairs where I can go and dry it. I felt so shy that night he came to me while I was washing my hair. Not shy for myself, but for his eyes. Still, I didn't put on my clothes. I did it on purpose. I *wanted* to shock him, I *wanted to hurt him, I wanted* to provoke him, so that he could take me and become just as bad as he thought I was. And he tried to provoke *me*, by asking me about all the other men I knew. What business is it of his? I *know* no other men. They just happen to be there, that's all. Sometimes one stays over, and it's good, and it's fun, and it's wonderful, and that's that. They're not important. And all the time I wanted to beg him to stop, and perhaps he wanted *me* to stop, but neither of us could. And then Stephen came to the door and he was furious with me. He thought it was Marc or someone I had with me, and he demanded to come in, but I wouldn't allow him. I wanted him to *admit* that he was jealous, and to tell me *why* he was jealous. But he only shouted at me that I was playing with fire. Did he think he could scare me with that? Then he turned round and stomped away. I went after him as far as the railings. When he reached the landing just below mine. I called out to him – softly, because I didn't want the Ambassador to hear. But he just ignored me. I nearly ran down after him. I wanted to beg him to wait for me. If he'd given me two minutes to dress. I'd have gone with him wherever he wanted, I'd have done whatever he wished. I couldn't bear that maddening conversation in my room any more. If he went on much longer, I was sure something would just snap. Then the Ambassador would get angry and take me, as I'd dared him to do. And then I wouldn't have any feeling left for him. He'd already lost all respect for me. And I didn't *want* him to. If only Stephen could take me away before that happened. I'd have gone back to his place with him if he'd wanted to, I'd have made love to him all night, anything, anything. But he'd already gone, and I had to go back. A few minutes later the Ambassador left anyway. For the last time, I thought. But it was for Stephen that I ached inside –

Shit, now I've splashed too much water on the floor and the magazine I started reading an hour ago is all soggy. I still wanted to cut out my horoscope. Not that it's really necessary, I suppose, for I know it by heart already. But I keep it every month. *Unexpected change of residence*. Would that mean these few days I've been living here in the Embassy? But the horoscope month only begins today. So it must mean I'm going back to my room, for I've made up my mind to leave tonight. He won't mind. He may even feel relieved, I'm sure my presence embarrasses him, although I hardly poke my nose outside the door. *Excellent month for money matters.* I can always do with that. And then: *Your romantic problems solved at last.* That's the bit that puzzles me. I haven't got any 'problems' that must be 'solved'! Unless it means I'm going to give Marc the sack. Perhaps I should. I like him very much. He's a wonderful lover, but I'm getting too used to him. And he's beginning to get used to *me.* That's the way it turns out time and again. There was Roger, I used to pose for him. At first it was a hell of a struggle to sell his photographs, for he was unknown and had to compete against all the famous ones. I was inexperienced too. Then some big shot or other saw one of the studies Roger had meant to keep for himself. A couple of them were published. The very next week he got an important contract. The wheels started rolling. And then I left. I didn't discuss it with him, for he wouldn't understand. But it was getting us both down. The work and the success and everything. We were no longer free. There was no uncertainty left, no adventure, no freedom. We no longer mattered to each other. OK. So I quit. Same thing in the Grande Chaumière. I modelled for the art students. Sometimes one would take me home with him. Then Jean-Paul became all jealous, wanted me for himself. Said I was the best model he'd ever had. But that was all he cared about: his painting, his model, his reputation – not *me.* So I quit again. And Claus, the German student. Worked himself half to death, night after night. Studying, writing. I kept house for him. Copied his notes. Washed and mended his clothes. We lived very chastely together. I enjoyed it, as long as I knew he needed me. But then he, too, started taking me for granted. So *voilà,* off I went again. Every single time. There's always an end, from the very first moment the end is *there.* Nothing *lasts,* I suppose one gets used to it and learns to accept it. If only, this time, it would last until Easter. It's not so long, only a few weeks. Yes, I think I'll talk it over with Marc. Stephen doesn't believe in the stars. I once read him his horoscope. Gemini. He said it was balls. We had quite a row about it. If only Stephen would listen. If only there was *something* he would believe in –

It must be time I got out. Shall I dry myself with the large new white towel he gave me? Or with his? I think his. And then I'm going to dress. He had a whole stack of clothes sent round this morning for me to choose from, I tried them on for hours. I don't know how I'll get it over my heart to send anything back, but it will be greedy to take them all. I adore clothes. Wearing them, and looking at them in the mirror, and going out in them and feeling them against my skin. A new dress is like a lover folding you in his arms. But then I also love being naked. It's all right to wear clothes to look beautiful or to feel warm, but it's not as necessary as being naked. That's the way one *is*. One has to breathe and feel and laugh with one's whole body. But it's impossible here in the city. I went to one of the nudist clubs once, but with them being naked is just like wearing a different set of clothes. Everybody is so conscious of it, so proud of it: 'Look how bloody natural we are!' One should be naked *without* thinking about it. Not to flaunt anything. Just to *be*. Stephen tried to peep at me the night I was having a bath in his apartment. Why the hell didn't he come in? I wanted him to come in. I wanted him to see me, I wanted to see him looking at me, desiring me, I wanted to be beautiful for him. That's why I went there. And I specially put on my red panties, those tiny, ridiculous, sexy red panties. I wanted him to see them, and to know what they meant. But he never even looked at them. He only wanted me, wanted to *have* me! The way one clutches something in one's hand, a bird or something, when you're small, until it stops struggling and is dead and no longer beautiful. He didn't realise how unnecessary it was to bind me to him. He already *had* me. Not because he was good to me; not because he was bad to me. But because I loved

290

him. I tried to convince myself that it wasn't true, because it's too much to bear. One can't live with it. It's not *right* for people to love each other, for then they *need* each other, then they can no longer live without each other, and that is killing. And I don't want that. And I want that. I love him. I want him. I want him to want me. Not to use me, but to know me the way I know him. And then it's all right for him to use me. Then I *want* to be a body to him, I, the whole I, his. I've so often tried to tell it to him, but he never understood, never wanted to understand. Just before Christmas I went back to him to tell him that I love him. And I took him an expensive Jacques Fath tie with a beautiful rough texture which would go well with his charcoal jacket. But when I showed it to him, he said: 'I suppose that's for the Ambassador?' And so I got mad and said: 'Of course it's for him.' But I didn't mean to say it. I told him about the Ambassador, thinking he would be jealous and try to take me back. But he merely jeered at me and made me feel as if I'd betrayed the Ambassador. Why must everything make me feel guilty? Why can't he under-stand? If I went to him and told him in so many words that I wanted him – would he believe me? He would just think I'm being vulgar, and then the words would no longer be true. And they must be true. It *is* the truth. That is what the stars meant. It must be what they meant.

No. I am not going to dry myself with his towel, but with mine. My clean, new, white one.

Mosaic

1

The first telegram, *en clair*, arrived on the morning of 3 April while the Ambassador was copying Nicolette's laundry list from a crumpled cigarette box onto a sheet of stiff official notepaper bearing the Republican crest at the top.

After Harrington, who'd brought him the telegram, had gone out again, the Ambassador sat studying it for some time as if to memorize the contents. Then he put it aside, under a paperweight in the form of a springbok head, completed the laundry list, drew a neat line under the last entry, and added the date. He folded the sheet and shoved it under a corner of his blotter to be handed, later in the day, to one of the servants at home who would take Nicolette's bag to the laundry that normally handled the official residence linen. Then he checked his watch, picked up the telephone and asked the girl at the switchboard to ring Keyter.

'Mr Ambassador?'

'Can you come up to my office for a moment, Stephen?'

'Straight away, Mr Ambassador.'

His hands folded on his clean blotting paper, the Ambassador sat waiting without any sign of impatience until the young man knocked on the door.

'Come in.'

Keyter stood in the doorway, waiting for the Ambassador to speak; but as nothing was said, he asked: 'Was there something you wanted me to do, Mr Ambassador?'

'No. No, nothing.' He moved the telegram across the desk towards the Third Secretary. 'Only – this. It's just arrived. I thought you might like to see it.'

Keyter tried to read something in the Ambassador's face – disapproval, hope, satisfaction, anger – but after a short hesitation he came nearer, took the telegram, glanced through it, nodded.

The Ambassador was waiting for his reaction.

But Keyter merely asked: 'May I keep it?'

'Of course.'

'Did you want to –? Have you –?'

'No, that's all, Stephen.' He leaned forward, almost reluctant, but said nothing more.

Keyter put the telegram into his pocket. 'How soon is "immediately"?' he asked without looking up.

'A week. Two at the utmost.'

'I see.' There was perspiration on his upper lip.

'Don't let it upset you unduly. I'll send the Minister a telegram to explain that your services are required here at the moment.' He got up to lend more emphasis to his words: 'There's no reason to be afraid of anything, Stephen. At the very least we can delay your return to Pretoria for a couple of months. Whatever happens then will be mere routine. It needn't have any influence on your career. I'll make sure the telegram is sent without delay.'

'No, Mr Ambassador.'

Puzzled, the older man looked at him. 'Why not, Stephen?' he asked. 'I can still protect you. And you know it.'

'How easy it is to destroy a person,' Keyter said quietly. 'It's not so easy to redeem oneself. But that is exactly what I have to do now. I'm sure there are other officials in Pretoria who can pull some strings for me. I had them in mind when I first drew up my report. But now I know something I didn't realize then: I can only live with my own conscience if I'm prepared to bear the consequences, alone.'

This was not the way one spoke in a crisis, the Ambassador thought. It was too well reasoned out, a recitation learnt by heart. The 'honourable' thing to do. The 'right' thing to say. Except it didn't sound like Stephen Keyter. However, he had learnt his recitation so well, no one would get him off it again.

Keyter was looking at him as if he expected an answer. But

296

after another moment he turned back to the door.

'I'm sorry, Stephen,' the Ambassador said behind him.

'Sorry?' He swung round. 'Why? Please, don't be noble now. There was nothing noble in what's happened. It's no use trying to fool each other. It just makes it more difficult.'

The Ambassador did not answer. Neither of them moved.

'It's all so petty,' Stephen said at last. 'A bit of jealousy. A bit of ambition. What else?'

'It's not as easy as all that, Stephen.' He knew very well he was saying it merely in an attempt to break the façade of bitterness in the young man. 'It's not so easy to diagnose one's actions,' he repeated.

'That's not true,' Keyter answered. 'That's the very reason why everything went wrong. We've always tried to find "difficult" explanations, even when we spoke about Nicolette. And all the time it was so terribly simple. As simple as love and hate.'

'Why do you mention her again?' the Ambassador asked, tired.

'What else is there to talk about?' After a moment he suddenly added, but not accusingly, a mere statement of fact: 'I saw her coming from your official residence a couple of days ago.'

'She is back in the rue de Condé,' the Ambassador said.

Their words were like lines intersecting: not a pattern of questions and answers, but a series of non sequiturs, as if each had memorized some lines from a different play and was now reciting them.

'She walked right past me, pretending not to see me.'

'She'd spent a few days in my house.'

'At the front door she stopped to talk to Lebon. I heard them laughing together.'

'She came after Erika had left.'

Only then did Keyter ask a question: 'Is she back in South Africa, or still in London – Erika, I mean?'

'In Johannesburg. At least she was when she wrote to me. I got the letter yesterday. You must look her up when you go back –' Repressing a strange feeling of anguish he went on hurriedly: 'She'll be lonely, I think. Annette's gone on to Cape Town. She wanted to be on her own.'

'It should do her good.'

'I suppose so.' Then: 'The divorce will be through soon.'

'I didn't know –'

'Neither did I. She told me in yesterday's letter. Not that it came as a surprise, of course.'

'No. Still –'

'It will be difficult for her to get used to South Africa again. One loses all contact. I'm sure she'd appreciate it if you visited her from time to time.'

Keyter nodded. 'And her operation –?' he asked.

'Soon.' With almost polite interest: 'Did she mention it to you, then?'

'Yes.' He looked at the Ambassador's averted face, and said softly, reluctantly: 'Did you know that Erika, and I –?'

In painful silence the Ambassador turned his eyes to him.

'Was it necessary to tell me this, Stephen?'

'I can no longer hide it from you.'

'I understand.'

'Please don't think – nothing ever *happened* between us. It was just that, at one stage, we needed each other.' Adding almost angrily: 'It makes it sound cheap to talk about it. But it wasn't.'

'Everything sounds cheap when one talks about it. But sometimes – you were right – one has to say it, in spite of all. We must learn to live with cheapness too.' Once again composed, he asked: 'Have you heard from her lately?'

'No. She avoided me ever since she came back from Italy. And I avoided her.'

'Because of me.'

'Because of everything. It could never have lasted anyway. And now I've done this to you too.'

The Ambassador shook his head.

'I could have saved you from it by saying nothing. Why is one always driven to confess? Why can't one learn to bear what is laid on one whatever is expected of one? Why is one always forced back to some sort of religious act just to get rid of one's burdens? It's humiliating. It's undignified. Just because I could no longer bear it, I had to unburden it on you, which is even more disgraceful. Why can't one be strong and brave and free? Free of guilt. There was no guilt while it lasted. But now, now that I've tried to get rid of what happened, because I could no longer bear it inside me, it's there. And it was the same with the report. I believed I was doing the right thing; and perhaps it was right – up to the moment when I began to put it in writing to confess. Then it all became a mess. But it was too late to stop. Suddenly it was all so complicated. It had been so clear before.'

Almost with a smile, but wearily, the Ambassador said: 'You should have been my son, Stephen.'

The young man looked at him, amazed, but without resentment.

'I don't know what I would have made of you,' the Ambassador said. 'But God knows, a man needs a son. To hold a small hand in yours and answer his never-ending questions. To rediscover the world through his eyes. To make him kites and catapults. A son who swims naked in a farm dam and comes to you for comfort and praise after he's shot his first bird. And who introduces you to the first girl who makes his head turn.'

'It doesn't work out like that.'

'No. Nothing works out. But if it *could*!' Almost wryly he remarked: 'That's what age does to one, you see?'

Stephen turned back to the door, then stopped again and uttered a brief, bitter chuckle. 'So now I'm going back.'

'When will you be ready?'

'Oh, I can arrange everything in a day or two. There's nothing which binds me. Nothing.'

'If there's anything I can do –'

'Thank you, Mr Ambassador,' he said formally.

The door was closed.

The Ambassador picked up the telephone. 'Mrs Smith,' he

said, 'I don't want to be disturbed by any calls or visitors.'

'But you have an appointment with those people from the arms firm –'

'They can talk to Colonel Kotzé. Otherwise they can see me tomorrow.'

'Yes, Mr Ambassador,' she said aggressively.

He leaned back against the high back of his chair. Outside there was sunshine and the distant noise from the streets. All round him were the musty corridors and offices of the Embassy, alive with the inscrutable activity of invisible people. Upstairs, somewhere, Le Roux, he presumed, was working through the day's newspapers to pick out reports on South African affairs, or, who knows, making notes of 'typical' events he could use in his writing. Verster would be preparing statistics for next week's commercial conference in Brussels, trying to make up his mind whether his son should go to a French school or be sent to boarding-school in South Africa. Colonel Kotzé would be studying specifications about the Mirage. Mademoiselle Hubert in the Hellschreiber's office would be typing Le Roux's report about a cultural exchange scheme between France and South Africa, interrupting her work at regular intervals to visit the toilet and readjust her hair. In the office next to his, he knew, Masters was studying recent shifts in French policy in Africa; on a memorandum sheet next to him lay the flight schedule of Sylvia's next shopping spree in London. Joubert, in his office, would be discussing his forthcoming home leave with some South African visitor. Harrington, ostensibly working on a financial memorandum, would undoubtedly be fretting about the fact that as a result of inadequate French contraceptives he was going to become a father in six months' time. The Registry Office was noisy, with constant coming and going, as Anna Smith and her typists and clerks were consulting files, typing letters, criticizing the latest plays, comparing France and South Africa to the everlasting detriment of the former. In the reading room downstairs the messengers were probably calculating the staff's postage expenses for the month and comparing their most recent amorous experiences with diverse men and women. In the first basement the typists would be preparing for the lunch break which was only forty-five minutes away. And behind the next door Keyter would be working on visa forms; or perhaps he was staring at his telegram through a cloud of smoke curling from the tip of an untouched cigarette.

And here he was sitting in his imposing chair behind the desk with the calendar which still showed the dates of January; in the still heart of all the activity in the concentric circles around him, yet isolated from it all; alone; gazing down at the folded laundry list on his blotter.

He studied his relaxed hands, the fine dust of hair on his fingers shown up by the light from the window. He made no effort to take up one of the pens from the heavy silver inkstand, or to open one of the files piled up near his right elbow. Instead, he just remained sitting, motionless, while the watch hands on the wall followed their circular course, until all sounds and suggestions of life had disappeared from the building, as water would drain from a bath. At one o'clock he got up, put the laundry list in his breast pocket and went through the empty building down to the dull sunlight on the grey cobblestones of the courtyard. At the main entrance Farnham and Lebon were chatting with a bored gendarme. They greeted him as he came past. He nodded, and crossed over towards the avenue Wagram where he often had his meals. As he waited to be served, he casually paged through a journal he'd bought at the kiosk outside. On the last page were the week's horoscopes. With a faint smile he started reading the forecasts for Scorpio and Leo. They didn't seem to have much in common. He took his knife and carefully tore out the page so that he could give it to Nicolette when he saw her again. Then he put the journal on his lap, ate his food, paid the bill, and returned to the Embassy. He went into the official residence and up to his bedroom. On the bed he opened Nicolette's laundry bag to check the contents against his list. As he'd expected, she had omitted some items and he carefully made the necessary alterations. There was something depressing about the heap of crumpled washing on the bed. It must have been several weeks' clothes, for they were damp with the heat of her little kitchen and there was a faint smell about them, a past tense smell, pathetically personal. Inexplicably an old broken sandal and a few crumpled bits of paper had also found their way into the bag. He took them out. The papers were covered with what seemed like little sums. Her budget? One scrap contained the undecipherable second half of a word followed by an exclamation mark. The Ambassador scrutinized everything very closely before he dropped the scraps into a waste-paper basket. At last he put her washing – including some sheets from the official residence he had given her – back into the bag, with the list on top, and took it down to the servant who would deliver it to the laundry.

Using the sandal as a pretext he went to the rue de Condé, but Nicolette was not at home and after half an hour's fruitless waiting he turned back and sauntered aimlessly towards the river. For a long time he stood leaning over the wall to stare at the long flat-bottomed barges gliding under the bridges. Later he went to a bistro for coffee. But before he had emptied his cup, he discovered that he'd forgotten her sandal on the river wall. It upset him unreasonably. Without finishing his coffee he hurried back to where he had stood. But the little sandal had disappeared. Perhaps it had fallen over the side, and drifted away, or sunk. Somehow the loss seemed irreparable.

With a heavy heart he walked back to the rue de Condé. But she had still not returned. In the boulevard Saint-Michel he entered a smoky cinema where a sentimental American film with an almost incomprehensible French soundtrack was being shown. Infidelity. Tears. Everlasting love. Suicide. Miserable, he sat watching it, resenting the lie of it all. Life was not like that, he thought; he knew. Or was it true after all: was everything essentially, no more than a melodramatic tale, told in clichés? And every anonymous little actor desperately did his bit, convinced that he was indispensable and contributing something important to the unintelligible whole; and after the last act, his costume – his wedding garment – stripped from him, he would spend his few coins in a bar, and curse, and stumble over a loose stone on his way home, and get lost in the dark.

By the time he came outside again his head was aching. Taking a short cut to the rue de Condé, he found her home at last, showing no traces of her day's mysterious wanderings through the city.

They had dinner together, and talked for some time; but he felt cornered in the little room, thinking of Keyter all the time. Everything had been so confused that morning. They would have to get together again to discuss everything in more detail. She soon sensed that he had something on his mind, but knowing that she hated the sight of Keyter, he didn't tell her about it. She became slightly irritated. And both of them felt relieved when, towards eleven o'clock, he suddenly made up his mind and left. He needed someone to talk to, and there was only Keyter he could think of.

As he entered the building in the rue Jacques-Dulud, he became almost unpleasantly aware of the total absence of smell in contrast with Nicolette's dwelling-place. Dispassionately the anaemic light illuminated the floor, the brown railings of the staircase, the narrow red carpet.

On the fourth landing he knocked on Keyter's white door. All was silent, and there was no light under the door. He could smell something, though. He sniffed, unable to identify it. After a minute or so he knocked again, this time with some hesitation, realizing that if Keyter was asleep it would be better not to wake him. It was almost midnight. Perhaps it would be better just to leave a note, and go. The smell was becoming unpleasant.

As he was tearing a page from his notebook he heard voices downstairs and leaning over the railing he could see a middle-aged French couple coming up, probably on their way back from a theatre or a concert. He wrote Stephen's name on the outside of the small folded page. The man reached the fourth landing a few steps before his mink-wrapped wife, and started looking for his key. Apparently they lived in the apartment right opposite Stephen's. The woman stopped on the last step, he dyed hair matt in the light. She sniffed, scowling.

'What's the matter?' her husband asked, unlocking his door and stepping aside.

'Gas,' she said, bringing her right hand with its large topaz ring up to her nose. 'Did you forget to turn off the stove again?'

He sniffed too. 'It's not coming from our apartment,' he said and turned towards the Ambassador. 'Have you perhaps forgotten to turn off the gas, monsieur?' he asked.

'I wasn't inside,' said the Ambassador. 'I only arrived a few minutes ago but there's no one at home.'

'These young people,' the woman said. 'Always going out and leaving the gas on. They never think of the neighbours.' She came to Stephen's door and gave a few delicate sniffs. 'No doubt at all,' she declared, pressing a perfumed handkerchief to her nose. Without waiting for comment she started rapping loudly on the door with her knuckle-duster ring.

There was no answer.

Annoyed, she looked at the Ambassador. 'Well?' she asked. 'What are you going to do about it?'

'Nothing,' he answered icily. 'Mr Keyter will turn off the tap when he comes back. I presume.'

'In the meantine we may all be gassed!'

Without answering he went to the staircase. But when he reached the first landing he realized that he was still holding his note for Stephen in his hand. He stopped. At that moment, for the first time, he was struck by the absurd, alarming thought: What if Stephen was *not* out? It must have been the melodramatic film that made him think such outrageous things. But whether his sudden anxiety had any foundation or not, it had now become imperative to find out what was going on. He hurried downstairs.

There was no light in the concierge's glass door when he knocked. But he heard a bed creak and a few minutes later the door was opened a few inches. 'What d'you want?' a woman's voice inquired. She was wearing a thick brown coat over her nightdress, her hair in curlers.

'I'm sorry to disturb you, madame, but there is a gas leak on the fourth floor and there doesn't seem to be anyone at home.'

'*Merde!*' she cursed and came out, buttoning her coat. With a single reproachful glance in the Ambassador's direction she went upstairs, muttering about the condition of her heart. He followed calmly. On the fifth floor, without waiting to ask for the facts, the concierge immediately entered into a heated argument with the middle-aged couple, interrupted only by sniffings and loud hammering on Keyter's door, which, in turn, caused various other occupants of the building to shout for silence from their apartments.

'Why don't you *do* something?' the woman in mink kept on asking.

'What can I do?' the concierge answered. 'I haven't got a key for the door. *Merde!*'

Whereupon the mink woman turned round to her husband, demanding peremptorily: 'Are you going to allow this person to insult me?'

In the meantime a number of other residents had also come upstairs and were adding their opinion to the general confusion. Only the concierge's curlers were visible in their midst, while regular *merdes* indicated that she was still involved in the argument.

'Shouldn't we telephone the fire brigade?' the Ambassador suggested at last, no longer able to conceal his irritation.

This led to a new discussion about whose duty it was to telephone, and whether it was the fire brigade that had to be summoned, or the police. But finally the concierge broke through the crowd and hurried downstairs, her coat flapping round her knees, her terrifying head bobbing.

Fifteen minutes later they all heard the braying of the fire engine outside, followed by the reappearance of the concierge, this time accompanied by two officers. Her attitude of great solemnity was ridiculously out of keeping with her appearance.

The door was opened. A sickening wave of gas engulfed them on the landing. One of the officers turned round briskly and motioned the spectators to stand back while he and his companions, their faces protected in their sleeves, rushed inside. A light went on. Almost immediately one of them came running out again.

'Get a doctor,' he called. 'And the police. There's someone inside.'

For a moment they were all too stunned to react. The concierge broke into hysterical sobs. The middle-aged man from the apartment opposite Stephen's led her away as the others all pressed forward to see. The fireman had disappeared again. A moment later he and his colleague came staggering out, carrying a body between them. Everybody crowded together.

'Stand back!' one of the officers ordered, pushing the man nearest to him out of the way. The body was carried into the apartment opposite.

'Stay outside!' the officer snarled again as the Ambassador tried to follow them.

Too hurried to care about his French grammar, he explained who he was. Still glaring at him suspiciously, the officer reluctantly allowed him to enter. The door was closed. The mink woman had already telephoned the police and was trying to decide which doctor to call when the Ambassador took the telephone from her hands and dialled the number of the doctor who usually attended the Embassy staff. Ignoring the rude remarks uttered by the woman beside him, he laconically explained to the doctor what had happened.

The firemen were already applying artificial respiration. The concierge, seated wide-eyed on an Empire chair, eight fingers crammed into her mouth, was mumbling alternately:

'*Mon dieu!*' and '*Merde!*' From time to time she removed one hand from her mouth to cross herself.

'And all this in our apartment!' the mink woman said, glaring at the Ambassador.

Her husband tried to calm her down, but she snarled so viciously at him that he resumed walking to and fro in the room, his arms behind his back.

Ten minutes later, while the two officers were still kneeling on the Persian carpet beside the inert body, the doctor arrived. The Ambassador opened the door.

Afterwards he retained only a confused memory of the hours that followed. The police. The trip in the back of the ambulance to the American hospital in the boulevard Victor Hugo. Waiting in a sterile corridor, oblivious of time. The doctor, at last, exhausted and matter-of-fact: 'I am very sorry, Your Excellency. There was nothing we could do.' The trip – by taxi, or in the doctor's car – to Master's flat in the avenue Malesherbes, through deserted streets with yellow traffic lights flickering monotonously on and off. Sylvia's face, without make-up, hideously distorted as she sobbed: 'I've always *known* something awful was going to happen –!' Douglas Masters in his blue striped pyjamas with the top button missing, revealing his white, hairless chest. The yellowish light inside a *mairie* where they tried to persuade a sleepy policeman to withhold the details from the press. The drive back to the Embassy in Masters's car in the early grey dawn. The chilly air on the sidewalk under the chestnut tree black against the empty sky. The thought: 'He's blaming *me* for it all –' The sensation of ice-cold perspiration on his face. And, as he put his hand into his pocket to find a handkerchief, the crumpled page with the horoscope he had forgotten to give Nicolette. (*Brilliant success in all spheres this week. Make full use of your opportunities. The world is smiling at you.*)

With a short, angry gesture he threw the page into the gutter. Then he turned round to the heavy, lugubrious entrance of the Embassy and pressed Lebon's bell to be admitted.

2

After Gillian had broken down everything in me – my convictions of morality and convention, my belief in tradition and religion and social institutions, and an existence devoid of all surprises – there was only one thing left: life itself. This small, indispensable fact, I thought, even she would not be able to deny. But she risked that as well, as recklessly as anything else she'd ever done.

Or was it, the first time at least, merely a dangerous game of which she knew that it would not be pursued to the end? It arose from a triviality: a quarrel which started when she sat next to me in a concert and kept on talking until I got angry and told her to shut up; she jumped up and went out; I followed. In the large empty foyer I tried to hold her back with force, but she broke loose. Outside on the broad steps she broke into a fit of cursing and screaming while I tried in vain to calm her. At last she cried: 'Why can't I talk if I want to? Are you ashamed of me? But why can't I be *me*? Nobody ever leaves me alone. I'm sick and tired of you and your nice manners. I'm sick and tired of everything!' Concluding melodramatically: 'I want to be dead! I'm going to kill myself!'

'Don't be foolish, Gillian!'

'You don't believe me?' she cried. 'All right. I'll show you –' And she ran off into the dark.

Go to hell, I thought. But after a while I began to feel uneasy. I realized how easily, in an inconsiderate moment, she could do something desperate. She had already defied everything my way of life represented in her eyes; who knew but she would get it into her head to defy life itself?

It was after midnight when I reached my room. There was light inside and the door was half open.

'Gillian!' I called. But there was no answer.

I hesitated, and went in. She was lying diagonally across the bed, fast asleep, still wearing her concert clothes. Something in her attitude scared me. It was no ordinary sleep. I went to the bed quickly. Under her shoulder I found the empty tablet bottle. I called out her name, tried to lift her, slapped her cheeks to wake her. But with barely a moan she slept on. I wasted no more time but ran to the telephone in the entrance hall.

It was more than an hour before the doctor said: 'She's out of danger now. We were damned lucky to get to her so soon.'

I sat at her bedside all night, watching her pale face, listening to her deep breathing.

'Why did you *do* it, Gillian?' I asked the next day. 'Don't you realize what could have happened?' . .

'I knew you would come,' was her only answer. It was impossible to make out whether she meant it or not.

That was the first time, and it had no serious consequences. But perhaps I realized, even at that early stage, that it had been a warning only, to pave the way for what was yet to follow. And when many months later, in Florence, I received the letter with the casual reference to her death, I knew immediately and almost with resignation: it had been inevitable from the beginning, I never found out exactly what had happened: whether it had been an accident, or illness, or whether she had indeed taken her own life. I could not trace anybody who had known her during those last few months when she had been living in Durban among complete strangers.

All I can remember is that on the very first day after my return to South Africa, leaving the boat in Durban, I took the bus from the city to the terminus where one boarded the smaller bus to the Stellawood cemetery. It was full; and everybody had flowers, except me. I spent more than thirty minutes in the caretaker's office at the entrance trying to trace the number of her grave. I had so little information to go on. When I found it at last I discovered with a shock that by the time I'd received the letter, she had already been buried three months.

An irritatingly jovial driver took us past the blocks of graves. Hers was right on top of the hill, where one could look out across green, grey sea. There was a gusty, chilly, unpleasant wind. A few seagulls were tumbling in the sky above, uttering their forlorn cries.

There was no stone, no sign, nothing except the number I had been given at the office. How could I know that she was really buried there? *She*? My only proof was a blotted inscription in an official book, and a number. How could I even know that she was dead? All I knew was that she had defied our ordinary forms of life, shedding them the way a snake gets rid of its useless old skin. It was my first confrontation with death: the sober fact of *not being*. I could not even rebel against it. And there was nothing I could do even to *try* understanding it. I would have to learn to accept again the very existence she had taught me to reject. Perhaps it was worthless; but it was all I had. That, and her memory. But the memories I stowed away. And it is only these last few months that I realize they have never left me completely. She has always been with me, like the number of her grave, waiting, a riddle to be solved, an answer to be found.

3

It was on the morning of Tuesday 9 April that the second telegram, this one in code form, was placed on the Ambassador's stinkwood desk.

4

She had just had her bath and was brushing her teeth when I arrived. Still naked, she opened the door to let me in, then darted back and went on brushing, her feet in the small red basin with puddles all over the floor, her smooth body and arms and long legs glistening in the light of the bare bulb in the kitchen, while her right arm was moving rhythmically back and forth. I sat down on a straight-backed chair beside the gas stove. Conversation was out of the question. Even if she heard me, which seemed unlikely with all the noise she was making, she was much too deeply absorbed in what she was doing. It went on for at least five minutes. Then she rinsed her mouth, gargled noisily, washed her toothbrush under the tap and began to dry her face with a flurry of movements.

At last her two green eyes peeped through the loose strands of hair over the wet towel, and said with a carefree laugh: '*Salut!*'

'I brought your laundry.'

'Thanks. Will you put my things in the cupboard for me? I won't be long.'

In the cosy confusion of her bedroom I emptied the bag on the bed and packed the stack of clean anonymous clothes into the wardrobe – no easy task, as every shelf and drawer was already overflowing with her incredible assortment of bric-à-brac.

'Where are we going tonight?' she called after a few minutes as she came in, dancing, threw down the towel on the bed and began to look for something to wear.

Remembering the macabre outcome of another evening in the early days of our relationship. I asked: 'Must we really go out?'

'Yes.' She was struggling with her head caught inside a jersey. 'It's so beautiful outside.'

'We're not going to a *cave* again. It was too dark for me.'

'No,' she laughed. 'No, tonight we'll look for *light*.'

'The Champs-Élysées?'

'Right. We can start at the top.' She pulled up a zip. 'At the American Drugstore.' She went on prattling, dressing, brushing her hair, applying make-up to her eyes, trying on one pair of shoes after another.

'I brought you some money,' I said, placing a small wad of notes on the table.

'Is it all for me?' she asked, amazed. 'Why?'

'You need it more than I do. That's why.'

Holding one shoe in her hand, she hopped towards me and kissed me. I smiled into her happy eyes, but could not suppress an unsettling feeling of guilt.

'*Allons!*' She skipped to the door and opened it.

Outside the tired old building the evening was young and cool, with a hint of spring. Bright low clouds reflected the city's light, lending everything a phosphorescence in the dusk. We took a taxi along the Seine to the pont Alexandre III. The Louvre, the place de la Concorde, the Madeleine on the opposite side of the river, the Assembly on our side, the Invalides, the bridges – everything was floodlit; the Eiffel Tower fingering the clouds with its rays of light; and in the streets, wet after an afternoon shower, everything was reflected brilliantly, blindingly, fantastically: the entire city transformed into a celestial carnival. From the avenue Alexandre III we reached the Champs-Élysées with a fluid movement of car lights gliding past us from the direction of the Arc. We ourselves seemed to lose substance and become part of one immense flood, everything dissolved into streaming movement, shimmering light. From the sidewalks came music: here a few street musicians, there a group of students making merry, or a clochard with a flute, and once a whole bus of singing children; piano or orchestral music from the cafés and the open windows on the floors above. She was leaning her head out of the window, her hair streaming in the wind, her eyes opened wide to allow the light to flood right through her. Once she looked round at me, blinking, laughing, tiny specks of light reflected in her eyes.

'It's blinding,' she said. 'Like looking into the sun. Now I see dots everywhere!' And she turned her head back to the window and gazed out again, while I sat watching her, so light and young beside my heavy years: a blithe Beatrice.

At the Étoile we got out, crossed the endless avenue of light between two waiting walls of traffic, and began to saunter down the opposite side towards the Drugstore. In front of an illuminated window a beggar in a moth-eaten tail-coat was playing sweet, nostalgic tunes on his fiddle. But suddenly he switched to something else as a nun approached from the opposite side – I first noticed it when Nicolette's hand formed the fica sign again – and started playing Ave Maria, his beady eyes wise and twinkling in his bearded face. The nun passed with downcast, disapproving eyes. But Nicolette stopped and urged me to give him something. And as we went on she sang softly to the accompaniment of his thin melody:

'*Sancta Maria, Mater Dei, ora pro nobis peccatoribus, nunc et in hora mortis nostrae* –' But her voice was light and playful, without the sombre melancholy I had sometimes noticed in it. And she stopped abruptly when we reached the Drugstore.

'Look!' she said, pointing to the sky. 'The moon is out!'

For a minute it gleamed through the clouds. Then the city lights were once more reflected from an even, silvery ceiling, and I opened the glass door and we stepped into the bright, neon-lit interior. It was crowded, but we found an empty table where she insisted on ordering enormous meringues. We were surrounded by chromium, and loud jazz, and a horde of strangers. And once again, as so often in the past, I was amazed by the fact that I could actually feel relaxed and even happy simply because she was with me, in surroundings which would otherwise have irritated me unbearably.

313

'Do you think it was wrong of the old man with the violin to play Ave Maria when the nun came past?' she asked suddenly, white crumbs on her tempting lips.

'Wrong or not, he got the tip he wanted.'

'I hope he's not going to be punished for it one day.' She shut her eyes, swallowing a large mouthful of ice-cream. 'Do you think it's true – *really* true – that one is resurrected after death?'

'Maybe.' Thinking back to it now, it sounds naïve; but at that moment it was, all of a sudden, so simple to believe anything, to see clearly into the heart of everything that normally appeared confused. And I could believe again what had already become impossible: that it was irrelevant whether there was a hereafter, or a God, or something-more-than-human or not; what mattered was not *what* one believed in, but the creative act of faith itself. And for that short while I did believe, because I was prepared to accept anything as long as she was there with me, in that gaudy interior with its too-high lights.

Her meringue was finished long before mine, and not wanting to keep her waiting (I couldn't stand the cloying sweet stuff anyway) I called the waiter. Like an eager child she took my hand, and we resumed our gay little pilgrimage of wonder and discovery.

We crossed the Champs-Élysées again to look at the shop-windows opposite; and leisurely wandered down as far as the Lido. Without going down to the night club we followed the arcade past the boutiques surrounding the central café. I duly admired the clothes and jewellery she pointed out, but most of the time my eyes were fixed on *her*. It must have been the artificial light which made her look so different, lending her an almost unworldly beauty as she gazed, enraptured, at the expensive wares aimed at feminine irresistibility. But those were only the first few steps into the little world of Venus. From there we went towards the Rond-Point, turning left in the rue du Colisée with its gigolos and pimps waiting on the illuminated sidewalks; past a night club with photos of breathtaking artistes posted at the door – 'girls' who in the course of their striptease acts would be transformed, unnervingly, into men.

Nicolette's only comment was: 'Angels are supposed to be like that too, aren't they? So what's wrong with it? Aren't they *beautiful*?'

In the rue du Faubourg Saint-Honoré we boarded a bus to the Opéra where she first took me to the Métro entrance in the centre of the square to show me the dazzling spectacle of all the concentric circles of light in front of us; then we walked right round the Opéra building, catching unexpected, exhilarating snatches of choir and orchestral music coming from the inside, until we arrived back on the brightly illuminated square.

I was beginning to feel tired. For the first time my thoughts went back – why? – to Stephen, to what had happened six nights before. She didn't even know about it yet and I didn't want to upset her with the news: I knew it would be a shock to her, even though she had detested the man. What little time we had left was too precious, too vulnerable for me to take any unnecessary risks.

I thought about the dreadful days behind me: all the red tape about returning the body to South Africa; followed by the inevitable anticlimax; I knew very well that the Minister's main reason for recalling Stephen had been to obtain first-hand information before the final move. And now –

But this was no time to think about such things. Stephen's very name had to be suppressed in my thoughts.

She took my hand to lead me further on our way. I looked at her, and smiled at her, and felt my momentary unrest ebb away. What did anything else matter while we two could still wander through the celestial city? It would end soon. It was inevitable. But at this moment everything was still precious and present.

We stopped at the Italian travel agency to look at the colourful posters. The great imperial eagle representing Rome. Rome – My thoughts threatened to start wandering again, but she was at my side, and I looked at her intently, urgently, seeing the reflection of all the lights around us in her beautiful eyes, and repeating in my mind the words she'd sung so lightly earlier that evening: '*Ora pro nobis peccatoribus, nunc et in hora mortis nostrae –*'

We wandered on, from light to light, window to window, poster to poster.

'It's so beautiful,' she sighed once. 'How I'd love to travel, all over the world, anywhere, everywhere, just travelling, travelling all the time –'

I listened in silence, thinking: She's even more beautiful now than before. But as I became more and more tired I realized more and more acutely that our journey must soon end: another predestination to which I had to resign myself.

We had a beer on a café terrace, resting for a while, staring at the people passing us in the luminous night. When we went down into the Métro fifteen minutes later, it was like a temporary blindness after all the light. But it was most welcome. The train was almost empty, so we could sit down, only half conscious of men with open newspapers held up like huge, sensational moths; and labourers in blue overalls.

At the Cité station she got out, without explaining why. But I soon discovered the reason, for when we came round the corner of the Préfecture de Police, Notre-Dame was in front of us, floodlit, drifting weightless in the dark. From the bridge there was also the rippling reflection of the cathedral in the water before us, more beautiful than I had ever seen it, a crown of light on a whole evening of light. She was very quiet beside me as if her rapture had turned more and more inward until, at last, it burned steadily like an unflickering candle inside her.

'*Messieurs-dames –*?'

From somewhere in the dark the gnarled old woman had made her appearance. Nicolette said nothing. It was strange, since she was usually so quick to prod me into buying something. Very serenely she just stood waiting as if words were not necessary. I gave the old woman a ten franc note, but took

316

only one rose in exchange: a white one, almost a bud still, with very tender petals. And I handed it to my little guide, who stood on tiptoe to kiss me, still without a word. The old woman had already disappeared. We set out on the last stage of our journey to her room.

There she carefully placed the rose in a glass of water and put it on the table. As she bent over she casually glanced through the window and said: 'You know, those people opposite –'

'No.' I went to her and put my hands on her shoulders. 'Forget about them. They're not important now. Nothing is important. Except you. Except us.'

She offered no protest when I began to unbutton her jersey. I turned her round so that she could lean with her back against me.

'Do you remember: once, before I'd been with you for the first time, you said –'

'I remember.'

Her eyes closed, she seemed to be listening to my hands. When she was naked, I lay down in the virginal little bed. And together we set out on a new journey, through another universe, a timeless journey, both ancient and very new, unhurried, filled with all kinds of discoveries and love, loneliness and comfort, despair and faith, just she and I, with our single shadow trembling on the wall. And at last, after a very long time – but time was not important – I said:

'You must believe me. I love you.'

'Yes,' she said. That was all: 'Yes.'

That was enough for the moment. But the rest, I knew, had to follow inevitably. And I had to tell her, as calmly as I could: 'The telegram came today.'

'What telegram?' She was tense now, no longer languid and sleepy.

'The commission will be here the day after tomorrow. Or tomorrow, rather, for it's almost morning.'

She did not answer.

'It shouldn't make any difference to us, though.'

Her head moved, but whether she shook it or nodded, I couldn't make out.

'Whatever happens, we're still here. Nothing will change for us.'

'It'll be over before Easter,' she said at last.

'A day before Easter. Why? What does that matter?'

'Nothing. I was only thinking.'

I made no movement, waiting for her to explain, but she said no more. If only I could grasp her shoulders in my hands, and hurt her, and force her to believe that nothing would make any difference to us. But it was like Christmas morning at the Mass, when she had entered into a dimension where I could not follow her. I could lie there next to her, hoping that this, at least, would last. But she was no longer relaxed and I had to let her go to put off the light. We didn't need it any longer: the early dawn was already coming through the window, greyish and new.

She came back and lay down beside me again: but we did not sleep. At last I got up and dressed. She made no movement.

When I reached the door I said: 'I'll be back tonight.'

She nodded.

'Early.'

'All right.'

And then I went out. The concierge's wife was on the first floor, scrubbing the steps, muttering a curse as she had to stand aside to let me pass. Outside on the pavement the rows of rubbish bins were waiting patiently to be picked up by the municipal trucks.

5

It was almost like before, the way the Ambassador did his work in his office that Wednesday. Not that he could hope to get through everything that had piled up during the previous weeks, but that was not so important. He merely wanted to keep himself occupied in order not to think again about things that had been thought through and resolved so long ago. He worked in strict isolation, having instructed Anna Smith to ward off all visitors and telephone calls and refusing to see even members of his own staff.

The telegram of the previous morning had supplied only the most essential information, omitting even the names of the commission members. But late in the afternoon he was told to expect a telephone call from London at eight o'clock that evening. That gave him a clue.

The call was unexpectedly delayed, however, and by the time he and his colleague had arranged about the commission's time of arrival at Orly the next morning, it was much later than the Ambassador had foreseen.

When, at last, he knocked on her grey door, out of breath from climbing the stairs too quickly, there was no answer. He knocked again, calling out her name, and waited; but there was not the slightest sound inside. He was puzzled, perturbed. Surely she must have waited. She'd been expecting him. What could possibly have happened? He knocked again, although he already knew from the texture of the silence that she was not there.

He went downstairs, not even bothering to put on the light which had gone out long ago. By this time he knew his way. Outside, he walked round to the opposite pavement of the rue de l'Odéon to make sure that there really was no light in

319

her window. For a long time he remained there, lighting a cigarette once, waiting, looking up every now and then, smoking, waiting. The window remained dark. He was still keeping all thoughts at bay. Perhaps she'd just gone somewhere to buy food, or a magazine, or something to drink. At last he stamped out his cigarette with his shoe and walked back towards the carrefour de l'Odéon. For a moment he considered going up to her room again, but he decided against it and went to the rue de l'École de Médicine instead, to a bistro they had sometimes visited. She was not there, and the *patron* couldn't recall having seen her earlier in the evening. The Ambassador left and went to the next possible place. She was not there either, nor had she been there. At last he ended up in the boulevard Saint-Michel where he looked in at every single bistro and restaurant, even those they'd never visited together. Most of the waiters to whom he put his question treated him curtly; a few grinned knowingly, or winked; but all the answers were the same. He went as far as the Luxembourg Gardens, and even crossed the boulevard to the shuttered newspaper and peanut stalls in front of the closed gates in case she might be there. The first few yards beyond the railings were dimly illuminated by the street lights, but further on it was dark, the heavy mass of trees an impenetrable screen against the sky. It would be desolate in there at this hour, all alone at the pond in front of the palace. The green chairs would be stacked up under the silent statues. Perhaps the dim glow of the night sky would be reflected in the pond, but all around it would be dark.

At last, with a shrug, he began to walk back, checking all the bistros on his side of the boulevard until he reached the river. And all the time he had the impression that she couldn't be very far away; that he would only have to walk a few more yards to see her blonde head bent over a glass of Coke or beer (or red wine tonight?); or to catch a glimpse of her legs in the crowd; or to hear her laugh or her voice. But he couldn't go on wandering about like this. Perhaps she'd already gone home and was waiting for him. So he returned to the rue de Condé, and, refraining on purpose from looking up at her window first, went up the staircase to knock on her door again.

There was still no sound inside, and no light.

Without waiting any longer he pressed the bell which rang on the landlady's side. Shuffling footsteps approached the door. A sliver of light fell across the landing.

'Who's there?' she asked.

The Ambassador went to the door so that she could recognize him.

'Oh, it's you,' she said; her voice sounded commiserating. 'No. she isn't here. She's gone.'

'If you care to open up for me again, I can wait for her inside.'

'I said she was *gone*. She's not coming back.'

He couldn't grasp it immediately. 'But she –'

'I can't stand here all night,' she snarled. 'Don't you understand French? She's gone, she left with bags and baggage, boots and all, this afternoon. Her place is empty. She paid me two weeks notice money: 'I'm sure she'd have cheated me out of it if I hadn't insisted. And where am I going to get another lodger? People are so damned fussy these days.'

'But she can't be gone,' he interrupted her. 'Didn't she leave an address or a message?'

'Why should she?'

'But we arranged –'

'That's your business, not mine. Perhaps she wanted to get away from you. Fancy a young girl like her going with such an old man anyway. I never liked the idea.'

'I'm not interested in your opinions, madame,' the Ambassador said sharply.

'So now you try to insult me. Why are you still standing here? *I* can't help you.' She stood back to close the door.

'Won't you let me go in just for a minute?' he asked in sudden panic. 'Perhaps she left a message there.'

'There's nothing. I've swept the floor and all.'

'Just one last look.'

'There's nothing, I tell you.'

He took a note from his wallet. Too much for a tip, but he had no change, and he was desperate.

'Monsieur!' she exclaimed, shocked. 'Do you think you can *bribe* me?' For a moment she glared at him. Then, with a flick of her plump hand she grabbed the note, slipped it into her apron pocket, took a bundle of keys from a nail beside the door and waddled past him with an attitude of offended dignity. Unlocking the door opposite, she pushed it open, switched on the light and stood back.

'Look for yourself!' she said.

Without waiting any longer, he went inside, through the little lobby to the bedroom. Four bare walls with the plaster peeling off in shreds in one corner. A scrubbed brown table with old ink and cigarette stains. A rectangular, heavy brown cupboard with one door hanging open at an angle. It was empty, the shelves and drawers covered with newsprint. A couple of chairs. A miserable little bed with a bare striped mattress showing several dark stains. The mirror in the gilt frame lay on the bed. The floor was swept, as the old hag had said. It was a room he didn't recognize, a place he'd never set foot in before. Not even a room: a small bare cage cluttered with junk.

In a daze, trying to compose his thoughts, he went over to the window. A light opposite caught his eye. Absently, he looked at it. The room was empty. But a moment later the young woman made her appearance from somewhere deep inside, wearing a loose faded gown, carrying a baby in her arms. She came to the window to make sure that it was closed; but she made no attempt to draw the curtains. Sitting down on the side of the bed, she opened her gown, took out a large, swollen breast and forced the nipple into the child's mouth. Then, oblivious of the suckling baby, she looked up, through the window, at the outer darkness, and at the man opposite.

Turning away, almost hurried, he went to the small

kitchen. The old blue gas stove stood primly against the inside wall, the grating blackened and greasy. In the corner, at the window in the slanting outer wall, was the washbasin, yellowish and impersonal. On the floor stood the little red plastic basin.

She was gone, then. And there was nothing left of her. Not a scent, not an empty lipstick, a crescent toenail, an old toothpaste tube, the core of an apple, a hairpin. Not even the question mark of a little hair curl on the side of the basin. *Nothing*.

It was as if she'd never been here. All he had left were a few memories. And how could he be sure even of these? And it came as a shock to him, this discovery that he felt the need of a sign to prove her existence. Was it really imperative, then, for one to leave something behind in order to have being? Could one not exist except through signs?

From the front door the old witch called out. 'What on earth are you doing? How long are you going to keep me waiting?'

'I'm coming,' he answered absently, continuing his search. But he found nothing.

He went back to the bedroom to start all over again, looking even on top of the cupboard and under the bed. Nothing; nothing. And when, at long last, he stood up wearily and saw the landlady's impatient face appear in the doorway, he was aware only of the slight, faded pattern the little cross had left on the wall; even the nail had fallen out.

'I found the cross under the bed,' the landlady said, adding with a sneer: 'What on earth would *she* want it for, I wonder? I can put it to much better use.'

Briefly, the Ambassador held out his hand towards her, half open. Then it fell back to his side.

'Come on,' she said irritably. 'I'm not going to wait any longer.'

He merely nodded. Without looking at the window opposite again, he went past her, aware only of the bewilderment in his heart about the girl: somewhere in this city, tonight, without her cross. How could she exist without her little set of superstitions and myths? Or would she simply go to the Flea Market next weekend and buy herself another crucifix? Could it really be so simple – even for her?

He waited outside until she had closed the door behind her 'Good-night, madame,' he said. 'And thank you.'

He went downstairs. Outside, he waited until the heavy door with its weathbeaten, beautiful old carvings had banged behind him; then he went away, aimlessly. Even familiar streets would be strange to him tonight. He went on walking merely to keep moving, wandering through the labyrinth, avoiding people and light. At last he reached the river near the pont des Arts, went up the steps to the deserted bridge and stopped in the middle to lean over the railing, his face towards the illuminated cathedral in the distance. He remembered another night on this bridge. And the many times she'd spoken of the river, and of the desperate creatures who flung themselves into it. She herself –? For a moment he felt afraid, paralysed, exhausted. Even that he did not know. He could merely believe, or hope, that it had not happened to her. But then, he'd never expected it of Stephen either.

Would that, in the end, be the simplest, perhaps the only, way out? What else was there left? Tomorrow the two members of the commission of inquiry would arrive. It shouldn't take long, perhaps a single day would suffice. Before Easter it could all be over. And then? What, what indeed, did he have left? Not even a little corpse.

For a long time he remained there, his hands clutching the railing. Then, with a brief, decisive movement, he turned away and crossed over to the opposite side, away from Nicolette's bank, back to his own. Perhaps he would regret this moment's decision in the days or years to come; he might never again find it possible to reach this point. But now, and for this moment, he had decided. There was still an irrational *lex humana* he had to respect.

He passed behind the Louvre and lost his way in the maze

around Les Halles; later he landed in the boulevard Sebastopol, but turned away again, towards narrower lanes in the dark, dingy quarter where young street-girls are initiated (who could have told him that?). All round him in the night invisible human activity was going on. He could hear his footsteps echo against the walls. Now and then, on the periphery of a circle of light, shadows skulked past. From an open window came the wailing notes of a cheap jazz tune with dark, undisguised lust. A man and a woman went through the door of an obscure hotel. On the curtains and blinds of the windows above were dancing shadows. How many people within the boundaries of this one city were not, at this moment, tangled in the processes and contortions of love? All the world was caught in it. And through it all, aware of it all, he was continuing on his long journey. *Amare liceat si non potiri licet* –! Endlessly the city stretched out around him circle upon circle, teeming with all its natural and unnatural lusts: those of Francesca as well as those of Pasiphaë.

Pasiphaë. This beautiful name from the readings of the remote past suddenly got caught in the web of his thoughts. And he held onto it, grateful to have *something* to occupy his mind. Pasiphaë. Mother of both the Minotaur and Ariadne; source of the Fall, and of salvation. Eve and Mary in one body. And without being aware of the transition, he thought: she, the false heifer, had lured him into the labyrinth; but without offering him the thread to lead him out again –

On a street corner under a lamppost a young girl stood watching him, waiting for him. He was so wrapped up in thought that he saw her too late to avoid her. She was thin, and wearing too much make-up, her mouth too large, painted too red. Her dress was tight and very short. She was smoking with a pretence of sophistication, but when he came up to her he noticed the uncertainty in her eyes and in her swift gestures.

'*Bonsoir* –?' she said, hesitant.

His first reaction was to walk on without answering, but troubled by her embarrassment, he stopped reluctantly.

Her lips formed a grateful smile.

'*Vous voulez* –?' she asked.

He resented his own weakness. But he was touched by her youth.

'You shouldn't be here, my child,' he said, uneasily, not paternally as he'd meant to.

Her face tautened. She half turned her back to him, trying to seem casual blowing the smoke through her nose.

My God, he thought, she can't be older than seventeen.

He felt an urge to talk to her, but knew it would be impossible to penetrate her resentment; it would merely make it worse for both of them. And so, although painfully aware of how futile and even abhorrent his reaction was, he took his wallet from his breast pocket and gave her all the money he had left. She opened her mouth and tried to say something, but couldn't.

Without waiting any longer, he walked away stiffly. Perhaps she was laughing at him. But he couldn't look back.

Having given all his money to the girl, he had to walk all the way home. It was like a penance. As he went on the streets around him gradually grew wider and more desolate. But he was hardly aware of fatigue, of anything but the city itself, surrounding him like a sacred wood. At the same time the city seemed to be absorbed into him, no longer out there but beside him, part of his body, with cathedrals and brothels, light and dark streets, everything.

Only when he finally pressed the bell at the main entrance of the Embassy did he become conscious of his utter exhaustion.

He had to wait a long time for Lebon to open, wearing a crumpled black overcoat over his pyjamas.

'It's the last time I'll be disturbing you at night, Lebon,' the Ambassador said, sympathetically. 'I've been making impossible demands of you lately.'

'That's nothing, sir,' Lebon said complacently, almost fraternally. 'I understand. If only women would appreciate what we have to sacrifice for them, that's what I always say.'

The Ambassador smiled wearily. 'One can't always have things the way one would like to,' he said.

'Still, it's worth while in the end. Cute little *gonzesse*, your Mademoiselle Nicolette –' The concierge made a vague, but eloquent gesture. 'She's got beautiful eyes, monsieur, don't you think so?'

'She has.'

'Unusual, like. The colour one doesn't see it often.' Closing the door behind them, he apologized: 'I don't want to keep you from your sleep, sir.'

'Not at all,' the Ambassador said, still lingering, as if he couldn't bear the thought of going on alone; and yet he knew the concierge must be eager to get back to bed.

'She was here this morning,' Lebon said suddenly.

'She.'

'Yes. We chatted for a few minutes.'

'What did she come for?'

'She didn't say. Perhaps she forgot, because after a while she went away again without coming in.'

'Didn't she – say anything?'

'How d'you mean, monsieur? We were just chatting. You know what it's like.'

'Was that all?'

'Yes.' Lebon scratched his head. 'I spoke to her about Mr Keyter. I thought she knew about it.'

The Ambassador nodded slowly. 'What did she say?' he asked quietly.

'Nothing much. Stood looking at me for some time. Then she suddenly seemed to get angry, and she asked: "What about it? Why did you tell me? What made you think I'd like to know?" And then she left. I'll never understand women, I tell you. No two of them are alike.'

'I must go,' the Ambassador said.

'Good-night, monsieur.' Lebon saluted. Then he thought of something: 'I've heard about tomorrow's business, monsieur –'

The Ambassador stopped.

'If there's anything I could do for you –'

'Thank you, Lebon.'

The Ambassador walked along the driveway, past the official residence, into the courtyard of the office building.

Behind him he heard Lebon bolt the door and disappear into his own quarters, whistling. There was something familiar about the tune.

Of course –

The Ambassador took out his keys to unlock the door. This was where she had come in, that first night. *Donna m'apparve –*, he thought with a smile, as if he'd just made a momentous discovery.

As he tried to find the right key, he stood humming Lebon's little tune, Nicolette's little tune.

> *Au clair de la lune, on n'y voit qu'un peu.*
> *On chercha la plume, on chercha du feu.*
> *En cherchant d'la sorte, je n'sais c'qu'on trouva,*
> *Mais j'sais que la porte sur eux se ferma –*

He unlocked the door and entered the dark reading room. Behind him the door clicked shut again. Without putting on the light he went upstairs to his office.

There was still work to be done.

November 1962 – August 1963

Also available from Minerva

ANDRÉ BRINK

An Act of Terror

'A massive apartheid thriller centred on a plot to blow
up none other than the State President outside the gates
of Cape Town Castle . . . Brink at his robust and
imaginative best'
  Adam Low, *Daily Telegraph*

'This is clearly André Brink's *tour de force* . . . A political
thriller, set in South Africa, laced with all the angst and
pain and lacerating emotion that comes from
attempting to intellectualise, and hence come to terms
with, living in that volatile, unnerving, but ultimately
fascinating land'
  Peter Browne, *Time Out*

'*An Act of Terror* is the work of a sane, civilised,
intelligent man – a story about events that are in the
process of becoming news stories. Brink . . . is a writer
of inspired violence, and his shifts of viewpoint are
thrilling and significant, and deeply honouring to the
profession of literature'
  Hugh Barnes, *The Times*

ANDRÉ BRINK

Rumours of Rain

Winter in South Africa – a time of searing drought,
angry stirrings in Soweto, and the shadow of the
Angolan conflict cast across the scorched bush.

Martin Mynhardt, a wealthy Afrikaner, plans a weekend
at his old family farm. But his visit coincides with a
time of crisis in his personal life. In a few days, the
security of a lifetime is destroyed and, with only the
uncertain values of his past to guide him, Mynhardt is
left to face the wreckage of his future.

'As complex and powerful as the African continent itself'
    Books and Bookmen

ANDRÉ BRINK

On the Contrary

'On the surface *On the Contrary* is a picaresque historical
novel, in which 18th-century adventurer Estienne
Barbier graduates from seducing French wives to South
African widows via a long and bruising association with
the Dutch East India Company. Underneath, of course,
the novel is about today's South Africa and the
dilemmas facing people challenging the status quo.
Brink has written a novel which entertains first and
only later assumes a political significance. To rake over
the old embers with such skill and ingenuity represents
a considerable achievement'
    Sunday Telegraph

'An immensely generous novel, vivid and adroit in its
use of history'
    The Times

'Unfailingly honest'
    Sunday Times

'Infernally beautiful'
    New Statesman & Society

AMIT CHAUDHURI

Afternoon Raag

'Enchanting, studded with moments of beauty more
arresting than anything to be found in a hundred busier
and more excitable narratives . . . Chaudhuri has proved
that he can write better than just about anyone of his
generation'
  Jonathon Coe, *London Review of Books*

'If there is such a thing as a betting certainty, it is that
Chaudhuri will win the Booker prize before the century
is out'
  David Robson, *Sunday Telegraph*

'Those who are always acclaiming the "poetic prose" of
Ondaatje would do well to study Chaudhuri's language.
Again and again, he produces the perfect adjective, the
stupendous adverb . . . radiantly exact'
  James Wood, *Guardian*

'As elegant and economical as the best poetry . . .
Chaudhuri's book is an astonishing accomplishment . . .
which seems to float tantalisingly above the usual
demands of fiction'
  Julian Loose, *Sunday Times*

'This immensely subtle novel both estranges and gently
strokes the surface of English and Indian life. I know of
nothing in English fiction that begins to resemble it'
  Tom Paulin

GITA MEHTA

A River Sutra

'This book is a delight. Written with hypnotic lyricism,
this is seductive prose of a high order. Gita Mehta has
written a novel which defies easy categorisation: its
central character is India's holiest river, the Narmada,
mere sight of which is salvation. The narrator, a retired
civil servant, has escaped the world to spend his
twilight years running a guest house on the river's bank.
But he has chosen the wrong place: too many lives
converge here. Minstrels, musicians, ascetics, monks –
everyone has their own story to tell . . .'
   Time Out

'The simplicity of the plots makes it difficult to express
the joy that one has in reading them. All India seems to
be there . . . I have a feeling, indeed a hope, that *A River
Sutra* will become a classic, revered and enjoyed by
young and old'
   Daily Telegraph

'A mesmerizing novel by a writer of prodigious gifts'
   Miami Herald

'Superb, profound, apparently effortless storytelling'
   Independent on Sunday

BAO NINH

The Sorrow of War

'*The Sorrow of War* vaults over all the American fiction
that came out of the Vietnam war to take its place
alongside the greatest war novel of the century, Erich
Remarque's *All Quiet on the Western Front*. And this is to
understate its qualities for, unlike *All Quiet*, it is a novel
about much more than war. A book about writing,
about lost youth, it is also a beautiful, agonising love
story . . . a magnificent achievement'
   Independent

'This hauntingly beautiful novel, written by a north
Vienamese Army veteran, manages to humanise
completely a people who until now have usually been
cast as robotic fanatics'
   Sunday Times

'An unputdownable novel. This book should be
required reading for anyone in American politics or
policy-making. It should win the Pulitzer Prize, but it
won't. It's too gripping for that'
   Tim Page, *Guardian*

'Is it too much to predict that this will become the *All
Quiet on the Western Front* of our era?'
   New Statesman and Society

A Selected List of Titles Available from Minerva

While every effort is made to keep prices low, it is sometimes necessary to increase prices at short notice. Mandarin Paperbacks reserves the right to show new retail prices on covers which may differ from those previously advertised in the text or elsewhere.

The prices shown below were correct at the time of going to press.

☐	7493 9931 7	**An Act of Terror**	André Brink	£7.99
☐	7493 9985 6	**Rumours of Rain**	André Brink	£6.99
☐	7493 9970 8	**Afternoon Raag**	Amit Chaudhuri	£5.99
☐	7493 9705 5	**The Name of the Rose**	Umberto Eco	£7.99
☐	7493 9792 6	**A River Sutra**	Gita Mehta	£5.99
☐	7493 9630 X	**A Way in the World**	V. S. Naipaul	£6.99
☐	7493 9731 4	**The Grandmother's Tale**	R. K. Narayan	£5.99
☐	7493 9604 0	**A Malgudi Omnibus**	R. K. Narayan	£6.99
☐	7493 9711 X	**The Sorrow of War**	Bao Ninh	£5.99
☐	7493 9966 X	**Lucie's Long Voyage**	Alina Reyes	£3.99
☐	7493 9641 5	**Aké/Isarà**	Wole Soyinka	£7.99
☐	7493 9710 1	**The Makioka Sisters**	Junichirō Tanizaki	£6.99
☐	7493 9774 8	**Grass Soup**	Zhang Xianliang	£6.99
☐	7493 9852 3	**Red Sorghum**	Mo Yan	£6.99

All these books are available at your bookshop or newsagent, or can be ordered direct from the address below. Just tick the titles you want and fill in the form below.

Cash Sales Department, PO Box 5, Rushden, Northants NN10 6YX.
Phone: 01933 414000 : Fax: 01933 414047.

Please send cheque, payable to 'Reed Book Services Ltd.', or postal order for purchase price quoted and allow the following for postage and packing:

£1.00 for the first book, 50p for the second; **FREE POSTAGE AND PACKING FOR THREE BOOKS OR MORE PER ORDER.**

NAME (Block letters) ....

ADDRESS ....

....

☐ I enclose my remittance for ....

☐ I wish to pay by Access/Visa Card Number ☐☐☐☐☐☐☐☐☐☐☐☐☐☐

Expiry Date ☐☐☐☐

Signature ....

Please quote our reference: MAND